DISCOVER TIME FOR LOVE

DISCOVER TIME FOR LOVE

FORWARD IN TIME, BOOK TWO

LOUISE CLARK

CONTENTS

Book and cover design by eBook Prep
www.ebookprep.com

January, 2020
ISBN: 978-1-64457-034-0

ePublishing Works!
644 Shrewsbury Commons Ave
Ste 249
Shrewsbury PA 17361
United States of America

www.epublishingworks.com
Phone: 866-846-5123

DISCOVER TIME FOR LOVE

THE FORWARD IN TIME SERIES

CHAPTER 1

"You want me to leave? Now?" The last word emerged as a squeak, caused, Liz Hamilton was quite certain, by shock, amazement and not a little horror. She stared at her boss, the paleontologist in charge of the dinosaur dig she was working on for the summer excavation season, unable to believe he had just told her she was being replaced.

An academic on the rise, Dr. Alfred Scarr was in his mid forties, a relatively young man in the academic world. He'd received his Ph.D. before he was thirty and Liz had heard that since then he'd not only become a full professor, but had achieved tenure, almost unheard of in the current academic scene. He was a man who would push your career upward as he rose in his. You wanted him as a mentor, not the man who was laying you off because someone better was about to arrive.

Being part of Scarr's dig was important—she'd only just defended her Ph.D. this spring—and she knew finding an academic position in a competitive market would be tough. She needed the reference Scarr could give her, so she swallowed hard and tried for compromise. "I'd be happy to stay and simply be one of the dig team."

But Scarr was shaking his head even before she finished. "Sorry, Liz, but we don't need any more diggers." He peered at her through black-framed glasses that never seemed to move on his beak of a nose. His eyes were dark and, Liz thought, beady, but that might have been the thick lenses. "Look, this doesn't have anything to do with you. It was just an opportunity came out of nowhere and begged to be grabbed."

"But Dr. Scarr..."

Scarr sighed. The expression on his round face said that Liz was being difficult and he wished she'd stop. "It's Zachary Doyle," he said. "Surely you understand."

Unfortunately she did. In the small world of dinosaur paleontology, Zachary Doyle was a comet that hadn't yet reached its apogee. Everyone talked about Zac, the papers he'd written, the talks he'd given. All the grad schools competed for his presence in their programs. Every day he received a new accolade. No one had a bad word to say about him. If she'd been in Scarr's place, she'd have wanted Zachary Doyle as a team leader too.

She couldn't bring herself to acknowledge Scarr's request, though. Zachary Doyle's career was everything she wished hers could be and she was super jealous of him. She straightened her shoulders and said instead, "We have a contract."

Scarr looked at her in amazement. Clearly he thought mentioning Zac's name was enough to get her acquiescence. "That's an internship agreement. It's not binding."

"Sure it is," Liz said. She sounded belligerent to her own ears. She knew that wasn't the way to deal with Dr. Scarr, but she was desperate. She needed this post. Needed to stay until the last day of her contract. Needed to receive a glowing report about her contribution and capabilities. Needed the recommendation for permanent employment that Scarr could provide.

He narrowed his eyes. "The internship agreement says you must complete six weeks on the site before I evaluate you. You have completed thirteen, more than enough for me to write my report. I sent it in last night. The contract, as you call it, is fulfilled. For both of us."

Blood flowed into her cheeks in a hot rush that left her feeling weak. She was contracted to stay for another six weeks. The whole department at the university would know that she had been let go early. They'd assume she hadn't been able to do her job adequately and she'd be shuffled to the bottom of the hiring pile. Her career was over. Nine years of post secondary education finished with no future in sight. "I'd like to see it."

Scarr blinked. "See what?"

"Your report."

He frowned. "I sent it to Dr. Benoit. It's up to him to decide whether to let you see it, or not."

Dr. Benoit was the Dean. This was bad, very bad. She gathered her courage. There was no way forward, no going back. She had nothing to lose. She set her jaw, jutting out her chin. "Freedom of information. If it's about me, I have a right to read it."

Scarr's brows snapped together in a frown and he pursed his fleshy lips together into a tight, annoyed line. "I'll forward it to your e-mail account."

Liz nodded. It was a small victory, but she didn't feel like cheering. If his assessment had been positive, Scarr wouldn't care if she read the report. His reluctance told her that he'd either torn her to shreds or he'd been so neutral that anyone reading it would think the worst.

"Zac arrives tomorrow on the morning flight," he said briskly. "I'll pick him up and bring him back to the site. I should be back by mid-afternoon. I'd like you to help him set up, show him around and introduce him to everybody. You can fly out the day after."

She stared at him. This was worse than she expected. "You expect me to smooth the path for my replacement?"

Scarr's mouth tightened even more. "He's not your replacement. He's a new, exciting, addition to the team."

"Since he'll be doing my job and I won't be here any more, he sure sounds like my replacement!" She needed to guard her tongue, considering whom she was talking to, but she couldn't do it. Disappointment, outrage and fear had her in their grip and she was reacting, not thinking, right now.

"You are not doing yourself any favors, Miss Hamilton."

"It's Doctor Hamilton, as you well know! I defended my dissertation and was granted my degree before I came out on this dig." She shot him a fulminating look as she spoke.

Scarr raised his eyebrows and smirked.

She knew what that meant. Yes, she'd achieved her degree, but she didn't have a hope in hell of getting a tenure track academic position. Not without a glowing recommendation from Scarr. He knew what was in that internship report and it wasn't enough to get her the job she so desperately wanted.

She drew a deep breath to stop herself from spitting out words that were somehow even worse than those she'd already uttered, then she turned and stomped out of the command tent where Scarr had his office.

As she left the admin tent she grabbed the keys for Scarr's pickup from the security cabinet. The undergrad seated at the long table where they catalogued finds, looked up and smiled, but didn't ask if Liz had permission to take the vehicle. Why would she? Liz often used it when she went out to scout new locations.

Liz nodded curtly to the girl as she passed, then grimaced, ashamed of herself. It wasn't the kid's fault she'd just been fired. She couldn't help the bitter anger that welled up inside her, though. The girl was so cheerful about the experiences she was having this summer, so full of optimism for her future. The contrast with Liz's own gloomy career direction was painful.

The pickup's powerful engine leapt into life as soon as Liz turned the key in the ignition. She drove out of the site, bouncing on the rutted dirt road that was little more than a track. She didn't have a particular objective. She just wanted to get away from everyone associated with the dig. Perhaps absconding with Scarr's personal vehicle was childish and maybe a bad idea overall, but right now she didn't care.

A curve in the road had the camp disappearing from sight and she heaved a sigh of relief. The sun glinted off the red sandstone rocks, reminding her to put on her sunglasses. She reached for her pack and grimaced. She'd left it at the camp.

The road forked. Since she had no particular destination in mind, she angled away from the sun. The track skirted around a rise where hoodoos carved by wind and weather over countless millennia rose in odd, twisted shapes. The sight made her sigh. She loved the other worldliness of this western landscape. She would miss it when she left.

In the shadow of the hill, she braked to a stop. She put her head on the steering wheel and closed her eyes, fighting not to allow the gathering tears to fall. She drew a deep breath. Then another. And another. One tear sneaked out, but that was all. After a minute she sat up. What was, was. Scarr wouldn't back down. She was going home two days from now. She'd better get used to the idea.

She put the pickup in motion and continued on. After an hour she knew she should be getting back. She wasn't quite sure where she was, but she knew she was off of the government land where Scarr's permit entitled his team to dig. The adjoining land belonged to a farmer who had leased his dig rights to a private exploration firm called Discovering Dinos. Both the farmer and Mike Edmonds, the owner of Discovering Dinos, were reputed to be fierce in their defense of those dig rights. Scarr's opening remarks on the day his team gathered had focused on the boundaries they were to work in and where they could explore. Stay on the government side of the line had been a mantra at every staff meeting since. Liz was pretty sure that even driving on Discovering Dino's leasehold would be a fighting offense.

She should head back. The sun was low in the sky and there were dark clouds building. The morning's weather forecast had predicted a thunderstorm and heavy rain for the evening. Downpours in this area could be dangerous. The light soils had a poor vegetation cover that made it easy for them to be washed away. Roads could disappear in an instant and crevices appear just as suddenly. She didn't want to be out after dark in the middle of a raging downpour.

Still, it wasn't dusk yet. She'd been gone about an hour, maybe an hour and a half. She had plenty of time to get back before darkness and the storm made it impossible.

She came to another fork and stopped. The terrain was open here and she could see the road twisting away, the gap between the two routes gradually widening. She stared at it for a bit, then pulled her phone out of the pocket of her jeans and dialed. She'd call her sister, Faith, before she turned the pickup and headed back to camp. That was, providing she had cell service.

She did and Faith answered on the first ring, saying her name.

Her sister's voice immediately took Liz back to her home in Lexington, Massachusetts. A vision of a white, colonial-style house, set back from the road and surrounded by green grass and mature trees, had her eyes tearing up again. Faith had been her champion throughout their lives, and that hadn't changed with her marriage to mathematician Cody Simpson.

"Hi. It's me. Have you got a minute?"

"Liz!" Faith's voice was delighted. "You have cell service. This is great. I tried calling you the other day, but you were out of range."

"It's the river valley we're camped in," Liz said, not for the first time. "We can only get service when we're away from the main site. Even then it's spotty."

Faith laughed. "The joys of being out in the wild west. What's up?"

"I... I'm coming home." As she said the words, the threatening tears leaked out. She dashed them away, angry with herself.

There was a pause. "Okay," Faith said, lengthening the word until it was a cautious statement. "When?"

"The day after tomorrow." She resisted the urge to sniff. Faith would know she was crying and that would upset her, something Liz wanted to avoid since Faith was heavily pregnant with her first child.

Another pause. "Why? What happened?"

Liz hesitated, then told her about the interview with Scarr.

"Bastard," Faith said.

Since she rarely swore, Liz realized how much angry her sister was on her behalf. It eased the sting—a little, anyway. "The thing is, this means I'm finished. My career is over before it's even begun."

"No, it's not." Faith's tone said she was stating a fact, not offering an opinion. "You spent the last thirteen weeks managing a bunch of inexperienced undergrads and a couple of first year post grads. What did Scarr do? He hid in his tent and worked on his findings. You managed the dig, not him."

"And now he's got Zachary Doyle, the wonder kid of the paleo community, to help him out. It will be Zac who gets all of the find credits for the season along with Scarr. My name won't be mentioned."

"But will Zac do as good a job of keeping the team on track?"

"Probably. His reputation says he will." Liz sighed. "Even if he doesn't, he'll have the benefit of my time on the site. He can't lose."

"Scarr is an idiot," Faith said.

Liz laughed, with some bitterness. "Crazy like a fox."

"Liz..."

She sighed again. "I'm okay, Faith. It hurts right now, but I'll get over it. The sun's about to go down, so I'd better head back. Thanks for listening."

"Okay. When you've confirmed your flight details, let me know and I'll pick you up at the airport."

"I will. Thanks again." She disconnected, then sat for a moment staring at nothing. Talking to Faith had made the whole situation more real, her upcoming departure inevitable. Something inside of her shattered and the torrent of tears she had struggled to hold back came flooding out.

She wiped them away with the heel of her hand and gave herself a talking to. Faith was right. Liz knew she'd done a good job this summer. So did Scarr. He was just a jerk who had grabbed a flashy opportunity. He was sacrificing her because she might be capable, but she didn't have star quality. Zac Doyle did, and having his name attached to Scarr's dig would boost the careers of both men.

She sniffed and put the truck in motion. Ahead of her, the dark clouds were thicker. She reversed and turned back the way she'd come.

The rough road kept her focus on staying safely on it, so she didn't worry too much about her own trials for a time. The hill with the spectacular hoodoos was ahead of her, a landmark that reminded her she was still on private land, when she saw the beam of a low lying light.

She frowned. The sun was behind her, descending below the horizon in a glow of oranges and reds. It wasn't dark yet, so the blaze of light ahead couldn't be the headlights of another vehicle. They wouldn't show up clearly until darkness had fallen.

The road curved and the location of the light became clear.

She was right. It wasn't the headlights of a car or truck, because it was some distance fro the road on an unsettled part of the open prairie.

The orb, for she couldn't describe the bright spherical glow any other way, was motionless. She stopped the pickup and stared at it, her heart pounding.

If this was what she thought it was, it could not be.

She opened the door and slid out of the cab. Slamming the door behind her, she rounded the hood. Then she stood and stared at the blazing beacon of light.

Her heart pounded, hard and fast. Her stomach churned, until she was almost sick with excitement.

And fear.

No, not fear. Terror.

What if she was wrong? What if she was hallucinating?

The light beckoned her. The desire to walk toward it fought with an instinctive fear of the unknown.

But it wasn't unknown, was it? Not really. Not if it was what she thought it was.

She drew a deep breath and began to walk.

With every step the light seemed to beckon her forward, to grow more welcoming, joyous somehow. The distance to it was further than she expected, but that didn't matter. By the time she neared it, her measured, cautious steps had turned into something closer to a skipping jog.

Close up, the blaze of the light should have seared her retinas, but it didn't. It glowed without fire and urged her forward. When she reached it, the light flowed around her, wrapping her in a blanket of love and pleasure.

Her heart thumping like a jackhammer, she stepped forward, into the past.

CHAPTER 2

*E*xcept she didn't.

Walk into the past, that is. She walked into the future.

Liz Hamilton came from a family with an extraordinary capability —they were able to travel through time. She had no idea if anyone outside of her family possessed the same skill, for it was a closely kept secret, only shared with those who could be trusted not to divulge it.

They called themselves Beacons and Travelers. Those who were Beacons generated a light that drew the Travelers to them. Once found and entered, the light acted as a portal. One moment the Traveler was in her own time, the next she was in the Beacon's.

Not everyone in their Beacon-Traveler family became one or the other. Up until a few hours ago Liz thought she was one of those destined to remain firmly fixed in her own time. The ability usually manifested in adolescence, when physical and emotional growth produced cataclysmic changes in the human body. Her sister, Faith, had become a Beacon in her early teens, during a dreadfully difficult time with their father, but Liz had sailed through her teen years without a lot of drama. She'd never become a Beacon and she certainly hadn't traveled. She had resigned herself to being the odd duck in the family.

Until today, when a Beacon had drawn her to this rough prairie, an open, empty expanse of dark red earth marked with the dusty green of sage and other scrub plants.

When she'd seen the light she'd known instantly that someone was calling her through time. She assumed she would be stepping into the past, most likely into an early paleo dig, perhaps one that had taken place during the first few years of the twentieth century. Instead, she found herself in a closed room that looked like a paleo lab. That meant a building and a building meant the future.

The room was large, bright, and filled with gadgets, whose purpose she couldn't even guess at. There were no windows, so she couldn't tell what the area around the building now looked like. All she had to indicate when she was in time, was this room.

She took a step forward. Somewhere in this vast space there was a person, the Beacon who had called her here, but right now she was alone. She spied what she thought must be a computer located on a desk on the other side of the room. She headed toward it. The computer would have information that would tell her what year it was. It might also tell her the name of the organization that owned this research facility. Both were bits of information that she would really like to know and that her Beacon would never tell her.

She reached the desk and looked for the keyboard that would activate the glowing screen that appeared to be nothing more than a clear panel of glass. She couldn't find it. It wasn't in front of the screen, and couldn't be tucked in a drawer, because the desk didn't have any. Desperate, she lifted the few papers scattered on the desk surface, surreptitiously looking over her shoulder as she did it, just in case her Beacon reappeared and demanded to know what she was up to.

She found nothing. Frustrated, she put her hands on her hips and glared at the blank screen. There was no answer there, so she bent to inspect the paper documents more closely. Perhaps she'd find a clue that would tell her what her Beacon had been working on before he or she left the desk.

She realized that the top document was a scholarly article by a well-known paleontologist whose discoveries in the late twentieth century had proved that birds were closely related to the dinosaurs and changed many of the assumptions formerly believed about dinosaur physiology and behavior. Since she'd not only read the paper, but had used it as part of her thesis, she let out a frustrated sigh and straightened. Unless she could figure out how to work the machine, there was no help here.

She stepped back and looked around the room again. Whatever the year was in the future, paper hadn't disappeared. Maybe there was a filing cabinet she could check. Beside the gleaming steel double pedestal desk was a cabinet. The closed double doors probably hid shelves and those shelves might very well hold paper files. She bent to grab one of the handles, then pulled—and discovered the doors were locked.

Resisting the urge to kick the sleek metal structure, she turned her attention to the equally sleek and shining lab tables. On one there was a plaster case that must surely contain a dinosaur bone, probably excavated in the area. She headed over to take a closer look. Maybe there would be documentation that would give her the clue she needed.

She had almost reached it when a male voice said, "Ah, you're here."

She jumped. She couldn't help it, even though she knew her Beacon must be somewhere nearby. She swallowed hard, suddenly nervous. "You were expecting me?"

His eyes lit up and he laughed. "Grandma, I've heard about this day since I was old enough to be told I would be your Beacon."

She stared at him. He was a tall man, with sharp, intelligent features and shaggy blond hair the color of her sister Faith's. He was wearing jeans and a t-shirt that did nothing to hide the muscles in his broad chest, which were evidence that he kept in shape or did work that required physical labor, like work on a dino dig. "I'm your grandmother?"

The amusement died out of his face, replaced by a deeper emotion. He nodded and said, "And it's damned good to see you again." He moved toward her as he spoke. "That's all that has kept me going through the last couple of weeks."

She frowned at him, but made no attempt to avoid the hug he so clearly wanted to give her. "I don't understand," she said, as he wrapped hid arms around her and pulled her close.

Perhaps he sensed her reluctance in the stiffness of her body. Or maybe he knew how this introduction had gone, because she'd already told him about it. Whatever the reason he gave her a final squeeze, then eased away. "Sorry about that. It's just... I loved you a lot. We all loved you a lot..."

"We?"

"The family."

She drew in a deep breath. "Okay, this is what I've got so far. I have suddenly—unexpectedly!—become a Traveler and I've come forward in time."

He nodded.

She did a quick mental estimate of his age and guessed he was probably in his mid-thirties. If she was his grandmother, that meant she was at least eighty-five or ninety years old when she died, so she was now about sixty years into the future, since she was almost thirty herself. She shivered with excitement. What advances could have happened between this time and her own? Finding out would be fascinating.

And forbidden. A time traveler could inadvertently change the future if she gained knowledge of it and used it in her own time. Both Beacon and Traveler knew that a Traveler could only learn what was necessary and nothing more. "Am I allowed to know who your grandfather is?"

He shook his head. The amusement was back in his eyes.

Feeling like she was playing twenty questions, she said, "Okay. You mentioned that it was good to see me again, and that the past two weeks had been hard. What was that all about?"

He hesitated, obviously deciding what he could and couldn't tell her. Finally he shook his head as he shrugged. "I guess it's okay. I mean, I don't think it changes anything." He paused and a muscle jumped in his jaw. "You died two weeks ago. We were really close when I grew up. Watching you fail..." He shrugged. "Well, it was hard. You were always so active and full of energy." His mouth quirked up in a half smile. "Seeing you as a young woman is amazing. The resemblance to my mom is so close, she's going to freak out when she meets you."

Liz didn't have a daughter yet and had no idea when the girl would be born, but the idea of getting to know the adult version of her child was curiously enticing. "It will be exciting for me, too," she said dryly, and the amusement leapt back into his eyes. He had a confident way about him, this grandson of hers. She wondered if that came from nature or nurture.

She turned back to look at the desk on the opposite side of the room. "Why don't you tell me what you can?" She wrinkled her nose. "Like what your name is. Or would that give me a hint I'm not supposed to know?"

He smiled that quirky smile again and held out his hand. "I'm Mark."

She smiled back and shook it. "And I'm Liz." Before he could say anything, she held up her other hand and said, "Don't tell me you're going to call me Grandma. I may be your grandmother, but I don't have any kids yet. I don't think I could handle being a grandma at twenty-eight."

He laughed. "I'll call you Liz, but think of you as Grandma. How's that?"

She made a face at him, but said, "It will have to do. So tell me, Mark. Why now?"

He knew exactly what she meant. "We're late bloomers on your side of the family. We've both just come into our powers."

"You mean..." She stared at him aghast. She thought she was an aberration. "So you weren't a Beacon before?"

He shook his head.

She considered him skeptically. "Maybe you were a Beacon, but you never had a Traveler around to visit you."

He shrugged. "Maybe. All I know is that you are my first visitor, from either the past or the future."

Odd to be considered the past when this was her future. Liz shrugged off the feeling and plowed on. "Can you tell me what year it is?"

He shook his head. "Not yet."

"Not yet? But later you can? Why?"

He hesitated again, carefully choosing his words as he had done earlier. "You have to deal with a few issues first. Once those are settled I can give you more information."

She crossed her arms over her chest. "Very cryptic."

"It's meant to be," he said, nodding.

She gestured at their surroundings. "Tell me about this facility."

"It's a state of the art paleontology museum and laboratory."

"It wasn't here when I left my time."

His smile quirked to life again. "No, it wasn't."

"That's it? That's all you're going to tell me?"

He nodded, the amusement in his eyes and on his face, deepening.

At her indignation, she supposed. She poked his chest. "Listen, bud. If I'm your grandmother, you're supposed to respect me and do what I ask you to do."

He raised his eyebrows and his eyes danced. "I do, and I am."

"What do you mean?" she asked, suspiciously.

"When I was thirteen you told me what I could and couldn't tell you at this meeting. I'm only doing what you made me promise I would do."

She stared at him. "Well, hell. Looks like I'm too smart for my own good."

CHAPTER 3

She stayed at the lab for another hour, but despite her interrogation, Mark refused to tell her any more of her life as he knew it. He managed to divert her attention for a time by giving her a guided tour of the lab and its high-tech tools. She was amused to discover that the screen she had assumed was triggered by a keyboard was actually voice activated. Beyond that detail, he wouldn't give her specifics about how the other tools worked, of course. She'd probably told him not to.

As she walked through the light and back into her own time her heart pounded with the same frightened rhythm that it had when she first entered the beacon. What would she find? Would the present truly be the same as it had been when she left? What if it wasn't?

Fortunately, nothing had changed. Back in her own time she found her truck was still some distance away, parked on the edge of the road. The prairie lay open and dusty. The sun, however, was almost down below the horizon. It bathed the sky in a glorious visual display of pinks, purples, reds, and oranges. Dark colors shot through lighter, indicating clouds, and trailing the glorious sunset those clouds were thick and black. Liz thought uneasily that the weather was about to turn nasty. Not only would they be missing her at the camp, but she didn't want to be driving through the predicted thunderstorm.

She jogged to the truck. As she turned the key in the ignition she took one last look at the beacon, still shining brightly in the distance. Mark had told her that he was there most days and that she was welcome to visit any time. She wasn't sure how she would be able to take him up on that, though, since she was leaving the area, probably forever. As she stared at the light, and thought how much she'd always wanted to be able to travel through time like her mother, who was both a Traveler and a Beacon, and Andrew Byrne, the eighteenth century gentleman who came through her sister Faith's beacon for regular, weekly visits. She decided she would somehow sneak in one last visit before Dr. Scarr shipped her back to Boston on the morning plane two days from now.

With the sunset rapidly fading behind her and the black clouds blotting out what little light remained in the evening sky, she guided the truck along the decaying asphalt road. The surface hadn't been renewed in years and she was sure she hit every pothole. As she bounced along, she began to worry about breaking an axle. That would be a disaster, since there was no cell service at the dig camp, so she wouldn't be able to call for a rescue. She'd be stuck until someone found her.

The wind picked up, battering the truck. She clung to the wheel, a new concern gripping her. Now she worried that she might lose control and go off the road. She slowed down and tightened her grip on the wheel.

She was guiding the truck into a twist in the road when lightening flashed ahead of her. Automatically she started to count in a rough attempt to figure out how far away the storm was, but still the crack of thunder made her jump. She loosened her hold on the wheel at the same time as rain pelted down. A sharp gust of wind had the truck slithering on the suddenly slick surface. Instead of navigating into the turn, she went straight.

She ended up in the ditch. Rain pounded on the windshield. Darkness had truly descended now. All she could see ahead of her was what the truck's headlights revealed, and that was pretty much nothing, just a long expanse of prairie that rolled off into the darkness. There were no landmarks to tell her where she was, or buildings to offer shelter. Shelter made her think of her Beacon. She craned around in her seat, but even though she checked out three hundred and sixty degrees, she couldn't see the comforting light.

She was alone, exactly what she had wanted to avoid when she started her journey back to the camp. Her hands flexed on the wheel as she fought down panic. It was a storm. People survived storms all the time. She'd driven off the road, but she hadn't wrecked the truck. She had protection. Even if it wasn't quite the shelter she wanted, she was out of the rain and wind.

Maybe her cell had service. She hadn't checked it since earlier in the day. If there was service, she could call the local authorities and ask for help. Hopeful, she pulled her phone out and logged on. Nothing. No Wi-Fi, no data. Hopefulness fled.

She stared down at the screen. She wasn't sure if she wanted to scream with frustration or moan in panic. Instead, she drew a deep breath. She'd driven off the road, she hadn't rolled the vehicle. Trucks were designed to handle all kinds of terrain. She'd try getting it back onto the road so she could be on her way.

Ten minutes later she gave up on that. The wind made controlling the big vehicle difficult, while the rain had turned the soil into a quagmire. She was not going to get the pickup back onto the road. Not tonight, not without a tow. With her options exhausted, she put her head onto the steering wheel and gave way to despair.

The blast of a horn, followed shortly afterward with a pounding on the window beside her, had Liz lifting her head. She blinked as she looked through the glass at the male figure outside. Shoulders were hunched against the weather. The face was obscured by a wide-brimmed, low-crowned hat. She should have been frightened by the advent of the stranger, but all she could feel was a dawning hope.

He signaled her to roll down her window, so she did.

"Are you hurt?"

She shook her head. "No. I'm okay." She had to shout to have her words heard over the roar of the wind.

He stepped back to scrutinize the situation. "You've got yourself in pretty deep," he said, turning his attention back to her.

She nodded again. "The wind caught the front end as I was rounding the curve and the rain made the road slick. I tried to back out —and go forward!—but neither worked. I'm stuck." She flashed him her widest smile. "Can you help?"

He didn't reply immediately. She hoped it was because he was figuring out how to haul her out of the ditch. Finally he shook his head. "Not tonight. I can't risk my truck getting stuck as well, if something in the tow goes wrong."

Disappointment made it hard for her to keep from protesting, but she did, because his reasoning made sense. "Right," she said. She couldn't manage a smile, but she could ask a favor. "When you get to wherever you're going, would you arrange for a tow truck to come out here in the morning?"

Amusement showed in the merest flicker of a smile on his hard mouth. "You want me to leave you here for the night?"

She frowned. "Do I have an option?"

At that he did laugh. "No. Roll up the window. Pull what you need from the truck and come with me."

Liz thought about psychotic murderers, trusting strangers, and never going anywhere with someone you didn't know. She rolled up the window, pocketed the keys, and hopped out of the truck when he pulled the door open and held it against the press of the wind.

"Where's your jacket?" he demanded as she reached the ground.

She was wearing jeans and a t-shirt. Her most sensible clothing was her scuffed leather boots. "It was hot when I set out this afternoon. I don't have one."

He shook his head, even as he pointed back to the road. "Never trust the weather out here. It can turn in an instant. The passenger door's unlocked."

After that comment she expected him to leave her to fend for herself against the pelting rain and battering wind, but he stuck close, helping her balance on the slippery footing and shielding her with his body from the worst of the storm. Even so, she was wet when they reached his truck. He hauled open the door and she scrambled inside with absolutely no grace or elegance.

She thought he would round the front hood to the driver's side, but instead he went to the back of the truck. She heard him bang something, then a few moments later he was pulling open the door to the driver's side. He tossed her a couple of packages, then levered himself into the truck.

She caught the packages with a woof, then said, "What's this?"

"Emergency kit." He started the truck. "I don't want to have to get out again."

She nodded and made sure her seatbelt was fastened. They drove for about fifteen minutes in silence. The headlights barely cut through the gloom, so his speed was necessarily slow. By now the wind was screaming a gale and her rescuer's mouth was set in a grim line as he focused on keeping the truck on the road. She rubbed her hands on her jeans. She was now desperately afraid that they were not going to make it to civilization tonight. In fact, she was wondered if they would be able to stay safely on the road at all. Her only consolation was that she knew, because of her visit with her Beacon, that she would have a long life with a husband, kids, and grandchildren. She wouldn't die, not tonight.

That didn't mean she couldn't be badly injured in an accident caused by the storm. Mark hadn't told her that she would be healthy, only that she would be alive. She worried about that while they crept along, battling the storm, struggling to survive.

A shadow loomed up ahead of them and she was shocked when her rescuer drove off the main road onto a dirt path that was little more than an animal track. They inched along, but as they drove the darkness deepened and when they neared the shadow she could feel the wind easing.

It wasn't long before she realized that he had directed them into the lee of a low hill. The land mass forced the wind to flow around it and where he parked the truck was sheltered and relatively quiet.

"Where are we?"

He gestured in a direction she thought might indicate north. "This is the opening to Roaring River Canyon. The creek is a little to the west of us, but it's also below us, so if it floods we should be safe. The rise behind us gives us shelter. We'll have to stay here for the night."

Roaring River was famous in the area for it's unpredictability. Usually it was a dry creek, but in the spring it flooded with winter run off, and in the summer a storm like the one battering them now could cause a flash flood.

She shivered. He'd cut the engine as he spoke and her t-shirt clung, cold and wet, to her skin. Roaring River Canyon was on the land that Discovering Dinos and Michael Edmonds, an independent paleontologist who sold his finds to the highest bidder, had the dig permit.

She looked over at her rescuer. She didn't know anything about Michael Edmonds except that Dr. Scarr considered him to be a rogue and a renegade—a mercenary in the paleontological world.

A rancher owned the land Edmonds was exploiting. Apart from the landowner and his ranch hands, the only other people who would be out in these badlands would be Edmonds himself or one of his dig team. She shot her rescuer a sideways look and wondered which of her options this man was.

She hoped he wasn't Michael Edmonds himself.

He indicated the emergency kit. "There's a thermal blanket inside."

"Great." Her shivering got worse and she fumbled with the fastenings.

He put his hand on her shoulder and she looked over at him to see that he was frowning. "You're soaked. Get rid of the shirt, then wrap yourself in the blanket."

Her fingers stilled. She stared at him.

He sighed impatiently. "I'm not going to try anything. It will be a cold night. I don't want you suffering from exposure."

She shivered again, adding a telling point to his argument. "Okay, but don't look." He snorted and moved in his seat so that his back was toward her. She saw that he was pulling off his jacket, probably because he was wet too, then turned away to remove her t-shirt. "I don't even know your name," she said in a conversational way, as she wrapped the thermal blanket around her shoulders.

"It's Mike," he said.

Her heart sank.

"Mike Edmonds."

Absolutely the worst person to be stuck with in the close confines of a pickup truck over night. Even worse, she found this paleo pirate's tough, self-confident manner way too attractive. His hat and the darkness made defining his features difficult, but she had a feeling that he was probably a good-looking man, as well as a very masculine one.

"I have the dig permit for this side of the property line, though I expect you are well aware of that, since you're one of Scarr's bevy of pretty undergrads. The question is, which one are you?"

CHAPTER 4

"I'm Liz." She hesitated, then added, "Liz Hamilton."

Liz Hamilton. The name rang a bell, but he couldn't quite place where he'd heard it, because he was too busy trying to ignore what her body was doing to his. He shrugged off his jacket. It was wet, not quite soaked through, but close enough that he was better off without it. He draped the dry side over his lap to hide his reaction to her as he opened his emergency pack and pulled out a thermal blanket to wrap himself in.

"Thanks for helping me," Liz Hamilton said from behind him. Her teeth were chattering now. He'd turn on the engine to give them some heat, but he'd have to limit the use. He had three quarters of a tank and carried an emergency can as well, but it would be easy to fall asleep in the warmth and forget about the idling engine. He didn't want to find themselves out of gas in the morning.

"Don't worry about it," he said gruffly. "It's what we do out here." He had the thermal blanket out and draped it over his shoulders.

She cleared her throat. "Well, okay. I just... I wasn't looking forward to spending the night in my truck. Alone."

He shifted in his seat. "Can I turn around yet?"

"Oh. Yeah, of course."

He turned to find that she was bundled up in the blanket and biting her lower lip. Her eyes, long-lashed and very blue, watched him warily.

"Sorry," she said. "I should have told you I was done." She sounded embarrassed, as if the thoughtlessness of the act was unusual for her. She confirmed his deduction when she continued on, "Today has been rather eventful. I have a lot on my mind."

He let that one pass. He didn't want to get into a deep discussion of Liz Hamilton's issues, whatever they were. He'd rescued her from her truck because out here you didn't ignore someone who was stranded. That she was a woman alone added an imperative to the need to act, but it wasn't the root cause.

He turned the key in the ignition and the engine roared into life.

"What are you doing?"

"Getting us some heat." He looked at her critically. Those gorgeous blue eyes were huge and her lips were pale. He hoped that the engine heat would raise the temperature in the cabin enough to warm her, because he didn't want to have to use body heat to warm her up. His memory of her nipples peaking from the cold and clearly outlined by the wet t-shirt was already playing havoc with his libido.

The clock on the dash was telling him that it was nine forty-five. The hours until sunrise, trapped in the cramped confines of the pickup's cab with an attractive, sexy female, stretched out before him, a long, slow torture as his senses demanded more than his mind thought it wise to take.

"Oh, that's lovely," she said as heat began to pump from the vents. She leaned her head against the seat. "I shouldn't have been on the road so late, but I was distracted."

"Can't afford to do that out here," he said. He stared out the windshield into the darkness. The rain was easing off. That might be a good thing, or a bad one. If the storm was moving away, he might be able to get them out of here before dawn. But if it was just a lull, they could be in for even worse weather conditions.

"No," she said on a sigh. "I found that out." She laughed, bleakly he thought. "I guess it's a good thing I was fired this afternoon. I can go back to Boston where I know how to deal with extreme weather, even huge mid-winter snow dumps."

Boston. Oh, hell. Now he knew who he had in the shotgun seat in his cab. Liz Hamilton, Dr. Liz Hamilton. The woman Dr. Alfred Snotty Scarr had hired on as supervisor of his exploration team, because the idiot man was better at scrounging up funding than finding dinos. He'd heard that Hamilton had the eye and that she'd found two promising areas this season. Areas that would probably keep Scarr busy excavating for the rest of this season and beyond.

And she said she'd been fired today. Interesting.

He could change the subject to something more neutral. It was what he should do, given who he was. He could ask her about Boston and if she was going home to family. Get her to talk about her siblings. Her parents. Her favorite aunt. Anything, but why Scarr had fired her.

He didn't care about her family though, and that conversation wouldn't keep his imagination off her curves and those peaking nipples. He cleared his throat. "Tough news." Should he admit that he knew her position in Scarr's hierarchy? If he did, would she wonder how he knew?

She took the decision away as she said, "Not unexpected. I'd hoped... The truth is, I just completed my Ph.D. and I need a job. I'd hoped my internship with Scarr would lead to something more permanent."

Internship? Really? He suspected that Scarr had been leading her on, ensuring he secured a highly trained individual at an inexpensive or non-existent salary range. That didn't sit well with Mike. He believed in paying people what they were worth. "You work on the dino dig up on the federal land?"

"Did," she said.

Apparently Liz Hamilton was a stickler for details. Maybe that was what had put her afoul of Scarr. He was a guy who liked to be praised, not bucked. Though Mike knew the answer already, he said, "Are you one of Scarr's dig babes?"

There was a minute of charged silence, then she laughed. "God, you're right. Virtually all the undergrads who are digging the site are female." She contemplated that for a minute, then she said, "No, I was his dig supervisor. He had me doing exploration work."

"Any results?" He was shameless. He knew the answer. Scarr had been working the federal land for the past five years. He'd found bones, enough to prove the area had potential, but there had been no spectacular finds under his administration. Not only that, but that bevy of beauteous undergrads he hired to work his finds tended to be entitled, stuck up pains-in-the ass who drove the locals crazy whenever they went to town.

Liz Hamilton shrugged. The thermal blanket slipped a little on her shoulder, exposing a sliver of pale, silky smooth skin. His mouth dried as other parts of his body leapt to attention. Hell, if he didn't keep his mind off her body and what it would feel like under his hands, he wasn't going to survive the night without embarrassing himself.

"I'd like to think I made a contribution," she said. "I found two really promising bone beds. I wasn't able to do much more than a cursory examination, but I think I may have stumbled on a nest."

He doubted it. From what he'd heard stumbling wasn't Liz Hamilton's style. She took her job seriously. In the few short months she'd been on Scarr's team, she shaped up the dig babes and made them treat her—and the local residents—with respect. If she thought she'd found a dinosaur nest, a reasonably rare occurrence, she probably had.

The cabin was now toasty warm. Mike switched off the engine. "So why did Scarr fire you?" Not the most tactful question and maybe he shouldn't have asked it, but he was curious. He wondered if Scarr had made a pass she'd turned down. He couldn't think of any other reason to let a productive member of the organization go.

She was quiet for what seemed like a long time. Finally she said in a neutral voice, "Zachery Doyle contacted him and offered his services."

Zachery Doyle. Oh crap.

"Zachery Doyle is a top scholar in our field. A star, you might say. Dr. Scarr didn't have the funding to keep both Zac and me." She shrugged and the blanket slipped a little further. "You don't say no to Zac Doyle."

The rain had eased to almost nothing, but the wind continued to whistle. "Do you think this thing has blown itself out?" Liz asked, changing the subject abruptly. "That we might be able to get home before morning?"

Now that they were no longer talking about that idiot Scarr, his awareness of the creamy flesh exposed by the loosening blanket was even greater. He'd like to be able to say they could make it to main roads and back to town. That would be easiest for both of them. He wasn't optimistic, though. The forecast had been grim and the signs were all indicating the weathermen were right for once. "Maybe. I'm not going to set off until I'm sure, though."

She nodded and fell silent. He thought she closed her eyes. He leaned back and stared out of the windshield. He glanced down at the clock from time to time, counting the minutes. One, then five and ten. The rain held off. There was quiet in the cab. Twenty minutes passed. The rain dried up completely.

A half an hour later he was contemplating leaving the sheltering shadow of the hill, when lightening streaked across the sky in a vivid display of nature's dangerous beauty. A crack of thunder followed.

Liz shrieked and sat up.

The heavens opened and rain came down in a deluge of big droplets that pounded the cab. It was the kind of rain that would wash away the surface ground, leaving great gaping holes behind. There was no way they were going anywhere tonight. It would be too easy to slip into a newly formed gully in the dark.

Another jagged flash of lightening was swiftly followed by the violent bang of thunder right overhead. He could hear the wind whistling around them and he thought it likely that the outside temperature had dropped significantly.

Beside him, Liz was shivering. He fired the engine again to warm the cabin and said roughly, "It's going to get worse before it gets better. Make sure you keep the thermal blanket tight around you."

She nodded. The engine chugged, churning out welcome heat. The rain hammered the roof, showing no signs of letting up. Liz was wrapped from chin to toes in the blanket, not a bit of her delectable body exposed to his eyes, but he couldn't stop thinking her breasts peaking against her wet t-shirt.

He shut off the engine and focused on worrying about the storm. Much better than fantasizing about a woman who was way out of his league.

This was going to be one of those storms that had rivers flowing down formerly dry streambeds, sweeping away everything in their path. A creek like the one that ran through Roaring River Canyon would be raging before night's end. The water would rush through the canyon on its journey out onto the prairie, and it would be headed their way. He'd deliberately parked them on a rise, but was it high enough to keep them from being swept away? He believed it was. He thought grimly that they were about to find out.

"Are we safe here?" Liz asked. Her voice was low and there was an underlying shake to it.

She was scared.

He glanced at her at the same time as she said, "I've never been in a storm like this, but I've heard of them. The rain creates flash floods that can wash out everything before them. How stable is the rise we're on?"

"Stable enough," he said. *I hope*, he thought, but didn't say the words. The cabin was warm now, but she was still shivering. He cut the engine. He thought that her shivers came from fear rather than feeling chilled. There was no sense in wasting gas.

Another flash of lightening, swiftly followed by the crash of thunder. The rain pounded harder and around them the wind screamed. Liz made a squeaking sound that he thought was a shriek she couldn't quite stifle. She was trying hard to be brave in the face of nature gone mad, but she was a city girl who had probably never been through a storm like this.

The next streak of lightening was followed by the roar of thunder, and both happened way too soon after the previous ones. The storm was right overhead and it was massive. Liz squeaked again and he slipped closer to her. She was shaking uncontrollably now.

He put his arm over her shoulder and pulled her gently against him. She stiffened and he said, "Relax. I'm not making a move. The wind's picked up and the temperature has dropped. We need to conserve heat and the best way to do it is to keep close."

She processed that and after a minute she nodded. "Okay." She shifted so her body pressed against his.

The next clap of thunder had her jerking in a startled way, even though she should be used to the sound of the storm by now. He automatically tightened his hold. She snuggled in close, burying her head in his shoulder. She was shaking hard, so he wrapped his other arm around her to comfort her. He felt her sigh and her body relax.

His didn't. Not only did he have a very attractive female nestled sweetly in his arms, but he had to keep that same female safe. Every male instinct he possessed was on alert and he knew that while the storm raged there was no way he would be able to let her go.

It was going to be a long night.

CHAPTER 5

She woke snuggled against Mike Edmonds warm body. He was still asleep. She knew that because she could feel the slow rise and fall of his chest under her cheek.

She should sit up. Pull away. Find her t-shirt and hope that it was dry enough that her bra wouldn't be perfectly visible beneath the thin cotton. Cover herself up before Mike's very masculine gaze saw way more than she was comfortable with.

But she didn't. His hold made her feel sheltered and cared for, a sensation she liked too much to move away from. She knew that it would be gone as soon as he woke and they were at odds with each other again. In the meantime she'd enjoy this quiet, stolen pleasure in the darkness of the now peaceful night.

She must have fallen asleep again, soothed by his steady breathing and the calm that had followed the raging wind and rain. This time when she woke, it was because Mike was easing away from her, shifting to open the cab door and leave the truck. She opened her eyes and stretched, then realized he must have gone out to relieve himself. That reminded her of her own needs, but she was careful to avert her eyes to give him privacy.

He was gone a long time. She'd pulled her t-shirt back on, finger combed her short blond hair, and started to wonder if something was wrong by the time he returned. Worry made her anxious, so that when he opened the cab door and poked his head in, she glared at him. "Where were you?"

"Scouting. The creek is still high, but the track is clear. We can get back to the road."

She hardly noticed what he'd said. By the time he was finished she had her door open and was scrambling out of her seat. "Great," she said, turning back to view him through the truck. "Turn around so I can use the bathroom."

He chuckled, annoying man, but he slammed his door and she saw that he leaned against it, putting his back toward her. She slammed her own door than moved away to find a place to do her business.

When she was finished she came round the bed of the truck to stand beside him. Sometime in the night he'd taken off his hat and he hadn't put it back on again, so she saw his face clearly for the first time now. The morning sun glinted off thick, russet brown hair that he wore cut short. His eyes were a warm hazel, his nose was straight, and his chin had a determined jut to it. It was his expression, though, that jarred Liz and made her swallow hard.

There was a confidence there that was all male. He was a man who was comfortable in his environment, and, she thought, in himself. He knew what needed to be done and he showed it in a straightforward way that she found very appealing. She resisted the tug of attraction and said, "Now what?"

"I'll take you back to your truck. I've got a chain in the back. I'll pull you onto the road and you can be on your way."

Excellent. Exactly what she wanted. Well, no, it wasn't. It was what she *should* want. The last thing she wanted was to go back to the dig camp where Alfred Scarr would be furious at her for taking off and not coming back. He'd probably be so mad he'd send her home today, rather than have her show Zachary Doyle around the dig site before she left.

She'd much rather stay with Mike Edmonds and find out more about him. Even though he was, technically, the enemy. At least, that's how Scarr had always described him. The marauding amateur who plundered ancient bone beds of their priceless relics and destroyed evidence that would enrich the world's knowledge of its origins.

Looking at Mike Edmonds now, amused hazel eyes seeing way more of her thoughts than she was comfortable with, long, lean body resting against the frame of the truck, his hands shoved into the pockets of his jeans, and one knee bent in a casual stance, she could believe he would be quite happy to manoeuver outside the law. She'd read his dig reports, though, and they gave her a rather different picture of him.

She said abruptly, "Sure. Let's go, then." She pulled her gaze away from his and turned to round the back of the truck to the passenger's side. Those eyes, that gorgeous face, were making her far too aware of him and of herself. The sooner they got back to her truck and she was on her way back to her own bleak reality, the better.

Before they'd gone a mile his mouth was a grim line and she was clutching the door handle for balance. The morning had dawned bright and clear. The sun was shining down from a cloudless blue sky. In a few hours the earth would be dry again, but now it was still heavy with rain and the track, never much more than earth beaten down by those traversing it, was now a series of rocks, potholes, and mud. Mike drove slowly, but still, they bounced over the surface until they reached the paved roadway.

Liz heaved a sigh of relief as the truck's wheels hit the asphalt. Mike picked up speed, but he still drove cautiously, for all around them was evidence of the storm. In places the side of the road was washed away. In others, there were rocks strewn onto the pavement, evidence of rushing water. Usually dusty, the road surface was greasy with dirt and water that had become a thin coating of mud.

By the time they reached her truck, Liz's stomach had started to growl. He drove past, found a place to turn around, then pulled up behind the truck and parked. They both got out and surveyed the damage.

She was lucky, Liz thought. The truck was off the road and leaning at an odd angle, but it was the same angle as last night. Mike walked around it, surveyed wheels, crouched down to test the firmness of the ground.

Finally he came back to where she was standing, observing him. "I think I can pull you out." Her stomach rumbled and his lips twitched. "Do you have emergency supplies in your truck?"

She nodded, even though she hadn't checked before she rushed away from the camp. There should be rations of some kind, and bottled water. If there wasn't, though, she wasn't going to admit it to Mike Edmonds who she was quite sure would never venture out into the wild without being prepared.

"Okay," he said, with a jerk of his head. "I'll get set up, then."

After considerable muttering that rose in intensity to a snarl and the occasional curse, Mike got her truck out of the ditch and onto the road. He inspected it carefully, then nodded. "You're good to go." His gaze was firm. "I'll follow you back to your camp."

She opened her mouth and he shook his head. "Don't argue. The truck looks okay, but there may be deeper damage I can't see. Plus the roads are dangerous. I don't want you to be stranded a second time."

When he was finished, she raised her brows and said, "I was about to say thank you. I appreciate that."

Color rushed into his cheeks. His mouth quirked up into a rueful smile, but he didn't say anything. Instead he nodded and turned back to his pickup. Liz climbed into hers and got the engine started. They headed off.

As she drove, Liz noticed what she hadn't been able to see in the dark. She realized she had been closer to the border between Edmonds' dig and her own than she thought when she went off the road. In fact, they were now right at the edge of the property Mike managed. She'd soon be back at Scarr's dig.

She was deep in her gloomy thoughts when ahead of her Mike's taillights suddenly flashed on. It was a good thing they were moving slowly, as she had to stomp on the breaks. Her truck skidded on the slick surface. When she came to a stop she saw what had caused him to stop so suddenly.

The road was gone. In its place was a gash where rushing water had torn through the countryside. As she opened her door and slipped out of the cab, she saw that he had also emerged to inspect the damage.

When she came up beside him, he flicked her a glance. He'd put his hat back on and the broad brim shaded his eyes, hiding the expression in them. "We'll have to detour around. There's no way we can cross this."

He was right. The hole in the ground had to be six feet deep and the sides were steep and jagged. To the north it extended as far as she could see. On the other side of what used to be the road, was the same view. They'd have to go miles out of their way to find a crossing.

As she scrutinized the newly exposed land, something caught her eye. "Hell," she said and ran to the edge of the gully.

Mike tore after her. "Careful!" He grabbed her arm to keep her from doing a header into the pit.

But she had already stopped. "We have to find a way to get down there." She glanced at him as she spoke.

He was staring into the rift, as she had been moments before. His mouth curved up into a smile that was pure glee. "I guess we do." He sounded as elated as she felt.

The flash flood had washed away dirt and gravel, exposing the rock beneath. From where they stood an ancient bone, preserved in stone, was clearly visible. And it wasn't alone. This had all the earmarks of a major find.

But was it on federal land, or private?

Mike Edmonds looked down at her. His grin was cocky. "Shall we go take a closer look?"

She was on the move before he was.

They found a spot where the slope looked reasonably stable and where they could scramble down into the gully. Before they set off, though, Mike scrutinized the scene through narrowed eyes. "No sense in going down twice. I'll get my tools from the truck. Wait here."

Liz frowned. "Like giving orders, do you, Edmonds?"

He raised his eyebrows. "I need to document the find. I don't want to deal with a female with a broken ankle instead."

"We," she said.

Amusement leapt into his eyes. "We're on my side of the boundary, lady. My find."

If she said, *I saw it first*, she'd sound like a whining eight year old. That was how she felt though, and Mike Edmonds was seriously ruffling her temper. She didn't know the details of his agreement with the old rancher who owned this land, but she knew that if he'd discovered a bone bed on federal land, Scarr would never let him work it, even as an associate. So he might have right on his side, but after her humiliating termination by Scarr yesterday, she didn't plan to give in easily to another pushy male.

So she said in her most professional way, "The actual location will have to be confirmed by GPS coordinates. Until it is, and even after, I believe I have a role to play in the excavation of this creature."

He looked down at her. "Do you now? And what would that be?"

"We excavate as equal associates. We document the find together and we publish together." Liz knew that what she was demanding was extraordinary, particularly in the hostile circumstances that existed between Dr. Scarr and Mike Edmonds. She didn't expect him to cave easily and he didn't.

"Let's find out how big this thing is and exactly where it is first."

Her turn to raise her brows. She added an expression she hoped was professionally neutral, but when anger flashed in his eyes, she figured she'd actually achieved disdainful. Not good for a working relationship.

Despite the temper lurking in his eyes, he managed to keep his tone even. "I'm going to get my tools." He paused, apparently wrestling with himself. "*Please* don't go down into the rift until I'm back."

She'd put a foot wrong and he was trying. She nodded. "Okay."

He cast her one last smoldering look, then he turned and headed back to the truck.

She watched him for a minute, enjoying the fluid way he moved his body as he walked, his broad shoulders and lean hips. Not to mention his very watchable ass. She turned away. Ogling the man would do her no good and he was manipulative enough to figure he could use her attraction to keep her in line.

Instead, she examined the rift, looking for other signs of dinosaur bones. Some distance away there was an anomaly that looked interesting. She memorized its location, then continued to scan.

As her gaze roamed the area, her mind wandered as well, going back to the extraordinary meeting she'd had before she drove her truck off the road. Mark, her Beacon, must have known about the accident, the rainstorm, and the find, but he didn't tell her about them. That meant they were important—no, life changing—events.

Her heart began to beat a little faster. In her family, people came into their time travel abilities as a result of a critical event in their lives. Her sister Faith had found her abilities during an argument with their father, Daniel, over her future. Would it be decided by Daniel or would Faith choose her direction? The way Faith told it, Daniel's decision had cast her into a fit of despair. She'd felt trapped and could see no way out.

Until Scarr had fired her yesterday, Liz had never fallen into such an emotional pit. She'd drifted through life, always getting what she wanted without too much effort. Sure, she had to work hard to get through a Ph.D. program, but studying for long hours and worrying about exams and her dissertation wasn't an emotional pit. Assuming that her career was over before it began was, and that was why she'd found her Beacon.

Time travel was an odd coping mechanism that she didn't think existed beyond her direct family line. The link between Beacon and Traveler began to help a Traveler deal with a crisis in his or her life. Once forged, the bond lasted a lifetime. She pondered that for a moment. Mark said he was her grandchild, which meant that she had been with him as an old woman during his childhood, but now, when she visited him they were both young adults and they would grow old together. She would never really leave him. That would be an incredible relationship. Not only would she see her grandson live to old age, but she would be able to watch her great grandchildren, and perhaps even her great, great, grandchildren, grow up.

The thought had her grinning at the scar on the landscape she was ostensibly scrutinizing, until she realized that she would only be able to connect with Mark if she lived here, or if he moved to Boston, where she'd be returning in about forty-eight hours or sooner. She doubted he was going to abandon that lab with all of its sleek sophisticated technology. If she wanted to continue to visit the future, she would have to find a way to stay right where she was.

She shoved her hands in her pockets and stared at the bone she and Mike Edmonds had found. There was no other option. She would have to convince Mike to include her on the dig, whether it was on his land or not.

CHAPTER 6

The find was exactly what it had looked like from the lip of the crevice—a femur from an enormous creature, probably one of the giants of the Cretaceous period. Mike slid an unobtrusive glance at the woman beside him. She'd stayed put at the top of the scar until he returned, as he'd asked, then she'd scrambled down the slope behind him, making no attempt to push past, and showing reasonable caution. He didn't think that came easy for her, which made him wonder why she was suddenly so respectful of his authority.

They both set to work, exposing as much as they could of the find without damaging it, cautiously exploring to discover the extent of the bone bed. The sun was high in the sky before Liz stepped back and said, "I think we have an almost complete skeleton here."

Mike nodded. He though so too. He also thought there might be more than one skeleton. This was a phenomenal find. "The only problem is the location."

Liz rubbed her forehead with her arm. The cool of the morning had given way to a hot midday. "I'm going to have to get back to Scarr's camp. He's probably frantic by now."

Apparently she hadn't called in, either because she couldn't get cell service or because she'd been so caught up in the find, she hadn't thought to. Whichever, her need to get to Scarr's camp suited Mike just fine. Once he was on his own, he'd be able to get his team working on staking out the find. Around here, possession was nine tenths of the law, especially when the person claiming that last tenth was not much respected in the area.

"So," she said, breaking into his thoughts. "Are you going to tell me what the GPS reading is?"

He looked at her blankly, his mind scrambling for a reply.

She laughed. "You don't think I missed you checking the readings earlier, do you? Come on, Edmonds, give. Who has the legal right to dig this creature?"

He cursed himself for assuming she'd be easily duped, just because her heart-shaped face, big blue eyes, and soft, lush lips were so totally feminine and, well, sweet, somehow.

She wasn't sweet or soft. She was prickly and tough. He knew that from last night and from her reputation as Scarr's site supervisor. She stood there, now, hands now in her pockets, her stance relaxed as she stared at him. There was challenge in those wide blue eyes, and the amusement in her expression somehow added a feminine power to her features. She was all woman, intelligent, strong, and determined. She wasn't going to give in easily.

Slowly, he smiled. Nor would he. "What makes you think I took a GPS reading?"

"Because I would have," she said with a shrug.

Well, that was unexpected. Still, he liked that forthright quality, so he said, "You're right, I did do a check."

She raised her brows when he didn't continue. "Are you trying to make me beg?"

At that he grinned. "It's a thought." She shot him a fierce frown and he laughed. "Okay, I'll give it to you straight."

"That would be appreciated," she said, her tone tart.

He chuckled again and touched the exposed bone that first drew them into the gully. "This is on my side of the border." He walked the length of the animal's body to the last bone they'd found, one from the creature's neck and pointed. "This is on Scarr's."

She sucked in a breath and her breasts swelled beneath the thin t-shirt. "Shared jurisdiction?"

He was momentarily distracted by imaginings that had nothing to do with the workplace. He dragged his mind away from her body and back where it should be, on this momentous find. "Most of the skeleton is on my side of the line. I dig the site."

She frowned at the bones for a minute, then looked squarely at him. Her expression was all business. "Scarr will dispute. He'll get an injunction to keep you from digging and he'll pull in every expert in the field he can to destroy your reputation before the case ever gets to court."

She was right. He'd met guys like Dr. Alfred Scarr before. "I don't have a reputation to destroy. I'm already an outlaw in the paleo field. What Scarr and his colleagues think doesn't matter to me."

She shook her head. Her short blond hair, cut long in the front, but short on the sides, fell into her eyes. She raked the bangs away in an impatient move. "You don't know Scarr. Whatever has happened before, he'll make it worse."

"I'll take my chances." She actually looked worried. He appreciated her concern, but he didn't think she had any idea of how far out of the tightly knit academic community he was. If Scarr dragged in professors and scholars to condemn him, they'd only be heaping their dirt onto an already huge pile.

"Look." She drew in a deep breath. "There's a good chance that there's more here than one skeleton. This area has tremendous poten-tial. It needs to be thoroughly explored. I think we'll find there are more bones on Scarr's side of the line and on yours. This will be a major site and you will have to work it with the professionals."

The word grated. "I am a professional."

She hesitated, then nodded. "Okay, my mistake. With academics like me, or Dr. Scarr. The relationship needs to be cordial—"

Still annoyed, he said, "Not likely."

She actually laughed at that. "Okay. You're right. It's hard to be pleasant to Alfred Scarr. Let's say polite, then. I can do that. I can be polite, even cordial. Let me talk to Scarr. See what I can work out."

"You want to carve out a place for yourself here." The flush that ran up under her tan told him he'd hit the mark.

"What's wrong with that? Yes, I want to stay. Yes, I want to continue a career in this field, and if Scarr sends me away before the season is over, I'll have zero chance of ever finding another posting. So, yeah, I'm going to do what I have to, to make this work for me."

Her jaw had hardened and her chin, which already had a determined jut to it, became more pronounced. Her expression had settled into bleak lines, exposing her desperation. He understood that emotion and he sympathized. Slowly he nodded. "Talk to Scarr, then. I'm willing to negotiate a compromise, but I'm not going to let him push me around."

A flicker of relief showed on her face, though a shadow of concern remained. "Thanks." She held out her hand. "Partner."

Slowly, not sure he was doing the right thing, he reached out and closed his hand over hers. They shook. The deal was done.

As she walked into the admin tent, Liz heard the sound of voices coming from the area Scarr had partitioned off for his office. The undergrad who had been cataloguing finds when she stormed out the day before looked up as she strode into the tent. Her serious expression brightened and she opened her mouth to say something, by way of greeting, Liz thought. She didn't want Scarr to know she'd arrived, though, so she put her finger to her lips. The girl frowned and closed her mouth. Liz smiled her thanks and continued on to the office.

The voices inside were male. She recognized Scarr's light tenor, but not the deeper one that replied. That could only mean one thing— Zachary Doyle had arrived. It fit. He was supposed to arrive on the eleven AM plane today. Scarr must have used one of the other vehicles to drive into town to pick him up. She hid a smile. Zac's presence suited her just fine.

Reaching the partition, she lifted the flap that served as a door and stepped into Scarr's office. The two men were huddled around the simple wood table that served as Scarr's desk. They both looked up as she entered. There was momentary astonishment on Scarr's face, then the emotion morphed into an annoyed frown that edged into narrow-eyed temper. The butterflies that had taken flight in her belly the moment she parked the pickup in Scarr's special spot, rioted in panic at the look. She fought the nerves they expressed. She wasn't going to be Scarr's victim. This time she was going to win their confrontation.

She smiled at Scarr, then she turned to Zac and held out her hand. "Hi, you must be Zachary Doyle. I'm Liz Hamilton. It's nice to meet you."

Zachary Doyle did not look like a man in his mid-twenties. His thick hair was blond and curly, even though he wore it cut short. On his round face a dusting of freckles marched from his cheeks across his snub nose, and there was a guileless expression in his wide blue eyes that Liz knew had nothing to do with the personality of the man himself.

He slid a look at Scarr before he accepted her hand. Liz glanced at Scarr too. He was watching the exchange with that same narrow-eyed look that promised painful repercussions, but he wasn't making his move yet.

"Zac Doyle," Zac said, completely unnecessarily. His voice cracked and he cleared his throat. "I understand you are going to give me a tour before you head off."

"Oh, yeah," Liz said. "Do I have a tour planned." Scarr was sitting behind his makeshift desk, while Zac had one of the two folding chairs on the other side. Liz grabbed the second chair and sat down.

"I wouldn't make myself comfortable," Scarr snapped. "You'll be leaving as soon as you pack your gear."

Now that she was into the confrontation, Liz was beginning to enjoy herself. The butterflies were still flapping around with more energy than she liked, but at least she could ignore them now. She grinned at Scarr. "You'll want to come along, Dr. Scarr. This is a tour you won't want to miss."

From the corner of her eye she saw Scarr and Zac share a confused look, then Scarr said, "You took my truck yesterday. I should have reported it stolen. You're lucky I didn't."

When she drove the long, roundabout detour from the washout back to the camp, she thought about how Scarr would react to her return and what he'd say. A less self-centered man would be frantic with worry about the absence of a team member during a storm of last night's magnitude, but she knew Scarr and was quite sure he wouldn't even think about the potential for danger. Scarr was a control freak. She figured he'd be angry that she hadn't fallen neatly into his plans. She'd structured her whole defense based on that assumption. It looked like she'd been right.

"No," she said, drawing the word out and smiling. *"You're* lucky you didn't."

Scarr was so enraged by that cocky and, yes, cheeky, statement that his face flooded a bright red. He opened his mouth to say something, then closed it again without speaking. He half rose from his seat, a threatening move meant to prove dominance. Liz stayed where she was and kept her smile in place.

Zac said, "I'm new here and out of the loop. Can you fill me in?"

Scarr subsided into his chair, though his expression remained thunderous.

Nice gambit, Liz thought. Zac's question had defused the situation and saved his mentor's dignity at the same time. "Sure. If Dr. Scarr had notified the cops that the truck and one of his team members was missing, they might have found me last night before the storm made travel impossible."

She paused to survey her audience before she delivered her punch line. "And that would have been a shame."

Her statement didn't make much of an impact on Scarr. His expression hadn't changed. He was still furious. She suspected he wasn't listening at this point. Zac, on the other hand got it. The guileless blue gaze sharpened, though his facial expression was still one of polite interest, nothing more.

"You see," she continued, "I wouldn't have found the washout this morning." She watched understanding dawn on both their faces. Washouts were a gift from heaven, nature's way of shifting layers of soil and exposing the strata beneath without any effort on the paleontologist's part.

Zac sucked in a breath and Scarr frowned. "You found something?"

She nodded slowly, still smiling. Smugly now, she thought. "One full skeleton, maybe more."

"Congratulations!" Zac said.

"You'll take us there now," Scarr said. He pushed back his chair, this time with the intent of leaving the office.

Liz didn't move. "There's a problem."

Scarr hesitated. "What?"

"The washout is huge. It stretches from federal land across the boundary."

"Into Discovering Dinos' permit area," Scarr said flatly.

"Discovering Dinos?" Zac said. "The paleo pirates?"

Scarr nodded. He pulled his chair back to his desk, then drummed his fingers on the rough wooden surface. He stared blankly, lost in thought for a moment, then he shot her a penetrating look and said, "Are you sure?"

She nodded. "Yup. We took measurements and GPS readings."

"We?"

That was Zac and Liz thought he had once again caught on faster than Scarr had. She said, "Mike Edmonds and I."

"Mike Edmonds!" Scarr sounded shocked and furious at the same time.

"The pirate himself?" Zac said. He looked amused. There was a sneer in his tone.

Liz resented that. She resented that these two men had dismissed Mike Edmonds so summarily. She'd worked with him for hours this morning and he'd been meticulous in his documentation as he explored the extent of the find, careful to damage nothing. Yes, he worked in the private sector, funding his excavations through the sale of the bones he found, but he wasn't a pirate. He didn't steal the finds of other paleontologists.

"How much of the skeleton is on our side of the line?" Scarr snapped, still tapping the desk with his fingers.

"Probably half, maybe a third."

"The head?"

She shrugged. "We couldn't find it."

More tapping, then Scarr pushed back his chair again. "We need to go out there and take a look."

Liz nodded. "Sure. The skeleton is almost completely intact. It's a huge beast. We'll have to work with Mike Edmonds to excavate. A joint project, with joint reporting."

"We?" Zac said. His tone was innocent. The word itself was a bombshell.

Scarr shot him a speculative look, then he nodded and said, "Zac is right. There's no 'we' here. You're headed home tomorrow."

Liz expected Scarr to pull something like this. She thought she was prepared for it, for how she would feel when he tried to snatch the find of a lifetime out from under her. She wasn't. She had to fight the rage that flooded through her and threatened to subvert her careful planning with a temper tantrum of epic proportions. She sat very still, breathed deeply and slowly.

She turned fire into ice before she said, "I'm not going home."

"Sure you are," Scarr said. "A find like this is too important to mess around with. Zac will be heading up this team."

She shook her head, slowly, emphatically. "No, Dr. Scarr, he won't, and I'm not going home, because the only person Mike Edmonds is willing to work cooperatively with, is me. If I'm not the one supervising our side of the dig, then you'll only have half a dino when you're finished."

CHAPTER 7

The building that housed Discovering Dinos was somewhere between a warehouse and a gigantic barn. It loomed on the outskirts of Roaring River, the closest town to both dig sites, and its size was silent testimony to the importance of dinosaur excavations to this tiny community. Mike parked his truck in the lot beside the building and strode inside.

The lobby of Discovering Dinos was a small space. There was a desk and filing cabinets, but no visitor chairs. People who came to Discovering Dinos either had an appointment and were immediately ushered into the guts of the building, or they simply wandered through after a quick wave to Barb Conway, the woman who was the lobby's sole occupant.

The room itself currently sported three lavender walls. An accent wall was papered with a scene of a flower filled country garden, complete with an arbor drenched in trailing vines, and a swing on which a girl in a poofy dress and a straw hat was being pushed by a silly looking boy in breeches. Mike thought the whole scene ridiculous, but Barb sighed with pleasure when she looked at it and said she loved it.

And if Barb loved it, the absurd scene was fine with Mike. He didn't care what his lobby looked like, as long as the appearance made Barb happy. Not only was she the mother of his best friend, but she organized his life, made sure all the correspondence that went out of Discovering Dinos was professional and correct, and she had a shrewd sense of when to push and when to back off that had secured him more than one lucrative contract.

A middle-aged woman with thick glasses and short, well-cut hair that was dyed a dozen colors, of which lavender was most prominent, she looked up as Mike pushed open one side of the double entry doors. The oversized oak partners' desk where she sat didn't fit with the décor of the room, but like the wallpaper mural, Barb loved it. "Morning boss," she said, with a smile. "Or should I say, afternoon?"

He grinned at her, not at all put out. Barb Conway was the general manager of Discovering Dinos. At least, that was what he called her and what appeared beside her name on the company website. She called herself his secretary and office dogsbody. "I spent the night in my truck, so I'm running late."

She frowned. "In that dreadful storm? What happened?"

"I was working the trackway, then rescued one of the diggers from the federal lands. The storm broke and we had to take shelter. When we set off this morning, I found the mother of all bone beds. Proof that good deeds do not go unnoticed."

Barb's eyes widened. "Where?"

"A washout on highway 25. Which is why I am so late. The girl—whose name is Liz Hamilton, by the way—and I did a quick survey of the find, then I had detour ten miles to get back here."

"Does Don know?" Don Conway was Barb's son and the county surveyor. He was also Mike's best friend.

"I called him on my way in, but he wasn't answering. I'm going to try him again now. The site is on the border of my uncle's property and federal land. I took GPS readings, but I want a proper survey. I wouldn't put it past that bast...rat Scarr to try poaching my find."

"If you can't get hold of Don, I'll find him," Barb said, as aware as he of the importance of having *T*s crossed and *I*s dotted. Alfred Scarr had a big name university behind him. He could play fast and loose with legalities and argue every little point, and even if he lost any legal challenges, he'd still have a job and continue to dig dinos. Discovering Dinos was a private company, with limited backing. All they had behind them was their reputation for doing business in a legal and ethical way. Smirch that reputation and their clients would disappear like water down a drain.

Mike nodded his thanks. "Anything I need to know about before I get settled?"

"Josh is playing with a new look for the website. He says ours is looking tired. Well, that's not exactly what he said, but that's what he meant. He wants to do something chill."

Mike raised his eyebrows. Josh was their computer guru, an eighteen-year-old techno wizard who worked part-time at Discovering Dinos while he coasted through high school. Like Barb, who redecorated the lobby at regular intervals, Josh liked to play with the website. As long as both remained happy, no walls came down and the website provided their information in a professional manner, Mike let them make whatever changes they wanted. "Any special reason this time? Or is he just bored?"

"He thinks it would be great to document the trackway find on line. You know, record all the steps you do as you excavate. The detailed documentation you take. That sort of thing. He thinks it would be an added selling point." She shot Mike a telling glance. "I think so too. Past time people started seeing you for the expert paleontologist you are."

Mike grunted, uncomfortable with the praise. "There's no way to mend my reputation now. I'm still the dropout who's a wannabe in the dino world, and I always will be."

Barb pursed her lips, her disapproval clear. All she said was, "Focus on the sales aspect, then. We're selling relics. As in the art world, provenance is everything. The better the documentation, the bigger the client list and the higher the price we can charge."

She was right, and Mike knew it. He nodded. "We won't start with the trackway, though." He was possessive about that trackway. Dinosaur footprints that had hardened into rock were rare and he didn't want to announce his find to the world until he knew what kind of creature had left its mark and how extensive the trackway itself was. "We'll do today's find. It's massive. Looks to be almost a full skeleton. I think the neck and shoulders are on federal land, but the rest of the body is on our side of the line."

Barb's eyes lit up. "Know the species?"

He shook his head. "At first guess I'd say it was a herbivore, but I can't be certain." He paused. Let a little of the elation that had been trailing him all morning show through. "It wasn't one I know on sight." Herbivores had less value than a carnivore like T Rex, but if this creature was a new species the find would be huge.

"Hot damn," Barb said, reverently. "Shoo. Go get Don on the phone and tell him to get moving and not be a lazybones."

Mike had no intention of calling Don Conway anything of the kind, but he nodded and headed to his office to phone.

Unlike Barb's lavender garden, his sported white walls, a double pedestal steel desk—a castoff bought at an auction at the county seat—an equally old upright filing cabinet, bought at the same auction, and a large table on which the toe bone of an iguanodon currently rested. The only modern thing in the room was the luxurious leather-covered, well-padded and sprung, executive desk chair, which was his pride and joy. It swiveled, had wheels that never failed to scoot him along the bare lino floor to whatever side of the office he chose, and his back never ached the way it did when he sat too long in his old desk chair.

He settled in his big comfy chair and reached for his desk phone. He didn't have to look up Don's number, so he simply dialed and hoped he wouldn't get another recorded message. He was in luck.

"Don Conway, speaking." The voice was brisk and sounded harassed.

"Mike here. I'm calling to report a highway washout."

"You and half the county," Don said with a sigh. "Where is it?"

"Highway 25, where it crosses into federal land."

There was a pause. He could almost see Don straightening in his is chair and paying more attention. "Any special reason you were in that area?"

"There is now. The washout uncovered a bone bed. A big one."

"Your permit or Scarr's?"

"Both."

Don whistled. "A jurisdictional nightmare in the making. You'll want to be sure both sides know who gets what."

Alfred Scarr had never hidden his disdain for Mike Edmonds and Discovering Dinos and since he was an outsider and Mike was a favorite son, most people assumed Scarr would do whatever was necessary to put Discovering Dinos out of business. Mike thought it too. "You're telling me. Don, the washout is huge. The rift must run a couple of miles or more and I don't think the bed I found is the only one. I need a proper survey of the area, the sooner the better."

His friend didn't disappoint. "I'll pull my team together and go now. Is the road passable?"

"No. It's gone."

"Good. Gives me the excuse I need if anyone bothers to complain."

By anyone read Alfred Scarr. On his way back to town Mike had thought a lot about the deal he'd made with the shapely Liz Hamilton. The more he thought, the more he considered it unlikely to hold. Scarr had invited Zac Doyle into his camp and from what he'd heard of Zac Doyle, he was an even bigger academic shark than Scarr was. Between the two of them Liz Hamilton didn't have much hope of keeping the rights to her find and sticking around to dig it. He figured Scarr would have her on the next plane out.

From his point of view, that would be a shame. He would have liked to get to know the attractive Dr. Hamilton better. He could even imagine working the site with her. He would not work it with Scarr or Zac Doyle.

Mike was a realist. He was pretty sure that as soon as Liz provided

Scarr with the GPS coordinates of the bone bed, the man would head right out to the site. He might even get there before Don had a chance to set up.

That wasn't going to happen. "I'll meet you there," he said to Don.

Don laughed. "I thought you would."

*L*iz drove Alfred Scarr and Zac Doyle to the washout using Scarr's truck. He sat shotgun. Zac wedged himself into the extra seat behind. She didn't bother with the long detour that would have brought her back onto Mike Edmond's permit land. Instead she took Highway 25, from the place where it met up with the road leading into Scarr's camp, all the way to the giant rift.

She parked well away from the edge, then turned to face the two men. "The washout is about six feet deep. The skeleton is on this side. We'll have to find a place to climb down, then I'll show it to you."

Scarr stared out the windscreen. "Why don't we use the path you found earlier?"

Did the man not listen? She dragged patience out from somewhere and kept her tone pleasant. "I was on the other side of the rift. To get there from our camp, we would have had to detour about fifteen miles. I thought you wanted to get here before Mike Edmonds came back and staked out his side."

Scarr considered that, then he nodded. "Good point. Okay, let's go look." He opened his door, then paused, shooting her a dismissive look. "You realize that this may all be for nothing."

Now what was he on about? "I don't understand."

Scarr shrugged. "You may have got it wrong. This may be a few bones from a previously well-documented species. It may not be the big deal you think it is." With that he climbed out of the cab, leaving Liz staring after him feeling a mixture of outrage and concern.

What if Scarr was right? What if she had discovered the skeleton of an iguanodon, or a hadrosaur, or some other well-documented species with plentiful finds? She watched Zac work his way out of the back seat and crawl out of the cab. Sure, it was almost a full skeleton and from her initial review it was well preserved. There would be useful information to be found, even if it was just a garden-variety hadrosaur. But it wouldn't be the find of a lifetime. A career-making find that would get her a teaching position at a reputable university and a guaranteed position on digs like this one for the rest of her career.

She watched the two men walk toward the rift and decided she should get moving. She slipped out of the truck and followed them along what was left of the road.

Scarr could be messing with her head. Priming her, so that she wouldn't put up a fight when he nominated Zac to supervise the excavation. Not that Zac Doyle needed the glory of the major find this skeleton could be. He was already on his way to a high-flying career. But Scarr would want his name associated with Zac the golden boy, not with a plodder like Liz Hamilton.

The men had stopped at the edge of the rift, where the highway was no more. Zac had his hand to his forehead, shading his eyes from the harsh sun, looking, she supposed, for a way down into the crevice. Scarr had his hands in his pockets and his head was bent. She couldn't see what he was looking at, but from his stance she thought he was tense. When she came up beside them, she saw the reason why.

There was a man in a hard hat standing in the bottom of the rift. His bright orange vest was blindingly bright in the harsh midday sunlight. He was looking up, presumably because he had heard Scarr and Zac's footsteps. Beside him were two other men, also wearing hardhats and vests, holding what appeared to be surveying equipment.

"Who the hell are these guys?" Scarr said, as she came up to stand beside him. His gaze never left the men in the rift.

"Mike Edmonds' survey team, I guess," Liz said.

As if to confirm her statement, the man who wasn't busy setting up equipment shouted, "One of you Alfred Scarr?"

Beside her, Scarr nodded. "That's me."

The man in the hard hat nodded. "I'm Don Conway, county surveyor. I'm here to see how bad the damage to the road is." He pointed to what must be the skeleton, though from where she stood, Liz couldn't see it. "Looks like there's a nice little dino here, waiting for you or Mike to excavate it. I'll take readings while I'm here and let you know the exact location."

"The dino is mine," Scarr shouted back. He gestured toward Liz. "One of my diggers found it."

Diggers! How dare he! She was the site supervisor and she'd been keeping Scarr's bevy of beauteous undergrads in line since she joined the dig after she'd defended her Ph.D. and become Dr. Elizabeth Hamilton, not just plain old Liz Hamilton.

Temper boiled and she brushed past Scarr, taking herself away from him before she said anything she would later regret. She saw Zac begin to move along the edge of the rift. He must have seen a path. She followed him and was rewarded when she saw him scramble down the rocky wall.

When he reached bottom she was already halfway down. He paused to wait for her. "Where's the skeleton?" he asked.

She pointed toward the surveying crew. "There."

Zac nodded. He was all business now and there was nothing of the innocent in his face. His expression was set, his eyes coldly assessing. He strode off to view the find, or maybe to confront the surveyor. Liz wasn't sure which, but she had no intention of being left behind. She hustled after him.

Don Conway glanced over at Zac and Liz as they neared. He nodded toward the skeleton and said, "Amazing what nature will throw your way, isn't it? I came out here thinking I had a pain in the ass problem, and what do I see? Something amazing."

And he was right. The find was amazing. Liz stared at it again, the sight reassuring her that her initial assessment had been correct. This *was* a career-making find. Now she just had to make sure it was her career it made, not Zac Doyle's.

Zac stepped closer to examine the exposed bones and she heard his intake of breath. Did he think it was a new species, as she hoped? Oh, how perfect it would be if it was!

She heard the rattle of sifting gravel and looked up. Scarr was no longer at his position on the lip of the cliff, so the sound must be him making his way down the path. Sure enough, when she looked over, he was down in the bottom and moving quickly toward them.

When he saw the skeleton, he sucked in a deep breath too. This was getting better and better.

Don Conway had moved off to instruct his crew, leaving Zac, Liz and Scarr examining the exposed bones. "Do you trust this local surveyor?" Zac said in a low voice. He was looking at Scarr. In fact, the two men were huddled closely together, with Zac's back toward Liz, excluding her from their conversation.

Scarr said, "He's a county official. I think he's all right."

Zac nodded, but his voice was tense as he said, "There's a lot riding on what this guy comes up with. We don't want to be shafted by some stupid yokel."

Honestly, Liz thought. Talk about a paranoid jerk. The conversation continued on in the same fashion, both men speculating on what would have to be done to get rights back if Conway put the skeleton on Mike Edmonds' side of the line. She listened idly, scanning the rift for the head of the great beast they were standing in front of.

Heads tended to get detached and drift away from the main skeleton. If they were lucky they would find it not far away from the neck, safely on federal land. She scanned the rift, looking for clues, hoping against hope something would catch her eye and tell her that the skull was close by, waiting for her to discover it.

No clues. No heart-stopping discovery, only the sound of Zac and

Scarr, droning on, as they plotted how to secure the site. Suddenly she heard the rumble of an internal combustion engine.

Conway looked up from his computations. "That's probably Mike Edmonds." He grinned, evidently pleased by this development. "Looks like we won't have to have a meeting in town. We'll be able to discuss who gets what part of this skeleton right now."

"Road repair, my ass," Scarr said. Loudly.

Conway raised his brows over the dark sunglasses he wore. "If you've got something to say, spit it out, Dr. Scarr. I'm a straightforward guy. I don't like hints and innuendo."

Scarr shot him a look of loathing. "Do you work for Discovering Dinos?"

The truck engine stopped and in the ensuing silence Conway's voice was hard. "I told you when I introduced myself. I'm the county surveyor. I work for the good people of this county and no one else. Understood?"

She thought Scarr understood perfectly well. Mike Edmonds was one of the good people of Twisted Butte County. Dr. Alfred Scarr was not.

There was another rattle of shifting dirt and gravel. She looked over, not at all surprised to see Mike Edmonds making his way down the path on his side of the rift, the one they'd used that morning.

The confrontation between Conway and Scarr was about to become a three-way battle.

CHAPTER 9

*M*ike eased his way down the rocky side of the rift, taking his time as he evaluated the scene before him. Liz Hamilton was standing to one side of Scarr and the man he thought must be Zachary Doyle. The two men stood closely together, clearly unified, while Liz was excluded from their pairing. That, he thought, was something he could work with. She'd have no reason to feel loyalty to Scarr and Doyle, so she'd be impartial. At least he hoped she would, because he had no intention of working with Zachary Doyle to excavate the skeleton.

Don's team was working near the road, so it looked like Don himself was taking the measurements of the bone bed. That was good. For all his apparent lightheartedness, Don was precise in his work, meticulous in his documentation. His findings could be relied upon.

Mike was very aware of Liz Hamilton's gaze on him as he slithered down the hill, even though she was wearing sunglasses. On the drive from town to the washout he'd had plenty of time to think about last night, the find, and what to do about both. He'd decided that the find took precedence over the lingering desire left from a night spent in close proximity to a woman he couldn't have. At the same time, he knew he would have to work with someone from Scarr's camp. The kind of complications Liz Hamilton would bring would be easier to deal with than the narrow-mindedness of Scarr, or the arrogance of the wonder kid, Zac Doyle.

When he reached the bottom of the rift, he ignored Scarr and Doyle, a deliberate move on his part, and strode straight to Don.

"Looks like you've got yourself a fine set of bones here, Mike," Don said, tilting his head to indicate the find. His sunglasses hid the expression in his eyes, but from his words, Mike guessed Scarr and Doyle were approaching. Don raised his brows, pitched his voice a little louder, and the corner of his mouth twitched, ever so slightly. "Have you got a buyer for the bones yet? Going to break up the skeleton? Hell, if you sold it piece-by-piece you'd make a killing."

"Don," he muttered, though he was resigned to his friend's antics. Don had an engineering degree from a top-notch university, and he was no country bumpkin, but Scarr and Doyle would expect a county employee in a rural, ranching area to be unsophisticated and ignorant, and Don knew that. He'd be quite happy to poke them until they were riled up and fit to burst.

Don flashed Mike a grin, then his expression became thoughtful. "There was that gentleman from China who was by some weeks ago. I bet he'd be right glad to learn of this here find."

Mike resisted the urge to shake his head. "This here find? Get real, Don."

Don choked off a laugh that he turned into a cough. Behind Mike a throat was cleared. He shot an impatient look at Don, who returned it with an innocent one. Then he slowly turned.

Scarr and Doyle stood shoulder-to-shoulder, presenting a unified front. If the expression on Scarr's face was anything to go by, Don had done a good job of irritating them. Scarr wasn't wearing a hat or sunglasses—stupid, in Mike's point of view—so Mike was able to see the disdain lurking in his eyes, as well as the pursed lips and flared nostrils that clearly showed what he was feeling.

Zac Doyle was younger looking than he'd expected. Mike kept up with the latest in his field, reading all the journals and published papers, so he knew of Zac through his published works, but he'd never seen a picture of the man. Unlike Scarr, Doyle was wearing sunglasses, so his eyes were shielded and Mike couldn't read the expression in them. His facial expression was neutral, but his stance and body language showed that he clearly sided with Alfred Scarr. It looked, though, that he was willing to let the older man take the lead.

Liz followed the two men. Now she stood to one side, between Scarr and Mike, on her own, siding with neither party. "Dr. Scarr, this is Mike Edmonds," she said, indicating Mike with a wave of her hand. "Mike, Alfred Scarr and Zac Doyle. Dr. Scarr leads the excavations on the federal lands. Zac just arrived to help him out."

When neither man offered his hand, Mike didn't either. "Your timing is excellent, Doyle, since Liz will be busy here."

"Miss Hamilton—"

"Dr. Hamilton," Liz said. "I was granted my Ph.D. in May."

She said that rather grimly, as if it was an ongoing source of conflict between her and Scarr.

"—will be leaving my team," Scarr said, not acknowledging her interjection. "Zac Doyle will be working this find."

"Really?" Mike pushed his hat back and took off his sunglasses. He wanted Scarr to see his eyes, to understand the expression in them. "Here's the thing. It was our find. Dr. Hamilton's and mine. Zac Doyle has nothing to do with it. I'll expect him to keep clear."

"You have no say in how this dig is run!" Scarr's tenor rose to an alto squeak as he spat out the words. "This is an academic find, not one of your pirate sites. Zac will manage this excavation."

Mike had a sense of movement behind him. A quick glance told him Don had ranged himself beside him. He was about to reply to Scarr's provocative statement when Liz Hamilton intervened.

"I will ensure that the find is excavated carefully and is properly documented," she said. Her voice was emotionless, but Mike thought she must be furious at being shunted aside so carelessly.

Zac Doyle spoke for the first time. "You're no match for a guy like this, Lizzy." His lips curled in what he probably thought of as a smile, but was more of a smirk.

The smirk and the deliberate use of a nickname was a classic strategy to undermine her credibility and her self-confidence. Contemptable, Mike thought, but it also confirmed to him that Scarr and Doyle wanted in on the excavation of this creature. These bones must be very special indeed.

Liz Hamilton's quick intake of breath indicated she was more angry than intimidated by Doyle's little ploy. Her eyes flashed, but she clamp down hard on her temper. Mike was impressed.

She shifted, moving her feet so her legs were set wider apart in a classic battler's stance as she glared at Doyle. "Since we only met this afternoon I'm not surprised you don't realize that no one—not my friends, not my sister, not my mother, no one—calls me Lizzy."

Beside him Don snickered. She didn't seem to notice.

"Another thing to remember, Zac. You're ABD, all but dissertation. One day you may be top of the heap, but right now? Right now, I out rank you."

She'd stuck home with that one, Mike thought, as Doyle's round, cherubic features twisted with temper. Too bad that Scarr's did as well.

"I decide seniority on my dig," Scarr said, outrage dripping from his voice.

Time to intervene. "Good thing this is my dig, then," Mike said.

"Outrageous! Half, perhaps two-thirds of the creature is on federal land, where I hold the dig permit. I will manage it!"

Mike allowed himself a smile. "Cooperation is key."

Scarr narrowed his eyes. "What do you mean? How is that relevant?"

Mike shook his head. He couldn't believe Scarr would be so obtuse, but he supposed that the man thought so little of him that he'd wasn't sensible enough to be wary.

Beside him, Don said cheerfully, "China calling."

Mike's lip twitched, but he didn't give into laughter. "He's right, you know. I could find a buyer for my part of the skeleton with a half-a-dozen phone calls. If I wanted to make a few more I could sell it one bone at a time." He stopped, let the words sink in, the way they hadn't earlier. Watched outrage take hold of Alfred Scarr, while Zac Doyle frowned. He almost had them.

Liz Hamilton said, "You wouldn't do that, would you?"

She was not looking at him, or at her boss, but at the remains of the great beast. Her expression was not only possessive, but nurturing, as if she felt a tenderness toward this long dead creature and wanted to be sure its remains were treated with respect.

He wanted to curse, because he couldn't, absolutely couldn't, taunt her the way he was Scarr and Doyle. He kept a rough edge to his tone, though, as he said, "Not if you are the one I'm working with, Dr. Hamilton."

She looked back at him, blinked, then smiled. He had a sense that he'd just been played, though perhaps it wasn't him she was manipulating, but Scarr.

"I told you," Scarr said.

"I know, I know," Mike said. "Dr. Hamilton is leaving your employ. Zac Doyle will handle the excavation."

"You understand me," Scarr said tightly.

"The thing is, Dr. Scarr, you don't understand me. The kind of man I am."

"I know exactly what kind of man you are," Scarr said. "You're an uneducated maverick whose desire for wealth leads you to destroy priceless artifacts. You indulge and encourage the greed and ignorance of those you sell to and make the jobs of professionals in the field that much harder. I abhor the kind of man you are and what you stand for."

"Now look here," Don began.

Mike put up a hand to stop him. He raised his brows and smiled at Scarr. "Then you won't be surprised when I let everyone who matters know that your arrogance and refusal to work cooperatively is the reason that the body of this creature was carved into pieces and separated. One half to you, and your museum; the other to me, and my customers. Each and every one of them."

From the shocked expression on Scarr's face, he hadn't thought quite that far ahead. "No one will listen to you."

Mike shrugged. "Some won't. Others will."

Scarr stared at him, his jaw working. Mike waited, let him stew.

Liz looked from Scarr to him, then back to Scarr again. "What if there was a contract?"

Scarr frowned. "What do you mean?"

The guy clearly wasn't a fast thinker. Mike pulled his hat back so it again sat low on his forehead, and replaced his sunglasses. The glare of the afternoon sun was giving him a headache. Or maybe it was that idiot, Alfred Scarr.

"You know, a legal document," Don said helpfully. "The kind that sets out rights and obligations that bind both parties so neither screws the other? A contract."

Scarr shot him a furious look. "I know what a contract is."

"A legal agreement between Mike Edmonds and you, Dr. Scarr, that sets out the terms for excavating this site," Liz said, breaking in before the comments became an argument. "Mr. Edmonds is a businessman. If he signs a contract, I think he'll abide by its rules."

"A contract will take time to put together," Scarr said. "I'll have to get the university's lawyers involved. One of them may have to come out."

"Or Edmonds' lawyer can go to the university," Zac said, his tone and cherubic expression innocent

"Ah, yes." Scarr strung out the words. He sounded pleased and he sent a warm smile Zac's way. Having Mike's lawyer go to his would show his power and put him in the top position. "Perhaps a contract would make this unfortunate situation workable."

He had no idea, Mike thought. Mike had a lawyer on retainer. The man had negotiated lucrative contracts with shrewd international consortiums. He doubted a couple of university lawyers would be able to best him. "Whatever works," he said to Scarr. "Dr. Hamilton and I can get started on taking measurements and reviewing the site while the lawyers do their thing. I'd like to get this skeleton out of the ground before the end of the dig season."

Scarr looked like he wanted to object, but he couldn't. The washout had exposed the skeleton. There was no telling what the harsh winter weather would do to it or what they'd find when the snow melted in the spring. He nodded. "Zac Doyle will do the work, however."

Mike slowly shook his head. "No need to get the lawyers involved, then."

There was a minute of tense silence, while Scarr glared at him. Doyle watched with an innocent stare and Liz had the sense to keep her mouth shut.

"Fine," Scarr said, snapping out the word. "Hamilton stays. But Zac will work with her. That's my last concession."

He heard Liz release her breath in a relieved sigh. He wanted to tell Scarr to go to hell, but he didn't think that would help Liz's cause. He'd make sure that his lawyer understood that having Dr. Elizabeth Hamilton heading up the excavation on behalf of Dr. Scarr's team was the only option he'd accept. He'd also make sure that it was stated clearly in the contract that Dr. Hamilton would be the one writing and publishing the field notes.

That was for later, though. For now he'd let Scarr have his little victory. Let him think he was the one in control. He'd soon find out he wasn't.

CHAPTER 10

As earlier, Liz drove back to the campsite. The trip was one of loud grumbling that would rise to outright venting, only to fall back to a grumble again, before cresting back up into a vent. Dr. Scarr was not happy about the situation and Zac Doyle made sure to keep his anxieties on high. There wasn't much Scarr could do to change it, though, no matter how many times he called Mike Edmonds a scam artist, a fraud, and pretty much any other slur he could think of. He'd have to rely on the university's lawyers and hope they got him the terms he wanted in the contract with Mike Edmonds.

When they reached the camp, Liz let Scarr and Zac Doyle off, but didn't leave the truck. When Scarr raised his brows and asked what she was up to, she said, "I have to call my sister in Boston to tell her not to pick me up tomorrow."

Scarr pursed his lips and nodded. With no cell service at the campsite you had to drive a few miles away to higher land or hike out of the valley and up a rise if you wanted to call out. Since it was nearly dinnertime, the second option wasn't viable.

As Liz drove to the spot where she'd be able to get steady, clear service, the emotions she'd been bottling up since last night fizzed free.

DISCOVER TIME FOR LOVE | 67

There was so much she had to tell her sister she wasn't sure where to start.

Faith didn't answer her phone when Liz called, but that wasn't a problem. They had worked out a system. If Liz needed to talk and Faith wasn't available, she'd send a text. The more imperative the text, the more quickly Faith would phone back.

Liz grinned to herself as she typed. *Urgent! Urgent! Urgent! Plans changed. Call ASAP!* That should do it. She leaned back in the seat and waited.

Sure enough, a minute later Faith's ring tone came through and her name flashed on the screen. Liz answered promptly.

"What's up?" Faith said, without preamble.

"I'm a Traveler."

"What!" The word was a shriek, then there was silence until Faith said, "Did I hear you correctly? You said you were a Traveler."

"You heard right. I walked into a beacon last night. I met my grandson."

"Are you sure you traveled? That this wasn't something...else?"

"At first I wondered if it was the setting sun. Except it was in the wrong place. I was intrigued, so I got out of the truck and walked toward it. It was just like Uncle Andrew describes it. The light drew me, made me feel better, loved and safe. I walked into it and found myself in a high tech lab sometime in the future. It must be years from now, because the man I met is an adult and he's my grandson."

"Wow!" Faith laughed. The sound was warm and affectionate. "So how does it feel? You must be the oldest first time Traveler in our family."

The time travel ability usually manifested at puberty. "Thanks a lot, sis, for making me feel ancient at twenty-eight."

Faith laughed again. This time it was more of a giggle. "Seriously, when are you going back?"

Faith was a Beacon like Liz's grandson, Mark. Her Traveler was their eighteenth century ancestor, Andrew Byrne. Andrew visited Faith weekly, if not more often. Though Liz liked the idea of a regular visit with Mark, she was still worried there was no way it could happen. "I don't know. The place where I found him was across the line, on Mike Edmonds' permit land. To get there I need access to a truck and Scarr isn't going to let me use a vehicle for a pleasure ride. I want to go back again before I leave this area, though. I'll work out something."

"Talking about leaving the area, what's this about plans changing?"

Liz stared out the windshield at the desolate landscape around her. "After I came back through the beacon, it was almost dark and there was a storm brewing. It broke on my way back to camp. I lost control of the truck on a turn and slid off the road."

"Are you okay?" There was alarm in Faith's voice.

"Yeah. I didn't roll the truck or anything. The wheels got stuck in soft mud and I couldn't get it back on the road." She paused to chuckle. "The enemy rescued me."

"The enemy?" Faith took a moment, then said, "Do you mean Mike Edmonds? Isn't he an uncertified paleontologist who has the dig permit beside yours?"

"That would be him."

"What was he like?"

"He's gorgeous." The description popped out unplanned.

"Whoa," Faith said. "That's a surprise. When you've mentioned him before, you made him sound like a wimpy wannabe. Gorgeous doesn't quite fit."

Had she talked about him that way? Probably. Before last night, she'd never met the man and, although she knew of his activities, hadn't really thought about him. Scarr often complained about the man, but after the first few rants, she tuned him out. "All I knew about him is what Scarr has said. Now I have a different image of Edmonds and I'm confused."

"Hang on," Faith said. "I'll do a web search on him while we're talking. I'll see what I can fill in." Liz heard the clatter of keys as Faith said, "Now, tell me what happened after Mike Edmonds rescued you."

"We spent the night together." There was silence on the other end of the phone connection. Liz laughed. "In his truck."

"Okay." Faith drew out the word, caution in her voice. "He's gorgeous and you spent the night in his truck. There's a picture forming in my mind."

"Well, haul your mind out of the gutter and erase that picture, stat. Nothing happened. The storm raged around us and we took shelter. That's it." Liz was glad she was talking to Faith on the phone, because her cheeks were red. It wasn't as if she hadn't had thoughts about the man she had spent the night beside. About the way his voice made her think of velvet sliding across her skin. What his body would look like naked. How his hands would feel on her skin. She swallowed hard. She was the one who needed to purify her thoughts, not Faith.

"Right. You have nothing to report. The incident was a non-event."

Faith's tone was mocking. Liz figured she deserved it.

"Tell me about the change of plans then," Faith added.

Liz envisioned the find and elation bubbled into her voice. "The storm was wicked. It caused an enormous washout, miles long and really deep. It exposed some strata that were hidden. I made a find. An almost complete skeleton."

"Way to go! That's exciting, Liz." Faith hesitated. "But—"

"Yeah, but I'm supposed to be coming home. Except I'm not."

"So Scarr isn't the jerk you thought he was? The find is yours, so he's letting you excavate it?"

"Oh, Scarr's a jerk all right. He planned to send me home and give my find to Zac Doyle."

"That sounds more like the Scarr I've never met, but already dislike intensely."

Liz laughed.

"So how'd you work the change in plans," Faith asked.

"Mike Edmonds and I ganged up on him."

This time it was Faith who laughed. "Mike Edmonds again. That must have been some night in that truck."

"Stop!"

"You're my kid sister. It's my job to tease. Hey, I'm getting some info on Edmonds. Okay, let's see. He owns a company called Discovering Dinos that works through a dude ranch in your area. The ranch specializes in paleo-tourism."

"You're making up words. Explain."

"People can do trail rides to dinosaur dig sites, or they can participate in a dig, for a day or a week. The longest is two weeks at a dig site. The company also sells bones and casts of skeletons to..." There a pause, then Faith said, "Huh. The clients listed are mainly museums. A couple of small colleges, too. They also sell videos that seem to be about paleontology. There's a list. According to another page, Mike Edmonds has a BSc. Oh, this is interesting. The site has a news and events tab. Let me see what's there."

Listening to her sister explore the Internet was excruciating. Liz itched to have a screen in front of her, so she could be the one to flip through the pages. It seemed to take an age before Faith spoke again, though it was really less than a minute.

"You know, Liz, this Mike Edmonds of yours may not be such a bad guy."

"What do you mean?"

"He does a lot of public speaking at schools and libraries. For free. And he's got a wad of testimonials from people raving about how great their experience was on one of his tours. How much they learned and how exciting it was to feel like they were part of unearthing the past. That sort of thing. Why does Scarr hate him so much?"

"Because he's not part of the academic community."

"Of course. He's different. A perfectly good reason to refuse to accept someone." Faith said. Sarcasm dripped from her voice.

Liz couldn't disagree. "Listen, thanks for checking for me. I'm going to have to get back. I'll keep you posted, but it looks like I'll be finishing out the season after all."

"Email me with all the juicy details," Faith said.

Liz laughed. "I will."

Just before she rang off, Faith said, quietly but with emotion, "And Liz? Congratulations on becoming a Traveler. I'm happy for you."

"Thanks, Faith." She had to swallow a lump in her throat as she disengaged the phone. For a moment all she could do was to sit and stare at the stark, beautiful terrain.

She had come into her abilities and become a Traveler. She'd discovered a skeleton that could be a career-changing find.

And she'd met a man who seemed to have more layers than an onion. He'd rescued her from the storm. He's supported her against her bully of a boss. He was gorgeous and he intrigued her.

She laughed a little at that thought. If she wasn't who she was, Dr. Liz Hamilton, apprentice paleontologist, desperate to create a career for herself, she might almost think she was smitten with the man.

The thought drifted through her mind.

Smitten. Could it be?

She sat up straight and started the engine. No. It could not be. She was career-focused. She didn't have time for a relationship.

She set the truck in motion and headed back to camp. Thoughts about last night and today chased themselves through her mind. As she turned into the lane that led to the camp, she grinned.

A relationship? No way. But sex with a gorgeous man? Who knew? She'd see how things went.

At the moment, though, she was open to sleeping with the enemy.

CHAPTER 11

At nine in the morning the sun already beat down with merciless power. To keep from burning her skin to a crisp, Liz was wearing a long sleeve shirt and jeans. As a concession to the heat, the front buttons were open, exposing the thin t-shirt beneath. A flat-crowned straw hat, the brim pulled low to shield her eyes, protected her head and on her feet she wore leather boots to keep out any small critters that might lurk in the dirt and rocks at the washout's bottom.

She and Zac had already been at the site for an hour. They'd come early to work in the relative cool of early morning. They'd take a break and find shade when the sun was at its highest, then snatch a few more hours as when afternoon eased toward night and the heat dissipated.

They were mapping the skeleton, analyzing the rock to see how friable it was, and how difficult it would be to remove the bones. At this point they weren't actively trying to identify the creature, but Liz was keeping a sharp lookout for clues. She desperately wanted to find the head. It was the key and so far, not in evidence. Somehow, over the millennia, it had been separated from the rest of the body. Without it the find would be interesting, particularly if it appeared to be a new species, but not definitive.

Figuring out where the animal had died was an important step. If it was in an ancient streambed, water could have washed the skull away from the body. If it was on land, it might be close by and just a matter of clearing away some of the hillside not exposed by the washout.

The creature, whatever it was, was one of the giants that lived at the end of the dinosaur era. It had large bones and strong hind legs. The neck was medium length, which meant that it wasn't one of the long-necked sauropods, but it might be one of the other herbivore species. Or it might be a carnivore. Now that would be exciting.

"Iguanodon family," Zac said, standing back to look at the whole creature, not just the rib cage where Liz was busy taking measurements.

"Possibly," she said. "I'm not ready to make a prediction yet."

"Unless we find the head, it's most likely that the final decision will be made in the lab. I'll let you know before we publish." He smiled when he said that, the cruel baring of teeth showing Liz that the jab was deliberate.

Creep, she thought. She hoped Mike Edmonds had thought to instruct his lawyer to include lab rights in his contract demands, because if the creature went back to Scarr's lab, he'd take all the credit for its find and the analysis of the remains. That was certainly the way Zac was thinking, and equally clearly, he planned to be part of the lab team.

She didn't reply. She kept her eyes on the dinosaur bones and tried to imagine what the area would have been like when this creature had lived. Over in the valley where Scarr was camped they'd found evidence that showed that 70 million years ago, this whole area had been on the edge of a waterway and covered in vegetation. There would have been plenty of food and water for the herbivores and lots of herbivores to feed hungry carnivores. Wouldn't it be great if this creature was a rare carnivore, not one of the many herbivores? Carnivore finds were unusual because the animals were apex feeders. In life they were few. In death they were almost never found.

"You're right. I shouldn't jump to conclusions. This might be a hadrosaur. Or even a parasaurolophus," Zac said, taunting.

"Yup," Liz said, and went back to her envisioning of an ancient world. No matter how brutal that distant time might have been, she figured it couldn't be much worse than working with the hyper-competitive Zac Doyle.

The sound of a truck engine, no, many truck engines, had her stepping back and straightening. She arched her back and stretched as she turned toward the sound, which was coming from the direction of Highway 25 on Mike Edmonds' side of the rift.

"Sounds like the guy's brought an army," Zac muttered.

Liz glanced over at him. He looked a little worried. As well he might, since he was checking out the hind end of the creature, strictly on Mike's side of the permit line. If Edmonds caught Zac at it, he'd be annoyed, if not worse.

The engines died as trucks parked. Men and women swarmed out of cabs and started to pull gear out of the backs. Liz decided to climb up to the edge on Mike's side of the rift. Not only would she be able to find out why he had brought such a big crew, but she'd be able to leave Zac Doyle behind. No small blessing, that.

She picked out Mike immediately. It wasn't just that he was tall—there were other tall men in his crew—or that his broad shoulders and slim hips stood out from the others. It was the way the mob of people reacted to him that identified him. They looked to him for direction, which he gave with good humor and attention to detail, no matter how small the query was. His crew was clearly used to him taking command and they were comfortable letting him have it.

She watched as he sent a large group away from the rim. The direction puzzled her, until she saw them placing stakes and realized that they were setting up a campground. A smaller group was wrestling with what looked like high tech equipment. That was even more puzzling. Liz couldn't find an answer. Mike and a skinny, quite young, male fell into a discussion. The male pointed in the direction of the skeleton and Mike turned.

Liz knew the moment his gaze fell upon her, because her whole body tingled. She swallowed hard. She was being ridiculous. His eyes were shaded by sunglasses and he was busy with whatever he was doing. He wasn't actually looking at her, but at the find. That was all. She was imagining that he was staring at her, that there was a mutual punch of awareness between them. Wishful thinking.

No, not wishful. Indulgent. She had a career to make. She didn't have time to fall into a relationship. With this man, or any other.

She walked toward him, setting a deliberate pace. Now that he had seen her it wouldn't do to linger at the edges of whatever he was up to. She was Scarr's representative on the dig. She'd needed to make her presence known and her position clear.

As she neared he nodded to the skinny kid and turned away from him, to watch her approach. A smile, slow, lazy, sensual, curled his lips. "Dr. Hamilton, I thought I'd find you here."

She nodded, wary of the promise in that smile. "You have a pretty big crew with you." A statement, but also a question. Why?

The smile lingered as he looked down at her. She wished she could see his eyes. He nodded toward the skinny kid. "I'm setting up a dino cam to cover the dig. It will live stream from Discovering Dinos' website once we are underway. Anyone who wants to tune in and watch us in action, can."

She frowned and looked down into the rife where the kid was pacing about framing angles with his hands. Zac had abandoned the hindquarters and was watching him warily. "Like the camera that documented the birth of some eagles in Florida a couple of years ago?"

Mike nodded. The sensual curve of his lips quirked up into amusement. "Josh—that's the kid I was talking to—is a computer whiz. He'll do all the technical set up. My video director will actually arrange the camera angles."

"Your video director?"

That lazy smile returned as he turned his attention back to her. "Hmmm. I've also brought the head of my paleo team. His name is

Will Lavery. You'll meet him later. He's going to explore the rift to see if there are any more remains that might be interesting."

Will Lavery. The name struck a bell, but at the moment Liz couldn't place the reference. She decided not to worry about it. "A good plan. I was going to do something similar down at my end."

"I thought you might," Mike said. There was a bit of mockery in his tone, but there was also approval. He did a half turn so he could point to the busy individuals setting up the camp area. "I like to keep my crew close to the dig. Saves time and makes it easier for everyone involved."

"Makes sense," she said. She thought about long hours in one of Scarr's trucks, driving back and forth with Zac Doyle. The mental image wasn't appealing.

"I've got an extra tent for you, if you want."

She pulled her gaze away from the builders, to look back up into his face. "What did you say?"

His mouth quirked. "You heard me."

She couldn't tell what he was thinking with those sunglasses shielding the expression in his eyes. "Take your glasses off."

After a moment, he slowly did as she asked.

"You offered me a tent. Why?"

"You are suspicious, aren't you?" There was amusement in his voice, but it was also there in his eyes, along with a warmth that was almost a caress.

The expression affected her in ways she couldn't allow. She swallowed hard, tamping down a stupid softening that had no place at this career-making dig. "We're enemies, Mr. Edmonds. You don't usually invite the enemy into your camp. It's dangerous."

"It could be," he murmured. "But I don't see us as enemies. Adversaries, perhaps, but not enemies."

She waved that away impatiently. "Semantics. Dr. Scarr does not see this as a cooperative venture."

"How do you see it, Dr. Hamilton?" His voice was silky, the amusement still there in his eyes. He was enjoying this.

How did she see it? How did she see him? She looked into those warm hazel eyes and thought about the night in his truck. He'd been protective, but respectful; commanding, but not overbearing. If she let him know where she stood now, she thought, he'd honor her position for the rest of the dig.

"Equals, but not partners." She watched his eyes, caught the arrested look there. "Not yet, at least."

"Well, well, well," he murmured. "An interesting answer. Not one I'd expected. The tent is still yours, Dr. Hamilton. If you want it."

That last statement sounded like a challenge and had something wild taking flight inside her. She went with her gut and nodded. "Thank you, I'll take you up on your offer."

He flashed her a grin that set that wild creature fluttering. "Good. We'll probably be able to move in the day after tomorrow. Bring your gear."

She swallowed hard and scrambled for someway to break the spell he'd put on her with a few words and a killer smile. "What about Zac?"

The smile hardened, then disappeared. "Not invited." He turned away, leaving her to wonder if sleeping with the enemy really was such a good idea.

CHAPTER 12

"Where's your associate?"

The voice shot a tingle of awareness down Liz's spine, but it didn't surprise her. That tingle had been there even before Mike Edmonds spoke.

She straightened and stretched, glad of the opportunity to do something other than peer at the ground looking for evidence that the creature's skull was still in the vicinity of its body. She took off her broad brimmed straw hat and ran her fingers through her short, blonde hair before she answered.

She resisted the urge to sigh. As he had yesterday, Zac drove in with her in this morning, but then he disappeared, leaving her to process the find on her own. He thought she didn't notice, but she did. She found his actions annoying. She'd intended to call him on it, but she'd discovered that he was very good at making himself scarce.

She slid a look at Mike Edmonds, who was quietly waiting for her reply. "He's somewhere down the rift." He opened his mouth to speak and she held up her hand. "On our side of the line. He's searching for new bone beds."

"If they're there, they are not on the surface," Mike said.

He was watching her face with a particular intensity that Liz found unsettling. The look was making her skin tingle and her throat dry. Her reaction was pure sexual awareness and she tromped it down. It had no place on this dig, between her and this man.

His statement gave her the opening she needed. "You've been looking on our side of the line yourself."

He grinned at her. "Did I say that?"

She snorted. "You didn't have to." He raised a brow and she relented. "Even if you'd done a little exploring when Zac or I weren't here, you wouldn't try to poach, no matter what Scarr thinks."

"Thanks for the vote of confidence."

Shrugging, she said, "It's more an observation." She cocked her head as she looked up at him. "You're a smart man, Mike Edmonds. You know that if Scarr believed you were taking bones from his side of the line, he'd have lawyers, and maybe the police, involved so quickly you wouldn't have time to hide them, let alone sell them."

"Pragmatic." He made the word sound like a caress.

Or maybe to her it felt like a caress. They were having a perfectly normal business conversation, not one filled with underlying sexual tension. Weren't they?

She felt his eyes following her as she went over to fetch the bottle of water she'd stashed in the shadow of the opposite wall of the rift. She uncapped the bottle and lifted it to her lips. The water felt good on her dry throat until she realized that Mike was watching her as she swallowed. Suddenly her skin was hot, too tight for her body, prickling with an awareness she couldn't ignore, no matter how much she wanted to.

She lowered the bottle. Mike leaned against a large bolder that the raging water had dumped in the middle of the rift. He appeared to be watching her, but it was hard to tell, because the brim of his hat and his sunglasses covered his eyes and masked his expression.

"I heard from Harvey Earnshaw this morning," he said.

This sexual fantasizing really must be all on one side. Her side. "Who is Harvey Earnshaw?"

"My lawyer." He stood up. Headed her way. "Harvey made contact with the university's legal team yesterday afternoon. He thinks the negotiations will be straightforward. He figures he'll have the clauses hammered out in a couple of weeks and the contracts signed within the month."

She stayed where she was, idly turning the bottle of warm water in her hand as she watched him approach. "Fast work."

"The university lawyers seem to be happy to cast Scarr to the wolves. Or in this case, to one wolf." He smiled.

Liz thought the expression singularly suited to the way he described himself. "You."

"Me. Harvey stressed that the find was being shared by the two people who discovered it. That Dr. Scarr would get a mention in the final dig report, but that the dig permit belonged to the university, and you work for it just as much as Scarr does."

She sucked in a breath. "You instructed your lawyer to cut Scarr out."

"Exactly what he planned to do to you," Mike said. He shrugged. "They don't want a lawsuit they won't win. Or one that would show them in a bad light. And not supporting a certified member of their own dig team would definitely put them in a bad light."

She laughed. "Scarr wouldn't agree."

He shrugged again. "The camp is ready. We're moving in tomorrow. You can set up any time you're ready."

She'd been thinking about how Scarr would direct his anger when he discovered that the lawyers were abandoning him. Now she felt nothing but relief. "Great. I'll bring my stuff with me when I come tomorrow."

He stared at her for a moment more, then he nodded and backed away. She drank some more water as she watched him move down the gully, deeper into his side of the line. He moved with determination and a lithe speed that appealed to her. She shook herself mentally, then put down the water bottle.

She needed to stop this now. Sure, the man had a great body. Sure, he was ridiculously attractive. Sure, he had that sexy way of talking to her as if she was the only person in existence who mattered to him. But —and it was a big but—he was, for now, her partner. A working associate who might not be as scrupulous as he should be. A colleague she would have to keep her eye on.

She sighed and got back to work.

By the end of the day she was tired. Zac complained about the lack of visible bones in the parts of the rift he'd explored, and told her again that the bones they had were from a commonly found species. Liz tried to tune him out, but he had a nasal way of speaking that rubbed against her nerves and made her skin crawl. She looked forward to changing her accommodation from Scarr's camp to Mike's.

Packing up her tent wouldn't take much time, so she'd wait until after dinner to put everything into her suitcase. First, she'd have to tell Scarr that she was shifting camps, though. If she put it off he'd be miffed. He liked to think he was the one in charge, making the decisions, even when he wasn't.

Perhaps she handled her explanation poorly. Or perhaps Scarr simply didn't like the idea of anyone making plans, but him. But a half an hour after she'd reached the camp she was staring at her boss and saying incredulously, "Again? You're firing me again?"

He stared back at her, his eyes hard. "You need to decide where your loyalties lie."

It was as if she was watching her career being washed away a second time. That was a shock when she thought she'd have charge of an important new dig. She scrambled to stem the flow and stop the damage. "I'm part of your team, Dr. Scarr. When I write my part of the dig report I will be citing you as the dig supervisor."

Wrong answer. Scarr puffed up like a fighting cock ready to do battle. "I will be writing the dig report. I will be citing you as the one to make the find and as an active member of the team that gathered the remains." He sounded absolutely furious. "It will be my lab that processes the bones found."

She eyed him warily. She wasn't sure how much he'd heard from the university, or if he knew how Mike Edmonds seemed to be manipulating the situation through his lawyer. At this moment it seemed prudent to keep her peace and agree with whatever he had in mind. "Okay. I don't know what the dig report has to do with my relocating to Mike Edmonds' camp. Or why you see it as a betrayal."

"You'll be working with him, discussing the status of the dig with him. In short, you'll be throwing in your lot with his."

"That couldn't be further from the truth!" At least, the throwing in with him was. The other? Talking about the dig, about the creature, speculating on its era, the cause of death, what the area had been like when it was alive? Yeah, she expected to talk to Mike about it. She couldn't see why Scarr would mind, though, since he never sought input like that from her in the past. "I thought you would appreciate my being on site. That way I can make sure he doesn't try to rip off our part of the dino."

"I don't want my name associated with his!"

Liz wasn't sure who was more shocked, her or Scarr himself. The outburst said a lot, but to Liz it didn't make sense. Mike Edmonds was involved, whether Scarr liked it or not. She was sure she looked quite astounded and wasn't surprised when Scarr spoke again.

"Having one of my team members living in Edmonds' camp will be misunderstood." He couldn't quite meet her eyes. "The community will think that I accept him as a colleague."

Understanding dawned. Scarr feared the tightknit academic world would evaluate him and find him wanting. It was a good point, one she would be well to consider, because that community would be analyzing her as well.

Shifting her domicile would be fraught with more dangers than she expected. Could she do it? Was she up to the challenges that would ensue?

Hell, yes. "Dr. Scarr, I'm moving over to Edmonds' camp. It will save me more than an hour travel time each day, so I'll be able to get more done, more quickly. I am not throwing in my lot with him. Nor am I abandoning academic methods. My goal is to retrieve the skeleton, as intact as possible. I think having a positive working relationship with

Mike Edmonds will make that easier, not more difficult." She hesitated, then added, "I think you are quite capable of making sure the academic community knows where you stand on the subject of Mike Edmonds and amateur paleontologists generally." She was throwing Edmonds under the bus and that felt wrong, but at the moment she was desperately trying to save herself.

Scarr thought about her comment, then he nodded thoughtfully. "I'll do a series of posts on the many ways amateurs hinder the gathering of knowledge." He pursed his lips, his expression satisfied. "Yeah. It's a beginning." He nodded decisively, then turned his attention back to her. "Zac or I will be at the rift site every day. I'll expect a regular report."

If that was what it took to keep her job, she'd do it. She nodded. "Of course." She wondered if she should warn him about the dino cam, but decided that could wait for another day. She hoped it would never come.

"Which tent is mine?"

Though Liz Hamilton smiled, there was a tightness in that smile that had Mike frowning. She had a backpack slung over her shoulders and a suitcase on rollers that she'd wrestled down into the rift and across it to the path up to his side.

He knew, because he'd watched her. And wondered why that idiot, Zac Doyle, hadn't driven the pickup along the detour to Discovering Dinos' side of Highway 25, then dropped her at the camp.

He had to force himself not to rush down into the rift, pluck the suitcase from her grasp, and haul it up to the camp himself. He didn't, because he couldn't. If he offered her extra help he'd acknowledge to her—worse, to himself—that he was interested in her as more than a colleague.

He gestured to a tent nestled in the middle of the half a dozen tents that made up the camp. "That one. The small one beside the admin tent."

When he'd chosen the location, he'd told himself he was putting her there so he could keep an eye on her. His tent was the one on the other side of hers after all, and with her lodged between him and the admin tent, there was no way she could do anything that might jeopardize his dig. The reality was that he wanted her close and he wanted her safe.

"Thanks," she said. "I'll just stow my bags, then I'll go down to the rift."

He nodded. No surprise there. It was nine in the morning and the day was already hot. She'd want to get as much done before the afternoon heat made time spent down in the rift a sweltering nightmare.

She gave him another fraught smile as she turned away. On impulse, he caught her arm. She stopped and looked back at him, wide-eyed.

"Is anything wrong?" he asked. It was a struggle to keep his voice even, as if he was just asking a casual question. He was congratulating himself on his professionalism when she frowned and looked down at his hand on her arm.

He let go, hastily. So much for being cool about it.

She smiled again and almost deliberately relaxed. "No. I'm fine. Thanks for asking, though."

So polite. The smile might have worked if he hadn't been watching her eyes. That shadow was still there, marring their vivid blue depths. Something was wrong. But what? He'd bet it had something to do with Scarr or Zac Doyle. The thought made his temper flare. She deserved better.

On her way to the tent, Josh Sheen, his computer wizard, greeted her with a shyness Mike hadn't seen before on the gregarious eighteen-year-old. Concern nibbled at the edge of his managerial self. He'd been eighteen once, too, too many years ago, but he could still remember how it felt to be awed by a beautiful older woman. Liz Hamilton was certainly beautiful and for Josh she was older, though to Mike she was just the perfect age.

Josh, though. If he did indeed have a crush on her, that could be a problem. He didn't want his team upset by emotional tangles caused by the new girl in camp. He headed over to intercede.

He didn't have a chance. Will Lavery, his chief of paleontology research, sauntered over to introduce himself.

Before that could happen Mike heard Josh say, "The camera will focus on Mike's part of the excavation, of course, but I used a wide enough angle that your dig will be visible." He grinned at her. "Don't worry, I'll make sure that you look good on camera."

Liz had let go of her suitcase handle. Now she slid the backpack off her shoulders. "Don't worry about that. I'm really interested in how the live streaming will document the dig. I'd like to talk to you about it, maybe tonight after we've quit for the day."

Josh's face fell. "I don't live at the camp. I set up the camera here, but I monitor it from the office in town."

Liz smiled easily. "Then I'll make my schedule work with yours. If you have a chance to give me a run down before you leave for the day, shout. I'd appreciate it."

Josh's eyes brightened and his chest swelled. "You bet!"

Mike felt an absurd flash of pleasure at how she'd handled the smitten teen. Respectfully, as an equal. It showed a side of her that he liked. A lot.

He reached the little group as she turned to Will and said, "Hi, I'm Liz Hamilton." She held out her hand.

Will took it. "Will Lavery. I run Mike's dig sites and his lab once the season is over."

"Nice to meet you, Will." Her smile was friendly and seemed genuine.

Will shot a look Mike's way, then he said casually, "Alfred Scarr was one of my profs at the master's level. I was glad he wasn't my thesis supervisor. He had a reputation of...interfering... in his Ph.D. students' study plans."

Mike knew why Will had brought up his degree work. He was letting Liz know that the Discovering Dinos team was professional and, unlike Scarr's assumptions, part of the community. He waited, curious to see Liz's reaction.

She raised a brow and said, "You worked with Scarr for your master's. Where did you go for your Ph.D.?"

Will's degree came from one of the top schools in the field. Liz tilted her head, her expression impressed. She smiled in that easy, friendly manner she'd used with Josh and said, "Since you run the site, I assume you're staying here at the camp."

"His tent is the other side of the admin tent," Mike said, drawing her eyes with his comment.

She nodded to them both. "Good, then we'll be able to talk this evening." She picked up the backpack by one of the straps and took a firm grip on the handle of the suitcase. "For now, I need to get to work. Nice to meet you, Josh, Will." She headed off to her tent, the suitcase bouncing and tipping behind her.

With the main attraction gone, Josh drifted away to the admin tent to work on some equipment. Will slid a look Mike's way. "Alfred Scarr is competitive, demanding, and ruthless about getting ahead. I wouldn't put it past him to deliberately insert a spy into our camp."

Mike stared at the open flap of the tent he'd assigned Liz. He could see her moving about inside. "I don't read her as being willing to cave into pressure like that." Then he shrugged. "But you may be right. I'll keep an eye on her." Why did that make him feel so very pleased?

Will turned toward the admin tent and started walking. After casting one last look at Liz's tent, Mike went along with him.

"I hated Scarr," Will muttered. "He was everything I disliked about the formal academic system. He was never around unless he wanted to pick your brain, or get you to write a paper for him. I couldn't wait to leave his program." He paused outside the tent. His mouth twisted. "Zac Doyle is supposed to be some kind of super hotshot, but from what I've seen so far, he doesn't do much."

"Guys like Scarr and Doyle are bottom feeders," Mike said. "Cheer up. Think how pissed they are that we have half of their find of a lifetime."

Will brightened. "It is, isn't it?" His eyes gleamed. "I think we've got a predator."

A smile slowly curled Mike's mouth. "No argument here. That femur and the muscular neck tell the tale. Theropod, no doubt. Now we just have to find out exactly which one it is."

"Look for the head." Will sighed. "It's probably on Scarr's side."

"Maybe. Maybe not." Mike's smile widened into a grin. "Wouldn't it be fun if it was on ours?"

Will laughed. "Bonus."

No, Mike thought. Having Liz Hamilton living in his camp, a potential spy, someone he needed to keep a close eye on.

Now that was bonus.

CHAPTER 13

Dusk drifted into the velvety darkness of a prairie night. The members of the Discovering Dino dig team and Liz gathered together in front of a campfire and talked. About the day, what they'd found, what they were expecting for the next day, about themselves. They were unwinding after a long, hot day in the sun and there was a sense of mellowness among them.

It was a very different atmosphere than the one Liz had learned to expect at Scarr's camp. There people broke up after dinner was over and the dishes washed and put away. A few worked in the lab tent, but most retired to their own tents. This friendly atmosphere that surrounded her now was as much a surprise to Liz as the quality of the team Mike Edmonds had put together.

His dig supervisor, Will, had a Ph.D. from a top school. The two summer students who worked with Will were also at top schools. That Mike was able to assemble such a well-qualified team was surprising, given the animosity Scarr—and, she assumed—other academic paleontologists had toward Mike and his business-oriented excavations.

Though she didn't express her surprise, Will caught on to it. Mike had moved away to deal with an email as they had Internet, thanks to the enterprising Josh. Will nodded his head in Mike's direction and said, "You wonder why I work for him and not an academic like Scarr."

Liz shrugged and said with a laugh that had an edge of bitterness she couldn't quite contain, "No one would want to work for Scarr if they didn't have to."

Will laughed too. The two students listened silently. "There are other paleontologists. Most of them aren't as self-serving as Scarr is."

"Yeah, that's true." As she moved through the various academic levels on her quest for her Ph.D., Liz had worked on other digs, in increasing levels of responsibility. As an undergrad, she'd simply dug where ordered and learned her craft. As a masters' student, she also dug, but she'd explored too, and worked in the site lab tent. Once she was at the Ph.D. level, she worked more closely with the dig's organizer and she'd had her name included in the dig reports. She worked, she achieved, she moved on.

She was proud of her accomplishments, but she was very aware that she wasn't the kind of splashy, spectacular person Zac Doyle was. Liz did her work, she didn't talk it up. As far as she knew, Zac worked hard at his craft too, but he was one of those people who excelled at making sure that everyone in the paleo community knew about his accomplishments, and that they realized this his were somehow more important than anyone else's.

There was quiet around the campfire for a minute. Liz looked over, past the flickering fire, to the shadows where Mike was still on his phone. She looked back at Will. "Why did you choose to work for Discovering Dinos?"

He prodded the fire with an iron poker that had come from town, like the wood burning in the firepit. There was not enough vegetation in this dry, dusty badland to supply wood for burning. "Why did I opt to work for a dino pirate like Mike, you mean?"

She flushed and hoped that no one would notice in the flickering light. "No. Why choose a private organization rather than a museum or a university?"

Will took a while to consider that. "The easy answer is that Mike had an opening and I needed a job." He shrugged. "That's part of it." He poked the fire again, his eyes on the flames. "The other part. Well, the other part was that I discovered I wasn't suited to the cut and thrust of academic life. I'm not particularly competitive. I love puttering around in my lab, cleaning bones, looking for clues about the animal's life. I like writing up what I find and knowing I can pass on my knowledge that way. I don't want to teach undergrad classes, or mentor grad students. Or go to conferences where I have to present papers to impress my peers so I can get ahead in my department." He shrugged. "Mike lets me do what I want to do."

"But he'll sell the bones you dig up."

"Will he?"

Liz frowned. "Doesn't he?"

"At times," Will said. "Discovering Dinos is a business. All of our digs are privately funded, either through the company or through investors."

Liz raised her brows. "I think you're proving my position."

Will shook his head. "How is Scarr's dig funded?"

"A grant from the university provides the base, but there are quite a number of smaller grants that top up the funds."

"From where?"

She frowned, thinking. "The second largest funding comes from a museum. Then there are several grants from private charities and donors."

"And they all want their piece of the pie," Will said softly.

She stared at him.

"Think about it," he said. "Say Scarr strikes it big on his dig here, the university gets its name mentioned in the news reports of a new dino find. They're also mentioned prominently in any papers that result from the find. The museum gets the bones. If our shared dino is a new species they will be able to display the only one on record in their museum. And then there are the private donors. They are also mentioned in the papers that are published and may have their names listed at the museum, along with the university's. Name recognition brings in more funding for the university and the private charities."

"The bones will stay here, in the United States," Liz said, a little desperately.

Will shrugged. "Who says they'll go out of the country under Mike's watch?" When Liz didn't immediately respond, he added impatiently, "All I'm saying is that no one is altruistic and the academic digs are doing it for the same reasons Mike is."

"And what's that?" She was rewarded by a long, *well duh*, look from Will.

But it was Mike who replied. "I'm fascinated by dinosaurs."

Nicely done, Liz! She felt herself go hot all over. Still, she didn't regret the conversation. And it was better that Mike should be part of it, rather than just being defended by his deputy.

Will shot Mike a glance, then grinned. "She has a somewhat... distorted view of what we do."

"Not surprising, considering," Mike said. He resumed his position by the fire, on the other side of Will, beside one of the summer students, who were taking in the conversation with wide eyes and closed mouths.

"So enlighten me," she said.

Will laughed at that and stood up. "I'm ready to head in. I had an early start today and I want to make another tomorrow. Good night."

The students decided it was a good time for them to slip away as well, leaving Mike and Liz in the darkness, lit by the stars above and the leaping light from the fire. For a time they sat silently, the only sound the crackle of the burning wood.

"What do you know about Discovering Dinos?" Mike asked finally.

Liz leaned forward, her elbows on her knees, as she stared at the fire. "Not much. I'd never heard of you until I ended up on Scarr's dig."

Mike poked at the fire, as Will had done earlier. "Did Scarr tell you that I sell the bones I find to the highest bidder?"

She nodded. "Usually dilatant billionaires from the third world."

"Hmmm. And did he tell you I'm destroying priceless evidence every time I dig, because I don't have the proper education?"

"Constantly." She was watching his face now, her attention completely caught. A smile flickered on the edge of his lips, but she wasn't sure if it was bitter, amused, or rueful. Perhaps it was a combination of all those emotions.

"I suppose he says my company is crass, commercial and making a fortune off of what should be a pure academic endeavor."

"Your dino tourism program," Liz said. "Yeah, he has mentioned it."

Mike laughed. Liz realized that the smile was amused, not bitter, because his laugh was clear of any darker emotions. "Those two who slipped away before our discussion turned into an argument—Justin and Maggy? They started coming to the Discovering Dino summer digs ten years ago, when I was just getting started. At first they came with their parents, but when they were older they came on their own. They're both in university now and they both plan to become paleontologists. And they'll succeed too, because they know what it takes to be a paleontologist. More importantly, they know what it means. The rough digging conditions, the long hours of backbreaking work. The nitpicky work in the lab. There's no romance in why they've chosen this career. Their eyes are open and they're prepared."

"You're saying you're a teacher as much as a prof in a university lecture hall is."

He cast her an approving grin. "Yeah. I'm hands on. I teach the basics, but I also instill a love for the craft, not just the technical details."

"There's no apology in your voice."

He raised his brows. "Should there be?"

She thought about that, then shook her head. "No, I suppose not. For selling bones to billionaires, maybe."

He made a derisive sound. "So the femur of a hadrosaur gets locked up in a case in some rich guy's mansion and he shows it off to all his friends to impress them. Is that any worse than the femur being put in a box and stored away in the basement of a museum, because the museum already has dozens of hadrosaur femurs? To be brought out once a year or three, if that, when a researcher decides they want to take a look at it?"

Put that way, he had a point. Liz laughed. "You're good at identifying the flaws in the system."

He shrugged. "I'm outside the system, so I see it differently."

"Nice of you not to say 'more clearly,'" Liz said, keeping her tone light.

Mike flashed her an amused smile. "Doesn't mean I wasn't thinking it."

She laughed again. "With that, I think it's time I turned in as well. I'll see you tomorrow."

"Good night," he murmured as she stood up.

She headed off. When she reached her tent, she looked back. He poked at the fire, spreading the embers, relaxed, a man comfortable in the world he had created for himself.

Something twisted in her stomach and she thought how very attractive that was.

Mike prodded the logs still producing a bright flame in the darkness. It was over a quarter of an hour since Liz had disappeared into her tent. She'd extinguished her light a couple of minutes ago and, except for the flames in the firepit, the camp was in darkness. He was alone with his thoughts.

That was fine with him. Though he enjoyed being around people and he liked the atmosphere of a camp on the open prairie, he found that he needed quiet at the end of the evening to recharge and think thorough the problems thrown his way during the day. Tonight his big problem was Liz Hamilton and his feelings for her.

When he'd met Liz Hamilton she'd been a woman in jeopardy. His mouth turned up into a wry smile as he thought the hokey words. As clichéd as the statement was, it provided a pretty good description of her situation. She'd been out on the prairie, in the open, with a major storm on the way, and no shelter in sight. He had stopped to help, because he would have stopped for anyone in the same situation. What happened after that had been a surprise. The instant attraction that caught him by the throat when he'd first saw her face, an attraction that didn't dissipate even when he learned who she was.

That attraction was still there and he fought it every time he was near her. During the day he hid behind his sunglasses and hoped she wasn't aware that he watched her more often than he should. When he invited her to move into the camp he told himself it was so he could keep an eye on her—and that was still true—but he also liked the idea of being with her outside of work.

A log crackled and shifted. He pushed it back to the center of the fire. Flames caught a fresh portion and blazed high. Tonight when he'd come back from dealing with Harvey Earnshaw's email about the contract negotiations, his damned ego had leapt when he realized that she and Will were talking about him. He liked that she was interested in him, that she was digging for information about him. He'd given her another nugget, let her see part of himself, before she retired for the night. He could have supplied more—all the details about how he'd formed Discovering Dinos, why he hadn't gone on to grad school after he completed his undergrad. But he held back. He wanted her to open up to him as well, and monopolizing their conversations wasn't going to do it.

It occurred to him that he was thinking about Liz a woman, not a paleontologist and colleague. He needed to get that sorted out in his head. They were locked together on this find, for the immediate future and very likely for a lot of time beyond it. Harvey had been practically rubbing his hands with glee tonight. He'd emailed that negotiations were going well and that all of the extreme, outrageous clauses he always included in his initial demands weren't causing so much as a ripple at the university's end.

It was Harvey's policy to include demands he was certain the other side would not be willing to meet. Then, when they protested and insisted those clauses be deleted, Harvey would concede—always with a great show of reluctance. Later, when the opposition wanted other concessions, he'd refuse, citing his earlier compromises, and the other side would back off. That way, he ensured that the really important stuff slipped through under the radar and he ended up with a contract that was tipped in Discovering Dino's favor. Tonight Harvey said it looked like he was about to get all of his must have clauses included, especially that one, really big, red herring.

Mike tipped his head back and smiled at the black, star spotted sky. If Harvey was right, he would be seeing a great deal of Liz Hamilton over the next months. Should he follow the attraction between them and see if it led to sex and a relationship? Or perhaps just to friendly sex with no ties between them? He mulled that over while the fire gradually die down.

As the flames faded into embers, he decided that casual sex between friendly colleagues was the best idea. No messy possessiveness on either side, so no painful emotional break up at the end of the season, but satisfaction on both sides.

He spread the embers, then dumped the last of the coffee from the urn onto them and added dirt on top for good measure. Then he turned in for the night, ready to deal with whatever the next day threw his way.

Tomorrow morning brought a sleepy-eyed Liz to breakfast and along with her a lot of thoughts about bed and waking up together that told him he needed to step up his plan to move their situation into his friendly colleagues and lovers scenario. He didn't have a lot of luck at breakfast. She ate quickly and disappeared down into the rift while he was still munching on bacon and eggs. Still, he figured he'd see her down at the excavation and didn't worry.

Forty-five minutes later he did find her there. He also found Scarr and Zac Doyle. He greeted them both politely. Zac nodded acknowledgement, but Scarr simply glared at him. Well, that was fine. He didn't care about Alfred Scarr. He went to work with Will on his side of the find.

Scarr shot them both a look, then grabbed Liz's arm and dragged her deeper into the federal side, away from Will and Mike.

"You'd think we carried the Ebola virus," Will muttered.

Mike laughed. "Wouldn't it be fun to find some way to make him catch it?"

Will laughed too, and they continued on, though Mike kept an eye on what Scarr was doing with Liz on the other side of the rift.

Whatever it was, he seemed to be deeply emotional about it. He waved his hands in the air as he talked and occasionally he pointed aggressively. It was that aggressive pointing that Mike worried about. But he stayed where he was and worked on clearing away debris, exposing more and more of the ancient bones that made up the skeleton.

Eventually Scarr nodded to Zac and they both headed down the rift, away from the find. Liz came back to her side of the skeleton and started working on the neck bones.

She was only a few feet away, but Mike couldn't read her expression. That worried him. She looked closed off, not simply focused on her work. He got a couple of bottles of water from the cooler and went over to offer her one.

She stared at it, then looked at him and smiled. "Thanks." She drank deeply, then said, "They've gone exploring."

He blinked. This was not what he expected. "Scarr and Doyle?"

She nodded. "Scarr figures that there must be more bones like these in the rift and he wants to be the one to find them."

While she drank more water, he tried to figure out if she was upset by this. "Shouldn't Zac be helping you with our dino?"

"Scarr and Zac want a find of their own. Scarr doesn't like the idea of sharing this one." She looked at her neck bones, then back at him. "Truth be told, Mike? I'm glad they're not interested in this creature. If exploring the rift makes them happy and keeps them from interfering in my dig, I'm all for it."

He laughed. "Me too."

She shot him a grin. "Besides, if there's anything on my side of the line, it's buried deep and not easy to find. I know. I've looked. Thanks for the water. I've got to get back to work."

As he watched her sashay back to her bones, a laugh rumbled deep in his throat. He'd thought she wasn't up to dealing with Scarr and Doyle, but it seemed there was a lot more to Liz Hamilton than he'd thought.

CHAPTER 14

"Things are looking good here." Zac Doyle's voice was encouraging, as if he actually cared about how the dig was going.

Liz had a soft brush out and was dusting surface debris away from one of the shoulder bones of her beast. Zac was standing to one side watching her work. He was supposed to be crouching beside her, engaged in the delicate work of releasing the fossilized skeleton from the rocks where it had rested for millennia. Instead she was doing the excavation all by herself while he went out and searched for a fabulous find of his own. With only her working on the skeleton, she'd be lucky if she was able to get it free of its burial place before the season was over and the early snows of winter arrived.

She didn't bother to look up. "Yes, they are." She kept brushing. Zac breathed and shuffled his feet, waiting for her to say something more.

What did he expect her to do? Beg him to give her a hand? Fat chance she'd do that. It had been over a week since she made the find and for all that time Zac had rarely been around.

"Al has decided we should do a thorough inventory of the area. He thinks this must have been an ancient river bed and he feels there's tremendous potential here."

There was. There were signs that other animals were buried here. The trouble was, they seemed to be up water from where her creature had died, on Mike Edmonds land, not Scarr's.

She kept brushing, focused on her work, ignoring Zac's shuffling feet and increasingly stressed breathing.

Interesting, that. He evidently wanted her blessing before he went off to do his exploring, even though Scarr—no Al!—had apparently already told him what his expected objective was. She brushed some more. Zac's feet shuffled, visible at the edge of her vision. She continued to work and eventually Zac went away. That was a relief. Having him hover encroached on her concentration and made her edgy. With him gone she settled in to get as much done as she could before the cool morning gave way to the heat of the afternoon.

Around mid-morning she surfaced for a water break. The sun beat down on her and her dinosaur, warming the pale sandstone walls of the rift, which then trapped the heat in the rift. She stretched, swiped her arm over her forehead, then went to get a bottle of water from the cooler. She was leaning on the boulder Mike had used the other day when she noticed Zac headed her way.

As she drank her water, she watched him idly. He was plodding, his head down as he put one foot in front of the other. His slumped shoulders told her that he hadn't had any luck finding another bone bed. Whether he was upset because his name wouldn't be associated with the local finds, or he was worried about how Scarr would react to his lack of success, she didn't know. Moreover, as she watched him, she realized she didn't care.

She went to the cooler to get another bottle of water. When he reached her, she handed it to him. He looked surprised, but nodded his thanks.

They drank in silence for a time then he said, "I'm going to have to go back to camp to report to Al."

There it was again. Al, the chummy short form of Alfred. Liz preferred the more professional, and possibly faintly derogatory, Scarr. "Find anything interesting?"

She saw him start to shake his head, no, then stop. "There are several formations where I'd expect to find bones. Once I report, I expect Al will want me to bring a mapping team in." He smiled, as if the task not only was of vital importance, but in a conspiratorial way, enlisting Liz's cooperation to make the mapping team's process easier.

Liz drank her water and didn't comment. Zac finished his and pitched the bottle toward the can they were using for recycling. It missed, landing beside and a little behind, but in full view of where she and Zac were both standing.

"Thanks for the water." He turned toward the path to the surface, ready to head out.

"Hey, Zac," she said. When he turned toward her, his gaze questioning, she pointed to the stray water bottle. "You missed."

He stared at her uncomprehending.

"The bottle goes in the can, not beside it."

He still looked bewildered.

Liz huffed out a breath and said, "Zac, take a moment and put the bottle in the can before you go." She felt a little petty saying that, until she saw the flash of annoyance in his eyes. Then she felt better. Zac was used to having others do his clean up for him. Being called on his skimpy performance was something he definitely didn't like. She was rather pleased she'd struck a nerve.

He stalked over to the can, picked up the bottle and ostentatiously crumpled it, before dropping it inside. Liz grinned and saluted him with her bottle. "Awesome, Zac. Thanks."

He nodded curtly, then made his way up the path. She wondered if he'd catch the underlying meaning to her little stunt over the bottle. That she knew he hadn't found anything significant when he went bone bed hunting down the rift and was just stringing her a line. She doubted it.

She finished up her water. As she dropped her own crumpled bottle into the bin, she heard the roar of an engine. It was coming from

Scarr's side of the ruined highway. Zac was on his way back to Scarr's camp.

Time to get back to work.

She glanced up at the sky as she moved back into the sunlight. Not a cloud in sight. She'd have another hour and a half or two hours before it became too hot to work and she had to retreat to the Discovering Dinos camp.

As if her thoughts of Discovering Dinos had conjured him up, Mike Edmonds' voice sounded nearby.

"Nice move." His tone was approving.

She knew he was talking about the water bottle, but she raised her brows anyway. She still wasn't sure how she felt about Mike Edmonds. He was good to look at and sexy in the extreme, and she was definitely attracted to him, but she wasn't sure if she wanted to see where that attraction went. Who knew? It might go nowhere. He might not be attracted to her.

"Do you think he really believes he's found some good potential sites?" Mike said.

He wasn't going to let this go. She shrugged. "Zac wants me to think he has. There's a difference."

"In the real world, yeah. For Zac Doyle? Maybe not."

That made her laugh. "You don't believe in bullshit, do you, Mike?"

His mouth quirked up into a half smile. "Not worth my time."

She raised her brows. "Is that why you're not in academia?"

He stared at her for a minute without answering. His eyes were covered by the dark sunglasses, so she couldn't tell what he was thinking, but she saw his mouth harden, then ease into a smile. "No. My cousin died." He pointed to the neck bones she'd exposed before her water break. "Want some help?"

She looked over his shoulder. Will was talking to the summer students, Justin and Maggy, giving them direction. Probably telling one of them to come over here to help her. That was sweet, but... "Scarr would go nuts if he knew I was accepting help from someone at Discovering Dinos."

Mike's smile broadened. "So don't tell him."

Liz's first instinct was to refuse, politely, but firmly. Then she looked at her massive dinosaur and thought about natural deadlines and the need to get the bones out of the ground before the short autumn turned into winter. She needed help. Usually she'd have a team of several diggers working with her. Scarr wasn't pulling anyone from his other site though, and Zac wasn't putting in any time.

Scarr wanted her to fail and on her own she probably would. Mike Edmonds was offering her a way out. "If Zac comes back I'll be in deep trouble."

"Do you think he will?"

"This afternoon maybe. Not before." Mike's eyebrows rose above his sunglasses. She felt her mouth twist into a rueful smile in response. "Yeah, okay, you're right. I'll be able to hear the sound of his engine if he comes back long before he sees anything. Okay, thanks, I accept your offer."

Was there approval in his smile? Or was she imagining it? Liz hoped it wasn't her imagination, because his expression made her feel warm all over. She went back to her neck bones and Mike followed.

She cocked her head. "Shouldn't you tell Will what's up?"

"Why?"

"So he can send Justin or Maggy over."

Mike looked down at her. "You'd prefer one of the kids to me?"

"What? No, of course not. I mean... I didn't think..." She shut her teeth over her babbling and willed herself to settle down. "I'm sorry. I didn't expect this." At his raised eyebrows, she said defensively, "You're the boss. I assumed you had other charges on your time."

"Will is supervising my side of the beast. My assistant has me listed as out-of-the-office, and she can handle pretty much anything that comes up, anyway." He shrugged. "My time is yours."

"You planned this," she said. She wasn't sure if she liked that idea or not. Part of her did. The part that liked the knowledge that he was noticing what she was doing. The other part wondered if there was an ulterior motive to his offer.

"I've been watching Doyle," he said. "And you. Doyle flits in, stands around the skeleton for a half an hour or so, then disappears on his own business. You work steadily, usually until long after you should be taking a break. From what I've seen you're careful and thorough. I respect that. I want to help."

His voice deepened as he said the last few words, sliding across her senses like an unexpected touch. Liz felt that change in tone like a caress that slid all the way down her body. She swallowed and said, "Thank you. I accept your offer." Her voice had softened in response to his and she knew she was replying to more than the simple words.

They got to work. Mike took direction from her, but added his own observations when he thought they were useful. They worked as a team, with surprisingly little conflict. Liz became absorbed in the work, hardly noticing the time passing. She was aware, though, of Mike's presence in a way that seemed remarkably natural. She liked having him beside her, focused on the same dino bones she was, intent, meticulous, and driven. Their conversation didn't stray far from a discussion of the state of the skeleton and what they found, but Liz felt as if they were speaking a deep emotional language just their own. There was absolutely no practical reason for her reasoning. It was all based on an emotional response.

When he put his hand on her shoulder sometime later, she didn't jump, though she felt the touch sizzle through her. She looked up, into his face. He was frowning. Her heart twisted. "What the matter?"

"It's well past noon. The sun's high and you're flushed. Time to break for lunch."

That little twist blossomed into a flight full of shy butterflies absurdly excited at being the focus of this man's caring. She sat back on her heels, then stretched, absurdly certain that his eyes were following her movements, even though his gaze was hidden by the dark glasses.

He turned away abruptly and she stood, suddenly feeling adrift. He'd just gone to the cooler to get them water, though, and those butterflies did a happy dance inside her as she watched him return. He twisted the cap loose, then handed her a bottle. She drank, tipping her head back, again feeling the warmth of his gaze as he studied her. The water slid down her throat, cool and refreshing as she swallowed. She lowered the bottle and smiled. Slowly. "Thank you."

"You're welcome."

His voice was rough. The edge of hoarseness told her that he was paying attention to every little move she made and the pleasure of it shivered through her. He turned away to pack tools neatly until they returned from the lunch break.

She took another drink, then capped the bottle and went to help him. They were very close, their shoulders almost touching, their hands brushing each other as they stored the tools. Each time they touched, they would smile. On the surface, the looks were an apology. In reality it was because the slightest caress was igniting new sensations.

At least, that was how it was for Liz. She hoped he was experiencing the same pleasurable feelings.

Too soon the area was tidied away and they were on their way up the path to the camp. They'd reached the crest of the ridge, and were back up at ground level when she asked, "Earlier you said you weren't a paleontologist because your cousin died. If you don't mind my asking, what happened?"

He stopped and stared out onto the prairie. Will and the students, Justin and Maggy, were already at the camp, moving around, organizing lunch. Liz thought Mike wasn't going to answer, then he said, "My uncle owns this land. Originally it was a cattle ranch, but when my cousin entered the army, my uncle turned it into a dude ranch. Less work, more stable annual income. From the time I was ten I worked here during the summer. I knew every inch of this place, and I was dino mad. After Uncle Ted turned it into a dude ranch I spent my summers leading trail rides to those places where the fossils were on the surface and easy to see. When I finished my Bachelor of Science degree I enrolled in a masters level paleontology program, but that summer my cousin died in Afghanistan. My aunt and uncle fell apart. They asked me to stay on that fall and help." He shrugged, and looked down at her.

"He was their only son and their daughters had moved away and had lives of their own. They didn't have anyone else. I stayed."

He started to walk. Liz followed. "You never thought of going back to school?"

"Oh, I thought. I just never got round to it."

There was more to this story. Mike Edmonds was a complicated man. One, she thought, with far more good qualities than the bad ones Alfred Scarr had decided to harp on.

CHAPTER 15

The morning began in much the same way as other mornings. She was up early to explore the rift before Zac showed up. She usually gave herself no more than an hour as she didn't want him to know that she was hunting for a new bone bed, just as he was. If something was to be found she wanted to document it and attach it to her name. Call it professional pride, competitiveness, or petty spite. It didn't matter. She wanted to be there first.

By the time Zac showed up, around nine o'clock, she was at her skeleton, working on the neck, while Will Laverty and the two students were working the beast on Mike's side of the line.

"Nice day," Zac said. He stood, his hands on his hips, examining the ever more exposed bones. "Cretaceous?"

All the days were nice. And they'd decided the creature was from the last age of dinosaurs a long time ago. "From the strata and the size of the creature, yeah, probably late Cretaceous."

He continued to inspect. Liz continued her careful exposure of the bones. She thought about suggesting he pick up a tool and get down to work, but she didn't bother. She knew he'd take off to explore in a few minutes anyway, so she just focused on her dino and pretended Zac wasn't even there.

Eventually, she heard him grab a bottle of water from the cooler, then he sauntered away, without mentioning to her what his plans were. She figured he didn't bother, because they both knew his pattern by now.

She settled even deeper into work mode, glad he was gone. Her thoughts drifted from Zac Doyle to a much pleasanter subject, Mike Edmonds. The man fascinated her. Last night as he and his crew sat chatting at the campfire, she'd learned more about his background and why he wasn't on the academic side of the profession.

In the aftermath of his cousin's death, he'd worked the ranch as he always had, running it with his uncle as a dude ranch and leading the popular dinosaur hunting trail rides he'd told her about on an earlier night by the campfire. On one of those excursions they found what Mike thought was an almost intact skeleton of a hadrosaur. He called in an expert, who confirmed his hunch. His initial idea was to arrange to have the skeleton excavated by a museum or university team, but the find generated little interest. Hadrosaur skeletons were fairly common and low priority.

The bones had eroded to the surface naturally. If they weren't excavated, the weather and natural forces would continue the process, exposing more of the skeleton, but also wearing away the already exposed bones. Mike decided to launch a rescue mission. He'd dig the creature, with the help of the guests at the dude ranch. He developed a plan to excavate the area over the next summer. He incorporated as Discovering Dinos, hired summer students to be teacher-excavators and set up the camping trip and dig program for families who wanted to do something different on their summer holidays.

The program was a huge hit, so Mike ran it again the next year, and the one beyond that. The whole area was rich in dinosaur bones and it didn't take a lot of effort to find other skeletons that could be used for the program.

Maggy and Justin, both graduates of these trips, had talked enthusiastically about their experiences. As they all sat around the campfire, there had been teasing and a lot of laughter, but Liz sensed that the excavation vacations taught elements of paleontology in an exciting, hands on way that stuck.

Around mid-day, Zac reappeared as he always did. He picked up a bottle of water and guzzled it down as he watched Liz at her careful work. She ignored him, as she had in the morning, and eventually he muttered something about going back to Scarr's camp to write up his scouting notes, and left. She listened for the sound of the truck engine that signified his departure, then she stretched, packed up her tools and headed up to the camp for lunch.

That afternoon, as other afternoons, Mike worked with her on her side of the line until it was time to break for the day. She loved working with him. For some reason, her senses were more alert and she noticed more details than she did when she was alone. Perhaps it was the act of sharing those finds, because she always mentioned them to him and he responded with enthusiasm, or thoughtful insights. Or maybe it was that his warm responses never failed to send shivers of pleasure cascading through her. Whichever it was, as the days passed she found herself looking forward to the afternoon session.

Between the long days at the dig site and the quiet evenings at the camp, she was getting a sense of the man Mike Edmonds was. He led without ordering, taught by example, was loyal to those he loved, and protective of those he considered to be under his care.

Like her. It amused Liz to think that she had become one of Mike's causes, but she had. He didn't like the way Scarr and Doyle were treating her, but he couldn't exactly go out and order them to change their attitudes. So he was ensuring she was well looked after by assisting her on her side of the excavation.

He divided his time between the site and his business. Usually he was at the dig, working his own side of the dino in the mornings, but this morning, two weeks into the dig, he had stayed in camp to return some messages left the previous day. One in particular was interesting. Harvey Earnshaw, the lawyer negotiating the future of the dinosaur skeleton, wanted a strategy session with Mike. Liz wondered what was up and if Mike would explain the details to his crew at camp and in front of her, or if he'd do it privately at some other time.

She shrugged the thought away and kept on working. Each evening, as she prepared for bed, she felt closer to Mike Edmonds the man, but he was still the owner of a private dinosaur excavation business and Harvey Earnshaw worked for him. She and Mike might be friends, but she wasn't his confident, and they weren't in a relationship where she'd expect openness.

Whoa, stop there! She paused, stretched and grinned at nothing in particular. She didn't think a relationship with Mike was in her future, but the attraction she'd felt from the time they met was strengthening with each day and as she came to know him better. If he asked, would she go to bed with him? She knew the answer to that, and it wasn't no.

She got back to work. The sun rose in the sky, the air down in the rift heated and she began to sweat. Still, she continued to work. Zac returned from his explorations, grousing about the glare of the sun and the heat. He snagged a bottle of water, then stood drinking it as he watched her work. When he finished, he announced that he was going back to Scarr's camp to write up his findings.

Liz moved away from her bones and nodded. She arched her back, got herself a bottle of water and said, "You had a successful morning, then?"

Zac sent her a condescending smile. "This rift is loaded with potential."

Well, they agreed there. She thought most of it was down at Mike's end, but she wasn't going to tell Zac and by inference, Scarr, that. So far this morning, everything was going to pattern. Might as well continue on the same way. "Did Dr. Scarr say anything about sending over a couple of students to work the site with me?"

"Al and I talk about the classifying the finds from this season. We don't discuss staffing," Zac said. He followed that statement with a disdainful shrug.

Since Zac had supposedly been brought on to replace her and her job had included supervising the students working the dig, this was a bit much, but she was discovering it was typical. She drank, then said, "I guess the answer is no, then."

Zac shrugged again. "I'm headed back to the main camp. Is there anything you want me to tell Al?"

Liz wanted to ask if Dr. Scarr knew Zac called him Al all the time, but all she said was, "Tell him I need a team."

"Yeah, sure." Zac crumpled his bottle then walked over to the recycling can to drop it in before he headed up the path to his truck.

The morning dragged on, the heat increasing with each passing minute. Mike didn't come down to the rift, and Liz was edgy without him working beside her. Still, she kept at it. She wanted her bones out before the summer dig season ended.

When Will Laverty cleared his throat to get her attention some time later, she was ready to take a break. There was an air of suppressed excitement about him, but all he said was, "We're heading up to the campsite to get some lunch. Are you coming?"

Liz nodded. She stowed her tools, then tromped up the path to the surface and on to the camp. They rested while the sun was high. Liz retreated to her tent to write up notes on her morning's work. She could hear Will talking to Maggy and Justin, then Mike's deeper voice joined the conversation and all of a sudden her concentration was shot. Idiot, she thought, and had to force herself not to rush through her task.

It was about three when they all headed back down into the rift. This time Mike came with them. As was usual he settled in, helping her with her neck bones. They talked about the creature they were excavating, what needed to be done next, but nothing about the telephone calls that had made him absent for most of the day. Down the rift, Will and his team worked steadily through the afternoon.

They were all tired and Liz knew she was ready to quit for the day when Will shouted, "Mike! Come see this!"

Mike looked at Liz and raised his eyebrows. "What's up?" he shouted back.

"It's a theropod. We have proof!" Will shouted back.

Mike was on his feet in an instant and Liz wasn't far behind him. Will stood by the hindquarters of the dinosaur, his body tense, but there was a silly grin on his face. Maggy jumped up and down, clapping with glee. She chanted over and over, "It's a meat-eater. We've got a meat-eater." Justin was still brushing away bits of debris, as if he wanted their discovery to be perfect.

When they reached the scene, Mike crouched down to inspect the exposed bone. The dinosaur lay on its side. The leg and hip Will had exposed was drawn up close to its chest and they could see the other leg peeking out beneath. Will touched the long bone with a gentle finger. "It's hollow," he said.

Hollow bones, the hallmark of a therapod.

He traced the top of the femur. "Body mass was toward the hip, so I think we've got a carnivore."

With the body mass centered on the hips, it meant the animal walked on two legs. They hadn't uncovered the front legs yet, but as Liz stared wide-eyed at the skeleton, she was willing to bet they'd be short and clawed, made for savaging prey, not running on all fours. The next step was to try to classify the animal. "I think we're looking at around seventy million years ago," she said.

Will nodded. "With the size of this bone and the length of the body, it's big."

"T-Rex big?" Justin said, sounding hopeful.

"Not a T-Rex," Mike said. He was studying the bones. "A species in the Daspletosaurus genus."

"I've never heard of a Daspletosaurus," said Maggy.

"Daspletosaurus was a tyrannosaurid dinosaur, meaning it was a meat-eater and in the same family as the T-Rex," Liz said. "It was a smaller creature, though, and not as well documented."

Mike nodded. "In fact, when it was first discovered in the nineteen twenties, it was classified as a Gorgosaurus, another predator which lived about the same time. It wasn't until fifty years later that it was finally given its own designation."

"Finds of Daspletosaurus are rare," Liz murmured, as she outlined the hip with her fingertip. "A skeleton as well preserved as this one will provide much needed information on the creature's life."

"Awesome," Justin said. His face glowed with excitement. "Maybe we'll find some of his prey further down the rift."

Maggy's eyes widened. "That would be so cool."

"First things first," Mike said, smiling at his two interns. "Let's focus on this guy and get him out of the ground."

Maggy and Justin looked at each other and nodded.

Will smiled faintly. "Back to work, crew."

Mike shook his head. "Time enough for that tomorrow. Let's head back to camp now and celebrate."

There were nods all around and they scattered to put away their tools for the day.

Mike strolled with Liz over to her side of the line. "Now, to prove this creature is a Daspletosaurus, all we have to do is find the head."

His gaze settled on Liz and he smiled.

CHAPTER 16

*D*inner that evening was a celebration. They were giddy with the realization that the beast they were excavating was a rare carnivore, and might even be a new species of carnivore. That thought was enticing, but they wouldn't know until—or if—they found the head. For now it was enough to know that they were working on something special.

For Liz this night was a stolen pleasure. Tomorrow, when Zac showed up, she would have to tell him what Will and Mike had surmised and that she agreed with them. She expected him to sneer and say they were wrong. She didn't intend to back down, so she figured tomorrow morning would be a battle.

Tonight, though, tonight she would let herself be happy. No, not happy, joyous. She absorbed the elation around her, let it flow through her, wrapped it around her. Lived for the moment alone.

They ate hamburgers and drank toasts with the bottle of Scotch Mike produced from the lockbox in his truck. While they ate they speculated about the great beast, what it was, how it died. Inevitably they wondered if there were other creatures nearby, perhaps the bones of its prey, or another carnivore who had fought their animal and also died of its wounds. With the help of a couple of shots of Scotch, Maggy drew a word picture of the last days of their dino, revealing a surprisingly fertile imagination and an eye for detail that was impressive. Not to be outdone, Justin invented another scenario, while Will cheerfully critiqued them both amid much laughter.

Darkness had fallen a long time since when Will, Justin and Maggy finally wound down and retreated to their tents. Even though she knew it would be a long day tomorrow, Liz wasn't ready to retire yet. She said goodnight to the others, but stayed out by the campfire.

Mike stayed with her.

Until they found the head, the most telling part of the skeleton was the back end, Mike's part of the dino. She could ask him what he planned to do with his section of their awesome find, but she wouldn't do it tonight. It would bring tomorrow and the conflict of shared owner-ship and the possibility of argument into this quiet evening. She was still fizzing with the excitement of the find and the energy of the evening. She didn't want to lose it.

The thought made her shiver.

"Are you cold?" Mike asked. His voice was low, rough with some-thing that sounded like concern.

Smiling, she looked over at him. What she saw made her breath catch and her smile fade.

"I can get you a blanket, if you need it."

His gaze seemed to bore into her, to strip away her outer shell and expose her inner self, shivering not with cold, but awareness. "A blan-ket? Like the emergency blanket you got for me the night of the storm?" Her voice dropped to a lower register, and she said the words more slowly than she normally would.

He stilled.

She wasn't surprised. She hadn't deliberately added that sexy edge to her tone, but now that it was out there she was ready to own it. Now it was up to Mike. The next move was his. She wondered if he would take what she was offering.

"Emergency blankets are warm, but they're not particularly

comfortable. I was thinking of something...softer. There's one in my tent." He waited a heartbeat, then two. Then he stood. "I can get it for you."

Liz stood too. "I'll come with you."

He stared at her for a minute, then he held out his hand. "Are you sure?"

"Yes," she said, and took his hand.

He didn't use it to lead her to his tent. Instead, he pulled her to him, buried his free hand in her hair and kissed her.

His lips were firm over hers, moving sensuously, inviting her to participate. She shook her hand free of his, then wrapped her arms around his neck. Her fingers played with the hair on the back of his head while she parted her lips and let his tongue sink into her. As his tongue stroked hers, she shifted her body closer so that her breasts were pressed against the muscular strength of his chest and her hips thrust against his.

Desire flooded through her, hot, demanding, urgent. "Michael Edmonds, if you don't get me into your tent and under that blanket soon, I can't be held accountable for what happens to us out here."

He laughed against her mouth, sound and sensation inflaming her. "Slow down, hot stuff," he muttered, then went back to ravishing her mouth.

She whimpered. There was no way she was going to break away from the kiss to protest verbally. Instead she let her body argue her case. She tightened her hold on him and pressed closer, until she could feel the throb of his erection making demands of its own. She moved her hips over his, showing his body hers was ready with what it wanted.

The kiss deepened. His mouth hardened and his tongue thrust deeper. She met it with her own, fighting for dominance, inflaming them both.

Mike was breathing heavily when he pulled out of the embrace. "Give me a minute."

She smiled at him and held out her hand. "Let's walk to your tent. Slowly."

He stared at her, then down at her hand. "If I take your hand, I'll take everything else you're offering, right here."

She laughed.

"I mean it, Liz. I'm that close."

She shot him a cocky, feminine, smile. "Hands in pockets, then," she said, shoving hers into her hip pockets so that her back arched a little and her breasts stood higher.

He sucked in his breath in a quick sizzle of sound. "Damn you," he said mildly. "You're not going to make this easy, are you?"

She laughed at the hungry look in his eyes and took a step back. "My tent's closer and I have a blanket too."

She took another step back as he watched her with an intent gaze. Then he swooped. His kiss was meant to push them both to the edge. To tease, to tempt, to promise.

When he let her go, Liz was panting. "Mike." His name was a plea and a demand all at once. More plea than demand, though, she thought, as her body throbbed with need.

"Your tent," he said. This time he took her hand and they ran.

Inside the tent he zipped the flap closed and stripped her, quickly. As his hands covered her breasts she moaned. He closed his mouth over hers, catching the sounds she made as his tongue ravished her mouth and his thumbs rubbed over her nipples. They hardened at his touch and she clung to him for support.

She was aware of nothing but sensation. The roughness of his clothing against her skin, the rasp of his stubble on her face, the pads of his fingers moving against her breasts. She shifted position, spreading her legs to stand without overbalancing, and was rewarded with the hard evidence of his arousal. She moaned. Mike did too. Then he pulled away.

She opened her eyes to look up at him. "Mike?"

His smile was tender. He scooped her up, then carried her over to her air mattress and gently lowered her onto it. A moment later he unzipped his jeans and pushed them off.

Liz shifted onto her side and rested her head on her hand while she watched him appreciatively. He was well endowed with lean muscle and, heavens, an erection that was proof that he really did want her very much indeed. She moistened her lips, then chewed the lower one nervously. Was she ready for this? For him?

She looked up, past his muscular chest, and caught him watching her. There was a lazy look in his eyes, but a tightness to his features that suggested pleasure desired, but held under strong restraint. She reached for him with her free hand.

He caught it as he lowered himself to his knees beside the air mattress, then he turned it so he could kiss her palm. She shivered. His mouth moved up to her wrist, pausing to kiss the vein beating heavily there. His tongue flicked out, stroking lightly, then he raked his teeth over the spot and her breath caught. Intent on his task he didn't look up, but moved along her arm to her elbow, where he kissed and licked and rasped over her skin. She sighed with pleasure and eased onto her back.

He came down on top of her, positioning himself carefully. She shifted, opening for him. He stroked her breast, then as she sighed with the pleasure of it, he caught her mouth with his and slipped inside. She was ready for him, hot and anxious to proceed. She wriggled and he laughed against her mouth. Then he thrust and gave her exactly what she wanted.

The fire that he'd let cool while he undressed returned, hotter than before. Liz gave herself to him, not just her body, but her emotions and her mind. She was aware of nothing but the two of them. If a bear had strayed into camp and attempted to tear an entry into her tent she would not have noticed. She was wrapped in Mike's arms and there was nothing but him.

Her climax came after minutes of ever growing exquisite pleasure. It cascaded over her, painfully intense as he emptied himself into the condom he wore, then easing to sweet pleasure as his climax crested with hers. He withdrew slowly, shifting to deal with the condom, then he moved her on to her side and nestled her securely against him. He covered them both with her sleeping bag, kissed the side of her neck where her pulse beat a slow, satisfied rhythm, and whispered, "Rest now."

She was asleep almost before he finished saying the word.

They made love again during the night. It was a slow, sensual joining, with each learning the contours of the other's body and what pleased them most. Like their first time, the pleasure was intense. Liz fell asleep cuddled against Mike, more relaxed than she could remember.

She woke to sounds of morning activities outside her tent, male voices and one chipper female one. She yawned and stretched, grinning at nothing in particular. Sometime today she was going to have to tell Scarr about the theropod theory. He'd probably throw a fit and refuse to believe it.

Didn't matter.

Zac would be arriving in another hour or so, sneering about her excavation, bragging about what he hadn't really found further along in the rift.

Didn't matter.

In fact, when she tried to work up any kind of stressful thoughts, she discovered they didn't matter. She'd had such an amazing night with a man she liked very much on so many different levels she couldn't work up the energy to be worried, even if she should be.

She got up, gave herself a rough sponge bath with bottled water she kept in her tent, dressed in her usual jeans and a t-shirt, then exited the tent.

Mike saw her first. He shot her a sly, but cocky, grin. "You up late. Too much partying last night?"

She raised her brows. They'd agreed some time in the darkness of the night, that they wouldn't broadcast their relationship to the others. Right now, though, Mike had the look of a man who had a really juicy secret he was dying to unload on someone and he wasn't going to be picky about who that person was. "Too much theropod," she said repressively. "I've been trying to figure out where the head might be."

Will looked up from the plate of bacon and eggs he was eating. "I dreamed about it last night."

Mike poured Liz a cup of coffee and looked at Will, his expression interested. "Dreams are supposed to be our brain's way of bringing buried information to the surface. Where did you find the head?"

Will's expression twisted into a grimace. "On federal land, a yard or so away from the neck."

Liz accepted the coffee from Mike with a smile of thanks. Their hands touched for a moment and awareness lanced through her. Mike's cocky grin turned into a slumberous smile. Her heart skipped a beat then started to hammer.

She sat down at the portable picnic table opposite Will, who hadn't noticed the exchange—thankfully!—because he was focused on finishing up his food. She shook her head at him. "It's not, though. Believe me, I've looked."

"Are you sure you didn't miss something?" Will asked. He looked over as Mike sat down. "It's logical it would be near the neck."

"I hope it's on Mike's side," Liz said. She was very aware of him beside her. She could feel the heat from his body, smell the scent of clean sweat and masculine hunger that was particularly him. Her body was responding outrageously. Her nipples were peaking, her pulse pounding and heavy with desire, and the blush that suffused her body was darkening with every wayward thought.

"Why?" Mike asked.

His voice was rough. Low. Full of innuendo. She cleared her throat and said, "Because if it's on the federal side Scarr will absorb it and make it his own."

"He can try," Mike said pleasantly. He even smiled as he said the words.

"What will you do with your part of the skeleton?" she asked impulsively.

He stared out into the prairie. "I have plans."

When he didn't say anything more, she said, "That's it? Nothing more, just *plans*?"

Opposite her, Will snorted.

Mike brought his gaze back to her face. There was amusement in his eyes. A smile twitched at his mouth. "Isn't it enough?"

As she sipped her coffee, her gaze locked with his. Plans. She put the bits and pieces of information from the last couple of weeks together and decided to leap into the void and hope there would be a ledge to break her fall. "Let me guess," she said, slowly stating each word. "You're going to build a state of the art museum to house it."

His reaction was priceless. His eyes narrowed and a frown darkened his brow. He shot a quick look at Will, who raised his hands in a gesture of surrender.

"Don't look at me," he said. "I didn't say anything."

Mike focused back on Liz. "How did you know?"

She put her cup on the table. "Let's say I have insider knowledge. Can I borrow your truck this morning?"

"Why?"

"I have an errand to run."

He pulled his keys out of his pocket and tossed them onto the table. "There's an extra can of gas in the back in case you get stuck."

She smiled at him, remembering the night of the storm, thinking about their lovemaking last night. "I won't. Thanks. I'll be back as soon as I can."

CHAPTER 17

Once she was on the road Liz wondered if she was doing the right thing. Her physical response to Mike hadn't surprised her last night, but the deep contentment that followed did. Now she had questions and she wanted answers.

The best place to get them was the future.

She drove back to the stretch of prairie where she'd found her beacon, wondering as she went if the beacon would be there again. After all, Mark worked in a museum. He might not be there at eight-thirty in the morning. She reached her destination, more nervous than she had ever been, fearful that she might have imagined the whole thing because she so desperately wanted to have the talent that her mother and sister did.

Keeping her eyes on the road ahead, she parked the truck. It was only when she got out and rounded the front end to face the open prairie that she realized she was holding her breath. That was because she let it out in a woosh when she saw the blaze of her beacon flaring in the empty landscape in front of her. Her heart began to pound as she headed toward it.

As the first time, she was in her own time in one instant, then in the future world in the next. In the high tech lab she stood for a moment to get her bearings. She looked around her. Nothing much had changed since she was here last, although she thought the bones on one of the stainless steel tables were new. Unlike the last time, though, this morning Mark was in the room, seated at the desk on the far side of the room. His back was toward her and he was touching the computer image in front of him, shifting from one screen to another.

She watched for a couple of minutes, expecting him to turn around and greet her, but he didn't move. She frowned, considering that. He had known she was coming the first time. Why was he unaware of her now?

She cleared her throat and his body jerked.

He swiveled the wheeled desk chair so that he was facing her. His expression was shocked. "Grandma. What are you doing here?"

She waved her hand, indicating their surroundings. "I wanted to talk about...this."

Mark narrowed his eyes. "I can't. You know that." Uneasiness flashed across his face and he shot a look over his shoulder at the document on his screen.

Liz took a step forward. He was worried about something on that screen. That meant she wanted to know what it was.

He must have caught her movement out of the corner of his eye, because he focused back on her as he said, "Shutdown. Authenticated restart required."

"Shutting down," said Liz's voice through invisible computer speakers.

She stopped and stood, staring at the now blank computer screen. "What the hell?"

He laughed. "You said that to Josh when he unveiled it, too."

"Josh. Mike Edmonds teenage computer genius?"

His brows snapped together into a frown, then he pulled himself together and blanked his expression. A moment later he was smiling and mischief danced in his eyes. "You're the voice of all of our automated dioramas too. You didn't like that either, but visitors love the way you speak. It must be the Boston accent."

"I suppose," she said uneasily. Then she shot him a frosty look, one her mother, Chloe, had used on her hundreds of times. "You didn't answer my question."

His only answer to that was a grin. He stood up. "It's early. It must be early in your time too. Would you like a coffee?"

Now here was an opportunity to get a little more information. "It is early. Any chance of breakfast?"

Mark cocked his head and raised his brows. "We do have a cafeteria, but it's not open yet. And no, I'm not going to take you on a tour." He gestured to a table not far from a sink. "There is a coffee machine, though."

She nodded acceptance and followed him over to the coffee station. The coffeemaker was a single cup brewer. She watched Mark insert a pod, set a coffee cup beneath, then push a button to get the machine started. The machine hissed and gurgled. Coffee spurted into the cup. She suspected that the technology, which had been a comparatively recent innovation on her side of the beacon, was old-fashioned here in her grandson's time. Intrigued, she looked over at him. "You don't talk to the machine to get it to start? You still have to push a button?" Somehow, knowing that you still had to physically touch the machine to make it work was a relief.

Mark frowned down at the coffeemaker. "This is a retro model. You told me it would make you feel at home." The gurgling stopped. A few more drops splattered into the cup, then the machine beeped. He handed her the full cup.

He headed back to his desk, indicated a square, upholstered guest chair beside it, and sat in the wheeled and padded chair he used. She held the mug between her hands, feeling the warmth, thinking about Mark's surprise at her arrival and the retro coffeemaker. "You didn't know I was coming this morning, did you?"

He met her thoughtful gaze with a blank one of his own. "You know the rules, Grandma."

Yes, she did. When someone visited you from the past, you couldn't talk about your present, especially if the knowledge might change the past and so also change the future. But then, when a crisis occurred in Uncle Andrew's life, Cody and Faith had proved that actions in the present had already affected the past, so it wasn't always a simple equation. Liz sat back in her chair and sipped her coffee, keeping her gaze locked with Mark's. When he started to squirm, she said, "I think it's interesting that you didn't know I was coming today. Was that because I didn't tell you? Or was it because I didn't make this journey before?"

He stopped squirming and looked intrigued. "I only know about three visits and this wasn't one—" He closed his mouth with a snap and glared at her. "That wasn't fair."

"Three!" Liz said. "Is that all? Andrew visits Faith all the time. At least once a week, if not more."

"I didn't say there weren't more. Just that you warned me about three specific visits."

"How do you know this isn't one of them then?" Liz asked, intrigued.

He reddened. "I just do."

Faith, Liz's sister, had been a Beacon to Andrew Byrne from puberty on. Liz knew all the rules about visiting the future and she'd seen first hand how the system worked. She figured she probably knew a lot more than her grandson. He might know she was coming because of a date. That was unlikely, though, because Liz herself had no idea when Mark's now was. Of course she might be able to figure out the date by counting the days that passed between her first visit and the next one.

Or it might be because she didn't come alone. "Do I bring Mike Edmonds with me on the next two visits?"

Mark frowned at her. "Why did you come, Grandma?"

He hadn't answered her question, which made her think that she probably had brought Mike. She wasn't sure how she felt about that. If she'd taken him into her confidence and told him about the Beacon, it meant she trusted him completely. That she was ready to commit to him.

Well, she already had, hadn't she? Last night, when their sex got way out of hand and turned into something much more emotional than just satisfying an itch. "I want to know if this museum houses my dino."

He raised his brows. "The Daspletosaurus?"

She sucked in her breath. "So it is a Daspletosaurus?"

"You already knew that."

"Yes, but..." He was right, she did. But it was nice to know that Mike had pegged it. She changed tack as quickly as Mark had. "So my Daspletosaurus is here, on display? Can I see it?"

"Your Daspletosaurus is in the literature," Mark said.

He wasn't answering her question again. "Is it here, in this museum?"

"Grandma, you have a great career ahead of you and you know I can't tell you anything about it."

Frustrated, she glared at him. She suddenly knew how Faith's traveler, Andrew, felt when he tried to tease information about his time out of Faith, Liz, and their mother Chloe. Annoyed, impatient, intrigued.

There was a clatter from deeper in the building. Mark leapt to his feet. "That's the staff, coming in for work. You have to go. No one can find you here."

Liz thought about refusing to leave until he'd told her what she wanted to know, but when all was stripped to the basics, Mark was family. And he was right. If she was seen there would have to be explanations. Better that she was a ghost, visible only to her grandson. "Okay," she said. "I'll go, but next time I come I want answers!"

He glanced nervously at the doorway as Liz turned and walked toward the far side of the room, where she'd first entered. Light flared. She went through it and was back in her own time, standing on the vast, open prairie.

There was not a building in sight.

CHAPTER 18

*L*iz cut the engine, but she sat for a minute in the pickup, thinking over her visit to the future, feeling the frustration. Finally she sighed and clambered out. After a brief visit to her tent to pick up her backpack, which was filled with the tools she used to excavate, she headed for the rift.

She knew there was trouble as soon as she stood at the top of the path. From her position on higher ground she could see that Zac and Scarr were standing by the skeleton, on the federal side of the line. On the other side, Mike, Will and the two students were diligently working on the back end of the dino. They were studiously ignoring Scarr and Zac, which was probably driving Scarr crazy. He was the only one who was allowed to ostracize another.

Her steps lagged as she headed down the path. She didn't want a confrontation with Scarr. Not this morning, not with Mike observing, not anytime or for any reason. Too bad her gut said she was about to get one. She kept her gaze on the path, as if she was watching her steps. That way she wouldn't catch his eye and have to talk to him any earlier than necessary.

He must have found out that they'd identified the dino as a Daspletosaurus, but how? The sound of the generator chugging away, caught her attention and gave her the answer.

Mike's dino cam. Somehow Scarr had linked into the feed. It would have been obvious to anyone watching that something momentous had happened. Scarr, expert paleontologist that he was, would have figured out the ramifications. He was probably miffed that she hadn't immediately informed him of the discovery.

That thought cheered her because the short answer was that she couldn't. It didn't matter that she hadn't thought of contacting him at any point. She was completely in the right here. She'd explain, he'd calm down, and everything would be fine.

After all, Mark said that the Daspletosaurus was in all of the literature and that she had a brilliant career. Obviously it was this find that started her on her path to success, so Scarr's annoyance would be smoothed over and she'd continue with her excavation.

She approached Scarr and Zac with a much more jaunty step then she had when she began her descent into the rift. Scarr glared at her. Zac's expression was carefully blank.

"You're late. Where have you been?" Scarr said. His tone was a combination of a snarl and a sneer. Out of the corner of her eye she saw Mike's head come up.

She stopped a little distance from Scarr, disconcerted by the open hostility. "I had an errand to run."

"Oh?" His tone was milder, but he raised his brows as he stared at her critically. "To where?"

Liz blinked. She had to suppress the urge to giggle as she imagined his reaction if she told him where she'd actually gone. "Does it matter?"

His eyes narrowed. "So you didn't come over to my camp?"

Too late she realized that he'd given her an out. He expected her to say that she'd borrowed Mike's truck, then driven miles to find Scarr and report. If she said yes, that's where she'd gone, he would be mollified, but it would be a lie. And Mike, who could probably hear every word they were saying since his team was close, and Scarr wasn't bothering to keep his voice down, would feel betrayed.

Choices. Which path should she take? She slid her backpack off her shoulders and took it over to the area where they kept the cooler. Then she knelt to pull out her tools. The actions gave her time to figure out what to do next. She decided she didn't like Scarr's tone. He might want an answer, but she wasn't ready to give him one.

She came back to the dino. "Zac is here every morning, at least for a few minutes. Why have you come today, Dr. Scarr?"

His eyes narrowed. There was a distinct menace in his voice, as he said, "Is there something you want to tell me, Miss Hamilton?"

That irked her. "If you're going to be formal, it's Dr. Hamilton. You know that, just like you know that I call you Dr. Scarr because I respect your reputation and your experience."

His jaw hardened, but he apparently didn't have a reply that would put her in her place, so she continued on. "Yes, I do have news. Mike and his team excavated the hip joint yesterday. They believe there is good evidence that this creature was a Daspletosaurus."

"You helped them," Scarr said.

"Yes, I did."

"It was not your place to do so!"

Well, put everything out front. If she accepted that statement, she would acknowledge that Scarr made the decisions. That this was his dino.

But it wasn't. The find was hers and Mike's and she felt a possessiveness for the ancient beast that roused her temper and made her say, "I think it was. This find may be shared by two permit holders, but it's one creature. It deserves the best I can give it. If that means helping Mike and Will—sorry, that's *Dr.* Laverty—that's what I'm going to do."

Fuming, Scarr said, "I'll remind you that the front half of this animal is on my permit land. I am the lead paleontologist on this dig. I deserved to know that this is a major find."

"You already knew that," Liz said, keeping her voice light and her tone mild.

"Yet I found out the details through that ridiculous dino cam feed!" Scarr shouted.

Liz took a step back and bumped against a large, warm body. She didn't have to look over her shoulder to know it was Mike. Some inner radar told her it was him the moment they touched. She did look though, just to bolster her confidence with his support. She realized that he was staring, no, not staring, but glaring, at Scarr.

"The dino cam is an educational tool that has an audience of tens of thousands," he said. His eyes were narrowed. His words clipped.

"People who don't matter," Scarr retorted, his lip curling into a sneer.

"People like my diggers, Justin and Maggy, who learn what the profession is really about and who decide to dedicate their lives to it because of what they've seen. People who are fascinated by dinosaurs and who go to museums and who support the field." He stopped then very deliberately added, "Spys like you."

Scarr went purple. There were snickers from behind Mike and even Zac, who was very obviously trying to keep out of the argument, choked on suppressed emotion.

After a minute, Scarr rallied. "Fine words from a man who betrays our scientific endeavors with every bone he sells and every dollar he makes. How much do you expect to get for your portion of the Daspletosaurus, Edmonds? Millions? Are you going to sell it as a full carcass or bone by bone? Which will net you more?"

"He won't do that," Liz said, before Mike even opened his mouth to speak. She thought about the sleek, sophisticated institution in her future. She had no proof that the Daspletosaurus would end up there, or that the museum had been created by Mike, but her gut told her both had happened, so she added, "This creature is for study and display and Mike believes in that."

"Yes," Scarr said, "because the lawyers will make sure that the university acquires custody of the full skeleton. They'll never allow it to be given to a marauding amateur like Edmonds."

"You're counting chickens," Mike said. He sounded remarkably calm for a man who had just been insulted.

"He's as professional as you are," Liz said steadily.

"He's a businessman," Scarr said. The sneer in his voice said he thought the occupation was something vile. "His goal is profit. Everything he does is solely to make himself rich."

"You don't worry about funding for your digs, Scarr?" Mike asked. He continued to sound amazingly cool and collected.

"My digs are funded by respectable granting authorities. Government, non-profits, educational charities. Profit isn't part of their mandate."

"Those worthy organizations don't care if you make any finds? They don't expect to see their names highlighted in the literature as funding bodies that supported the dig?" Mike queried.

Scarr's nostrils flared. Mike had scored a hit. "That's different," he said.

"How?"

Scarr didn't deign to answer. Thoroughly furious, he turned to Liz. "Think it over, Miss—pardon me! *Doctor*—Hamilton. You need to decide. Are you part of my team? Or do you want to throw in your lot with Edmonds? Remember," he added, "if you choose Edmonds your chance to be come something important in the paleontological world is over. You'll be nothing more than a jobbing digger, like Dr. Laverty here."

A quick glance at Will told Liz that Scarr's gibe had struck home, but he set his jaw and didn't respond. Anger at Scarr's casual dismissal of people she both liked and respected had her fighting back. "There's nothing to decide. I am part of your team and that didn't change because I helped Mike and Will expose the hip. I have nothing to prove and no decision to make."

"You've been sleeping with the enemy," Scarr said, more furious than before, if that was possible.

Liz stared at him, horrified. How did he know she'd made love with Mike? His next words made her relax, but only a little.

"Prove you're part of my team. Move back to my camp. You have until tonight to decide."

CHAPTER 19

This was crazy. She knew Scarr was obsessive about this find, that he had a pathological dislike of Mike, and what Scarr thought Mike stood for, but to make accusations like this? "Dr. Scarr, I really don't think—"

"No, you don't." He turned, showing her his back, shutting her out. He edged closer to the skeleton, then turned to face her. "Until you make your decision, stay away from my dinosaur."

"Your dinosaur?" Mike said from behind her. His voice was silky smooth over an underlay of menace.

Scarr's eyes narrowed. Clearly he was willing to take up the challenge.

They'd be wrestling in the dirt in a minute. "Okay, fine. I'm going to take the afternoon off. I've got some stuff I need to do." She looked at Mike, then at Scarr. "Things need to cool off here and I think it will happen faster if I'm not around. Dr. Scarr, I'll let you know my decision later today."

She turned to walk away.

"Decide carefully," Scarr said to her back.

She hesitated momentarily. She heard the derision in his voice and knew that he expected her to use her afternoon to pack up her stuff. Part of her was prepared to do exactly that. The other part wanted to turn around and tell him to take his ultimatum and stuff it.

"Liz," Mike said quietly as she hovered.

She knew what he offered with that single word. Refuge, a place with him. She shook her head, but she softened it with a half smile. "I need to think, Mike. Somewhere private. Do you mind if I borrow your truck again?"

"Go ahead," he said, but there was despair in his eyes.

She wished she could change that, but she couldn't, not here. Not now. Scarr had been right, she was sleeping with the enemy and there was no way she would ever let him know how accurate his words had been.

She nodded her thanks, then headed up the path.

She drove back to the empty prairie where the sleek museum of the future would someday stand. Though she parked the truck, she didn't get out. Nor did she walk toward and into the beacon, though it burned brightly, indicating Mark was working in his lab. Instead she stayed in the truck and thought. Then she called her sister, Faith.

"Hey you, what's up?" Faith's voice was disgustingly cheerful, particularly when Liz was facing a decision that would affect the rest of her life in more ways than the obvious one.

"Things are getting tense around here. I need clarity. Do you have time to listen?"

"Always," Faith said. "Is it about the dig? Or...that gorgeous man you spent the night with in his truck?"

Liz drew a deep breath. She hadn't talked to Faith since the day she'd called to tell her she had become a Traveler. So much had happened since. "Both," she said. "And they're intertwined."

"Work and gorgeous men," Faith said. "It happens."

She was obviously thinking of her relationship with Cody Simpson, which had developed while Faith was the office manager at the company where Cody was the head software developer. "Yeah," Liz said. "And supervisors tend to get in the way."

In Faith's case it had been her manager, Ava, who Liz had nick-named the tyrant lizard, after T-Rex, the most famous of the carnivo-rous dinosaurs. Like Scarr, Ava liked control, and to be the one in control, and she could be ruthless in the pursuit of her objective. She had made Faith's life miserable until Faith climbed out of the box Ava had put her in and taken charge of her own life.

"Did Scarr fire you again?" There was indignation and worry in Faith's voice.

Liz laughed. Somehow, as she sat here in the middle of nowhere, talking to her sister while she stared at a beacon of light no one but she could see, the dreadful feeling of being trapped eased. "Sort of." She explained what had happened over the last few days. She didn't leave anything out, including the night with Mike. She concluded with her visit to the future this morning. "So I don't know if the Daspletosaurus is what makes my career or if it is something else. On top of that, I know I'm involved in the museum where Mark works, but I don't know how. It's on Mike's land, but that doesn't necessarily mean that it's there because of him. Or because of the Daspletosaurus."

"Mark can't tell you, you know that, Liz."

She snorted. "Of course I do. But now I also know how Uncle Andrew felt when he tried to find out what happened between him and Mary Elizabeth. It's so frustrating! The information's there, I just don't know how to tease it out."

Faith chuckled. "From what you've said, you taught Mark well."

Liz sighed. "I know. It's annoying. I only have myself to blame. Why didn't I tell him to fudge his answers? Give me a clue which way I should turn."

"Don't you know?" Faith said. It was formed as a question, but it sounded like a statement.

"You think I've already made my decision," Liz said, as her whirling thoughts slowly settled down into a pattern.

"Haven't you? What did you do when you wanted to sort out your thoughts and feelings?"

Liz stared at the bright, steady light across the prairie. "I came to the Beacon."

"Exactly. What does that tell you about yourself?"

"I want someone to tell me what I am going to do?"

"Well, I suppose that's true, but it's not what I meant." Faith hesitated. "You're a risk-taker, Liz."

"What? No! I'm not. I'm a step-by-step plodder."

"Yes, you are. When you came into your power, it wasn't as a Beacon, like I am. It was as a Traveler. Think about it. You walk into a portal hidden in a ball of light, without any assurances that what is on the other side is safe. You didn't know what you would find, yet you walked through without hesitation."

"Okay." Liz said the word slowly, drawing it out. "I get what you're saying, but what does that have to with my decision and whether it's made or not?"

"Down at the dig site you had Scarr pressuring you and Mike behind you. He was offering support, but that was a kind of pressure too. What did you do when you wanted to clarify your thoughts? You went to the place where you have taken the greatest risk of your life. Why?"

"I feel peace here." The words popped out, surprising Liz. It wasn't what she planned to say. In fact, she didn't know what she had intended, if anything at all.

"Go with your gut, Liz. Don't fight the decision you've already made, because it isn't what other people will say you should do."

She drew in a deep breath, then let it out again with a woosh. "I'm going to stay with Mike."

Faith laughed. "Figured that."

"And I'm going to finish excavating my Daspletosaurus."

"You go, girl!"

"Then I'm going to write and publish the excavation report."

"I know you will. I believe in you, Liz."

Liz looked at the glowing beacon and thought about walking into the light. Faith was right. If she had the courage to cross the barrier of time into the future, she could deal with a selfish prig like Scarr. "Thanks for being a sounding board, sis."

"Anytime. When do we get to meet your Mike?"

"He's not *my* Mike yet!"

"Yeah, yeah, so you say."

She could imagine Faith smirking as she spoke. Sisters, especially know-it-all older sisters, were a pain sometimes. "After the season is over. We can both probably take time off then."

"Good," Faith said. She uttered an evil laugh. "Maybe Dad will join us. You can tell him you're a Traveler. Won't he be pleased?"

Liz laughed. Their father, Daniel, had never reconciled to the exotic talent his wife and daughter Faith possessed. He had long held up Liz as the only other reasonable member of his family.

"Mom's delighted by the way. She wants to hear all the details. Wait till I tell her there's even more exciting news."

"Don't! I'll fill her in when I can. Listen, I'm going to go and inform Scarr I won't live in his box anymore and that he's welcome to come into the one I've designed, but if not..." She shrugged, then realized Faith couldn't see her. "If not, it doesn't matter to me. It's his choice."

"Have fun," Faith said. "Call me when you've worked it all out."

"I will." She disconnected, then stared at the beacon, letting the rightness of her decision seep into her.

Then she started Mike's truck and headed off, not to the rift, but toward Scarr's camp.

CHAPTER 20

She was taking too long. Mike considered, not for the first time, whether he should contact local law enforcement and report Liz missing. Sure, the weather was fine, but accidents happened and cell service was spotty. If she lost control on the road and drove into the ditch the way she had on the night they met... Just the thought of what could have happened made him shudder.

He put the pot containing premade stew onto the burner of the camp stove. It was his turn to cook, which meant he had plenty to do with his hands, but not much for his brain. He was overthinking this. Liz was fine.

Maybe he was fussing about her absence because he couldn't allow himself to believe that she would choose Scarr over him. There he went, overanalyzing again. If she went back to Scarr's camp, it would be because she chose a career in academia over a somewhat dubious future with him. He couldn't blame her for that. She'd worked hard to get her Ph.D. She'd want to make use of it in the best way she could.

He set a pan of water to boil on the second burner for noodles to go with the stew. His problem was, he wanted too much. He'd long ago given up the idea of an academic career and he didn't regret that. He enjoyed the combination of creativity and management that was needed to make Discovering Dinos successful. And while he didn't teach university students, he did give guest lectures at high schools and then there were the week-long digs at the dude ranch. So he was passing on his knowledge and helping young minds learn.

There was a part of him, though, that craved the excitement of the big find. When he'd descended from the truck on that first day when he and Liz found the rift, his heart had pounded and he had wanted to dance a jig, there, in the middle of the road, in front of a woman who was pretty much a stranger. That she was as excited as he had been was as potent as an aphrodisiac. She'd been in the forefront of his thoughts ever since. He'd watched her work long hours, always meticulously, and oh so very, very carefully. That quiet, skillful style called to him, captured his interest, then deepened from initial attraction into respect and something more profound, and far more emotional.

When he kissed her, he realized that attraction had become desire. Desire that he couldn't sate in one night with her. Desire that told him he needed months—if not years—to explore her, physically and emotionally.

He hadn't told her, of course. He shredded lettuce into a bowl of water to wash it. He realized he was ripping the leaves into smaller and smaller bits. He paused to take a deep breath and regain control. Then he told himself, again, that Liz deserved her chance at success. By returning to Scarr's camp she wasn't rejecting him, what he stood for, or the relationship that had borne fruit last night. She was looking at the rest of her life, not a short-term romp in bed.

Being rational sucked. He wanted her with him. At his campsite, on his dig, in his bed.

Jeeze, he had it bad.

It. His hand, until then, still busily shredding lettuce way too fine, stilled. What was *it*?

Obsession? Lust? Desire? Passion?

None of the above, but something far more important?

What was that? Love?

Nah. Couldn't be. Love took months to develop and was based on mutual respect. Well, they had the respect thing. Or at least, he had it. But they didn't have the months.

So he was safe. Whatever he was feeling, it wasn't love.

If he'd fallen in love with Liz Hamilton, he'd made a big mistake, because she was focused on her career, not a relationship.

He looked down at the little bits of lettuce in the bowl and sighed. His green salad was going to look more like coleslaw than a traditional salad. He swirled the bits around in the water, then dumped them into a colander and shook out as much water as he could. He set the colander onto a towel to drain and tossed cherry tomatoes into the bowl to wash while he chopped up an onion.

He was scrubbing the tomatoes when he heard the sound of a truck engine. He jerked his gaze toward the road, noticing out of the corner of his eye that Will had emerged from his tent to see who was arriving, while Justin and Maggy, who were sitting by the firepit, both jumped to their feet.

The engine belonged to his truck and the driver was Liz. Mike felt the little knot of worry in his gut dissolve at the site of her as she jumped down from the parked truck.

She half ran, half skipped to the camp. "I'm sorry I'm late! Did I miss dinner?"

All those emotions that he'd been brewing up while he cooked, boiled to the surface, hot and bubbly and ready to burst. "That's it? Did you miss dinner? That's all you have to say?"

She blinked at him, then she smiled. "You're grouchy."

"I am not grouchy," he said, realizing as he said the words that was exactly how he sounded.

Her smile widened. She said softly, so only he could hear, "You were worried about me."

"Damn right," he snapped back, but he kept his tone as low as hers.

Her smile brightened to megawatt level and he realized she was riding an adrenaline high. "Tonight," she said, her voice low again, but this time full of promise. "My tent or yours?"

"Mine. I have a bed and it's bigger, and sturdier, than your air mattress." He must be drawing on her excitement, because a few minutes ago he hadn't even considered the possibility their relationship would continue.

"Deal," she said. Then Will came over from his tent and Maggy and Justin drifted over from the firepit.

"We didn't expect you back," Will said, when he reached them.

Liz turned her blinding smile on Will and Mike was overwhelmed by a moment of intense jealousy.

"It took me longer than I expected to sort out Scarr," she said, with a wink.

Amusement lightened Will's expression. "How did you do that?"

"Yeah, how did you?" Mike echoed. "Scarr sounded pretty firm when he laid down his terms."

She shrugged. "I reminded him that neither he, nor Zac wanted to do the actual digging work to get the skeleton out of the ground."

Mike grunted. "Good point, but I expect Scarr could have assigned some of his delectable diggers to work the site."

"Delectible diggers?" Liz said, a laugh mixed with amazement in her voice.

Mike refused to be embarrassed. "That's what the townsfolk call them."

"Huh. I didn't know that. I suspect Scarr thinks of them that way, but I've never heard him use the term." She grinned. "You're right, though, he didn't take that argument very seriously because of his... interns. So I reminded him that the university and its law team know that the find is mine and that I'm the lead on this skeleton. That made him think. I made him really consider when I suggested that if he tried to cut me out, it would be his reputation that would suffer, because everyone would wonder why he'd done it. I even speculated that he might become known as uncollegial. You know, someone who refuses to share his results and knowledge with others in the field, or withholds support for a colleague. Students wouldn't want to work with him. Colleagues at his level would shut him out. Funding would dry up.

He'd have his tenured position at the university, but he'd be out of the mainstream in our field."

Midway through her recital, Mike started to laugh and Will's amusement turned into a low chuckle. As she talked, the water for the noodles boiled over, while the stew rose perilously close to the top of the pot, bubbling and spitting. Mike rushed to save his meal, lowering the flames on the burners and adding noodles to the boiling water.

When he had food under control he looked over at her and grinned. "So what was the outcome of your blackmail conversation?

"It wasn't blackmail! I was merely pointing out some of the difficulties that could arise if he banished me from the site."

Mike raised his eyebrows. "And?"

She shrugged. "Things continue as they did before. I stay here at night. I dig the Daspletosaurus during the day." She looked round at each of them, and smiled. "I'm very glad to be back."

Later that evening, after Will and Maggy and Justin had turned in for the night and the camp was in darkness, Liz and Mike quietly made their way to his tent.

"I thought you weren't coming back," he murmured when they were inside and alone together. His hands were on Liz's waist and he'd positioned her so that her hips rubbed against his. He slid his hands under her t-shirt, up her bare skin, savoring the sensation of silky skin under his fingertips.

She sighed with pleasure. "I was always coming back. I had to figure out how to make Scarr understand I would be doing it on my terms, not his."

"You were gone all afternoon." He set his lips to the pulse beating in her neck and nibbled.

Her breath caught. "Scarr is stubborn and for some ridiculous reason he decided today that he was going to linger at the rift, instead of vacating as soon as I wasn't around. I had to wait for an hour before he showed up." She rubbed her hips against his, amusement sparkling in her eyes as she watched his eyes glaze and his expression harden in reaction. "I'm not the most patient of people, so I was pretty grumpy when he finally showed up."

"Guess you're going to be grouchy with me, then, because I plan to take my time." He moved his mouth to the underside of her chin, then kissed his way up to her lips. His tongue flicked out to stroke the edges and she put her hands on his shoulders and clung.

She opened her mouth to invite him in, but he nibbled on her lip, scraping with his teeth, soothing with his tongue. Her eyes closed and her grip on his shoulders tightened. "Let go," he murmured. "I've got you."

With a little groan, she did. He wrapped one arm around her waist to hold her steady, while with the other he slipped inside her bra to cup her breast, teasing the nipple with his thumb. She murmured low in her throat and her tongue came out to touch his lips in a tentative way that he found far more erotic than an aggressive approach.

He pulled away to lift her and carry her over to the camp bed. There, he sat her on the edge and knelt down before her so they were at eye level. He stripped off her t-shirt, then unhooked her bra and slipped it off her shoulders. He paused to look and be dazzled. "You're so beautiful."

She smiled that cocky, feminine smile at him and put her hands behind her so her breasts stood high. "Touch me," she said, her voice husky with the same desire that was coursing through him.

He did, with pleasure. He put his hands on her breasts to stroke and fondle and tease her nipples until both stood puckered and taut. She dropped her head back and closed her eyes. He saw her swallow hard, then he lowered his head and took one nipple into his mouth.

"Oh, my God," she whispered. She arched into his mouth, demanding more. On her other breast, he pinched her nipple and her breath caught. "Mike. Michael. What you're doing to me. Stop that or give me more."

He didn't stop, but he didn't give her the *more* she wanted either. He continued to suck and play while she shivered and moaned.

"Please," she whispered. "I want to get my jeans off. I want your clothes off. I want to touch you. All over."

"You want a lot," he murmured, but with one last flick, he drew away.

Her hands were trembling as she tried to unfasten her jeans, so he took over the job. It gave him the added bonus of an opportunity to stroke hips and thighs, and to test out her most private place. He wasn't surprised to find that she was wet and ready for him.

When he stood to strip off his clothes, she settled on the cot. He lowered himself to her, positioning himself so that he was on his knees, spread wide so that they were on either side of her hips. "You wanted to touch me," he said.

She did. She slid her hand over his erection, already full and ready. It grew under her touch, straining his control. It was his turn to groan. "You have about one more minute then I'm going to break."

She chuckled. To his regret, she abandoned his cock to slide her hands up his chest, lingering at his nipples to tease and taunt as his hand played with hers, then she caught his shoulders and drew him down to kiss him.

He slid inside her as their lips caressed each other. She closed around him, heightening his pleasure as he thrust. As the tempo increased she writhed beneath him. The kiss deepened as they both fought for release.

When it came, it was shattering. They lay panting as pleasure eased and finally died away. He slid off her, drawing her against him for a cuddle.

"Mike," she whispered.

"Hmmm?"

"Do you have time tomorrow morning to go somewhere with me?"

"Why?" He frowned. She sounded uncertain.

"There's something I want to show you. Something important. Will you come?"

He stroked the hair that had tumbled over her forehead, the short strands silky beneath his fingertips. "Of course. Will you tell me what it is?"

She looked into his eyes. He saw worry in hers and that made him very nervous.

"I can't. It's...well, it's complicated." Her gaze searched his face, begging him to understand. "Will you trust me?"

"Yes."

"It's that simple?" she said, with a little laugh.

It was, he realized, that simple. It didn't take months. All it took was acceptance and realization.

He was in love with Liz Hamilton.

"Yeah," he murmured before he kissed her again. "It's that simple."

CHAPTER 21

They wrangled over who would drive the truck the next morning. Mike insisted, his truck, he'd drive, but Liz pointed out that the destination was hers, so she should be the one behind the wheel. Since Will had already departed with Maggy and Justin down to the rift, the argument became a discussion filled with considerable touching, kissing and laughter. In the end Liz did drive, because she refused to divulge the destination to Mike.

When they reached the open stretch of prairie and parked she turned to Mike. "We're here."

He stared out at nothing and said, "Why here?" When he looked back at Liz there was a frown in his eyes.

She grinned at him. "You'll see," she said, and hopped from the truck.

He followed her out. She came around the hood to stand beside him. He looked at her, his brows raised. "Now what?"

"We walk." She looked ahead to the bright orb of light only she could see, then turned to him. "Take my hand and don't let go. Okay?"

He was staring at her as if she had temporarily lost her mind, but he clasped his hand around hers. His touch warmed her, filling her with so much contentment, Liz knew she was doing the right thing. There was a risk, of course, in taking Mike into the future with her. He might react like her father had when her mother confessed to him that she both traveled through time and brought time travelers into her own time. Daniel Hamilton couldn't handle the strangeness and the result had been divorce and a strained relationship with his daughter, Faith, who was a Beacon, like her mother. Chloe Hamilton had made the mistake of not telling her husband-to-be this important part of herself before they were married. Liz wasn't going to make the same mistake with Mike.

Yesterday's crisis had made her realize that she'd slipped past attraction and great sex into an emotion that she thought was remarkably like the one her sister felt for Cody Simpson. Lust, affection, respect, pride, and tenderness all wrapped up together in a package called love. She knew Mike wasn't ready to take their physical relationship into an emotional one, but she thought he was drifting in that direction, even if he didn't actually know it yet.

So she was going to show him her newly found time traveling ability and ask him to accept it as a big part of who she was.

A few feet away from the Beacon, she stopped. Showtime. "What do you see ahead of you?"

He frowned, looking around the open prairie. "Sagebrush. Some dried grasses. Red earth. Hoodoos over to the east. What's this all about, Liz?"

Her mouth twitched up into a rueful smile. "I see a great round orb of light. It's a beacon and it's waiting for me to pass through."

"Liz," he said. He sounded impatient, definitely disbelieving. "You're having me on. Why? What's the real reason we're here?" He turned so they were face-to-face, then he lifted his free hand and dug his fingers into her hair. "Whatever is going on, you can tell me." His gaze locked with hers. "Did you make another find, here on my permit land? Are you worried about telling me?"

She laughed. "Kind of, but not what you think." She touched his cheek in a gentle gesture. "There's no easy way to explain this. I think we should just do it." She turned back to the beacon. "Walk with me. And remember, don't let go."

She tugged at his hand to be sure he was following, then she stepped into the beacon.

And was inside the sleek, stainless steal lab.

Beside her Mike said, "What the hell?"

Mark was sitting at his desk, but he had his chair positioned so he could see the place where she always arrived. He smiled and said, "Welcome. You must be Mike."

Mike was staring at Mark as if he was prepared skewer the other man if he did anything untoward. The only problem was, he'd have to let go of Liz's hand to do it and once he no longer had physical contact with Liz he'd revert back to his own time. "Who are you?" he said suspiciously.

Mark raised his brows. "Oh, I forgot." He shot an amused look at Liz. "You didn't prepare him."

"Doing works better," Liz said. "Mike, this is my grandson, Mark." Mike snorted with disbelief. Liz continued on as if he hadn't made the sound. "Mark, this is Mike Edmonds."

"I know," Mark said. "I'd shake your hand, Mike, but if you aren't in physical contact with Liz all of this will disappear."

"Yeah?" Mike said.

There was a gleam in his eyes that Liz didn't like. "Mike, don't—"

He jerked his hand from hers and was gone.

Mark laughed. "You'd better go get him."

Liz shot him a fulminating look. "You knew this was going to happen."

"I did, but I had no idea it would be such fun."

"Great," she muttered. "Another tease in the family." She went through the beacon back into her own time. She found Mike standing on the prairie.

He was frowning, but when she suddenly appeared, his eyes widened. "Where were we?"

"In a museum, in the future." She waited patiently while he digested that information.

His frown turned into a brooding stare. "You mean we just traveled through time?" She nodded. "That's a lot to take in. I'm fairly certain that it's generally accepted that time travel doesn't exist."

"It does in my family." She hesitated, then said, "We keep it pretty quiet."

"I can imagine," he said. He looked over her shoulder at the place where the beacon was, though she knew he couldn't see it.

She took a deep breath. "We only tell people we care about. People we love and trust."

"Love and trust?" He looked as if she had knocked him on the head with a frying pan and addled his wits.

She held out her hand. "Come back into the future with me."

Bemused he slid his hand into hers and she walked through into Mark's lab.

He grinned at Mike. "Family lore says it gets easier to accept with every visit."

"Really?" Mike looked around the room. He headed over to the computer, tugging Liz behind him.

"Security close," Mark said before he got there. The screen went blank.

"Now that wasn't fair," Mike said. "When in the future are we?"

"About sixty years from your time. I'm sorry, I'm not allowed to provide you any specifics that might influence your present."

"Family rules," Liz said, smiling faintly.

Mike looked around the gleaming room. "I want to do this again."

"What do you mean?" Liz asked.

"Test the system," Mike said, and let go of her hand.

"Mike!"

"He's gone," Mark said.

"You knew that was going to happen." Liz put her hands on her hips, annoyed.

Mark raised his brows and grinned at her.

Liz walked into the light and back to Mike.

He was standing with his feet spread and his hands on his hips. This time he was waiting for her. "I don't feel any differently than I did before. Is there no physical repercussion? Surely traveling through time would be hard on the body."

"I've never heard of any problems." She held out her hand. "Come back with me."

He took it and they returned to the lab. Mark was now sprawled in his desk chair, clearly waiting for them. "Welcome back."

Mike nodded. He looked around and his gaze focused on the plaster cast on the stainless worktable. "This is a paleo lab. Is there a museum attached to it?"

Mark stared at him for a moment, then he nodded.

Mike's eyes narrowed. "Is it my museum?"

"Mark can't tell you that," Liz said.

Mark nodded agreement. "Grandma warned me you'd ask that."

Mike looked down at Liz. "Grandma? Really?"

She laughed. "It's sixty years in the future."

"So it is," he said, and let go of her hand.

She stared at the empty space where he'd been while Mark laughed at her disbelief. "What is the man thinking?" She headed back to her present.

Mike was waiting for her. His expression was smug. "It's kind of fun making you chase after me."

She glared at him. "You're acting like a kid who has just discovered that the garden gate opens and closes."

"I want to know what I'm getting into," he said.

"And what do you think?"

He answered her question without words. He reached for her, then drew her against him. He kissed her slowly, but with a passion that had Liz wrapping her hands around his neck and surrendering to the physical response he drew from her.

When they came up for air, she smiled at him. "Does this mean that you aren't freaked out about my ability?"

He nuzzled the side of her mouth. "I have to admit I'm amazed that I've traveled through time, but freaked out? No."

She pulled away so she could search his face. "You won't judge me? Think I'm crazy? Be uncomfortable with what I can do?"

"No, no, and no. I admit it's not a skill I expected my woman to have, but—"

Liz frowned. "Your woman?"

He had that smug look on his face again. He held out his hand. "Let's go back into your future."

She took his hand. "Okay. Why?"

He just smiled.

They went back to the lab. Mark was sitting as before. "Having fun?" he asked as they reappeared.

Mike nodded. "I was wondering how often Liz would be coming back to visit."

Mark shrugged.

"Throughout her life?"

"Mike, Mark can't—"

"I know, he can't tell me what happens in the future."

"It's all right, Grandma. I can't tell, because I don't know. You warned me about your first visit, and this one, but you told me it was safer if I didn't know all the details of our lives."

"But you do know who your grandfather is," Mike said.

The color drained from Mark's face and Mike grinned. He lifted Liz's hand and kissed her knuckles. Then he turned back to Mark. "I'll say goodbye for now. Grandson."

He let go of her hand and disappeared.

Mark said, "You didn't tell me this was going to happen!"

Liz stared at Mark. "Is it true? Is Mike your grandfather?"

Liz's shock seemed to help Mark recover. He blanked his expression—or he tried to. Amusement twinkled in his eyes. "Shouldn't you go and find out?"

CHAPTER 22

He was waiting for her. Kneeling on one knee in the classic proposal pose. Liz stared at him.

Mike smiled and held out his hand. "Elizabeth Hamilton, will you do me the great honor of becoming my wife? In sickness and in health." Mischief danced into his eyes and into his smile. "In our present or *our* future."

Her heart pounded. Emotions picked her up, shook her, dropped her back into amazement and shock. "I didn't tell him because I didn't want to spoil this moment for myself." She put her hand in Mike's.

He stood. "The ground's kind of hard," he said.

She choked and laughed.

"You haven't answered my question."

"Yes," she said. She searched his face. "Are you sure?"

He smiled and this time the expression was tender. "Very sure," he murmured. He stroked his thumb along her cheek, then he bent, moving slowly and deliberately, and kissed her.

At the touch of his lips any reservations she still harbored flowed away. It felt right being here with him. It wasn't just the affirmation from her visit to the future that they had a long and evidently successful relationship, but the look in his eyes before he kissed her. A look that said he was the luckiest man alive because she had just said yes.

As he kissed her she let her body melt into his and mischief drove her as the evidence of how she affected him pushed against her. She pulled his shirt free from the waistband of his jeans, then slid her hands up his warm skin. He made a little sound of protest and pleasure. He deepened the kiss, teasing her lips open with his tongue, then plunging inside. It was her turn to sigh as pleasure took her.

When he lifted his head they were both breathing hard. He glanced around, his eyes gleaming. "Too open, I'm afraid."

She laughed and cuddled closer. "There's nobody here but prairie dogs."

"And our grandson on the other side of that beacon of yours."

"We could move far enough away that we wouldn't accidentally roll into the light."

Mike looked skeptical. "What if he moves around? Does the beacon go with him?"

"Of course. He *is* the beacon."

"What if this is a parking lot and he comes outside to get into his car? Or to a picnic area where he takes his morning coffee break?"

Liz began to laugh. "I guess you're right. Seeing Grandma and Grandpa making love could scar a guy for life."

"Wouldn't want that," Mike said gravely, but his eyes danced with amusement.

"I suppose we should go back and tell him our news," Liz said.

"I'm pretty sure he already knows," Mike said, holding her close. "Or he's guessed. But yeah, let's go back. It seems rude to leaving him hanging."

She reluctantly eased out of his arms. "How did you know he is your grandson too?"

Mike pulled his cell out of his pocket, flipped through some pictures, then showed one to Liz. "My mother," he said.

The picture showed Mike standing next to a woman with dark hair and Mark's eyes. "The family resemblance is strong," Liz murmured.

Mike nodded. "So is the name. Mark is my middle name." He shrugged. "Put together, it was a pretty sure bet."

"Is that why you kept coming back and forth?"

He smiled at her. "There was a lot to take in. I needed to know this was real, then I needed space and time to think. To decide how to handle this."

She looked up into his eyes. "Are you sure?"

He touched her cheek again, stroking down to graze his fingers along the line of her jaw. "Yes. I make decisions quickly and this one was easy."

They hovered there, on the edge of kissing again, both of them fighting the urge to give into the desire that pulsed between them, both of them aware they could not. Finally Liz cleared her throat. She held out her hand. "To the future again?"

They found Mark as they'd left him, in his lab, but his screen was alive with images and he was working it with fingers and voice. They were too far away to be able to see the contents of the files he had open, but the technology was dazzling. Mike headed for the desk, intrigued. Liz had seen it before, and understood the fascination, so she went along. Mark heard them though, and ordered a security shutdown before they could see anything interesting.

"You're back," he said. "I didn't expect you."

Mike raised his brows. "You thought we'd leave without saying good-bye?"

Mark grinned. "I thought you'd be distracted."

Liz smiled up at Mike. "We were."

"We are," Mike said. He returned her look, tenderness in his. He glanced at his grandson. "Wish us happiness. Your grandmother and I are engaged."

"Congratulations," Mark said. The dismay of a few minutes ago was gone. Amusement had taken its place.

Liz leaned forward and kissed his cheek. "We have to go, but we'll be back."

"I know," Mark said.

"Of course you do," Mike commented. His expression was wry.

They left a short time later. Moments after they returned to the present, Mike's phone rang. He held on to Liz's hand, refusing to let go, as he answered it. "Harvey! Good to hear from you. How are the contract negotiations going?"

They wandered back to the truck as Mike talked to Harvey Earnshaw, the lawyer who was negotiating with the university on behalf of Discovering Dinos. Most of Mike's side of the conversation consisted of "yeah," "right," and "okay," so Liz couldn't get a sense of what Harvey was saying on his end of the line.

As they neared the truck, Mike said, "I can be there in an hour or so. Email the documents to me. I'll read them over, then sign them and send them back." He disconnected, but it was a minute or so before he spoke. "That was Harvey Earnshaw."

"Your lawyer."

He nodded. They reached the truck. He stopped, but didn't get into the cab. "He has a deal. A compromise that is a fair deal."

"What are the terms?" Liz asked.

"You and I are the main authors of the dig report and any other research papers that come out of the find."

Liz nodded. This was a good clause.

"We are both involved in the lab work."

Liz nodded again. The scientific work that went on after the excavation was finished and the bones were safely secured in a laboratory setting was even more important than excavating the find itself. Having Mike included in the lab work was a major compromise, one that she was sure would infuriate Alfred Scarr.

"The location of the head determines who gets custody of the whole skeleton."

That surprised her. "The university was willing to risk giving you control of the creature's fate?" She wrinkled her nose. "Evidently they don't have as many prejudices as Dr. Scarr does."

"They do," Mike said. "But they're playing a hunch. The way the body is lying, the head could be on either side of the line. The shoulders and neck are within Scarr's permit area, though, so they think the odds are on their side."

"What do you think?" Liz asked, searching his face for clues.

He shrugged. "Could go either way. If the university wins, the skeleton is processed in Scarr's lab and then will be displayed or archived at the university's museum."

"If it's on your side?"

His smile was mischievous. "It comes to Discovering Dinos' lab, then I build a museum to house it."

Liz's breath caught, then she laughed. "Do you think that's what happened?"

He looked back to the open prairie where they had so recently been inside a state-of-the-art paleo lab. "It could be." He looked back at Liz. He touched her cheek. "But we won't know until it happens, will we? We were both very careful to make sure our current selves wouldn't know what our future selves did."

Liz frowned. "Some times I'm a pain in the ass."

Mike laughed. "Come on. I'll drop you at the site, then I have to go back into town to read that contract and get it back to Harvey."

"In a minute," Liz said. She reached up to tangle her fingers in his hair, then she pulled his head down. "I want a kiss first," she murmured against his lips.

He wasn't hard to persuade.

CHAPTER 23

*M*ike dropped her at the campsite. Before leaving for town he gave her a kiss, which he said was to remember him by. That made Liz laugh and somehow the kiss went from being quick and affectionate to being leisurely and passionate. She was humming to herself as she sauntered to her tent to pick up her tools before she headed down to the rift.

A quick look at her watch told her that it was nearing ten. That wasn't surprising since she and Mike had left for the museum about eight this morning. She estimated the time it would take him to get to town, read and review the contract, possibly discuss it with Harvey the lawyer, then, once it was signed and off, to get back to the site. She decided she couldn't expect him until after one, or maybe two, this afternoon. Since she was starting late on her excavation, she decided she'd work for an hour or so after the others stopped for lunch. That way she'd be able to share her own break with Mike when he returned.

Satisfied with this plan, she made her way down into the rift.

There was no evidence of Zac or Scarr over on her side of the line, so she wandered over to where Will and the students were working. "Morning." She watched Maggy carefully brush away grains of earth that were disguising the fossilized bone beneath. The steady clink-clink of a hammer hitting a mallet indicated that Justin was hard at work chipping away surrounding rock on another part of the skeleton.

"Morning," Maggy echoed, while Justin simply looked up and smiled.

Will lowered the book in which he was doing a sketch of a recently exposed bone and smiled at her as Justin had. He added, "Morning, Liz. Is Mike coming down to the site soon?"

She shook her head. "He's on his way to town. Harvey phoned. The negotiations have been finalized. He sent the contract to Mike for review and signing. Mike's gone into the office to print it off and read it. He'll probably be back out by mid-afternoon."

Will started to frown as she spoke and both Maggy and Justin stopped working to listen in. "Do you know what the terms were?"

Liz wondered if she should divulge the terms, then decided that there was no harm in letting Mike's team know. "Mike and I are the lead authors on the dig report and the analysis of the skeleton. The location of the head is the determining factor on where the creature's bones will be analyzed and eventually displayed."

"Our side of the line and Discovering Dinos handles it. Scarr's side and the bones go to his lab?" Will's frown deepened. "And Mike is okay with this?"

Liz nodded. "He thinks the head is on his side."

"Maybe. Maybe not," Will said.

Liz laughed. "Yeah. That clause took my breath away. It's so risky. On the other hand, I am really happy that Mike will be included in the final report, with his name ahead of Scarr's. That's so important in academic writing." She smiled a little smugly, a lot mischievously. "Scarr must be furious that he won't get star billing. He's probably thinking that the university sold him out." In academic writing the first name on a paper was usually the most senior academic. The names following might be the people who did the actual research or experimentation, but unless they were full colleagues, they never got star billing.

She was at her own side of the line when Zac reappeared from his usual morning scouting trip. His expression was bleak and his trudging walk told her that he hadn't had a good morning.

"So you actually decided to come into work," he said. He had to shout the words since he was still a distance away from her. Liz heard Justin's tap-tap, stop and glanced over at Mike's site. Will had edged a little closer to her, while Maggy watched wide-eyed, and Justin stood stiffly, a worried expression on his face.

She turned back to Zac. "As you can see, I'm here. Did you find anything interesting this morning?"

He went over to the cooler to grab a bottle of water. When he came back he said, "I was looking for the head."

She was about to say he wasn't going to find it half a mile away down the rift, when he added, "It's on this side of the line. Both Scarr and I know it. If it isn't close to the body, something must have carried it off. A predator. Or if the dino died in a streambed, the current." He shot an evil look at Will. "It's not on that amateur's side of the line. I'm sure of it."

"I'm not an amateur," Will said, wading into the conversation. "My credentials are as good as yours."

Zac snorted. "Yeah, sure. You work for the paleo pirate. Any credibility you might have had was zeroed out when you took the job." The sneer in his voice made Will flush.

"You and Dr. Scarr hope that the head is on this side," Liz said. She shrugged. "I've been hunting for it since I found this creature and I haven't had any luck. The way the washout carved open the site left fewer parts of the dino exposed on Mike's side. They have more area to explore. Our side is pretty clear. I don't think it's here."

"It can't be over there," Zac muttered, glaring.

"You've heard about the contract," she said, suddenly understanding. If the head was on Scarr's side and the skeleton went to his lab for processing, Zac would have his name included in the dig reports for what could be the find of the decade. His career would shoot up like a nasty, encroaching weed that happened to receive the same dose of fertilizer the rest of the garden did. If Liz hadn't still been feeling mellow from her night with Mike and his morning proposal, she would have been upset. As it was, she knew that the museum was here, on Mike's land. That mean the odds were very good that the head actually was on Mike's side of the line.

"There's no point in my hanging around here any longer," Zac said, over the crackle of crumpling plastic. He took his bottle over to the recycling can and dropped it in. Disdainfully, with a smirk that was designed to show he was doing this to annoy her, not because she'd shamed him into it days ago. He trudged up the path to the top of the rift without saying good-bye.

Will watched him go, his eyes hard. "What a piece of work he is."

"Amen to that." Liz hesitated, then added deliberately, "I meant what I said. I believe the head is on your side."

"I do to," Will said. Then he sighed. "But we haven't found it. What happens if neither of us discovers it before the season ends?"

That was a good question and one Liz had asked Mike earlier. "Until the head is found the skeleton is divided. The hindquarters go to Discovering Dinos' lab, to be worked on here. The neck and front quarters go to Scarr's lab. Each side is allowed to display their bones, augmented with plaster casts of the rest of the skeleton."

Will raised his brows. "So for Mike, it would be better if the head is never found, than to have it found on Scarr's side."

"Yeah, I guess that's true." This was a perspective that Liz hadn't considered. As she got back to work, she wondered if she should continue to look for the head. Or if she was better to focus on the bones she had and leave finding the head for some future, unspecified date. There was no clear answer to her internal question. Finding the head would confirm Mike's assertion that this was a Daspletosaurus and increase the value of the skeleton. On the other hand, it could mean that Mike lost control of his portion of the bones. Not the scenario she wanted.

They worked steadily for another hour, then Will called a halt. "We're heading up for lunch, Liz. Do you want to join us?"

She smiled at Will and shook her head. "I started late, so I'm going to for another hour of so. If Mike gets back before I come up, would you let him know I'm down here?"

Will nodded. He and the students put their tools away tidily, then headed up the path. Liz paused to drink a bottle of water, then she went back to work.

She was clearing the area around one of the upper vertebrae when she realized she was exposing another fossil. She brushed further, revealing more of the bone. Her heart began to pound. The curve of the fossilized rock looked remarkably like the rounding of a jawbone. Was it possible that she had found the head? Or at least a portion of it?

She sat back on her heels and stared at what she had uncovered. If this was the head, then it was on Scarr's side of the line. That meant he gained custody of the entire skeleton, leaving Mike with nothing.

The head would confirm the species of dinosaur they were excavating. The head could prove that this was the body of a rare carnivorous dinosaur. The head would make her career. Her name would be associated with this creature forever. She would be an in-demand paleontologist. She could write her own ticket.

She wanted to be with Mike. To work with him, not be an ivory tower academic whose closest friends and associates were as predatory in their own way as the Daspletosaurus she was excavating.

She stared at that curved sweep of exposed bone. Despair settled over her, depressing her earlier high spirits. She had been so sure that the museum meant that the head had been found on Mike's side. She still could hardly believe that it hadn't been. How could this be? A museum that sophisticated meant lots of funding, not just from Mike's Discovering Dinos profits, but also from granting institutions. Those institutions wouldn't touch a commercial organization, unless it had something very special to exhibit or contribute to the field. She assumed it was this creature. What else could it be?

Nothing that she could think of right now, but maybe Mike would find something as significant as the Daspletosaurus further down the rift, on his side of the line. So far nothing had come to light, but it was a long gouge in the earth, so there was always a possibility that more skeletons would be exposed as time and weather wore away the surface. But there was no guarantee it would ever happen.

Another, more devastating, thought occurred to her. What if she'd somehow changed the future by exposing the head—if finding it meant that the museum was never built? What if the head was never found in the timeline she'd visited just this morning? If the museum had been built to house the hindquarters of their dino?

Her hand crept to her throat in an unconscious act of dismay. If she had changed the timeline her own future might have changed. She might not marry Mike. Mark might not exist. Her beacon might have gone dark.

Horror engulfed her.

CHAPTER 24

*W*as there any way to cover up the skull so it was never found?

She peered at the stone surface. She couldn't put back the rocks she'd chipped or dusted away, but perhaps it wasn't too noticeable. If she worked in another area, maybe Zac or Scarr wouldn't see that curved sweep of fossil and wonder if it belonged to the dino. She studied the scene. The trouble was, the neck vertebrae above the skull were exposed and when they lifted those bones to take back to the lab, they would have to scrutinize the area to make sure they weren't damaging other bones that hadn't been excavated yet. Then the skull would be found.

Feeling sick, she stood staring at the skull and despairing. She turned away to get a bottle of water and stand out of the midday sun while she figured out what to do. As she turned, she noticed the dino cam and her heart sank further. The camera was always on during the day, recording every movement. Sure, she was on the periphery of its main coverage, but she was the only person here, so her actions would be noticed. Even if she figured a way to rebury the skull, the camera would have recorded its discovery. She knew Scarr watched the daily footage, so by tomorrow, if not sooner, he would be over here gloating about the find. With the winner-take-all terms of the contract, he'd have a renewed interest in excavating the bones and getting the creature out of the rock and into his lab.

Unless... Could she persuade Mike not to sign the contract? She had assumed that it would take him a half an hour tops to read it through, sign it, then send it back. He'd been gone for more than two hours though, and the only reason she could think of was that there were clauses he couldn't accept and he was busy strategizing with Harvey the lawyer to reopen negotiations.

If that was the case, she had a chance to tell him not to agree to the stipulation that the skull location would determine the fate of the skeleton. She chugged water and felt her spirits rising. There was a chance to save the future. She couldn't get phone service down here, but she could at the top of the rift. She'd hustle up the path and phone Mike.

She finished the water and tossed the bottle into the recycling can. Then she turned toward the path. And stopped in her tracks. Mike was scrambling down the slope with a clatter of small pebbles rolling away under his feet.

If he was here, he must have signed the contract. For a moment she felt nothing. She was hollow. Empty. Then despair came roaring in, filling the hole with such dark emotion she didn't know how she could handle it.

"Mike!"

He turned at the sound of her voice. His smile was intimate, tender, pleased, and it fell into a frown when he saw her stricken expression. "Liz! What the hell?" He strode over to where she was standing and caught her shoulders in a firm, comforting grip. His eyes searched her face. "Tell me what's wrong."

"Did you sign the contract?" Her voice came out as a thick, hoarse croak.

He nodded. "The terms were exactly as Harvey said, no surprises. Why?"

She moistened her lips as she stared into his face and felt like a traitor. "I found the skull," she whispered.

Pleasure lit his expression. "That's terrific. Where?"

She wanted to cry. Instead, she sniffed. "It's on Scarr's side of the line."

"Yeah," he said. "I was prepared for that." He smiled at her and rubbed his thumb over her cheekbone. "You weren't, though, were you?"

She frowned. "It must always have been there, where it is now, but I shouldn't have discovered it."

It was his turn to frown. "Why not? The skull is a tremendous find. It will confirm the species and prove that we really are dealing with a Daspletosaurus."

"It changes the future!"

He stiffened, his frown deepening. Then understanding dawned. "You're worried about the museum."

"Why else would it be there? We must have made a tremendous find in order to have an instillation like that out here, in the middle of nowhere."

"We," he said. His slow smile replaced the frown and the tenderness returned to his gaze. "I like the sound of that."

"Mike! I changed the future. We may never get together. Mark might never be born because of this find!"

"Why wouldn't we still get together?" He sounded puzzled. "How will the skull keep us apart?"

She drew a deep breath to steady herself. "The bones will go to Scarr's lab for analysis and preservation."

He nodded. "And you and I will go with them."

She frowned. "What? Scarr's lab is back east. You live here. Discovering Dinos is here."

"Liz," he said, smiling and caressing her cheek, "working on a find like this is a tremendous opportunity for me personally and for Discovering Dinos, as well. My participation in the analysis will enhance my reputation, perhaps more than it will yours, since you've already got a doctorate to prove your skills. When Harvey and I discussed the terms we wanted out of the contract we took into account the strong possibility that the head would be found on Scarr's side. Harvey's a bright fellow. He made sure the contract was a win for me and Discovering Dinos no matter where the skull was found.

She put her hands on his chest and chewed her bottom lip. "I thought I'd be working with you, at your lab here."

"Maybe someday you will," he said, his voice husky. "I'd like that very much."

"I would too," she whispered. "But..." She shook her head. "The museum. The Daspletosaurus will be displayed back east, not here. There is no museum now."

"How do you know that?" he asked gently.

"How could there be?"

He looked up and around. "This whole region is full of dino bones. Who's to say that this is the only find you make around here? You don't know what's inside the museum, only that there is a spiffy lab with all the latest tech that you never went beyond."

A little bit of hope flickered into life inside her. "That's true, but..."

Amusement danced in his eyes. "I guess I'm going to have to convince you. Come on, let's find your Beacon."

The afternoon wasn't going exactly as he'd planned. Beside him, on the shotgun seat in the cab, Liz was strung as tight as a piano wire. He could practically feel the anxiety flowing off her in waves. He wanted to reassure her, but he didn't have the proof, and he wasn't about to make promises he couldn't be sure he could keep. So he held her hand in his as he drove closer and closer to the prairie where the museum would one day be.

He believed it would still be there, mainly because he had information she didn't. Since his abrupt introduction into Liz's world of time travel this morning he'd done a lot of thinking—about the museum, about Liz's future, and how tightly it would intertwine with his. Now he had a hunch how the museum would come to be and what its feature exhibit would show.

As they neared their destination Liz's grip tightened around his hand. He squeezed back reassuringly and turned his head to smile at her. "Another mile or so and we'll be there. Are you ready?"

She swallowed convulsively and nodded. Then she shook her head. "Yes. No. I don't know! Mike, what if it's not there?"

That was a question he had no answer to. If her connection to the future was severed that would mean other unforeseen changes in the established timeline. He didn't like to think that something he and Liz had done had changed everything. On the other hand, if there was a change, maybe it was meant to be. And the change was part of the established timeline.

He wasn't a physicist or a philosopher. Figuring this kind of stuff out was way above his pay grade. He took a deep breath and said, "My dad always says, 'Don't count your babies before they're born.' I think it's a pretty good way of thinking."

That distracted her, as he hoped it would. "Isn't it chickens and hatching?" she asked, sounding puzzled.

He grinned. "Not when you father's a small town doctor. He leaves the chickens to the farmers and ranchers."

She laughed, again as he had hoped. The road twisted around a curve that circled the range of hoodoos to the east of the prairie. As he drove out of the shadow of the low hills, Liz sucked in her breath and made a sound that could indicate hope or dismay.

Mike couldn't see the beacon, of course, so he couldn't tell if it was there, ahead of them, or gone forever. "Well? Is it there?"

She sighed and the panicked clutch on his hand loosened. "Yes."

"Good." He pulled over into the spot they'd used that morning. Lifting her hand to his lips, he kissed her knuckles before he released it. "Come on. Let's go." He climbed out of the truck, leaving Liz to follow.

He waited for her by the side of the road. When she was beside him, he reached over and took her hand. He smiled down at her. "Ready?"

She smiled, a little shakily, he though, and nodded. They set off in the same direction they'd followed this morning. When they had almost reached the place where they'd crossed through the beacon, he tugged her hand and led her away from it, toward the hoodoos.

She followed in his wake, stumbling a little with the unexpected change in direction. "Where are we going?"

"Just taking a short detour," he said. He hid a smile. He thought what he had to show her would have her forgetting all her worries about the fate of the Daspletosaurus.

They reached a gully and he scrambled down the side, helping Liz keep her balance as she skidded down behind him. On the other wall there was a spot where it was clear the ground cover had been disturbed. He went over to the spot and took out a small spade he'd put in his hip pocket when he rounded the back of the truck to wait for Liz to get out. He quickly removed a small section of the surface dirt and grasses, then he brushed away the remaining dirt with his fingers.

As he stood back to let her see what he'd exposed, he said, "What do you think?"

Frowning she crouched down to look. Slowly she reached out and touched the rock. "It's a footprint. A dinosaur print, from the size of it." She glanced up at him. "Are there more."

He nodded and gestured ahead. "I did a few spot checks. I think it extends quite a distance."

She stood and slowly brushed off her hands, looking in the direction he indicated. "Then it could be a trackway."

A trackway was a length of dinosaur footprints, probably made in wet sand or a soft river bottom, then preserved for millennia. Trackways helped paleontologists estimate the size of ancient creatures, ways of movement, and how they traveled. Finds were as rare as the Daspletosaurus. "Yup."

"When did you discover it?" She was looking at him now, her expression thoughtful.

"Earlier this summer. I haven't had time to do any proper work on it, so I covered it up to protect it." He drew a deep breath. "Liz, I think the museum is here because of the trackway, not the Daspletosaurus."

She glanced toward where the museum would eventually be, then up at him. "Makes more sense for the location."

She looked back down at the footprint and he could sense her curiosity, and the urgent desire to investigate further, now. He chuckled. Catching her chin, he gently directed her so she was looking at him again. Her eyes were sparkling with excitement. He said, "I think we excavate the trackway together, as a husband and wife team. I also think that it's the reputation you gain from finding and excavating the Daspletosaurus that gives credibility to our work and increases the value of the find."

She reached up to cup his cheek with her palm. "Your reputation too. I think you are just as good a paleontologist as I am. Or as Scarr or Zac Doyle is."

Deep inside something warm and special uncurled. "Liz Hamilton, do you know how much I love you?"

She shook her head, but she was smiling. "No. Why don't you tell me?"

"You make my day brighter by just being there, my nights wonderful with your touch."

Emotion darkened her eyes, softened the tension in her features. Her tongue came out to moisten her lips and he followed the movement with his eyes. "Oh," she said, with a small sigh, "that was so beautiful. You lovely man, I am so lucky to have found you."

She reached up to drape her arms around his neck and press her body against his. He wrapped his arms around her waist to hug her closer. He heard her whisper in his ear, "I love you, Mike. With all my heart."

He knew it was time. He moved his head so his mouth met hers and kissed her with lips and tongue and a passion that couldn't immediately be fulfilled. She was loose and pliable in his arms when he raised his head.

She sighed and said, "I guess we should head back." But she didn't make any move to leave his embrace.

"In a minute." He dropped a light kiss on her chin, then he eased her out of his embrace so he could reach into his pocket. "Liz, this morning, when I asked you to marry me, I had no token, no ring to give you." He pulled out a velvet covered jeweler's box and flipped open the lid. Inside was a stunning square cut diamond ring. Liz gasped, her gaze riveted to the box and the ring inside.

He slipped it from the holder and held it between his thumb and finger. "Liz, will you wear my ring, today and for the rest of our lives together?"

"Oh, Mike! Yes, and yes, and yes again!"

Feeling giddy at the step they were both taking, and perhaps a little shaky, he slipped the ring on her third finger. He noticed, with some relief, that her hand trembled as well.

"It's beautiful," she whispered, touching the diamond gingerly with a finger.

Relief washed over him. He'd spent an hour choosing the ring. Fretting over cuts and styles, worried that she wouldn't like what he'd chosen. He'd even extracted a promise from the jeweler that he could bring it back and let Liz choose the ring she actually wanted if she wasn't happy with it. Still, her reaction added to his confidence, making him feel that he understood her.

He brushed his fingers along her cheek, then down to her chin in a tender caress. "I think the trackway is the key to our future, but why don't we go back to your Beacon and find out?"

She turned her face into his hand and kissed his palm, before she said, "Mark will never tell us. He's not allowed."

Mike's mouth twitched up into an amused smile. "He's not supposed to, but I bet there's things we can coax out of him if we try."

Liz laughed. "Today proved something to me."

"What?"

She looked at her ring, then at Mike. "Let's live our lives and let the future take care of itself." She held out her hand.

He took it and they started walking. "No counting babies, then?"

"No more than three," she said casually, letting go of his hand as she scrambled up the side of the gully.

Flummoxed, he stood frozen, then he shook himself back to life and followed her up. "Three?" he said, as he reached her.

She grinned at him. "I don't think I could handle more than that."

"Three kids," he said, as they walked back the way they'd come. He was still shocked, though he knew he shouldn't be. After all, he'd met his grandson this morning. To have a grandson you had to have a son or daughter to start with. Still... "When do you want to start?"

She shot him a look, then laughed. "Not right away. I want lots of practice, first."

"I have to admit, that's a relief," he said. They were nearing the area where Liz's beacon had been before. "Is it there, your light?"

She nodded. Stopping, she turned to face him. She caught hold of his hands and looked up into his eyes. "I believe in you, Mike. I believe in us. Whatever the future brings."

He squeezed her fingers. "You're the best thing that has ever happened to me, Liz. I love you."

She glowed with emotion. "I love you, Mike." Then she laughed. "Shall we go into our future and show our grandson my ring?"

"He's probably seen it," Mike said, dryly.

She laughed again. "So what? I want to show it off. Besides, his grandfather, who is way more romantic than I ever expected, probably told him to be waiting with a bottle of champagne to celebrate."

"And maybe all the rest of the family too," Mike murmured. He watched Liz's eyes widen. "After all, now that we've decided how many kids we're going to have there's no need to keep them all a secret."

"Oh!" She was positively bouncing with excitement. "Come on, let's go!"

"In a minute," he said, drawing her into the circle of his arms. "I think I need to calm you down, first."

And he did, with a kiss that pledged his love now and into the future before them.

CLAIM TIME FOR LOVE

THE FORWARD IN TIME SERIES

CHAPTER 1

"This will end, Mary Elizabeth." Though George Strand's features showed no emotion, his tone was full of arrogant demand and he skewered her with eyes that were a pale, icy gray.

She stood before him fighting the panic clawing through her, trying not to show this man how anxious he was making her. This was her father. Why was he so cold toward her? Why did he not care about her desires? She was his daughter. His only child.

She stared back at him, defiant, even though her heart was pounding and she had to fight to keep the hands she clasped in front of her from trembling. He sat stiffly; ramrod straight on a ladder-backed chair behind a walnut desk, the glossy sheen of the wood the only ornament to the solid construction. The desk was designed to intimidate—and it was working. He watched her silently, his thin, carved features expressing nothing but disdain mixed with a little boredom. She squared her shoulders, struggling to keep that defiant expression, and not let him see how dismayed she really was. If he knew, he'd push her harder, tell her how selfish her behavior was, how it was upsetting her mother, make her feel guilt when she had every right to be angry. It was always this way when her father took her to task.

She opened her mouth to speak, then closed it again when he slowly raised his eyebrows. She remembered a time when he was willing to listen to her defense of whatever scrape she'd gotten herself into, but not recently. Not since he'd been elevated to the Governor's Council in Boston and his position in the government had added more responsibility, as well as power.

"You are a granddaughter of an earl," he said, his tone critical. Although it was his wife, the Lady Elizabeth, Mary Elizabeth's mother, whose father was an earl, George Strand certainly liked to act the part of a wealthy, titled gentleman. Though only a member of the landed gentry, he dressed like a aristocrat. Mary Elizabeth had never known any man as fastidious as her father when it came to attire. His coat was a dark, forest-green silk, braided with gold thread. His embroidered-silk waistcoat was the shade of a leaf in spring. His shirt was of the finest linen, and at his throat and wrists lace frothed. His wig was curled over his ears and tied with a black bow at his nape. It was perfectly powdered and gleamed white in the afternoon sun streaming through the windows.

He would not have looked out of place in the most fashionable salon in London. But he wasn't in London. He was in America, in the small town of Lexington, to be precise, in a country home he had purchased to provide his wife a pleasant escape from the sweltering summer heat of Boston.

"You have a responsibility to your name. To your mother's name. You are not some hoyden who can misbehave with impunity."

His sharp, critical, tone rubbed Mary Elizabeth's nerves raw and made her want to cry out in denial. What did she care about a grandfather she could barely remember? Or a society that had nothing to do with the world she now lived in? This was her life. Didn't she have a say in it?

"How did I misbehave?" she challenged, desperate now to stop this conversation before the weight of his disapproval overwhelmed her into agreeing to something she did not want, just so she could escape him.

He shifted in his chair and studied her critically. Though he appeared unemotional, when he spoke she could hear anger underlying his cool words. "You wish me to itemize each of your indiscretions? Or simply start with the most heinous one?"

Heat rushed into her face, burning under her skin. He had a way of making her feel worthless and of no account. "N-no, Papa, you don't have to list the details." She knew them as well as he. Refusing to snub local colonists whose political views were considered radical. Consorting with one particular colonist in a way that could certainly be called flirtatious. Speaking privately to said colonist at parties, dancing with him more often than was proper. Best not to let her father become even angrier than he already was by reciting the many ways she had failed him. "But I don't understand why you are so set against Andrew."

He sat forward with the speed of a pouncing wolf, making her gasp and stumble back. Her hand fluttered upward, then fell, heralding her dismay. She drew a deep breath to compose herself, then deliberately smoothed the figured peach silk of the wide overskirt of her gown. Peach was not the best color on her, but her mother insisted she wear soothing pastels, for darker, brighter colors were, she said, only for married ladies. Mary Elizabeth knew many young American women who chose darker shades for their gowns, and she resented their freedom, especially when her mother was adamant, and the colors she was forced to wear were not flattering to her dark hair and warm-toned skin.

She folded her hands in front of her again. His quick movement had been done to discompose her, she knew, but she suspected he also required a way to spend some of the anger that he kept so carefully leashed. She needed to be careful, or she would push him too far.

"Andrew, is it? A man who gives a woman leave to use his Christian name is expecting certain familiarities. And the woman who uses it, welcomes them. Tell me daughter, just how intimate have you been with this jumped up colonial popinjay?"

Heat rushed up into Mary Elizabeth's face, making her cheeks burn. She swallowed guilt that shouldn't have existed. "N-none, Papa. I am chaste and Andrew...I mean...Mr. Byrne has made no attempt to taint my virtue."

Her father sat back. She was relieved to see some of the tension easing out of him. "See that it remains that way. And I will not hear you referring to the fellow in that common manner again."

"No, Papa." She lowered her gaze, relieved.

He nodded briskly, then proceeded with his lecture as if she had never spoken. "You are a lady and will behave as one. That means you will no longer consort with the colonial underclass who persist in thinking themselves the equals to gentlemen such as myself. You will be modest, polite, and you will speak when spoken to—and not before."

She'd heard this lecture before. Children have their place, girls have their place, women have their place. Learn it. Accept it. Do not stray from it. She waited a heartbeat and then another to be sure her father had finished speaking, then she curtseyed and, still keeping her eyes lowered, said in a subdued voice, "Yes, Papa."

"Look at me, Mary Elizabeth."

She did as he demanded, raising her eyes once more. Usually at this stage in his reprimand, he would point to the door and she would make her escape. This time he studied her. "I wonder..." he said, after a few moments of silent reflection.

She watched him with a frown, waiting to hear what he would say next. This was a new twist and she wasn't sure what was running through his mind.

He smiled faintly. It wasn't a nice smile. "You promise so easily, daughter. As you have all of your life. I do not for one moment believe that you are truly sorry for your behavior. Or that you will obey me."

"Papa! That is not so—"

He held up his hand. "Please do not insult my intelligence with false protests." He considered her as if she was an insect impaled with a pin, viewed with the unrelenting clarity of a magnifying glass. "You are a handful, Mary Elizabeth. Beautiful, charming, and far more intelligent than a woman should be. Much like your mother, in fact."

She watched him, her gaze riveted to his, her breath coming faster.

Her father never complimented her—or her mother, for that matter. Beautiful and charming were positive adjectives, the kind of words a woman wanted to hear. But there was nothing complimentary about her father's expression, or the contemptuous edge beneath the even tone.

"Your mother has a redeeming feature that you lack, however."

He paused, waiting. She knew her cues. She was expected to respond. Her voice was thick with rising emotion when she spoke, knowing where this was heading. "What is that, Papa?"

"She knows her place."

The words were a whiplash of disdain. Mary Elizabeth colored. "Papa, I—"

He didn't let her finish. "As your father, the law gives me complete control over your person. I choose your friends. I choose where you will reside. If I wish, I can choose what gown you will wear today. Your future belongs to me. Remember that, Mary Elizabeth, and your life will be a comfortable one. Resist me and you will regret it."

She did not doubt a word of what he had said. There was no paternal love in his gaze. He wasn't just a father frustrated with a child who was willful and disobedient. He was a man for whom everyone served a purpose, a man determined to be obeyed, no matter the cost. "Yes, Papa," she whispered. She stood, motionless, even though instinct told her to flee.

"This Byrne fellow is a hothead. He consorts with ruffians who think the law does not apply to them. They demand representation in His Majesty's Parliament. What nonsense! They are colonists, pure and simple. They are governed, they do not govern. I will not have my daughter associated with such riffraff."

It was an explanation and a command.

"Yes, Papa," she said again, trying without success to keep the despair from her voice. Andrew Byrne was the best person who had ever come into her life. Oh, he was definitely a pleasure to look at, with his wicked, laughing blue eyes, deep set above high cheekbones and framed by thick black lashes, a firm masculine mouth with lips that were neither too thick nor too thin, and a chin that jutted just enough to express strength of character. But more importantly to Mary Elizabeth, he was a delight to be with. He made her laugh. He made her feel cherished. He made her feel wanted. He made her feel desired.

Her father's lip curled and her heart sank. He'd heard the false meekness beneath the pliant agreement and she knew he would never allow Andrew to court her.

The door opened and her mother poked her head. She was wearing a gown of figured silk, a lovely green that brought out red highlights in her dark hair. Her eyes were dark too, usually warm and caring, but right now shadowed with worry. Still she smiled as she said in an overly cheery voice, "Darlings, have you finished your private conference?" Her gaze moved from her husband's hard features to Mary Elizabeth's face and she faltered. "Am I too early? You did say, Mr. Strand, that you thought your conversation should only take a quarter of the hour."

For an instant the unrelenting expression remained in his eyes and the sneer on his lips, then he assumed the pleasant mask he used to cover the authority he wielded with such cold brutality. He nodded to his wife. "Do come in, my dear. I believe our daughter understands her position now." He returned his gaze to Mary Elizabeth, his brows arched.

Mary Elizabeth was under no illusion that his anger and contempt had taken flight. She turned to her mother with considerable relief. "Hello, Mama. Have you come to collect me for our walk this afternoon?"

Lady Elizabeth Strand's smile faltered as she shook her head. A fresh wave of anxiety washed over Mary Elizabeth as she braced herself for what was to come.

"No, child. No walk today," she said softly. "Your papa and I are agreed that when we finish here you are to retire to your room."

"But—"

Her father held up his hand. "As I told you when we began this conversation, this Byrne fellow had the effrontery to ask for your hand in marriage and he claimed that he had already spoken to you. You admitted that was true, did you not?"

"Yes," Mary Elizabeth whispered. She glanced at her mother and the sadness she saw in her eyes was more painful to her than the anger in her father's.

"I have told him that it is, of course, quite impossible for such a union to occur. I am sure he understands his place now."

"What did Andr—Mr. Byrne say, Papa?"

She should not have spoken Andrew's name. Fury blazed in her father's eyes. "You require time to reflect, girl. To remember who and what you are. Be thankful we believe that your contemplation can be conducted in the comfort of your own chamber."

Panic shot through her. Normally after a lecture on misbehavior she was assigned some form of penance, usually something that would remind her of what she *should* be doing, like sending her to the school room to write *I will not misbehave* a hundred times in perfect copperplate handwriting. Or more lately, sewing a similar phrase into a sampler that could be framed and hung in her room as a daily reminder. Once the task was done she was free to go about her regular routine.

This time there was no task to perform, no moral to learn. There was just time and reflection and one room to do it in. As if he was sending her to prison. "How...How long?"

Her father didn't pretend to misunderstand. His voice cold, he said, "Until you understand your responsibilities and where your loyalties lie."

Until you obey. That's what he truly meant. *Obey. Learn your place.* She swallowed hard.

Her mother said gently, "You will, of course, attend church tomorrow."

So there was a time limit on her banishment. Relief made her knees weak.

"Your behavior will be impeccable and you will be everything a properly brought up young lady should be," Lady Elizabeth added in that same quiet voice.

Mary Elizabeth nodded, careful to keep her expression contrite, but her mind was already skipping ahead to tomorrow. Church offered many opportunities for communication. Somehow, she would have to find a way to meet privately with Andrew.

"You will stay by my side and you will not sneak away to be with Mr. Byrne," her mother said as though reading her mind. "I know he is a handsome young man, Mary Elizabeth, and that you are much taken with him...but he is not for you." She glanced at her husband. "Your father has generously agreed to allow you to speak to him in order to break off whatever connection you have made with him."

"You are telling me I must say good-bye," Mary Elizabeth said around the lump that had lodged in her throat.

"Yes, my dear." Her mother gave her a brief nod, her eyes reflecting the pain that Mary Elizabeth was feeling. "There can be no other conclusion to this wayward friendship and Mr. Byrne must not continue to think that there is any possibility that he might marry you. I will allow you as much privacy as a few feet of separation can provide, but you are to remain within my sight and hearing while you speak with him."

Mary Elizabeth choked back a sob. "He won't understand, because I don't understand."

"Then you'd best figure it out before morning," her father said, that whiplash tone in his voice again. "Because if you do not, I'll have to deal with Byrne more firmly than I have already done. I can assure you that neither he, nor you, will like the consequences!"

CHAPTER 2

Mr. Ian Turner, the minister at St James the Redeemer church, was an intelligent man whose Sunday services were neither too long nor overly religious. Which was why Andrew usually made an effort to listen to him and pay attention to his sermon. Not today, though. Today his brain could think of nothing but Mary Elizabeth and the complicated problem of how he was going to marry her.

The concept of marriage had not come swiftly. In his late twenties, he was focused on managing the estate he had inherited from his father, whose death some four years earlier had left him in charge of a large and prosperous property that included rich acres for growing crops, a dairy herd, and several thriving side industries. Furthermore, he was much sought after by the young ladies—and had been since he first reached manhood. He did not need marriage to satisfy his needs, and he was quite sure that he didn't have the time to woo a wife.

Then Mary Elizabeth Strand moved to Lexington and that was the end to all of his sensible bachelor ways. Dark, mischievous eyes set in set in a delicate, heart-shaped face, midnight hair she wore neatly pinned up, but which he knew was thick and luxurious. He could imagine it loose, falling to her waist, and the silky feel of it on his finger tips as he buried his hands in the thick mass while he kissed her. His imagination supplied other images too—a dreamy look in her eyes when she'd been thoroughly kissed, the pleasure of her lithe body pressed against his as they embraced. But that was his imagination, based on the proud way she carried her slender form, as if she were gliding over the ground, not walking upon it as other women did. Then there was the warmth of her smile to capture his attention, and the way she understood what mattered to him—his lands, his businesses, and the freedom he prized so highly. She caught every nuance, and even though his views were at odds with her father's she accepted them, because, she had told him one evening, she believed in him.

At their first meeting, she had shown him she was attracted to him, with shy glances from beneath the thick fringe of her lashes, and as they got to know each other, she blossomed. Her reticence warmed into quiet confidence and her gaze reflected her complex nature, at times twinkling with humor, or thoughtful in reflection. But it was the innocent passion in her magnificent, dark eyes that took his breath away. As they got to know each other, they managed to find private places where they could whisper their shared longings and dreams and he could steal a kiss or two at the social events they both attended.

He wasn't sure if it was her honest admiration that made him look at her differently from the other girls who had pursued him over the years, or if it was simply the connection they'd forged together, but he was certain of one thing—Mary Elizabeth had changed his thinking about marriage. He wanted her in his life forever.

At first their attraction went unnoticed, or at least unremarked. Inevitably it came to the attention of her mother, the Lady Elizabeth, and then to her father, George Strand, even though he visited his family at his summer home only occasionally. Unfortunately, Strand didn't see Andrew's union with his daughter in as positive a way as Andrew did. Or indeed, as Mary Elizabeth herself did.

When Strand realized that one of the American colonists he despised was courting his daughter—and that his daughter was not

averse to the match, he chose to act. He paid two ruffians who masquer-
aded as servants to send Andrew a message. They had assaulted him as
he was leaving a party where he and Mary Elizabeth had been trysting.
There were two of them, great hulking lummoxes with fists like hams
and the cauliflower ears of boxers. They issued their warning, then
followed it up with their fists. Andrew fought back, landing a few good
blows of his own, before the miscreants scuttled away, but he was quite
sure they would try to waylay him again.

Having Mary Elizabeth's father so violently opposed to the match
would have been an impediment if she were a colonial girl and her
father a prominent American. But she was the daughter of an English
official, while he, Andrew Byrne, was an American colonist who
fiercely believed that the American colonies deserved representation
and the right to govern themselves. Mary Elizabeth delighted him. Her
family did not. Should he continue on in the face of such vehement
opposition from her father?

He needed to decide and he could not do it here in Lexington
where there was a very good likelihood that they would meet, and then
he knew he would fall under her spell all over again. He had decided to
go away to somewhere he could brood and decide.

Rather than go to Boston, where George Strand held sway, or to
Concord where his closest relatives lived, Andrew chose to go farther
afield, or rather, to a place where distance didn't matter, time did. He
would stay in Lexington, but he would visit the one individual who just
might be able to offer assistance in his decision-making, Faith
Hamilton.

Faith was a special person blessed with the power of a Beacon. She
was quite literally a portal of light who could bring certain ancestors
from their era into her own time period. Andrew was one such ancestor, a Traveler who had the ability to see Faith's light and propel
himself into her present. As far as Andrew knew, this unique gift
existed only within his own bloodline. It was hard to tell, though, for it
was a closely guarded secret, shared only within the family.

He was certain that in the future he would be able to learn more about the outcome of his relationship with Mary Elizabeth. He would also be out of temptation's way, which would save him from another possible altercation with Strand's henchmen.

Andrew had returned to his farm where his housekeeper fussed over his disheveled state and her husband, the farm manager, made dire comments about the infernal British. He told them he would be going away for a few days, allowing them to believe that he planned to raise awareness of Strand's high-handed behavior through neighboring towns. Bidding them adieu, he told them he would walk to the general store to wait for the public stagecoach. In actual fact, he made his way to a particular stand of trees on his property. There he found a glowing ball of light that only he could see shining through the trees. Warmth and a sense of unreserved welcome flowed from the light. The frustration, anger, and impatience of the day flowed out of him as he stepped into its hospitable glow.

There was no impression of movement, no alteration of his senses to indicate he was moving through time, though not through space. One moment he was in his wood, the next he stood in a cozy house that was both familiar and strange. Familiar, because he'd been there so many times. Strange, because it did not yet exist in his own time. This was the home of his dear relative, Faith Hamilton, the woman whose light shone in that forest grove.

He'd met Faith when she first came into her powers, as an emotional young woman of some ten and four years. Only a couple of years older himself, he'd been in the woods, avoiding the chores his father had set him. Suddenly light blazed through the trees, setting the leaves aglow. It called to him, that light, and he'd rushed forward only to find himself in a strange house. In front of him stood a large, red-faced man and a harried golden-haired girl. They were arguing. He'd immediately jumped to the girl's defense and somehow that had brought them together, allies against the dark force of the man who was, it turned out, her father.

Not long after that event, the father, whose name was Daniel, had abandoned his family—something Andrew disapproved of, though he thought it best the fellow was no longer around to cause trouble. Andrew had taken to visiting Faith every week, and over the years they became friends. Now Faith was like a sister to him.

He had stayed with Faith almost a week. He could only remain in her time if he was close to her, so Faith had taken him into the city with her and to the place where she went to work each morning. The visit had been enlightening. Not only did he meet Cody, the excellent fellow Faith was in love with, but he'd also seen how dedicated Faith was to her position and how jealous certain persons in the organization were of her.

Despite the dangers his presence brought her, Faith had given him sanctuary and helped him sort out his tumultuous feelings. Try as he might, however, he could not persuade her to provide him with solid details about his future, and Mary Elizabeth's. Nor would she allow him to consult the marvelous information-gathering device she called a computer. He knew as well as Faith did that for their powers to remain secret, Beacons and Travellers must strive to ensure that they did not change the past or the future through their actions. That meant remaining silent and keeping secrets. He learned little during the week he spent in the future, despite Faith's technologically advanced world, Frustrated, he had found himself wishing for his own rural agrarian one. His time away did help though, for he missed Mary Elizabeth so much that he realized that she was the love of his life and the woman he would marry.

He'd returned to his own time two days ago, and immediately sought her out. He found her at a ball put on by Franny and Maurice Hodder. Maurice Hodder was a sedate and conventional man with a high standing in the community and conservative views. Lady Elizabeth Strand enjoyed the Hodders' company and never objected to Mary Elizabeth participating in a social event that Franny organized. However, Franny was the sister of Andrew's closest friend, Ronald Aiken, and she had been quietly helping Andrew court Mary Elizabeth, providing secluded places for them to meet.

Friday night had been no different. Franny loved to organize social events and the more people she could convince to attend one of her grand evenings, the happier she was. It was a formal affair, so Andrew dressed in a coat of dark-blue velvet, with a waistcoat of white brocade. He'd paired it with black silk breeches and white stockings. The deep cuffs of the coat sleeves showed off the lace at his wrists and at his neck, lace also frothed. He didn't powder his hair, but he tied it neatly at his nape with a black ribband. He had a mission that evening. He planned to dance with Mary Elizabeth, then steal her away to a quiet place to propose. He wanted to look his best.

Franny, apprised of his desire to single out Mary Elizabeth, advised caution. Not only was her mother, the Lady Elizabeth, attending the ball, but so was George Strand. Moreover, while Andrew had been away, Strand had made it clear that he did not approve of his daughter consorting with a colonist and he'd let it be known that he would not be pleased if members of the local community aided and abetted the romance. He implied there would be repercussions. Franny was worried.

So, Andrew didn't dance with Mary Elizabeth that night. But he did manage to meet with her in the garden. There, near a little clump of rose bushes, he told her of his love for her and asked her to marry him. To his great delight she said, yes.

Being a man of honor, Andrew did the proper thing and called upon George Strand the next morning to ask for Mary Elizabeth's hand in marriage. He knew Strand would not easily accept his suit, for the man had already expressed his disdain through his ham-fisted henchmen. However, with Mary Elizabeth's sweet declaration of her love for him humming through his brain, he'd assumed that Strand would be willing to unbend to ensure his daughter's happiness once he knew how she felt.

He was incorrect. If anything, Mary Elizabeth's declaration of her feelings for Andrew, and his request for her hand in marriage, inflamed Strand's ire to the point that he became so red in the face that Andrew had wondered if the man would suffer an apoplectic seizure. Sadly, he did not. Instead, he set his pair of brutal ruffians on Andrew once more.

The second scuffle resulted in the considerable discomfort Andrew was suffering from even now as he sat in the church listening to the words of the service, but not hearing them.

George Strand, Andrew thought as he sat in the church pew, would regret the order he had given—twice!—to have an upstanding citizen beaten, simply because Strand thought he was somehow better than Andrew was. This was the kind of injustice that infuriated Andrew and other men of like mind. America was no longer a simple colony of farmers, traders, and explorers, living on the edge of the wilderness. It was a wealthy society, growing wealthier every day, and men of substance, such as himself, were as educated and cultured as any Briton from the old country.

The Reverend Turner began his sermon, a homily on the benefits of repentance and forgiveness. The topic grated and Andrew shifted uneasily on the hard maple seat. He couldn't see Mary Elizabeth from where he sat. George Strand had claimed one of the private boxes at the front of the church when he'd first arrived in the area and it was too far Andrew's own place for him to see how she was responding to the sermon. It didn't matter in any case, for when it came to his courtship of Mary Elizabeth, he refused to ask forgiveness for anything he'd done these past weeks.

Mr. Turner's strong tenor voice thundered from the pulpit and he gestured emphatically toward his rapt audience, indicating he was coming to the climax of his sermon.

Andrew grimaced to himself. George Strand had made a great fuss over Mary Elizabeth's lineage when he turned down Andrew's suit. True, her mother was the daughter of an earl, but Strand's family was merely landed gentry, no better than Andrew's ancestors had been. And now, here in the new world, Andrew's standing in the community made him at least the equal of George Strand.

The sermon ended and the chastened congregation rose to sing a hymn. That was much more to his taste and he joined in with hearty enthusiasm. No, there would be no repentance on his part, no matter how good for his soul the excellent Reverend Turner thought it would be.

The hymn singing over, they sat again. Andrew stole another look in the direction of the Strands' pew. He wished he could see Mary Elizabeth's face. Had her father told her Andrew had asked for her hand? He had reacted angrily to Andrew. Had he taken his ire out on his daughter?

Andrew believed completely in Mary Elizabeth's assertion that she loved him, but did she have the resolve to stand up to her domineering father? She hadn't been in the churchyard prior to the service, so he'd had no chance to speak with her. In fact, the Strand family, George strutting proudly at the head, had marched into the church moments before the service began. The small parade consisted of the odious George with his wife on his arm, followed by a fellow in scarlet regimentals liberally covered with gold braid who walked beside Mary Elizabeth. Her hand was on his arm in much the same way her mother's was on George Strand's. That worried Andrew. Who was the man and why was Mary Elizabeth paired with him?

As the Strand cortege had walked down the long aisle to their pew near the front of the church, she looked neither left nor right. That was not like his Mary Elizabeth, who was friendly, social, and curious. Normally she would have been nodding and smiling at those she knew, but not this morning. Her stiff reserve, paired with presence of the unknown English officer beside her, made Andrew fearful that George Strand had decided to punish his daughter. But how?

When the service ended Andrew rose with the rest of the congregation, then waited his turn to leave the church. The Strand family had lingered near their pew, so he emerged out into the sunshine earlier than Mary Elizabeth. He hovered near the door, determined to speak to her before Strand hustled her into his carriage and back to his home.

"If you don't want to call attention to the fact that you're mooning over the lovely Miss Strand, you'd best mingle with your neighbors awhile until the lady leaves the church."

Andrew turned to see his friend Ron Aiken standing to one side of him. Ron was a landowner close to him in age and deeply involved in the politics of the day. They had been friends for years and held similar views on many subjects, particularly those relating to Britain's arrogant mismanagement of its American colonies. On one subject they differed radically, however, and that was Andrew's courtship of Mary Elizabeth. Though Ron's sister Franny was delighted by the romance—not surprising since she was the wife of the deeply conservative Maurice Hodder—Ron disapproved. He thought Andrew should dally with Mary Elizabeth and nothing more. He disapproved of Andrew's desire to wed her and ally himself to a family so deeply committed to the British point of view.

Despite this disagreement, Ron was a good friend, and his advice came from a place of affection, even if aimed to ensure that Andrew didn't lose his standing with the more radical members of the community.

"I fear you are right, my friend," Andrew said. "Mr. Turner is feeling chatty today. He seems determined to spend at least five minutes conversing with each member of his congregation."

Aiken laughed. "It's not that the good reverend is chattier than usual, Byrne, but that you are impatient. Come, let us have a word with Mr. Turnbull, while his lady wife is busy comparing recipes with her sister."

Andrew nodded agreement and the two men moved across the churchyard, pausing to greet friends and neighbors on their way.

"Well met," Fletcher Turnbull said as they joined him. He studied Andrew's still bruised face with raised brows. "Took a tumble off your horse, Byrne?"

Ron Aiken snorted. "More like took a beating from two lackeys. That English popinjay, Strand, ordered his ruffians upon him yesterday."

"I gave as good as I got," Andrew said as he touched the bruise high on his cheek along with a black eye that couldn't be missed. He'd noticed curious looks aimed his way all morning. Fletcher was the first to make mention of it though. "There were two of them, however, so they were able to land a few blows." The ache in his ribs testified to that.

Turnbull's expression darkened. "What did you do to cause Strand to waylay you?"

Andrew drew a deep breath. Not many people knew he'd been courting Mary Elizabeth. He wasn't sure he wanted to circulate the news to all and sundry, but it wasn't a secret either. "I asked for his daughter's hand in marriage."

Turnbull's brows flew up again and his eyes brightened. "I had no idea! She's a pretty young woman and a kind one too, I think. My congratulations to you, but I take it Strand turned you down, if setting his lackeys on you is any indication."

"He did," Andrew said, nodding gloomily.

Turnbull looked from Andrew to Ron, then moved a little closer and lowered his voice. "Did you see the fellow in uniform who followed Strand into church?"

Andrew and Ron nodded. Turnbull moved even closer. "He is a colonel of dragoons, I heard. He and his regiment arrived in Boston town less than a se'nnight ago. He's here, I'm told, to keep the peace, and Strand is mighty familiar with him. His father is a nob, they say. A member of the government and a friend of Strand's father-by-marriage, the earl."

Andrew listened to this with grim dismay. The unnamed colonel was just the sort of man Strand wanted for his daughter. Was that why she had entered the church on the colonel's arm? Why she didn't look his way as she passed his pew? Was the colonel with the Strands because he had come to Lexington to court Mary Elizabeth with the full approval of her father? Panic at the thought tied Andrew's stomach into knots.

He shifted uneasily, turning so that he could watch the door where Mr. Turner chatted cheerfully with his parishioners as they emerged from the church. As the queue slowly moved through the door and out into the churchyard, Andrew cursed inwardly at the reverend's friendly nature and his willingness to converse with each of his parishioners in turn.

Finally, George Strand stepped out of the dimly lit church, his wife beside him. He stood in front of the minister, his back straight, his expression haughty. Lady Elizabeth said something to the reverend, then they both stepped aside. Mary Elizabeth and the colonel appeared in the doorway and paused. With the dark interior behind, the outdoor light shone upon them, a handsome couple linked together. Her hand was on the officer's arm and there was a small smile on her face. The colonel's proud military bearing seemed to claim the woman beside him, while the expression on his face was one of smug satisfaction.

As they hovered in the doorway, the babble of voices in the church-yard died down as though the interest of the entire congregation was fixated on the young, handsome pair. The knot in Andrew's stomach tightened, for Mary Elizabeth and her colonel resembled a couple emerging from church on their wedding day.

George Strand gestured toward them, urging them forward, as he said something to Mr. Turner. The minister looked surprised, then he smiled in a congratulatory way and patted Mary Elizabeth's hand as he spoke to her.

Andrew's heart sank. The colonel wasn't in Lexington to court Mary Elizabeth. The decision had already been made. He was here to marry her.

CHAPTER 3

*M*ary Elizabeth blinked as she and Colonel Jonathan Bradley emerged from the cool dimness of St. James Church. She had spent most of the service forming sentences, tearing them apart, then reforming them in a vain effort to put together a speech that would convey to Andrew that she still loved him and was simply trying to placate her beast of a father.

After a day and night sequestered in her room with only the necessities of water and a little bread to take the edge off the worst of her hunger, Mary Elizabeth's mood was bleak.

When her mother tapped on her door at sunrise that morning Mary Elizabeth had already been awake. Lady Elizabeth hadn't bothered to wait for her to give permission to enter. Instead, she opened the door and swept inside. There was a smile on her lips, but no light of laughter in her eyes. "Have you decided what you will wear to church this morning, my dear?"

Mary Elizabeth had opened her mouth to reply, but her mother waved her hand dismissively. "The pale blue muslin with the underskirt figured with spring flowers, I think." She flung open the door to

Mary Elizabeth's wardrobe and found the articles of clothing. Scrutinizing them, she'd nodded decisively. "Yes, exactly what the day requires. Not overly ostentatious, but flattering to your coloring. Such perfect stitching, as well. The gown is beautifully made and the fabric is of the finest quality."

Mary Elizabeth had sat up in bed, staring at her mother in consternation. "But that gown requires panniers, Mama."

The gown was one of Mary Elizabeth's fancier garments. Panniers were a frame-like structure worn around the hips and used to push out the skirts on either side of the body. Wearing them made movement awkward, forcing a woman to be very aware of her surroundings, since it was very easy to knock against nearby objects or people. They were all the rage in fashionable society, but impractical for everyday activities, so Mary Elizabeth rarely wore them.

"Yes," Lady Elizabeth had said, contemplating the gown. "A simple, dark-blue ribbon around your throat for decoration, I think. That will set off the sash at the waist."

Her words pulled Mary Elizabeth out of her personal nightmare and caused her to focus on her mother. She realized that Lady Elizabeth was dressed in a gown of rose silk, with a richly brocaded underskirt of pale cream. And she was wearing panniers. Her stomach did a little flip and she'd had to swallow hard. "Mama, we are attending church this morning, are we not? You have always said that when we attend services, we are worshipping God, not attending a ball. Surely, there is no need for such extreme finery?"

Lady Elizabeth had turned to face her daughter, her expression austere. "Your father has specifically asked that you look your best. We have a visitor he wishes to impress." She'd swept toward the door without waiting for a reply. Her hand on the knob, she'd paused and looked back at Mary Elizabeth. Though her features were set, their expression implacable, there was a flicker of sadness in her eyes. "I will send my maid to help you dress. She will be here to carry out my orders. You will not protest her dictates. Is that understood?"

"No! Mama, what is going on?"

"You will obey, Mary Elizabeth," was all her mother had said, before she left the room, closing the door with quiet finality.

Mary Elizabeth had discovered her father's plans at breakfast an hour later. Her hair had been artfully arranged to show off her large brown eyes, heart-shaped face, and delicate chin. The blue ribbon had been tied around her slender neck, the pale blue gown emphasizing her creamy complexion and dark hair. Though she loved the gown, she hated the cumbersome panniers, which forced her to take small, careful steps as she negotiated the narrow staircase and the doorway to the breakfast room.

Her father's visitor was an officer, one Colonel Bradley, who had recently arrived from England. His features were hard, but he smiled at her warmly when they were introduced. Breakfast had been a polite affair but had reminded Mary Elizabeth of the fashionable dinners she had attended when her father had sent her back to England for a London Season in a vain attempt to secure her a husband. Everyone was pleasant enough, but there was an undercurrent that flowed through every conversation, as if they all thought she was a mere country cousin and not up to snuff.

Mary Elizabeth's stomach was in knots throughout the meal. Though she'd joined the conversation when asked direct questions, she hadn't paid a great deal of attention to their chatter. She was polite, she smiled at all the right moments, but her mind had been focused on what she would say to Andrew.

She couldn't break with him. She wouldn't do it. Andrew was the finest man she had ever known. He was held in high regard by the community here in Lexington. He respected others. He did not jump to snap judgments, but considered options. He was intelligent and caring, and oh, so fun to be with. Just being in his presence filled her with a passion she had never experienced before. He completed her. She would be lost without him.

After breakfast, as they had prepared to make their way out to the waiting coach that would take them to the church, her father caught her arm, holding her back.

"You remember your duty, Mary Elizabeth. You will break with Byrne today. If you do not…the consequences will be severe."

"Papa, surely you cannot mean this."

His icy gaze did not waver. "I have never been more determined, daughter. Andrew Byrne is not for you and you will tell him so. Do I make myself clear?"

She searched his eyes for some inkling of kindness or regret that she could latch onto, but all she could see was cold condescension. "Yes, Papa."

And now she was standing in the doorway of the church and the moment she must break with Andrew was upon her. The service hadn't been long enough to tame the emotional chaos in her mind. She drew a deep breath to help steel herself for the role she must play. To rescue herself, to save the love she felt for Andrew, she would have to pretend, and she'd never been very good at that.

Somehow, she would have to come up with the words that would satisfy her mother and father and yet convey to Andrew that she needed to speak with him in private so that she could explain herself. She pasted a smile on her face, one that was supposed to look relaxed and happy, and hoped that Andrew—and everyone else—would see through it and understand.

Beside her, the colonel patted her hand in a way that seemed disturbingly possessive for a gentleman she had only just met. When they rose from the pew at the end of the service he had bowed elegantly to her and asked her if she would do him the honor of allowing him to escort her from the church. As her mother had put her hand on her father's arm Mary Elizabeth had little option but to agree. Colonel Bradley smiled and placed her hand on his arm, with all the reverence of a gentleman for a lady he had special feelings for. But that was absurd. No one could discover love in an instant. She had no choice but to smile back, though, if she was to play the part she'd given herself. As they strolled down the aisle she nodded to whatever he was saying to her, all the while wondering desperately how to alert Andrew to the disastrous situation she was now in.

With the sunlight warm on her face, she scanned the crowd in the churchyard, searching for Andrew. Her heart leapt as she spotted him under a tree speaking with his friend, Mr. Ronald Aiken. That was unfortunate, as Mr. Aiken was another young man her father disparaged as a damned rebel, and no friend of England's. Seeing Andrew with Mr. Aiken would do his cause no good in her father's eyes.

Reverend Turner said her name, bringing her back into the moment. "Miss Strand, how delightful to see you this fine morning. And Colonel Bradley, it is a pleasure to make your acquaintance. How long will you be staying with Mr. and Mrs. Strand?"

"*Lady* Elizabeth," George Strand said sharply. "May I remind you, Reverend Turner, that my dear wife is the daughter of the Earl of Alesford."

Since Mama never bothered flaunting her aristocratic connections and Papa wasn't in Lexington all that often, the minister was very properly flustered by this admonishment. "Indeed, sir. My very great apologies, Lady Elizabeth."

Mama waved her hand in that airy way she had, bestowing a warm smile on the minister. "It is no matter, Reverend Turner."

Papa frowned at this exchange. Mary Elizabeth saw a reprimand coming and quaked at the possibility. When her father was in a rage, his words could cut with the precision of a sharply honed sword.

Colonel Bradley saved the moment by answering the minister's question. "I am here for several days, perhaps a se'nnight or more, Reverend Turner. I hope within that time to be able to make a very happy announcement."

As he glanced at Mary Elizabeth at the end of that statement, no one in their little group could help but understand his meaning. Her father nodded, his eyes gleaming with satisfaction. Her mother lowered her eyes, carefully avoiding the minister's gaze. Mary Elizabeth herself stared at the colonel, horrified.

Reverend Turner's eyebrows rose, though he smiled politely. He was one of those who looked favorably on Andrew's courtship of her. He must have been surprised by the colonel's announcement. "Indeed! How very unexpected. I look forward to being one of the first to hear your news."

Her father inclined his head as though he was a king bestowing a favor. "Indeed."

"Come darling," her mother said in a breezy tone. "Let us go and greet our friends." She smiled at the colonel. "I must spirit my daughter away, Colonel Bradley. My deepest apologies."

Mary Elizabeth withdrew her hand from the colonel's arm. Her heart was pounding so hard she missed whatever Bradley said to her. Her mother linked arms with her and moved them both away from the doorway.

"Mama," Mary Elizabeth said, feeling faint. "I...I can't..."

"You can and will." A fleeting look of sorrow crossed her features before it was replaced with her usual friendly expression. "You have no choice, Mary Elizabeth. Be kind to your young man, but be swift and clear," she whispered, even as she waved and smiled at an approaching matron. "Why, Mrs. Yonge, how delightful to see you. How is your dear mother? Feeling better these days, I hope?"

Mary Elizabeth wanted to shake her head at her mother's ability to smile and converse while they were in the middle of an emotional crisis. Indeed, her mother could have made a grand actress of the stage.

Their progress through the churchyard was necessarily slow as Elizabeth paused every few feet to speak to neighbors and acquaintances. Even though they were fairly new to the Lexington area, Lady Elizabeth had wasted little time in creating a large social circle around herself. George Strand might be roundly disliked, but few found fault with Lady Elizabeth.

Or her daughter. Mary Elizabeth knew that she was accepted in this community and that Andrew's friends all approved of a marriage between them. That made today's action doubly hard. She would be cutting herself off from not just Andrew, but from the friends she had made here. For that reason, every one of these small social visits was a blessing to cling to, while postponing the inevitable.

But she could put off the dreaded conversation for only so long. The crowd in the churchyard had thinned as parishioners made their way to their carriages, or set off to walk home. It was impossible to avoid Andrew now for he was heading toward her, his stride determined. She watched him come, enjoying the way he moved with such supple strength, but she frowned as he neared, for his beloved face was bruised and swollen.

She turned to her mother. "What happened to Andrew?" Fury ripped through her, for she thought she already knew the answer. "Was this Papa's doing?"

"Your father did not lay a hand on Mr. Byrne," her mother said calmly, though her eyes were watchful.

"Did Papa tell you of this?"

She said carefully, "Your father mentioned that he'd heard Mr. Byrne had been beset by footpads."

Mary Elizabeth saw the resignation in her mother's eyes. She knew the explanation for it what it was—an excuse. There were no bands of robbers working the area. If there had been, she would have heard of it, since keeping the town safe was of great concern to Andrew and his friends. He would have mentioned it to her.

"Was Papa behind this?" She kept her voice low, but there was furious demand in it, nonetheless.

Her mother shrugged. "Darling, please. This is not the time, nor the place for such a discussion. Mr. Byrne is fine, as you can see. You must do what your father has requested of you today."

Anger made Mary Elizabeth's cheeks heat. *Requested?* Her father had *ordered* her to break with Andrew. And her mother was evading her questions. The one person she trusted the most next to Andrew, was lying to her now. Mary Elizabeth's heart broke as outrage simmered in her mind, clarifying her thoughts as the quiet calm of the church had not.

"Concentrate instead on saying your goodbyes to Mr. Byrne," her mother said patting her hand. "It's for the best, my dearest."

Before Mary Elizabeth could reply, Andrew was upon them. The bruises on his face could not detract from how handsome he looked in his dark blue coat, and contrasting gray waistcoat. His breeches were blue, like the coat, and his black boots, polished to a high shine. His thick black hair was tied back at his nape with a black ribbon.

Her breath caught as her eyes met his. Her stomach felt as though butterflies were flitting around inside as he drew near. She loved him. She could not let him go.

She removed her hand from her mother's arm and extended it for Andrew to take. He lifted her fingers to his lips as his gaze captured hers. "Mary Elizabeth." The way he said her name was both an endearment and a caress. It made her shiver. Made her yearn for more stolen kisses.

Her mother cleared her throat.

Andrew lowered Mary Elizabeth's hand and shot a polite glance her mother's way as he amended his greeting. "Lady Elizabeth," he said with a nod. He turned back to Mary Elizabeth and smiled warmly. "Miss Strand. I hope I find you well?"

"You do," she said, "but Andrew, your poor eye! What happened to you?" She used his Christian name deliberately. He would expect her to, for they had been calling each other by their intimate, personal names for weeks now. When she said her little good-bye speech she planned to change how she addressed him, using his more formal surname. She hoped he would understand that the switch was purposeful and that her words were not really hers at all.

She hoped.

He looked at her steadily. She thought she saw a message in that look, but she couldn't be sure. It seemed that they were both talking in code today.

"I was set upon by ruffians," he said, with a deliberate glance at her mother. "I believe a request I made to a mutual acquaintance caused him to resort to uncivilized tactics."

Mary Elizabeth's eyes widened in shock. So, she had been right to question the story about footpads operating in the area. She looked at her mother in dismay. When she turned back to Andrew her eyes were blurred from unshed tears. "Andrew, I am so sorry."

He reached for her hand and kissed it once more. "Fear not, my dearest lady, I am resolute. It would take more than a pair of black-guards to turn me from my path." His lips turned up in the insouciant grin she loved so much and her heart did a little flip. He was so very dear to her.

"Mr. Byrne!" her mother said. Her voice was frosty. Though Andrew was a head taller, she managed to look down her aristocratic nose at him. "You forget yourself. Mary Elizabeth, we must return to your father. Do you have something you wish to say to Mr. Byrne?"

She almost said no. Then she sighed. "Andrew..."

Her mother cleared her throat.

"Andrew," Mary Elizabeth said again. This time she stared deliberately into his eyes, then flicked her gaze toward her mother before she began again. "Mr. Byrne, I am sorry to say that I cannot speak with you again. I believe we must part." Another flick of her gaze toward her mother. "Forever."

His dark brows met in a quick frown. "You do not wish to receive my courtship any longer?"

She carefully arranged her features into the saddest expression she could manage without her mother protesting. "I—It is necessary. You understand, do you not?"

"No, I do not," he said. He cast an angry glance at her mother. "However, I am not surprised, given your father's frosty reception to my request for your hand."

"We wish you good day, Mr. Byrne," Lady Elizabeth said curtly. "Come, Mary Elizabeth. We will not remain here to listen to this young upstart disparage your father." She caught Mary Elizabeth's elbow and turned her toward their carriage where George Strand and Colonel Bradley waited.

She had one last chance. "Andrew—" Surely, he would see the

despair and desperation in her expression and know that she was being coerced.

Her mother tugged her arm, frowning prodigiously.

Glancing from her to her mother, his eyes widened as he suddenly realized the message she was trying to convey. He nodded, then said in a low voice that only she could hear, "Be well, sweetheart."

Her heart swelled. "I'll wait for you, Andrew," she whispered, choking back a sob as her mother towed her toward the carriage.

CHAPTER 4

The carriage lurched over yet another rut, jarring everyone inside. Mary Elizabeth gritted her teeth and thought, not for the first time, that it would have been much easier to walk to and from church. The day was beautiful and sunny, the temperature not too hot. Her father, however, believed that walking would diminish their status in this small community. Servants, he said, walked. Their masters did not. So the Strand family endured the rutted road home.

Lady Elizabeth had kept the conversation flowing. She was doing it, Mary Elizabeth knew, to allow her to regain her composure after the emotional conversation with Andrew. She was also doing it to show her daughter what a fine catch Colonel Bradley was.

He was certainly well-bred, holding up his end of the conversation Lady Elizabeth initiated with a quiet ease. Several times Mary Elizabeth caught her mother looking at her with a glance that said, '*See what a charming man he is? The kind of man who would make a woman an excellent husband.*' She also felt the colonel's thoughtful gaze on her several times. She tried to ignore it, but she knew the man was trying to read her emotions, to decide if she was as willing to receive his advances as, no doubt, her parents had said she was.

The carriage ride seemed interminable. The conversation inevitably had to include Mary Elizabeth, even though she didn't want it to. "Mary Elizabeth was able to enjoy several weeks in London last year while we were visiting my brother, the earl, and his family," Lady Elizabeth said.

At that, Colonel Bradley smiled. "How did you enjoy the city, Miss Strand? I am desolated to say that I was stationed abroad at the time. I would have liked to have shown you the sites."

Lady Elizabeth answered for Mary Elizabeth, bestowing an approving smile on him. "Your escort would have been much welcomed, Colonel, particularly by my brother, who said that there was little in London to hold one's attention beyond the fashionable salons of the beau monde."

Mary Elizabeth's memory of her uncle was of a portly man who didn't like to be bothered with anything that didn't provide him with his own entertainment. Still, she couldn't say that to a stranger like Colonel Bradley. "The parties were quite magnificent, sir. We regularly were out half the night and slept the day away as a consequence." She smiled at him. "Quite different from my usual schedule."

He smiled back. In fact, he chuckled sympathetically as if he found her observation quite entertaining. "I have heard my mother and sisters complain that the fashionable season can be exhausting. Yet they love it and insist on joining my father in town when he is there to deal with matters in Parliament."

"Your father is elected to the House of Commons?" Mary Elizabeth asked. She knew nothing of Colonel Bradley's family, only that her parents approved of him.

"The Lords," her father ground out.

Colonel Bradley smiled gently. "My father is the Viscount Camberly. He is a friend of your uncle's. Indeed, your mother's family and mine have a long history of alliances."

The word hovered in the coach, simple, but ambiguous. "Alliances, Colonel Bradley?" she asked. The question came out breathlessly, because her heart was racing with dismay. Was the man proposing to her? Here? In the jostling coach, in front of her parents?

"Why yes, Miss Strand. Their political beliefs tend to coincide and I know that your grandfather and mine worked together to ensure important bills were passed."

Her heartbeat slowed down and she stopped feeling as if she couldn't breathe. "Of course," she murmured. Her father shot a sardonic look her way. She pressed her lips together. She'd had enough of this conversation.

"I believe my husband said that you have been offered a position in the Horse Guards after your mission here is completed?" Lady Elizabeth remarked, when it was clear that Mary Elizabeth had nothing more to say.

The colonel inclined his head slightly. "Indeed, my lady, you are correct." He turned his gaze back to Mary Elizabeth. "When you are next in London, Miss Strand, I will be able to escort you to the park or to see the sites. And I hope that you will allow me to dance with you at the many balls."

Mary Elizabeth managed a slight, smile. It would certainly be a change from her only Season. She'd spent all those hours at fashionable parties standing on the edge of the dance floor overhearing the other debutantes gossip that she was nothing but a vulgar colonial, while their mothers whispered behind their fans about how sadly forthright she was, not to mention that she was quite on the shelf. She'd even heard one grand lady say that there was nothing a man found quite so dull as an assertive, intelligent woman.

While Mary Elizabeth liked the idea of being defined as intelligent, she hated being the object of speculation and derision. So she spent the parties and grand balls standing apart. No young men asked her to dance and no one asked for her hand, much to both her father's and her uncle's annoyance. A waste, of his time, her uncle had complained. Later, her father, writing from America, chastised her for not making suitable use of the investment he had made in her future.

Except that the future he had invested in wasn't the one Mary Elizabeth wanted. She was one and twenty years old. Her family had come to America when she was only four and ten. In the years before the family left England she had spent most of her time in a select school for girls and had seen her parents very little. The school had been pleasant enough. She was the granddaughter of an earl, which gave her more rank that some of the girls in the school, but less than others. Still, she hadn't been picked on or ostracized. She'd enjoyed learning, but had made no close friends.

Then her father had decided that he would bring both his wife and daughter to the colonies with him and she'd come to Boston. Instead of a school, she'd had a tutor for her lessons and her mother to teach her how to manage a household. She and her mother had become close, though her relationship with her father remained cool. She met and became friends with the daughters of prominent Bostonians. While her father associated with men who were committed to retaining British rule, she found the American girls friendlier and more open. They were also far more forthright English ladies of her acquaintance and far more likely to express their views and take a stand on an issue.

It was a trait Mary Elizabeth loved, but one that brought her into conflict with her father far too often. Eventually, he decided it was time she wed and she was sent home to England for the wretched Season.

It didn't take several months in overheated London ballrooms for Mary Elizabeth to know her own mind. She'd grown into a woman in the colonies and she had discovered that she thrived in the freer society. She didn't want to return to England. Nor did she want a marriage within the English aristocracy with a man who cared nothing for his wife or what she believed in.

No. She wanted Andrew. She wanted to marry him, to create a life together with him. Here. In America.

The carriage turned ponderously into the lane leading up to the house. Mary Elizabeth breathed a sigh of relief. The strained conversation would soon be over. She would be sent back to her room to serve out the punishment her father had meted out to her. She welcomed it.

The solitude of her bedroom would be a welcome relief to the subtle pressure of the colonel's courtship.

It was the colonel who handed her down from the coach. She thanked him with a polite smile and a slight curtsey. After they entered the house, she headed for the stairs, knowing she must return to her chamber.

"You will join us for the mid-day meal in one hour, Mary Elizabeth," her father said.

She looked at him, wide-eyed.

"See that you are not tardy," he said, his tone sharp, his words a brisk command.

She fought down a momentary panic. It was only lunch, after all. She shouldn't be surprised that her father would provide Colonel Bradley another opportunity to court her. She lowered her eyes and curtseyed again. "Yes, sir."

The luncheon was a substantial repast. George Strand had brought a French trained chef with him to America, so the many courses were more like those served in an aristocratic household in England, than in an American one. The first course was a smooth and savory beef bouillon. That was followed by at fresh-caught trout, pan-fried with thyme and lemon. The meat was roasted lamb, served with a mint sauce. At the end of the meal, cheese and biscuits followed a fresh baked apple tart. Mary Elizabeth ate heartily, not sure when she would next enjoy a feast such as this. There were a few times when she noticed the colonel watching her with raised eyebrows, but she didn't care.

The conversation at the table flowed steadily thanks to her mother. They discussed the current political situation in the colonies and Mary Elizabeth was not surprised to learn that the colonel held similar views to her father. The colonists needed to be taught a lesson, he said at one point and she thought how much fun Andrew and his friends would have had with a comment like that one. They would not allow it to pass without a response, she was sure. She considered asking why it was so important to suppress the aspirations of the colonists, rather than treating them as equals and allies, but knew that she would be thoroughly denounced if she did. So, she remained silent and continued to fill her belly with delicacies while she could.

When the meal was over, her mother remarked the afternoon was so fine that the colonel and Mary Elizabeth should take a turn about the garden.

Mary Elizabeth frowned. "But, I thought—" She expected to be banished to her room. This change in scenario was bringing butterflies to life in her stomach.

"I should be delighted if you would walk with me," the colonel said.

"Of course, she will," her father said. He shot Mary Elizabeth a cold look she interpreted to mean she should remember her place.

"Yes, of course." She agreed, but all those warning butterflies were telling her this stroll did not bode well.

They stepped onto the terrace at the back of the house that led to the gardens. As they walked down the stairs onto a graveled path, Bradley took her hand and settled it on his arm. He held it there with his hand over hers as they strolled. "Your father has very kindly allowed me the opportunity to speak privately to you."

That was true. They were out of earshot of the house, even though they were in full view of her parents, who were sitting on the terrace. "It is a very pleasant afternoon," she said, rather desperately trying to keep the conversation to unremarkable topics.

The colonel wasn't about to play along. "My father has reached old age and his health is no longer as robust as it once was. I am a second son, but my brother does not enjoy good health either."

He paused and Mary Elizabeth took the opportunity to leap in. "I fear that you must worry about your family, Colonel Bradley. I trust that your brother regains his health."

The colonel stared ahead. "Thank you. Your warm heart speaks well of you. I do not expect—That is to say, I believe that my wife will one day be Lady Camberly. As such it is important that I marry into a good family, although at the moment my prospects are only those of a serving officer and younger son."

"You...You are very practical about the subject of marriage, Colonel."

"As I must be." They had reached the end of the garden. Here the path rounded an ornamental bush. While they made the turn, they would be obscured from the prying eyes of her parents on the terrace. He stopped and shifted so that they were facing each other. "My brother's ill health is not widely known. As well, he may yet marry and sire children. My accession to the title is not guaranteed. An alliance with your family would benefit me and marriage to me is perhaps a better match than you might expect, having spent so many years here in the colonies."

When he first began this speech, Mary Elizabeth thought that he was complimenting her, but by the time he was finished she realized what he really meant. "You have not been able to find a wife high enough to suit you and your aspirations, have you, Colonel Bradley?"

His face flushed scarlet. "I am offering you the chance to marry well and perhaps to gain a title. I have nothing to apologize for."

"No." Sadness and perhaps resignation filled her. "You are asking me to settle, as you have decided you must settle, for second best."

Anger sparked in his eyes. "I assure you, madam, that I have done nothing of the sort."

"Then you are very fortunate, Colonel. I, on the other hand, do feel that marriage to a man I hardly know and one I do not love, would surely be settling for less than I deserve and desire."

"The American," he said, his tone clipped.

She lowered her eyes, but didn't respond. He was an officer in the army, after all. He could easily make life very difficult for Andrew if he so desired.

"Your father informed me a jumped-up colonist had set his cap for you. The effrontery!"

She looked into his face and realized that he would use the excuse of another man to ease his damaged pride. The danger to Andrew seemed to grow with each passing moment. "I have no desire to be a titled lady, or to live on a great estate in England and be a member of the beau monde. I am happy here, in the colonies. It is where I feel most comfortable, most at ease with myself."

Relief chased affront from his expression and a smile lightened his face. "I have pressed my suit too ardently, too quickly. You need time to reflect. I understand that. I shall not ask for your hand as I had planned, nor will I demand an answer. Not today. But I assure you, sweet lady, I will not value you any the less."

His reaction wasn't exactly what Mary Elizabeth wanted to hear, but at least he was no longer focused on Andrew as a rival. That meant Andrew was safe, at least for the moment.

They strolled back to the house. Mary Elizabeth had her hands clasped in front of her; the colonel's were behind his back. As they mounted the stairs to the terrace Mary Elizabeth saw that her father was frowning.

"What news?" he said, scrutinizing them both from beneath his brows.

"Miss Strand is a very charming young lady," Bradley said. "But I fear she has no desire to live in England. I hope to convince her otherwise, however."

"How very kind of you, Colonel," her mother said brightly, but her eyes were wary.

Her father's frown turned into a glare. "Mary Elizabeth, a moment in my study, if you please."

"Yes, Papa." She knew what the visit to the study meant. She was being banished to her room again after a lecture on the evils of refusing the Colonel's offer of marriage. She turned to Bradley. "Colonel, it has been a pleasure meeting you." She didn't add that she hoped he would be gone by the time she was allowed out of her room.

The colonel smiled and bowed. "The pleasure is all mine, dear lady."

Her heart sank. He had the look of a man who had made a decision.

And it wasn't the one she wanted.

CHAPTER 5

As Andrew watched George Strand's large, ponderous coach lumber away from the church, he realized the man's desire to rise within the ranks of the elite would mean he would never allow his daughter to marry a colonist.

In that moment when Mary Elizabeth and Colonel Bradley had emerged from the church looking like a newly wedded couple, his heart had fallen to the pit of his stomach. Her clumsy attempt to convince him that she no longer wanted to marry him, combined with her cautious glances at her mother, had relieved him of that worry. She had obviously spoken the words under duress. She was as much his today as she had been before he asked her father for her hand.

So how to overcome the obstacle of her father? By law, the man had every right to choose his daughter's husband. However, society was changing. To coerce a daughter into an unwanted marriage was becoming less common. Still, it did happen.

Deep in thought, Andrew strolled to the hitching line where his horse was tied. Thanks to his weeklong visit with his Faith in the twenty-first century, he'd gleaned that he and Mary Elizabeth would eventually marry. He also knew that the ceremony would take place in

New York City. How they would get there, however, he had no idea. Nor, for that matter, did Faith.

He mounted his horse as he contemplated how much easier it would be if he could simply recreate what he already knew had happened. As it was, he would have to figure out something himself. Annoying, but certainly not beyond his imagination and capabilities.

New York City, he thought, was many days distant by horse or coach. A post road from Boston to New York through Hartford and Springfield had been established a hundred years before to ensure the mail was delivered between the two cities in a timely fashion. Mr. Benjamin Franklin had reorganized the postal system, and now post riders on fast horses could travel the route in four days, riding day and night. A coach, carrying two passengers and traveling only by day, would take much longer. It would be easy for a mounted man—or one with a troop of dragoons behind him—to overtake a carriage.

They would have a better chance traveling by sea, which was not only faster, but it was safer as well. However, to sail down the coast to New York would mean going into Boston town and finding a ship's captain who was willing to brave the wrath of George Strand, who was an important member of the government.

Riding slowly, he considered that idea. Though Boston might be the obvious choice as a departure point due to its size and busy harbor, it could be risky as well, given George Strand's influence in the city. If they were to travel to New York by sea, perhaps they should leave from another, smaller seaport. Salem, in the north, for instance, or one of the ports farther south. There were drawbacks to that option as well. While it might be easier to find a captain and a ship to sail in at one of those ports, the overland journey from Lexington would be longer. And the longer he and Mary Elizabeth were on the road, the more likely it would be that George Strand would catch up with them.

There was also the problem of the other end of the sea voyage. Would Strand think to have a message sent to the harbormasters at all the major cities along the coast? A message that requested Andrew

Byrne be detained and Mary Elizabeth Strand be sent back to her father in Boston?

The more he thought about getting married in New York, the more fraught with danger the idea became. According to Faith and her family, it had happened, but how had he managed it? He snorted at this thought and the horse pricked its ears. How *would* he do it was more to the point.

Spiriting Mary Elizabeth away from her parents' home was as complex a problem as transporting her safely to New York. Strand knew he wished to marry her. He must also know that his daughter reciprocated Andrew's feelings. He would keep a close eye on her to ensure she didn't slip away into her lover's waiting arms.

He sighed. This problem had so many levels he wasn't sure he would be able to find a safe path forward. He knew something of his future, but not enough for the information to be helpful. In fact, it would have been easier if he'd known nothing at all. Rather than tying himself into knots trying to figure out how he would get her to New York City, he would have simply figured out how he would marry her.

He kicked the horse into a run, enjoying the rush of wind against his face they galloped down the road. A turn was ahead and he suspected that he'd soon see the Strand's coach. He didn't want to pass it, so he aimed the horse toward the fence that separated the road from a field. He reveled in the soaring motion as they leapt over the fence, man and beast as one. Making a smooth landing, Andrew kept his horse at a fast clip.

He reached home, exhilarated by the headlong gallop across country, but with no good ideas on how to get himself and Mary Elizabeth to New York City. By Wednesday evening he'd completed a prodigious amount of work on his accounts and in the management of his acreage, but no flashes of inspiration had come to him. He decided to go into Lexington to see what news he could ferret out.

His destination was the Moon and Stars tavern where he often met with friends like Ron Aiken. Men who believed as he did that America was the equal of Britain and deserved a representative government of its own. There they would share a mug of ale while they discussed the issues of the day. Upon arrival, he tied his horse behind the building and strode to the front entrance. He'd discovered on a previous visit to Faith's time that the building still existed. It was no longer called the Moon and Stars, and people labeled it a restaurant, not a tavern, but its purpose was the same—a gathering place that served excellent food and drink.

He liked that some parts of his time still existed in the future. The twenty-first century was so very different from his own that those few remnants of his world were a reassurance of continuity.

Inside, the tavern opened into one large room. At the back was a long oak bar, with shelves holding various bottles of spirits. Round tables sturdily built of local pine and darkened with smoke and age, dotted the room. Most of the seats were taken and the tables were loaded with tankards of ale and plates of hearty stew with baskets of crusty bread. To the left, on the far wall, a doorway led into a smaller snug for men who preferred to engage in private conversation.

Andrew cast a quick look around. Windows were small and spare and the candle sconces that fixed to the walls didn't shed much light into the depths of the expansive room. He thought about the twenty-first century restaurant that had replaced the tavern. There had been fixtures designed to replicate the candle sconces of his time utilizing a magic current Faith called electricity—energy that flowed from the ground and into the wall where it connected to various fixtures and generated light so strong it mimicked daylight. It was remarkable really. Faith had told him that Mr. Franklin was most known for working with electrical currents. That surprised Andrew, who thought his work with the postal service much more practical.

In Faith's time the old wooden beams in the ceiling were darker and absorbed some of that bright electrical light, adding warmth to the room. Though the wood was newer and paler now, in his time, it had no effect on the light quality. He cursed the dim light provided by the candles and narrowed his eyes, searching for congenial company.

He spied Ron Aiken sitting with a group of men in a far corner.

Ron raised his hand in greeting and Andrew made his way over to the table.

"Sit, my friend," he said. "What brings you into town on this fine evening?"

Andrew shrugged. "I felt the need of a pint with friends." He signaled the barmaid for a drink. She knew his preferences and nodded. Andrew turned back to his friends. "What news?"

There were shakes of the head, frowns and cautious sideways glances. The talk, then, was about the injustices perpetrated by the British overlords. Voices were lowered and someone always kept watch to ensure no one came too close and overheard.

Andrew didn't mind talking sedition, which was how George Strand would brand the conversation, should he happen to overhear them. Andrew called it asserting the rights that every landowner and free Englishman expected. There was a pause in the conversation when his pint arrived and was paid for, then they were back at it.

It wasn't until much later that the topic of George Strand and his daughter came up. It was Ron Aiken who did the talking. "You know Lucy Weaver—she works at Strand's place over by you, Andrew."

Andrew nodded.

"Well, she was in town for her afternoon off and stopped in for a bite to eat. She mentioned that old man Strand has decided his daughter is to marry that officer who's visiting them."

Andrew nodded again. "I suspected it after the way Strand was showing him off at church on Sunday. Before they left the churchyard, Lady Elizabeth had Mary Elizabeth make a stiff little speech about not seeing me again, but I didn't believe it."

His friend sighed. "She may not want to marry the fellow, but Strand is determined that they wed and has taken action accordingly."

"How?" Andrew asked, dreading the answer.

There was compassion in his friend's expression. "Lucy said he's locked Mary Elizabeth in her room and won't allow her to leave until she agrees. She said that he's put her on short rations, hoping that hunger will make her more pliable."

Andrew stared at his friend. This was terrible news, indeed. He knew Strand was ruthless, but to treat his daughter this way showed a coldness that sent a cold shiver down Andrew's back. It was followed by fury. "The bastard!"

"Aye," his friend said, and the others at the table nodded agreement.

"I'll kill him," Andrew said, through tight lips.

"Not the best idea," Ron said. "The English colonel would seek you out and you'd find yourself strung up for a certainty. Then what use would you be to Mary Elizabeth?"

Ron was right. The future that he knew depended upon his marriage to Mary Elizabeth. If they did not wed, he might never have children—or descendants. When his sister and her husband died far too young, her children would be orphaned. He would raise them, of course, but their lives would be the lesser without Mary Elizabeth to love them as their mother would. Faith might never be born and he would not travel into her future world.

If he and Mary Elizabeth did not marry, the time line would be changed irrevocably. Who knew how that would change other lives, both those with direct connections to the Beacon-Traveler network, and others who had no idea that travel through time was even possible. He drew a deep breath. He would not change the future, he could not.

What he could do was plan to get Mary Elizabeth to New York and once there marry her as quickly as possible. He nodded to Ron. "Good advice. But mark my words, gentlemen. I will wed Mary Elizabeth Strand. Sooner, rather than later."

Aiken raised his glass. There was a twinkle in his eyes. "To marital bliss."

Andrew laughed. "I can drink to that."

CHAPTER 6

The next morning, having accepted that his marriage to Mary Elizabeth would be both hasty and stealthy, Andrew set about planning how he could make it come to pass. He knew he must spirit Mary Elizabeth away before her father forced her to marry Colonel Bradley, and to do that he had to make sure that George Strand couldn't intervene. That's where the stealthy part came in. He and Mary Elizabeth would have to slip away without anyone the wiser so the alert would not be raised too swiftly, thus allowing them to put a good distance between themselves and their pursuers.

If Ron Aiken was correct, and George Strand had locked Mary Elizabeth in her bedchamber, slipping away would be difficult. Opportunities would be few and perhaps unexpected, so he would have to be prepared.

His first task would be to arrange their wedding in New York. He wrote his sister, explaining the situation and asking for her help to procure a special license so that he and Mary Elizabeth could marry upon their arrival in the city. As he dusted sand over the paper to blot the ink, he decided he could not entrust a missive as important as this one to Mr. Franklin's postal service, even though it was now much more efficient than it once had been. He'd ride into Boston himself and arrange for a courier to deliver it to his sister directly. Still, it would take more than a week for it to arrive and a response to be returned. He shook his head as he sealed the letter with his signet ring. Time was not on his side.

With the letter written, he immediately set off for Boston. As he rode he considered his next steps. Contact Mary Elizabeth first? No, much as he wanted to speak to her, to reassure himself that she was all right and that she was still committed to their union, he knew he should have his plan made and the details organized before he took the risk of reaching out to her.

The more he thought about it, the more he wished he knew the exact date he and Mary Elizabeth would marry. He could then work backward to figure out what had to be done by when. By the time he'd reached Boston and left the letter with the courier he regularly used to send messages to New York, he'd made up his mind. When he returned that night he would look for Faith's beacon shining in the grove that would lead him to her home in the twenty-first century. He would visit her tonight and he would find the answers he sought.

It was just before six in the evening when he stepped through the center of the beacon into Faith's kitchen.

She was standing by the stove and she wasn't alone. Her lover and now fiancé, Cody, was standing at the big maple table and he was opening a bottle of wine with a corkscrew.

Also at the table were Faith's sister, Liz, her mother, Chloe, and her father, Daniel. At the sight of Daniel Hamilton, Andrew almost groaned. What the devil was he doing here tonight of all nights? He did not get along with the man, and never had. Daniel refused to accept that being a Beacon for a Traveler who moved through time was a blessing and that traveling itself was an opportunity only given to a few. No, Faith's father considered it a freakish disability that diminished both his ex-wife, Chloe who was a Traveler, and his daughter, Faith who was a Beacon.

To be sure, he had apparently mellowed since Faith's fiancé Cody had joined the family group. Cody, himself a mathematician of considerable repute, was fascinated by Faith's ability and never hesitated to defend her from Daniel's occasional swipes.

It was Daniel, dressed formally in a well-cut dark blue suit in the twenty-first century style that Andrew thought efficient, but dull, who noticed him first. "What the hell are you doing here? This isn't your night. You're not due until tomorrow."

That was true. His regular visiting night was Friday. "Needs must, my dear Hamilton," he said, then bowed with a flourish that involved considerable hand movements and bended knee. He kept his eyes on Daniel as he went through the motions and was pleased to see the man's cheeks redden and anger flash in his eyes.

"Andrew!" Faith said. She had turned away from the stove and was staring at him, a frown between her eyes. "Is there a problem?"

Faith was dressed in what she'd once described as a cocktail dress. Cocktails, Andrew had learned on a previous visit, were potent alcoholic drinks that eased a person's inhibitions and sometimes made them forget their manners. The dress, therefore, was worn for festive occasions. Short, figure hugging, and black, the neckline dipped to a vee and had three quarter length sleeves. Her golden blonde hair was loose, curling over her shoulders. The contrast with the black fabric made it gleam in the overhead lights. Andrew thought, with some amusement, that the garment was meant to appeal to Cody, but be formal enough for an occasion as well.

"Of course there's a problem or he wouldn't be here," Daniel said, impatience in his voice.

"That's not true, Dad. Andrew is my dear friend. He knows he can come forward any time he needs to."

"Thank you, dear lady," Andrew said as he sauntered over to Faith. He lifted her hand to his mouth and pantomimed kissing the back. He knew the gesture would annoy Daniel even more.

Faith sighed and murmured, "Andrew," as she shook her head.

Andrew straightened and grinned at her before he turned to face the others. He noted that Daniel had snapped his mouth shut in a hard line and his whole body had tensed. More and more pleased by how his arrival had been received, he said, "Mistress Chloe, well met. The lovely Miss Elizabeth, it is a pleasure as usual." They too were wearing cocktail dresses. Since Cody, like Daniel, was dressed in a suit—his was a dark gray, matched with a pale blue shirt and a dark blue tie—Andrew was quite certain an event was in the offing.

Cody finished pouring a glass of wine and brought it to him. A glint of amusement flickered in his eyes. "Your timing is impeccable, Andrew. I can hardly wait to see how my parents react to you."

"Oh!" Faith put her hand to her mouth. "They'll be here in a half an hour. I'd forgotten."

"I thought you might have," Cody said without apparent dismay. He brushed a light kiss on Faith's lips. Daniel made a harrumphing sound that had Chloe shooting a dirty look his way. "We'll tell them that Andrew is an actor prepping for a role," Cody said. "That will explain the velvet coat, gold braiding and ruffles, not to mention the extravagant manner."

"Why would some random actor be here when this is a dinner for family?" Daniel said, not about to be placated.

"He's not random, Dad! He *is* family," Liz said. She was able to get away with the defense because she was the only one of Daniel's family who wasn't a Beacon or a Traveler.

"Long ago," Daniel said, his tone softening as he turned to his daughter. "Now he's just a pain in the butt."

Andrew raised a brow at Daniel's crudeness and sipped his wine as Cody grabbed another glass and went back to pouring. "I'll not stay long enough to be introduced to your excellent parents, Master Cody, my friend. I've a request to make and then I'll be on my way."

"You should stay," Cody said, passing a glass to Chloe. "They'll have to meet you sooner or later, since I've asked you to be my best man."

"How will he host the bachelor party?" Liz wondered.

Cody grinned. "Now there's a thought, since he can't be in this time unless Faith is nearby. Maybe she'll have to hide in the cake." He passed glasses to Liz and Daniel.

Hide in a cake? Andrew looked at Faith and thought about the size of the average cake. He raised his brow. "That would be a feat of some considerable engineering skill and one I would like to see."

Cody chuckled and Daniel snorted with disdain.

Andrew opened his eyes wide and taunted, "I think it is a task for an engineering expert such as yourself, Hamilton."

He was rewarded when Daniel burst out, "Why you—"

"Dad, he's teasing," Faith said. She shook her finger at Andrew. "Behave."

"But he is so easy to raise to anger," Andrew murmured wickedly.

Cody picked up two glasses, came over to stand close to Faith, and handed her one. As he sipped, he looked at Andrew over his glass. "Since you didn't know that we were having a family introduction and wedding planning session tonight, is there any particular reason you decided to visit?"

He couldn't lie to Cody, whom he admired. "It is Mary Elizabeth."

"Ah," said Cody.

"Chloe has already told you too much!" Daniel grumbled.

"I have not," Chloe retorted indignantly.

"Did you not tell him about his marriage last time he was here?"

That had been the day George Strand had rejected his request for Mary Elizabeth's hand and had set his henchmen to assault him. He had come forward to seek sanctuary, unaware that Faith had planned an intimate evening for two with Cody. His arrival filled Faith's house with family members, all determined to add their input on how he should proceed in his quest for Mary Elizabeth's hand. The quiet dinner Faith had planned became a riotous evening of family squabbles and, eventually, delight, as Cody proved his love to Faith.

It was while Faith and Cody had stolen away for a few minutes of privacy that Chloe provided Andrew with a few clues about his future with Mary Elizabeth. To Andrew's mind they were far from enough, tantalizing, not definitive.

Chloe must have thought the same way for she tightened her lips at her ex-husband's taunt, and shot him a fulminating look.

Daniel pressed harder, forcing her to answer. "Didn't you?"

"Well, maybe," she hedged.

"That's a yes," Daniel said, looking pleased.

If he didn't wrest the conversation back to his reason for being here this evening, Daniel would continue to complain about the Beacon and all that it entailed until Master Cody's family arrived. "Mary Elizabeth's father is keeping her prisoner in her bedchamber and allowing her only rations of bread and water," he said. That statement produced the effect he wanted. Conversation stopped. All eyes focused on him. As he continued, anger had his voice rising, but he didn't care. "He has found a suitor for her, but she refuses to accept the fellow's offer of marriage. Strand wishes to starve her into obedience."

"That's terrible!" Liz said.

Cody sipped his wine and watched him over the edge of his glass. Faith opened the oven door and pulled out a cooking tray.

Andrew sniffed and focused on the contents. Sausage rolls. His favorite.

"You can't tell him anything," Daniel said, mainly to Chloe, but also to the room at large.

Leaving the sausage rolls to cool a moment, Faith turned back to Andrew. "Unfortunately, Dad is right. The less you know about your future, the better."

Andrew glared at Daniel, who returned the look with a sneer of his own.

Chloe sighed. "Though it pains me to do it, I must agree with Daniel. Things will play out as they are supposed to. You have to be patient, Andrew."

"Patient! How can I be patient when the lady I love, a gentle kind lady who has done nothing wrong, is being abused by one who should be her steadfast protector?"

There was silence for a moment. It was Cody who broke it. His tone thoughtful, he said, "I suspect the answer is less than you desire, Andrew, and more than you would allow, Daniel."

Faith slid the sausage rolls onto a platter, then held it out to Andrew. He took one and popped it into his mouth. The ease of food preparation was one of the best things about the twenty-first century, he reflected, along with vehicles that moved swiftly along paved road-ways and information machines that contained all the knowledge of the universe. "Let me use your computer, Faith."

"No," she said, and passed the platter to Cody.

Cody plucked a roll from the tray, "What is it you want to know, Andrew?" he asked, taking a bite

"The date of my wedding."

"You already know it's in New York City," Chloe said. "Why do you need to know the exact date?"

"New York City is far distant and the man Strand intends for his daughter is a colonel in the dragoons—"

"Jonathan Bradley," Chloe said, thoughtfully. "He becomes a viscount."

"Really?" Liz said, sounding intrigued. "I didn't know that!"

"Mom!" Faith said.

"He's to be a lord?" This was getting worse and worse. "No wonder her brute of a father is so determined to force her into wedlock. I will have to steal Mary Elizabeth away, but to get her to New York without being captured by Bradley and his mounted soldiers is well nigh impossible!"

"I've wondered about that," Cody said. He wandered over to the table where Faith had deposited the platter and helped himself to another sausage roll.

"If I know the date it will help me decide if I should try to spirit her away by sea or try the longer, slower overland route," Andrew said. "I will also know when we must escape her father's clutches." He looked around, deliberately making eye contact with each of them, including Daniel. "Don't you see? Everything hinges on that date. Everything."

CHAPTER 7

"$\mathcal{M}$y dear, come and sit beside me." Lady Elizabeth patted the empty spot beside her on the rustic wooden bench.

After days locked in her room, Mary Elizabeth wanted to run through the gardens like a hoyden, not sit demurely beside her mother. The day was perfect, the blue sky cloudless, a light breeze offering a cooling contrast to the warmth of the mid-morning sun. Everything about the day raised Mary Elizabeth's spirits and urged her to move, to celebrate her brief freedom.

Her mother patted the seat again. Mary Elizabeth reluctantly gave up the notion of stretching her legs. Instead, she glided over to the bench, perching on the edge of the seat at an angle so that her mother was able to see her face as they spoke. She knew she looked and acted like a proper lady. A good thing, since she thought there was as very good chance that if she behaved in an ill-bred way, she'd be banished back .to her room immediately.

"Thank you for allowing me to spend some time in the garden today, Mama." She was careful to arrange the wide skirts of her pretty gown so that the fabric was not bunched up, creating wrinkles. The moss-green linen overskirt paired with a white underskirt embroidered with pale yellow roses was a favorite of hers. She'd chosen it this morning to buoy up her spirits. Her incarceration was beginning to seem endless and she knew she had to do something to keep her resolve not to bow to her father's demand that she wed Colonel Bradley.

Lady Elizabeth smiled. "You have been in that stuffy room for almost a week, Mary Elizabeth." She tapped her daughter's wrist with her fan in a teasing way that nonetheless conveyed a warning. "I thought an hour or so in the fresh air would do wonders for your attitude."

Mary Elizabeth looked away from her mother's gaze. She'd been allowed this respite so she would understand all that she was giving up by refusing to accept Colonel Bradley's proposal. "You are most kind, Mama." The simple joy of being in the outdoors was a seductive entice-ment indeed, compared to sitting in a locked room for hours on end with no pleasures to look forward to.

"Darling, I am so glad we have this opportunity to spend some time together." Lady Elizabeth beamed at her. "We'll have a lovely chat and I shall try to make you smile. Perhaps I shall even coax a laugh from you."

"I do not think that will be possible, Mama." Now she was here, in the garden, with the sunshine bathing the gravel walks, and lush flower beds perfuming the air, Mary Elizabeth was prepared to do what she could to prolong the reprieve, but laugher? There was no laughter in her heart when the purpose of her incarceration was to separate her from her beloved Andrew and force her into wedlock with a man she hardly knew.

"Darling." Lady Elizabeth sighed. "You must look at this from your papa's point of view...and mine."

Mary Elizabeth raised her brows—and bit her tongue.

"We both care for you greatly, daughter. You know that."

Did they? Her mother perhaps, but her father? She was nothing but a pawn in whatever game he was playing to advance his future prospects.

Lady Elizabeth cocked her head. "The young man you met here in

Lexington is charming in manner and very pretty to look at, but what do you know of him?"

"You wish me to list his virtues, Mama? That is most kind of you, for I believe we will be some hours in the detailing."

Lady Elizabeth pursed her lips in annoyance. "Come now, daughter. He cannot be such a paragon as that."

Mary Elizabeth looked out into the garden and sighed. "He is not. He is, as you say charming, having a delightful manner about him that is impossible not to like. More than that, though, he makes me feel needed, but also safe, when I am with him. He makes me smile, too." Unconsciously her mouth turned up at the corners, as her eyes grew dreamy. "And sometimes we laugh at the most absurd things. He is passionate in his beliefs..."

Lady Elizabeth drew in a breath to interrupt. Mary Elizabeth held up her hand to still her. "Yes, I know. He is one of those who believe that America should govern itself, which is something Papa deplores, but—"

"Your father does condemn those who indulge in rebellious behavior, Mary Elizabeth. There is no way around it. Consider this. If you were to marry your American charmer, you would be cutting yourself off from your family, for Papa would disown you."

"What about you, Mama? Would you disown me?"

Lady Elizabeth hesitated for a moment. "Yes."

Her mother's response caused her to suck in her breath. "Surely not, Mama!"

"I would have to," Lady Elizabeth said. Her voice was low, almost melancholy.

Mary Elizabeth's hand crept up to her throat, signaling her vulnerability.

"Your father is my husband, Mary Elizabeth. I must obey him in all things." She watched her daughter as she added with careful deliberation, "As you must."

"Mama, I do not dislike Colonel Bradley, but with him I do not feel the same wonderful emotions I feel when I am with Mr. Byrne.

Marriage is for a lifetime. My lifetime. How can I spend it with a man who is a stranger to me? One I care nothing for?"

Lady Elizabeth studied her for a minute, then she once more tapped Mary Elizabeth's hand with the fan. "Very easily, daughter. The passionate feelings Mr. Byrne has roused in you will fade with time as the troubles and problems of life pull you apart. Those troubles will make you realize that you and Mr. Byrne come from very different backgrounds and have interests that do not coincide. Colonel Bradley, however, is a man of our world. His family and mine have long been intertwined. You will have common expectations of life and how it should be lived."

"What if we do not?"

"It is up to you to ensure that you do."

"Ensuring the marriage works is my responsibility alone?"

"Of course not." Her mother eyed her critically. "But you must expect your husband to be focused on life outside the home. Colonel Bradley will have his career in the military, then later, he is pledged to embrace a political career. Your father expects him to become a powerful force within the government." She smiled at her daughter and reached for her hand. "You would be an excellent political wife, Mary Elizabeth. You are bright and your manner is charming...when you are not being difficult, that is."

Mary Elizabeth eyed her mother dubiously. Being labeled as charming when not being difficult was faint praise indeed.

"You will live in London, of course, with all of the social events that coincide with the parliamentary sessions," Lady Elizabeth continued. "Colonel Bradley has agreed to bestow a substantial sum on you upon your marriage. The amount indicates how wealthy his family is and how much they value him, as a second son who may or may not inherit. You would become a leader of the beau monde. Your influence would be great."

Mary Elizabeth had the distinct feeling that her mother was itemizing a future she had wished for herself. It certainly wasn't one Mary Elizabeth wanted. During her one season, when she'd travelled back to

England with her mother, she'd felt out of place at the dozens of balls they'd attended. There had been snide comments from the other young women, mocking her for being a mere colonial. As for dancing, Mary Elizabeth had spent most of the time sitting in one of the chairs lined up against the wall, with all the other wallflowers.

She'd hated everything about her season and the though of making her way to the forefront of London society was not a dream, but her own personal nightmare. She knew her mother wouldn't understand, however. "But what if I wish to remain here, in America, Mama?"

Lady Elizabeth raised her delicate eyebrows. She tapped her fan on Mary Elizabeth's wrist. "La, girl. What nonsense. Of course, you want to return to England. It is where your home is. Your family."

"We have lived in America eight years, Mama. I was a child when we sailed into Boston harbor. I grew to womanhood here. This is my home. My friends live here." She drew a deep breath. "The man I wish to marry lives here."

That statement hung heavily in the silence that followed. Her unrepentant gaze clashed with her mother's disappointed one, but she refused to look away.

It was Lady Elizabeth whose gaze shifted first. She stared out at the garden, rich with the vivid colors of late spring. There was frustration along with sadness in her voice as she said, "Marriage to that man is out of the question."

"Why, Mama?"

She turned then, to look at Mary Elizabeth, her brows arched. "I have explained. It is your father's wish. No, his decree. There will be no alliance between our family and Mr. Byrne's."

"Alliance! I love Mr. Byrne, Mama. I do not wish to marry him for his connections or the money he might bestow upon me."

Lady Elizabeth looked away again. "That is not the way society works, daughter." She drew a deep breath and when she looked at Mary Elizabeth again she smiled brightly, as if she were determined to seek and find the best of the situation. "An arranged marriage, such as the one your father has made with Colonel Bradley, is often the most satisfactory of partnerships. Neither party is blinded by strong emotions and they are able to work together in mutual respect."

Such a marriage sounded awful. Though Mary Elizabeth didn't say the words, the thought must have shown on her face for her mother rose from the bench with a look of finality on her face. "Marriage to Mr. Byrne is out of the question. I am sorry, Mary Elizabeth."

Mary Elizabeth rose too. "I cannot marry Colonel Bradley, Mama. Not when my heart belongs to Mr. Byrne."

"Think carefully, dearest." She cupped Mary Elizabeth's cheek. "There are many advantages to a marriage with Colonel Bradley. It is more than likely he will inherit his brother's title. He will be wealthy, a man of power. You would be pampered, your every need attended to."

"I cannot, Mama."

Her mother shook her head, and heaved a deep sigh. "You must change your mind, or you will be far worse off. Return to your room, now, but think on my advice."

Mary Elizabeth swept her mother a deep curtsey, her head bowed in submission she didn't feel. "As you wish, Mama."

As she turned away and headed for the house, she thought she heard her mother sigh and murmur, "Not as I wish."

She had been out in the garden less than an hour.

CHAPTER 8

On Sunday morning the maid who brought Mary Elizabeth a breakfast tray that consisted of the usual stale bread and a jug of water, told her that Mr. Strand and the Lady Elizabeth were expecting her to travel with them to church. She was to be in her mother's sitting room in precisely one hour.

Mary Elizabeth was both surprised and not surprised. As all members of the congregation attended the weekly church service, unless they were ill, her absence would be noticed. Questions would be asked. However, her father cared little for the good opinion of the citizens of Lexington. He was an expert at dampening pretentions and avoiding questions. If anyone inquired about her absence, he would simply raise a brow and shoot a disdainful look at the person who had the temerity to ask.

It must have been her mother who made the decision, she decided as she ate her meager rations. The food would ensure she didn't starve, but it wasn't enough to fill her belly. Nor did it lighten her mood as she considered what to wear. She knew that whatever she chose would be critiqued, but she couldn't bring herself to pick one of the gowns that featured bright colors, or a joyous riot of flowers embroidered into the cloth. Instead she picked a dun-colored gown that she paired with a leaf green underskirt. The dress was designed to be worn with narrow panniers. Her mother would know that she had chosen clothes more in keeping with a sensible countrywoman than the daughter of a man of influence, one who had the ear of the royal governor, but she hoped her father would not remark upon it. As the bodice was square and cut low, she added a fichu of the finest linen to fill it in and cover her respectably.

When she reached her mother's sitting room she discovered both her parents were waiting for her. That was curious. The room was small and boasted only a daybed for reclining and two armless chairs, along with an elegantly simple lady's writing desk. This was her mother's personal space, the place where she retired when she wanted to read quietly, or work on letters. Occasionally she invited Mary Elizabeth to join her. Then they would talk about practical things, like running a household or what attributes to look for when hiring new staff. They would also share thoughts about their neighbors, the social events they had participated in, and those that were upcoming. Until the issue with Colonel Bradley had occurred, Mary Elizabeth had believed that her mother enjoyed living in Lexington and valued the friends she'd made amongst the residents.

Perhaps she did value her connections in Lexington, but that hadn't prevented her from bowing to her husband's wishes. Over the past week Lady Elizabeth had made it very clear that the person behind the arrangement with Colonel Bradley was Mary Elizabeth's father, and that whatever her feelings, she must obey him in all things, even the ruination of her daughter's future.

As the parlor that opened off the entry hall was the room in which the family gathered, finding her father in her mother's domain alerted Mary Elizabeth that whatever message was about to be passed to her was one she could expect not to like.

Lady Elizabeth was seated on one of the armless chairs, the more comfortable one with the brocaded back and seat. Her hands were clasped in her lap and her expression was unreadable. Mary Elizabeth couldn't tell if she was uncomfortable with her husband's invasion of her small domain, or indifferent. She was wearing a gown cut on severe lines and as muted as Mary Elizabeth's own. It was different enough from her mother's usual style to be worrisome.

Her father, however, was dressed with his usual wealthy elegance. His coat was velvet, his shirt snowy white, the lace at his wrists and throat of the finest quality. His breeches were silk and there were silver buckles on his shoes. He stood with his back to the window, his hands clasped behind him, his face in shadow. Mary Elizabeth found it impossible to judge his mood. However, it did not take her long to discover that he wasn't happy.

"Your inappropriate rebellion has gone on long enough, daughter," he said in a clipped tone. "Colonel Bradley has returned to Boston as his duties did not allow him to remain any longer."

Mary Elizabeth bowed her head, but didn't reply. She was relieved that the colonel had departed. She hoped he had also decided that marrying her would be a bad idea for all concerned.

"He was not pleased," her father went on, his voice icy cold. "In fact, he expressed a certain reticence to continue with the betrothal, since he refuses to marry a reluctant bride."

Colonel Bradley went up a couple of notches in Mary Elizabeth's estimation, but only a couple. He didn't reach the level of being an acceptable life partner. No, only Andrew held that title in her mind and heart.

"What have you to say to that, daughter?"

Obviously, a cheer wasn't the answer her father wanted. She swallowed hard and said as politely as she could, "Colonel Bradley shows his honor and truly excellent breeding, Papa."

Her father eyed her critically. "Yes, he does. Indeed, his exemplary behavior exposes the shallow pettiness of yours."

She pursed her lips, biting back a retort. There was nothing shallow or petty about her refusal to accept Bradley's proposal. This was her future. She didn't want to spend it in England as wife to a professional soldier or a budding politician. Or, for that matter, as a titled lady of the *ton*.

"Well?" her father said. "What have you to say, daughter?"

"I'm sorry, Papa." She didn't think the words would pacify him, but it was at least worth a try.

It didn't work. Unfortunately, it enraged him further. "I was able to convince Colonel Bradley that your behavior was simply that of a timid and naïve young girl afraid of such a major change in her life," he said, biting out the words through stiff lips. "He allowed me another week to soothe your fears here, in Lexington. I have promised him that at the end of the week you and your mother will return to Boston. There you will accept his proposal in as pretty a fashion as any man could want. You will be married before he returns to England."

Mary Elizabeth's gaze flew to his. "And if I do not, Papa?"

Her father's features twisted with anger. "If you refuse Colonel Bradley's offer, you will be sent to England on the next ship out. There your uncle has promised to find you a husband. His steward needs a wife. As does the fellow who manages his stables." He paused to let that sink in. "Think on it, daughter. Marriage to an aristocrat? Or to one of the lower orders? Which would you prefer?"

She didn't wish for either. "Papa—"

Her mother, who had remained silent through her father's lecture, interrupted the entreaty that hovered on Mary Elizabeth's lips. "All will be forgiven if you repent, Mary Elizabeth." Her voice was low, husky with suppressed emotion. "Attend church with us this morning. Use the time for prayer and reflection. I am sure you will come to understand what course you must take." Her expression was grave as she took Mary Elizabeth's hand in a comforting way. She tried to smile, but her expression—and the comfort offered—failed.

George Strand muttered, "What nonsense," under his breath. Louder, he said, "You spoil the girl, Lady Elizabeth. She'll come to heel, or she will regret it."

The look her mother shot her father was anger veiled in deference. "You are, of course, correct, Mr. Strand. I do believe, however, that reflection in a sanctified place cannot help but to build understanding of what is important. I am sure that once the service is over, Mary Elizabeth will feel able to make the decision she must." She looked back at her daughter. "Won't you, my dear?"

What could she say? Eyes lowered again, Mary Elizabeth dropped a curtsey and murmured, "As you say, Mama."

Her father made a derisive sound, but Lady Elizabeth rose and said, "Come then, let us be on our way. We would not want to be late for the service."

"The Reverend Turner knows better than to start before we are seated," her father snapped.

Lady Elizabeth flushed, but she managed a small smile and was able to keep her tone light. "Nevertheless, it is always an excellent strategy to be on time, if possible."

The subject of Colonel Bradley and her betrothal to him was not brought up again during the carriage ride to the church, but Mary Elizabeth's thoughts never strayed far from it. She had friends in Lexington, but no way to alert them to her plight. There had been no time to write a note to Andrew, one that she could pass to one of her friends with a request that it be given to him personally. She knew that her father would keep her close while they were in church, and later in the churchyard, minimizing her opportunity for private conversation to little or none. No matter which way she examined the problem, she could find no way to escape.

By the time the church service began she was resigned to accepting Bradley's proposal, because she certainly didn't want to be packed off to England for a humiliating marriage to a complete stranger. At least she knew Colonel Bradley was an honorable man.

As she sat through the service, she did as her mother had asked and prayed for guidance, and for the humility to accept an arranged marriage she didn't want. It was then that the daring thought entered her head.

She could promise to wed Colonel Bradley, but she didn't have to actually go through with it.

How could she not, though? She had such a short time left here in Lexington. She could not conceive of a way that Andrew could arrange for them to be married in that time. She took heart from the thought that they did not have to be married here, in Lexington. Andrew could travel to Boston and they could be wed there. She would have to jilt Colonel Bradley, of course. That would infuriate the colonel and send her father into apoplexy. She refused to let that thought influence her. Whatever she did to avoid the arranged marriage would infuriate him. There was no way around it.

There was another issue that would come from jilting Colonel Bradley. A betrothal was as binding as a marriage. To accept, then refuse would dishonor her, make her suspect in the eyes of many. Was Andrew one of those? He was a man of principles and strong beliefs. Would her subterfuge make her less desirable to him? Would he think her fickle?

Was there a way to make the colonel refuse to marry her? Perhaps when she was in Boston, she could encourage other suitors to court her and turn Bradley against her. That was a dangerous plan, as both the colonel and her father were men of influence. There would be few suitors willing to approach her. Besides, if she encouraged other courtships she would be down the same road of tarnishing her reputation. Her goal was to marry Andrew if he was still willing to have her. Other suitors would only complicate an already confused situation and might turn Andrew away as well.

The thought of Andrew made her realize that there was only one solution to her dilemma. The only solution as far as her heart was concerned. Andrew would have to find a way to marry her now, here in Lexington, before she returned to Boston. For such a marriage to take place she would have to be able to speak to him.

She considered ways of arranging a meeting. Through one of the servants or a mutual friend? Either was possible, but to actually get to the meeting she had to be able to move about freely. While she was locked in her room that was impossible, but the only way out of seclusion was to accept Colonel Bradley's proposal.

She sighed inwardly. So be it, she decided. As soon as the service was over she would tell her father that she would wed the colonel. Perhaps then she would be allowed some freedom of movement and she could steal away to have a few words with Andrew before they left the churchyard.

"Mama," she whispered, as the congregation was rising to its feet and people began to shuffle from the pews into the aisles. "I...You were right. Reflection did help. I...I will marry Colonel Bradley."

Lady Elizabeth sighed. She put her hand to Mary Elizabeth's cheek. "A wise decision, child." She glanced at her husband. "Mr. Strand. We must plan a wedding!"

Her father frowned as he looked over at Mary Elizabeth. He apparently wasn't as trusting as his wife. "Indeed?"

"Yes, Papa," Mary Elizabeth said, making her expression as dutiful as she could.

"Very well," Strand said with a firm nod. He hailed the minister, who was heading down the aisle to his post at the door. "Mr. Turner, I have news of some import to relay."

"Indeed, sir," Turner said. He smiled a greeting to the two ladies. "And what can that be?"

"You remember Colonel Bradley who was staying with us this past week?" Strand pitched his voice loud. It echoed throughout the church.

Mary Elizabeth was uncomfortably aware that his words captured everyone's attention as the other members of the congregation waited to hear what was so important that the minister would be stopped in his normal execution of his duties. Mary Elizabeth caught sight of Andrew near the doorway. His expression was guarded, his body tense. She suspected he had guessed her father's news and her heart clenched at the pain she would soon be causing him.

"He has requested the hand of my daughter in marriage and I have agreed."

Mr. Turner raised his brows. He cast Mary Elizabeth a searching look. "And what of Miss Strand? Has she agreed as well?"

Mary Elizabeth lowered her eyes and swallowed. The lie was a lump in her throat that wouldn't go away, but she knew she would have to speak around it. She looked up into the minister's eyes. She hoped he —and certain other members of the congregation, most specifically, Andrew—would understand the real meaning of what she was about to say. "My father has convinced me that Colonel Bradley would be a fine husband, well able to provide for me, and one who is most acceptable to my family. Though I hardly know the good colonel, I must trust in my father's judgment and believe in his choice for me." She stopped, swallowed hard and added, "I must thank you, Reverend Turner. Your service today helped me to understand what I truly wanted."

"I am glad of it, my child," he said, though he looked confused. His sermon had been on the value God placed on hard work and honest toil, hardly the stuff to soothe the fears of an anxious bride-to-be. He looked at George Strand, his brows raised. When he spoke, his voice was sharp with authority. "It will be a long engagement, I presume. I hope that the lovely Miss Strand will be wed from our church here where she has made such a positive impact on our community."

Her father colored at the tone. He said briskly, "She will be wed in Boston, as soon as the banns can be read."

That snapped the minister' brows together in a frown. "Does Colonel Bradley believe the lady will change her mind?" Disapproval of such a hasty marriage was evident in his tone.

"Colonel Bradley wishes to have his affairs in order before he returns to England," her father said curtly.

The minister's frown deepened. A low hum of displeasure could be heard from the congregation, still listening to the polite sparring with unabashed interest. Out of the corner of her eye, Mary Elizabeth saw Andrew push past his friend Ron Aiken. Aiken caught Andrew's elbow and shook his head. Andrew shot him an angry look and jerked from Aiken's hold.

Now was the moment for Mary Elizabeth to send her message and hope that Andrew would understand her concealed intent. "If Colonel Bradley was not so anxious, I would prefer a longer engagement," she said. She allowed a tremulous smile to play on her lips as she looked first at Reverend Turner, then turned to face the members of the listening congregation. And, most importantly, Andrew. "I would like the opportunity to celebrate with friends and to adjust to this momentous decision I have made."

Mr. Turner nodded emphatically and the hum from the crowd grew louder. She saw several influential women nod as well. One of them was Franny Hodder. As the wife of a confirmed Tory and the sister of Andrew's dear friend Ron Aiken, she was the link to both Mary Elizabeth's parents and the man she loved. If Franny was on her side, perhaps there was hope yet.

Her father's mouth flattened into a straight line, but it was Lady Elizabeth who responded. "Before we return to Boston, we will have a tea, for all of my daughter's friends here in Lexington."

The excited murmur of approval ensured George Strand couldn't squash the suggestion of a party. Lady Elizabeth smiled cheerfully at the rapt audience. "We will begin the preparations this very afternoon." She slipped her arm through Mary Elizabeth's. "Come daughter. We have much to do."

CHAPTER 9

*H*e has requested the hand of my daughter in marriage and I have agreed.

George Strand's words to the congregation echoed in Andrew's mind all the way home. The effrontery of the man. *He* agreed, not Mary Elizabeth. *He* was choosing how she would spend the rest of her life, not Mary Elizabeth. Although it was true that she had announced that she had decided Bradley was a desirable husband.

No, she'd said that her father had convinced her he was.

He'd wanted to push his way through the crowd to where the Reverend and the Strands stood. What he would have done he wasn't sure—punched George Strand in the nose, probably, but Mary Elizabeth's final words had stopped him.

I would like the opportunity to celebrate with friends and to adjust to this momentous decision I have made.

Celebrate didn't exactly fit with adjust, so there was an ambiguity in her words. Was she sending him a message?

The town's gossip mill had informed him that Strand had kept Mary Elizabeth locked up in her room all week. She'd lost weight and her expression was strained. When she'd emerged from the church, he'd tried to catch her eye, but she had been surrounded by excited young ladies and matrons, chattering about the upcoming tea that Lady Elizabeth announced. He doubted Mary Elizabeth had made her decision freely, but he must know if her true choice was to wed him.

He had to speak with her.

The next day, it was not hard to discover what was happening at the Strand mansion. The town was buzzing with talk about the betrothal. George Strand had already relocated to Boston, presumably to meet with the future bridegroom and organize the marriage contracts. Lady Elizabeth and Mary Elizabeth would be following him in a little over a week, after the grand tea Lady Elizabeth was planning, but before then, she had accepted several invitations to visit on behalf of herself and Mary Elizabeth. These included the ladies sewing circle, a matron's tea, and a luncheon with the wife of the Reverend Turner and the ladies of the church enhancement group.

The social gatherings would bring Mary Elizabeth into Lexington, but they were not the sort of events he would also be invited to. What Andrew had to do was find a way to meet with Mary Elizabeth privately. Once he had her word that she truly desired marriage with him and understood all it would entail, he would put his plan into action.

There were some problems with this scheme. First, his current plan hinged on taking Mary Elizabeth to New York. He hadn't yet received a letter from his sister, so he couldn't be sure she would harbor them if he and Mary Elizabeth escaped there. He also had no idea how he would get them both to New York. He could, he supposed spirit her away to another town and prevail upon the minister there to marry them, but he doubted anyone would be willing to act so precipitously. To wed, the banns must be read in the church, in the presence of the congregation, three times on successive Sundays. The purpose was to allow anyone who disputed the right of the betrothed couple to wed to make their concerns known. Exceptions happened, of course, but only if there were strong reasons for them. Andrew didn't think eloping was one of them.

Then there was his concern about disrupting the timeline. He knew from his visits to Faith and her family that he was to wed Mary Elizabeth in New York. If he altered that action, what would happen to the future? Everyone who was a Beacon or a Traveler knew that maintaining the timeline was of paramount importance and he was loathe to be the one who broke that rule.

So, he must find a way to transport Mary Elizabeth to New York City. He just didn't know how.

His first break came when he was at the tavern pondering his situation over a glass of ale.

Ron Aiken entered the establishment and sat at Andrew's table. "A word in your ear, Byrne."

Andrew raised his eyebrows. Ron was often stealthy in his way of phrasing things. He was a dyed-in-the-wool rebel and he was all too aware that should he be arrested, the authorities would not go easy on him.

The serving wench came by and he ordered a pint. While he waited for it to arrive, he talked about the weather, the state of the crops, and the outrageous cost of the farrier. The girl brought his beverage. He flashed her a big smile and dropped extra coins in her hand. She knew what that meant. He wanted privacy. She wouldn't be back until he flagged her, even if his tankard was empty.

"My sister is holding a dinner party." He lifted his mug and sipped, watching Andrew over the rim.

Ron's brother-by-marriage, Maurice Hodder, that most conservative of gentlemen, assumed all sensible men were supporters of English rule. He refused to acknowledge that his wife's brother was plotting the downfall of the British colonial government and Franny made sure that he never fully understood how rebellious Ron was.

Andrew raised his glass and looked at Ron over it. "A party, you say."

Ron nodded. "She's invited the Lady Elizabeth and her daughter." He paused to drink. Andrew waited. "A going away party, as it were."

"I thought that was supposed to be the tea Lady Elizabeth was giving."

"That's the final do. They'll leave for Boson the next day." He leaned forward. "This gathering of my sister's is the start of the town's send off. Franny wanted to make it a widely attended celebration, but my dear brother-in-law thought that inviting a select group of local landowners would be more appropriate."

Andrew raised his brows. "And am I considered to be an appropriate landowner?"

Ron grinned. "Well, you're a landowner of some consequence." His expression sobered. "Maurice may not hold with rebellion, but he doesn't accept that everything the English do is suitable. He doesn't like how Strand is treating his daughter." Ron paused to drink a hearty draft of his ale. As he set his mug down on the table, he slanted Andrew a shrewd glance. "There's an opportunity here, if you're willing to take it."

Andrew raised his brows. "I should be delighted to attend your sister's party. When is to be held?"

"Friday. I'll let my sister know. She'll be pleased. She likes the idea of playing matchmaker."

Andrew frowned. "Are you suggesting that she'll find a way for Mary Elizabeth to be alone with me?"

Ron sent him an amused look. "You know my sister."

Yes, he did. She had been a hellion before she married her very respectable husband. Ron never understood what she saw in Maurice, but Andrew always assumed it was his steadiness and confidence. She might no longer be a hellion, but she had a mischievous sense of humor and a strong sense of right and wrong. If she'd decided that Mary Elizabeth deserved the opportunity to plan her own life, she'd act to ensure it happened.

Ideas began to form in his head. He finished his ale with one last gulp, then set his mug back on to the table with a determined thud. "Thank you for the conversation, Aiken, but I must leave you now. I've arrangements to make." His friend nodded and raised his own tankard in salute as Andrew rose from the table.

Night was chasing away evening dusk as he rode back to his farm, indicating that the hour was growing late. Despite the dim light, the horse trotted along peacefully, clearly knowing the way. Andrew let the animal pick out the path as he thought about timing. The Hodder's dinner was in two days' time. He needed his plan in place before he spoke to Mary Elizabeth. Formulating it would be so much easier if he had more details.

Faith knew those details. He had to talk to her, to convince her to tell him everything she knew.

The horse stumbled on a stone. He steadied it, then drew it down to a walk. He was almost home now and darkness was falling fast. He didn't want to take the chance of the rest of Faith's interfering family being there when he asked her for assistance. Madame Chloe would shake her head, denying his request, while the objectionable Daniel would blather on about influencing the future and then declare it wasn't allowed. Mistress Liz would follow her mother's lead, even if she wanted to talk to him.

However, today was Wednesday, mid-week. Faith rarely entertained or went out on Wednesday evenings, so it was likely her beacon would be waiting for him if he went to the grove. He urged the horse back into a trot and changed direction.

He was right. Her light blazed through the woods. He dismounted and tied the horse to a tree, then he walked into beacon.

In an instant he found himself in Faith's living room. The electric lamps were turned low, but he was still able to see Faith and Cody entwined on the couch, in the middle of what appeared to be an intense embrace. "Dear God," Andrew said and stepped back out of the beacon.

He gave them enough time to untangle themselves before he stepped into the light once more. Faith and Cody were still on the couch, but now Faith sat up straight and Cody had his arm draped across her shoulders. Though Cody didn't appear upset at the intrusion, Faith was clearly flustered. Andrew made haste to apologize.

She unbent a bit at that and said, "We weren't expecting you."

"Yes, we were," Cody said. "We just didn't know when you'd show up."

"Cody," Faith said, frowning. She poked him in the ribs with her elbow, turning the word into a warning.

He turned his head and kissed her temple. "You know my thoughts on this."

"Yes," Faith replied. "But..."

Andrew took heart from the conversation. Faith knew when and where he and Mary Elizabeth would wed. She and Cody must have been speculating on the details that were never written down. They'd come to some conclusions, that much was apparent. Now he just had to coax them to reveal what they'd guessed, as well as what they knew.

He sat down on the chair that faced the couch. "I won't be visiting as usual on Friday." He paused, waiting to see if that got any response.

Cody raised his brows. Faith said, "Oh?" in a casual way. Her face showed polite interest and nothing more.

"I've been invited to a dinner party."

Faith and Cody's expressions didn't change. He wondered if Friday was significant as more than just the day he discovered whether Mary Elizabeth was truly willing to defy her parents in order to marry him.

He tried again. "I wrote my sister in New York and asked her to arrange for Mary Elizabeth and me to be married."

"And did she respond?" Faith asked.

He'd learned from Chloe that he and Mary Elizabeth would wed in New York, but she had not said how he would arrange it. He assumed his sister would help, but he couldn't be sure. Her husband was a merchant whose trade was dependent on England's good will. Though he sympathized with much of what Andrew and the other rebels believed, his brother-in-law had a business to run and a family to support, so he stayed neutral. Andrew wasn't sure he'd condone a runaway marriage that involved the daughter of a senior British official in Boston.

"Not yet," he replied, answering Faith's question. He watched her expression, hoping for answers. There were none. Annoyed, he said, "Mary Elizabeth will return to Boston town with her mother next week. I need to act quickly. I had a thought that I'd bring her here and abide awhile, until the hue and cry from her disappearance died down. Then I'd find a way to get her down to New York to be wed."

Faith sat up straight at that, sliding out from under Cody's arm. She said urgently, "You can't, Andrew. You know you can't! Mary Elizabeth can only travel through the Beacon with you. She can only stay in my time if she is touching you. You know that!"

He nodded. "Of course I do. But, Faith, I'm desperate. I have not had a moment of privacy with Mary Elizabeth since the night I asked her to marry me. Her parents kept her under lock and key all last week, until they forced an agreement from her to marry the English colonel. Even now she is never out and about unless she is with her mother. I do not know what Friday will bring, but I must be prepared for any and all contingencies."

Faith drew a deep breath, then let it out slowly. "Andrew, if you are here, in my time, and you break physical contact with Mary Elizabeth, she will pop back into the eighteenth century. Have you any idea how difficult it will be to keep her here with you? For a short time, it is possible. But to remain long enough for people to stop searching for you both? Impossible!"

"She's right, you know," Cody said. "When you come into our time you need to have a limited purpose."

When Cody agreed with Faith, Andrew's fantasy of escaping to the future dissolved. Faith understood the Beacon and its rules, but Cody was a logical man of science. If he was siding with Faith, it meant there were too many difficulties for the plan to succeed. "What am I to do?"

"Go to your dinner on Friday," Faith said. "Find out how Mary Elizabeth wants to proceed." She reached out and caught his hand, squeezing it. "She may want to find a way to marry you without breaking with her parents."

"That would be impossible. George Strand would never allow us to wed. He'd rather disown his daughter than have it happen."

"What about Lady Elizabeth?"

Andrew thought about Lady Elizabeth, whose charming, friendly demeanor seemed to hide a dislike of her husband. She and Mary Elizabeth were close. To forever be unable to communicate would be heartbreak for both of them. "She does what her husband tells her."

Cody raised his brows. "Does she?"

Andrew sat up straight. "Are you telling me—"

"We're telling you nothing," Faith said hastily.

"Then it's possible that Lady Elizabeth will help us elope," he said. He looked from Faith to Cody, but Faith had her stony expression firmly in place and Cody's face was alight with laughter. Andrew couldn't tell if that was because his probing amused Cody, or if he and Faith had just sent him chasing after a phantom possibility.

Either way, he thought he'd discovered as much as he could tonight. He stood. "Wish me luck on Friday."

Faith stood and kissed his cheek. "You don't need luck, Andrew."

Cody grinned at him. "She's right. A plan is better than luck."

Conversation stopped when Andrew strolled into the Hodders' formal front parlor on the day of Franny's dinner party. Although Maurice Hodder was a prosperous gentleman, and his home was substantial, the parlor itself was not overly large. At the moment there were seven other people in the room, a comfortable size for the space. Andrew's gaze quickly found Mary Elizabeth, who was sitting on a brocade-covered sofa beside her mother.

He drank in her appearance, from her pretty sky-blue gown and embroidered underskirt, to the way her dark hair was elaborately dressed so that lustrous curls fell over one of her bare shoulders. Though she was smiling, her skin was paler than usual and the soft rose that pinkened her cheeks was absent. Her warm brown eyes, usually so bright and lively, were shadowed.

She had glanced his way when he'd arrived—he knew because his skin had prickled with awareness—but now she kept her eyes averted, obviously careful not to appear interested in him.

He knew differently, though, and it made him glad that he'd taken care with his appearance, choosing to wear a dark, wine-colored coat that Mary Elizabeth had once told him made him look very fine. He complemented it with a white, figured silk waistcoat and black silk breeches. His shoes were polished to a high sheen and his hair was tied at his nape with a black ribbon.

Her studied disinterest told him that he needed to tread carefully if he wanted to make this evening a success, so he focused his attention on his hostess and tried to act normally when all he really wanted to do was to sweep Mary Elizabeth away with him. "Good evening, Franny, Maurice."

Franny Hodder beamed at him and said, "Welcome, Andrew. We are delighted you were able to come tonight." She held out her hand to him.

Andrew captured it in his, then executed his most sweeping bow over it. Franny, who had known him since they were both children, giggled. Her husband Maurice shook his head. "If a fellow didn't know you were as sensible a farmer and as canny a businessman as was ever born, I'd have you down as a popinjay, Byrne."

Franny shot her husband a flirtatious look from blue eyes that danced with mischief as she said, "Really, Mr. Hodder, to chastise one of our guests in such a way!" She shook her head. Maurice grinned at her. They had been married less than a year and he was clearly besotted with his lively blonde bride.

Her brother Ronald wandered over. "Well met, Byrne. You know everyone else here, I think?"

Of course he did, but Ron's question allowed him to bow to the Reverend and Mrs. Turner before he focused on Mary Elizabeth and her mother.

Lady Elizabeth's mouth was set in a straight line and her expression was haughty. "Mrs. Hodder," she said, rising from the sofa and drawing Mary Elizabeth up with her. "I fear that my daughter and I must excuse ourselves. I do apologize—"

Mary Elizabeth shot her a distressed, look. "But Mama!"

Lady Elizabeth put her hand on her daughter's arm. "Hush, child." She didn't take her eyes off the little group around Andrew. "I was not aware of the company—"

"But surely, dear lady, you cannot object to Mrs. Hodder inviting her brother, Mr. Aiken, to dine," the reverend said innocently.

Lady Elizabeth's eyebrows shot together into a frown at that. "No, of course not..."

Smiles wreathed Turner's cheerful countenance. "Nor can it be Mr. Byrne, whose family has been prominent in the community for two generations and more."

Lady Elizabeth stiffened and her frown deepened. She opened her mouth to reply. The reverend rolled on. "It must, therefore, be myself and my wife. I am desolated, dear lady. Pray tell, what must I do to return to your good graces?"

Andrew blinked. It appeared that Reverend Turner had decided to be one of his champions.

Color crept up into Lady Elizabeth's cheeks. "My sincere apologies, Reverend. I have nothing against you and Mrs. Turner," she protested.

Andrew took the opportunity to ease closer to Mary Elizabeth. He hoped to have a moment to talk to her while Turner distracted Lady Elizabeth, but she was not about to be outflanked.

Her glance was steely as she said, "Everyone in this room is aware that Mr. Byrne has been turning his attentions to my daughter. Now that she is betrothed it is inappropriate for them to be together."

"Surely not, Lady Elizabeth," Mrs. Turner said. She was dressed in a dark gown with a matching underskirt and if she wore panniers they were tiny compared to the fashionably sized ones that added such width to Lady Elizabeth's skirts. She was sitting on a comfortable wing chair positioned opposite the sofa. "Mr. Byrne is a gentleman and Miss Strand has been brought up most graciously. Nothing could happen during a dinner amongst friends."

Mrs. Turner was wrong. If he had the chance, he'd spirit Mary Elizabeth away in an instant. At her mother's comment, she had clasped her hands in front of her lap and lowered her eyes. Color stained her cheeks and she was worrying her lower lip between her teeth. She looked miserable. Then she lifted her head, found his gaze and smiled. His heart turned over and started to pound.

"Mama, we are to leave Lexington in another week," she said, her voice husky. "Do allow us to stay. Mrs. Hodder has been a particular friend since we came here and once I am wed, I will be returning to England. I will not have an opportunity to visit with my friends here and I will miss them when I am gone."

Lady Elizabeth studied her, then she pursed her lips and shot Andrew a narrow-eyed glance. "Very well. We will stay, provided Mr. Byrne promises to acknowledge your betrothal and behave appropriately."

Andrew didn't hesitate. He bowed with an elegant flourish and said, "As you wish, my lady." Even as she tilted her head in stiff acceptance, he was plotting ways he could draw Mary Elizabeth for a private conversation. In his heart, she was engaged to him, for she had agreed to marry him. Nothing else mattered.

Ronald Aiken sauntered over to hand him a glass of rum. "Don't rush your fences, Byrne," he murmured. "Between us we'll ensure you've a moment or two alone with Miss Strand. Give it time."

Andrew tipped his glass in salute. "My thanks, Aiken."

Ron nodded and moved away. Mrs. Turner continued to chat with Lady Elizabeth, who had returned to her seat on the couch, while Franny drew Mary Elizabeth off with the excuse that she wanted her to look at her embroidery work. Andrew joined the men and found they were discussing a new family who had recently moved to the area.

By the time dinner was called, the initial tension had dissipated. It wasn't precisely a jolly meal, but conversation flowed without restraint. Inevitably, Mary Elizabeth's betrothal became a topic of discussion. "Do you expect a long engagement, Miss Strand?" Franny asked as the girl she'd hired to serve for the evening brought in the final course, a syllabub made with rich cream and flavored with wine and lemon.

Mary Elizabeth smiled her thanks to the girl before she said, "My father is having the banns read now. The colonel and I are to be married as soon as that process is completed."

In less than three weeks, then. Andrew knew a moment of panic. That was hardly enough time to organize an escape to New York and a clandestine marriage there. Of course, he didn't really have three weeks anyway, since he needed to get Mary Elizabeth away before she left Lexington for good.

"That is rather soon, is it not, Lady Elizabeth?" asked Mrs. Turner. She'd couched the words as an innocent query, but Andrew caught an undercurrent of disapproval.

Lady Elizabeth must have caught the inference too, for she put her spoon down, then patted her lips with the starched white linen napkin. "My daughter can hardly sail for England with Colonel Bradley as an unmarried girl," she replied stiffly. "I believe, as well, it is best for her to be settled with her new husband before they travel. The first weeks of marriage can be difficult for a young couple."

Mrs. Turner nodded. "That is true," she said in a thoughtful tone. "It is wise to have family and friends around while the young people make adjustments. However," she paused, deliberately Andrew thought, before she added, "Her betrothal is one of the highlights of a young woman's life. It seems a shame to rush the process in the case of Miss Strand."

"Needs must," Lady Elizabeth said. Her tone was cool.

"Surely, Miss Strand will have an opinion!" Franny said.

Mary Elizabeth blushed as everyone turned to her. Her voice was composed though, as she said, "My father has made all of the arrangements to ensure this marriage comes to pass. I believe he will continue to do so."

"Do you feel you have no say in the matter?" Ronald Aiken asked. Of those at the table, only Lady Elizabeth reacted with any dismay. Aiken was known to be a radical in his thinking. No one was surprised by his outspokenness.

Lady Elizabeth glared at him. "Sir! You are impertinent."

Ron smiled, not in the least put out.

Mary Elizabeth said slowly, "I agreed to the marriage, though it is closer to my father's heart than mine."

"This is the new world!" Reverend Turner said. "Such old-fashioned ideas do not belong here. Miss Strand, if you are not agreeable to
this marriage, you must say so!"

"Dear Reverend Turner," she said, smiling. "Your kindness on my
behalf warms me, truly it does. I believe I have as fine a champion in
you as any woman could wish. Rest assured, I would call upon you if I
felt I needed to, but..." She looked down at her half-eaten dessert for a
moment, then she raised her gaze to the assembled group once more.
"Events have already been put into motion. I do not think you need to
brave my father's wrath for me."

"I would do it," the reverend said stoutly.

"And I would support him," Mrs. Turner said, nodding.

The others at the table murmured agreement. Andrew remained
silent. He knew Lady Elizabeth would focus on him if he joined in and
she would be even more vigilant about keeping them apart during the
evening. He had plans to talk to Mary Elizabeth privately, and he
wasn't going to risk losing the opportunity by blurting out his support of
Mary Elizabeth.

It appeared, though, that his caution would be wasted. Lady Elizabeth set her spoon down and pushed back her chair. Her expression
was as cold as any Andrew had ever seen. She was about to bolt, taking
Mary Elizabeth with her. He mentally cursed Ron Aiken's determination to stir the pot.

After a hasty glance at her mother, Mary Elizabeth said, "I am
deeply touched by the affection all of you have shown for me. Thank
you." She turned to her mother. Putting her hand over Lady Elizabeth's
she said gently, "Mama, we have made true friends in this community. I
am grateful for that. The decision is made. Let us enjoy the rest of our
time here."

Lady Elizabeth looked at her daughter and the anger in her expression melted. She took a deep breath, then nodded. The awkward
moment passed and the evening continued with tea and coffee being
served in the parlor.

As they moved from the dining room to the parlor, the Reverend

Turner engaged Lady Elizabeth in conversation. That provided Andrew with the opportunity to speak to Mary Elizabeth. "We must talk. Come with me into the garden. We can be private there."

"Until Mama comes to drag me back into the house. No, Andrew, come to my house tonight. Mama will go to bed not long after we return. She is no longer locking me in my room, so I will be able to slip out to meet you. Can you do this?"

His heart soared. "I can."

She nodded agreement, blessed him with a tiny, intimate smile, then nodded toward her mother, at the head of their small procession with the minister on one side and Maurice Hodder on the other. "I must ensure my mother is not suspicious. Approach me in the parlor, but do not be daunted by what I say!" When he nodded, she hurried ahead so that Lady Elizabeth would not realize that she and Andrew had spoken.

Andrew slowed his pace. His heart was pounding with excitement, for he was sure—though not completely certain—that Mary Elizabeth would agree to elope with him. To separate herself from her family by such an act was a momentous decision for a woman to make, and he knew she could not do it lightly. He would treasure and protect her for the rest of her life once she did, but the choice and the spoken decision must be hers to make.

When he entered the parlor no one was yet seated. Mary Elizabeth stood by the tall French doors that led out to the terrace behind the house, talking to Fanny Hodder. Maurice Hodder was chatting with Lady Elizabeth as he led her to the sofa, which was positioned so that there was a good view of the outside through the leaded glass in the French doors.

No time like the present, Andrew thought. He ambled over to the French doors, deliberately trying to appear unthreatening, knowing that everyone in the room would see through his subterfuge immediately. He smiled at the two women. "My dear Fanny, may I steal Miss Strand from you for a moment?"

Fanny frowned as her shrewd blue eyes scanned his face. "Andrew, I don't think that would be a good idea…"

Mary Elizabeth flipped open her fan and said loudly, "Mr. Byrne, I am a betrothed lady. You know I cannot speak with you privately."

Fanny's eyes widened, then narrowed, speculation in their depths. She moved a little closer to Mary Elizabeth. "My dear, I'm sure he meant nothing untoward."

Playing along, Andrew bowed. "My apologies, Miss Strand. I overstepped."

"Indeed, you did, sir." She turned, apparently to face Fanny more directly, but in reality, to wink at Andrew. "I think it best if I join my mother on the sofa. You do understand, Mrs. Hodder?"

"Of course," Fanny said. She shot Andrew a disapproving look for all the room to see, then, her arm linked with Mary Elizabeth's, she bustled over to the seating area near the fire to join the others.

Andrew had to struggle to keep his face grave, but he managed it. The play-acting had been effective. Lady Elizabeth was nodding approvingly at her daughter, her earlier wariness assuaged by Mary Elizabeth's apparent compliance. As the evening continued, all he could think about was meeting Mary Elizabeth tonight. In the moonlight. Privately, where he would finally gain her agreement for their runaway marriage.

CHAPTER 11

*T*he carriage ride back to Strand Manor should have been a strain on Mary Elizabeth's fraught nerves. Her mother spent the whole drive complaining. Not about the meal, or their hosts, or most of the other guests, no, her focus was on Andrew and by extension his friend, Mr. Ronald Aiken. Lady Elizabeth saw both men as examples of the dangers of extremism and said more than once that she could not understand why the Hodders would condescend to associate with either one of them.

Since Mary Elizabeth had plans for the remainder of the evening, plans she didn't want her mother to know, she was careful not to say anything that would cause Lady Elizabeth to consider her to be as rebellious as Andrew and Ron Aiken. As she was certain her mother would expect her to champion her American friends, at least in some small way, she took a moment to deliberately point out that Mr. Aiken was a blood relative to Mrs. Hodder and therefore someone she would find difficulty shunning. When Lady Elizabeth waved her perfectly good objection away with one elegant flick of her wrist and said, "Nonsense! Everyone has unacceptable relatives. One simply learns to avoid them and they go away over time," she knew she had hit just the right note.

Personally, Mary Elizabeth thought Franny Hodder actually supported her brother Ron. She doubted the woman wanted him to go anywhere. She didn't voice that thought to her mother, of course. It wasn't part of her strategy. She wanted Lady Elizabeth to feel comfortable retiring for the night at her normal time. She didn't want her fussing and worrying about the outcome of the evening and staying up late. So, she listened to her mother grumble, interjected a comment here and there when she thought it would seem odd if she didn't speak, and for the most part held her tongue.

Once they reached Strand Manor, Lady Elizabeth spent a half hour planning the next day's meals with their housekeeper, then discussing the activities she and Mary Elizabeth were committed to, before she followed her usual pattern and retired to her bedchamber for the night. Mary Elizabeth went up at the same time, kissed her mother good night and retreated to her room where she made ready for bed.

As the maid she shared with her mother unfastened her stays, then brushed out her long hair and braided it, she fought to keep her nerves steady. Tonight, she would meet with an unmarried man unchaperoned, in the darkness of the night. If the maid had even the slightest inkling of her plans, it would be her duty to inform Lady Elizabeth. It was important, then, that she not allow any of the building excitement and fear to show, for she did not want anyone to stand in the way of her rendezvous with Andrew.

Finally, the woman finished. Mary Elizabeth bid her good night, climbing into bed as she spoke, following her usual evening routine as closely as possible, even to the point of taking a book to bed with her. When the door closed, Mary Elizabeth leaned back against the pillows, the book unopened on her lap. She made her plans while she listened as the house quieted for the night.

She sat for a very long time before she slipped out of bed. Clad only in her white linen nightgown, she picked up her candle, and went to stand in front of the window. The garment was voluminous, long and shapeless, but she knew the pale color combined with the candlelight, would ensure she was seen by anyone outside, watching. After a minute or two, she deliberately blew out the candle. But still she stood, sure her form would be visible even in the darkness. Then she moved back into the room, to the wardrobe. She reached up to the high shelf where a spare blanket was stored for cold nights. She had to stand on her tiptoes, for she wasn't a tall woman, but her fingers caught the edge of the wool fabric and she tugged, pulling the bulky folds down into her arms.

Clutching the blanket to her breasts, she breathed deeply, calming the butterflies in her stomach. What she was about to do was an act of defiance so outrageous that it was unprecedented in her life. It was the right thing to do, but oh, how nervous she was. She folded the blanket and set it on the bed so she could don her night-rail, a lovely silk garment that was a deep, sapphire blue. It was tied at the waist with a sash, which she knotted with great care, then she pushed her feet into slippers, picked up the blanket, and crept to her door.

She cracked it open and listened. The house was quiet. Clutching the blanket to her chest with one hand, she carefully closed the door, ensuring that it was on the latch before she hurried toward the stairs.

She left the house through the tall French windows in her father's study. They opened out onto the terrace that faced the back garden. Beyond the formal walkways and plant beds was a forested area, which her mother liked to call her wilderness. It was not, of course. The grounds at Strand Manor had all been manicured to mimic those on a proper English estate. The real forest had been cleared, with the dead-wood hauled away and the undergrowth removed. Still, the trees would provide shelter and privacy for her meeting with Andrew.

She flitted down the steps from the terrace, onto the graveled path below, then hurried toward the woodlands. As she ran, her feet crunched loudly on the gravel. Her heart pounded and she glanced over her shoulder, fearing discovery. Then she saw a figure step from the sheltering trees and her heart leapt.

Andrew! He had come as he promised he would. One part of her soared at the knowledge, while another shuddered at the enormity of what she was about to do. Her breath caught and panic hovered, then she was wrapped snuggly in Andrew's embrace, the blanket falling to the ground as she threw her arms around his neck.

He drew her into the shadow of the trees, then he kissed her with all the pent-up emotion she knew he must be feeling. His mouth was rough on hers, his tongue pushing aggressively at the seam of her lips so that she opened to him. He thrust deeply, and she thought she heard him groan. With pleasure? She was too inexperienced to know what the sound meant, but she did know that after she settled from the shock of that invasion, the kiss was doing things to her senses she had never expected. Tentatively she rubbed her tongue against his, hoping that she was doing the right thing and Andrew would enjoy her touch.

At her action, Andrew's body went still. His kiss eased, the roughness turning into coaxing. His tongue retreated. Hers followed, sliding delicately over the top of his. He chuckled—chuckled! What did that mean? —and moved his lips seductively over hers as he touched the tip of his tongue against hers, then caressed it. His hands slid down her back to cup her behind, then he pressed her forward so that her belly and hips pressed against his body. She realized what the groan and chuckle meant. Andrew desired her. The evidence was there, pressing hard against her soft flesh.

The kiss seemed to go on forever and as Andrew caressed her, her body warmed, then heated with desires she didn't know existed, much less know how to manage. Her senses were aflame, each one bombarding her with impressions. The rustle of the leaves emphasized the soft caress of the warm breeze, and filled her nostrils with the scent of pine and roses. In the trees, the darkness was profound. She had had a fleeting glimpse of Andrew in the moonlight before he drew her into the shadows and she sensed he was dressed as he had been at the dinner. He must have come straight here after the party, to be with her. Her heart soared with the reassuring thought.

When Andrew eased away, leaving her lips parted, wanting more, she whispered his name.

He dropped a light, caressing kiss on the corner of her mouth, then another on the edge of her jaw. From there he moved down to her throat where her pulse beat strongly. The kiss sent a jolt of feeling through her body. Her eyes slid closed to allow her to better savor the sensations he was creating and she arched against him. This time when he groaned, elation and a primitive feminine power rushed through her.

He drew a deep breath. "Before Colonel Bradley arrived in Lexington, I asked you to marry me, Mary Elizabeth."

"Yes," she whispered. He'd stopped kissing her, so she opened her eyes. Gazing up into his, she saw that his expression was serious. She pulled her scattered senses together and did her best to concentrate.

"You said yes." He shifted his hips. Pleasure flashed through the tender core of her that was already pulsing with heat.

"Yes! I still say yes." She moved against him, meeting the pressure from his body with hers.

Even in the dim light she could see that desire flared in his eyes, but he said, "Stop, love. I want you so badly I fear I will not be able to control myself if we continue this play much longer."

She shifted so that her body made full contact with his, crushing her breasts against his chest and grinding her most private area against the bulge in his breeches. "I don't want to stop." She eased her fingers into his dark hair and pulled his head down so they could resume their kiss. The wonton statement echoed in her mind, sounding just right to the emotional, physical part of her, but shocking the properly brought up granddaughter of an earl. It was the loving part that won out, for being with Andrew this way felt so right, so exactly what she wanted, that the respectable young lady surrendered without a fight.

Andrew, though, might be a more difficult foe to conquer.

For a minute she thought she had succeeded in convincing him. She took the initiative this time, drawing her tongue over his lips in a teasing caress that had him groaning again and opening to her. She slipped inside, glorying in the taste of him and the way she could feel his body tremble from her touch.

He pulled away too soon. "Mary Elizabeth. Miss Strand! We must stop."

"I brought a blanket," she said, rather breathlessly. Admitting she was prepared for what was to come, had even been planning it, made her heart race.

He stepped back, a hint of a frown between his eyes. "A blanket? Miss Strand—"

"Call me by my name, *Mary Elizabeth*. We are to be married, are we not?"

He nodded, his expression still serious and reserved.

She reached for him. "Andrew," she said. But he did not move back into her arms. Her hand dropped to the tie on her night-rail. She pulled it loose.

This was it, the true moment when she committed herself to Andrew, tonight and forever. One day they would say their vows in a church, before the congregation and God, but tonight she would say her vows to him, and him alone. For her, the words were as binding as any spoken in a church. "I agreed to be your wife. From that day forward I have believed myself to be bound to you. I do not care what my father wants of me. I am yours, Andrew."

The sash fell away. The garment opened, exposing the thin linen nightgown beneath. His breath caught. She said, "If you want me."

His breath hissed out. "God, Mary Elizabeth. Want you? You have no idea how much I want you, on how many levels."

She stepped closer, her head tilted up so that she could look into his eyes. "Tell me then," she whispered. As she spoke, she reached back and pulled the braid over her shoulder. She tugged the ribbon, untying it, then slowly, deliberately, loosened the braid. All the time she watched his face. His gaze was fixed on her, and once he moistened his lips and swallowed hard. When the braid was undone, she shook her head and the waving locks tumbled over her shoulders.

Andrew reached up with both hands to slide the tangled locks through his fingers. In a low voice, he said, "I want you to be the woman who is with me every day for the rest of our lives. The one who shares my dreams and my triumphs, bears my children, accepts me as the man I am. I ache to become your lover, to be the one who brings you the pleasure of the marriage bed. I want to be your friend, to support you in all you dream of for your future. I need a partner in my life, Mary Elizabeth, equal and valued and desired."

As he spoke, she shrugged the wrapper off her shoulders, so that only her elbows held it up. By the time he finished his voice was hoarse. She had the sense that he was holding on to his self-control by an increasingly thin thread. She straightened her arms and let the garment fall, so that it pooled on the ground around her feet.

His eyes followed its descent, then travelled back up slowly. The linen of her nightshirt was very fine, so fine that it was almost translucent. She knew he could see the dark curls at her core, the swell of her breasts, and the dark puckers of her nipples. "Andrew," she whispered.

His gaze had lingered on her breasts. Now he raised it to look into her eyes.

"My mother and I leave for Boston the day after the tea she is holding. That is in four days from now. I want to give myself to you. Tonight." She drew a deep breath. "Tomorrow night. And the night after, and the one after that, until I go away. I want you to make me your wife, because in my heart that is what I am."

"Mary Elizabeth..." He had to pause to clear his throat. "I had thought to wait until our wedding night." He cleared his throat again as he gestured at the trees around them. "To make love for the first time, here, on the ground...Mary Elizabeth, you would not be happy. The first time should be special—"

"This is special." She stepped closer and felt his hands tighten in her hair.

"Memorable—"

"How will this not be memorable?" Her breasts brushed against his chest.

"In a bed," he rasped.

She laughed at that, the amusement dancing in her eyes. "I cannot counter that, husband of my heart." Of its own accord, her smile turned sensuous as she reached up to caress Andrew's cheek, while her gaze searched his. "All I can say is that a bed doesn't matter to me now, in this moment." She drew a deep breath and pushed through the last, feeble barriers her proper self had erected. "Please, Andrew. Make me your wife."

For a moment he did nothing, then he lowered his mouth to hers. At first the kiss was a light caress, a mere brushing of his lips over hers. She kissed him back, opening her lips a fraction to allow him access. He hesitated, then seemed to come to a decision. His tongue teased her mouth and when she parted her lips wider, he plunged inside. Her spirit soared as he wrapped his arms around her and pressed her body hard against his.

When he broke the kiss, he was breathing heavily. He stepped away and she suffered a sudden dismay—had he changed his mind? Then, when he picked up the blanket and shook it out, she understood his intentions. Her pulse echoed in her ears and her breathing quickened as she watched Andrew lay the thick cloth down on a soft area cushioned by fallen leaves. Slowly, deliberately, he removed his coat and waistcoat, then folded them both to make a pillow for her. Seeing him so intimately attired in his shirtsleeves brought a quickening between her legs. Her heart pounded with excitement, knowing the moment of surrender would soon be upon her.

He came over to her. His gazed burned with intensity. Her breath caught.

"Are you certain?" he asked.

She reached for him. "Yes." She could hear the desire in her voice. She hoped Andrew could hear it too.

He came to her then, kissing her with a slow sensuality that made their previous caress seem merely affectionate by comparison. She allowed herself to go pliant in his arms. Indeed, it was not a matter of allowing at all, but the inevitable result of the most sensual embrace she had ever had. He lifted her without breaking the kiss, then he laid her on the blanket.

He knelt beside her. "Your breasts are beautiful," he murmured, his hands cupping their fullness.

Amazement had her arching as his thumbs teased her nipples, while his fingers caressed her soft, rounded breasts. She had no idea that a man's hands, stroking her body through thin linen, would affect her so. When he stretched out beside her and lowered his head to take one sensitive peak in his mouth she whimpered. Her hands clenched, then opened to touch him. She wanted to feel him, all of him.

His skin was warm beneath his shirt. She tugged at the fabric, wanting no barriers. Andrew chuckled deep in his throat as he sat up, grabbed his shirt, and pulled it over his head.

Mary Elizabeth stroked his chest. There was wonder in her voice when she said, "You are beautiful."

This time Andrew laughed aloud. "You do me a kindness, sweet lady. Lift your hips."

She did as he asked and he used the moment to drag her nightshirt up to her shoulders. When she'd settled again, he slid his hand up her stomach to her breasts. Skin to skin, warm flesh to warm flesh. The sensation was shocking. Wonderful. "Oh, Andrew," she whispered. Then he tugged her gauzy gown over her head and tossed it aside. His mouth closed over her nipple and he sucked. She drew in a shocked breath. This was even more evocative than his earlier caress. Her fingers dug into his hair, holding his head there. "Don't stop."

Her eyes closed, she didn't see when he shifted so that he could draw a hand down her belly to the curls at the apex of her thighs. She felt every inch of the caress, though. By the time he had reached her most private part, instinct had told her to open her legs to him. His fingers played with her moist, swollen folds, then penetrated. She sucked in her breath, shocked at the invasion. He moved his thumb over her swollen nub, rubbing rhythmically. Need pounded through her, growing as his tongue stroked her nipple while he caressed her. She arched against his questing hands and mouth.

She had never felt such pleasure. She wanted it to go on forever, building, making her want more. She was panting, her head thrashing from side to side when he shifted, moving away to pull off his breeches, then he was beside her again, his mouth on hers, stretching out over her.

He intensified the kiss. His tongue eased into her mouth, stroking in a leisurely way that made her want to move beneath him. Her moist folds met the hardness of his erection and he slipped into her opening. She stiffened as her body stretched to accommodate him, but his tongue began working its magic again and his hands massaged her breasts once more. He pinched one of her nipples and she gasped and arched. He slid in farther, then drew back. The friction made her moan with pleasure. He moved again and so did she, establishing a rhythm that brought those pleasurable feelings of earlier back to life. When he broke the barrier of her virginity, she felt the stab of pain, but it was nothing against the rising pleasure that was demanding...something. She didn't know what. All she knew was that she didn't want him to stop. Ever.

With her virginity gone, his thrusts deepened. He felt huge inside her, and each stroke was filled with wonder until suddenly she felt her body tighten. As his shaft pulsed inside her, desire broke, pleasure cascading through her as she convulsed around him.

Andrew dragged his mouth from hers. She opened her eyes to see him throw back his head as he groaned with supreme pleasure and called out her name. Then he slumped on top of her, breathing heavily. She wrapped her arms around him, enjoying the weight of him pressing her into the ground.

"So, husband," she said, her hand stroking lazily along his back, the contentment deep inside her turning her voice into a seductive murmur. "Tell me how you plan to spirit me away from my family so that we might wed properly."

The cool of the night had settled over their bodies, reminding Andrew that they were both naked and in a decidedly compromising position in the Strands' garden. He kissed her and said, "We need to get to New York. My sister and her husband live there and they will help us marry."

She stirred and stretched, lazily, like a satisfied cat. "Will your sister approve of me?"

Andrew had no idea. He hadn't even considered the possibility. "Of course she will. Who could not, dear heart?"

His Mary Elizabeth chuckled. "You are sweet, Andrew, and I love you for it."

She kissed his jaw. The skin there tingled, reminding him they were both bare in some very appropriate places. His hand crept back to her breast to cup it. Her flesh was warm beneath his, and he felt himself stir. She murmured approval and moved suggestively against him. Her lips grazed along his jaw until they found the corner of his mouth. Hers opened, allowing her to stroke that tender place with her tongue. Caught up in the pleasure she was giving him, Andrew rubbed his thumb over her nipple and she sighed. The soft exhalation tickled and teased. He shifted so their mouths met, then he kissed her deeply.

This time when they made love he was better able to control the pace, guiding her upward, then as she neared her climax, pulling back. He teased them both until neither could stand it any longer, then he quickened his strokes until she gasped and he could feel her falling over the edge into ecstasy. Her pleasure triggered his and once again he spilled his seed in her.

She fell asleep in his arms afterward. He lay awake, listening to the sounds of the night, every protective instinct alert. Absently he stroked the silken skin on her shoulder as she cuddled beside him. His thoughts drifted. If they did not make a baby out of this night's work, he would be very surprised. That added yet more urgency to planning their wedding.

Should George Strand ever learn that Mary Elizabeth had given herself to Andrew, there was no telling what he would do. He would be outraged that his daughter had defied him after she had promised to wed Colonel Bradley. He wanted the alliance with Bradley and he was a man who did not like to be thwarted.

Would Colonel Bradley be willing to marry a woman who was no longer chaste? Andrew didn't know him well enough to be certain, but he could guess. Bradley had agreed to a convenient marriage with Mary Elizabeth to take advantage of her mother's social position in England. That Mary Elizabeth had given herself to another man would not change her birth or her heritage, so Bradley might still be willing to go through with the wedding. If he was, Andrew was quite certain that George Strand would do everything he could to ensure the marriage took place.

Andrew had no intention of allowing that to happen. Not only would Mary Elizabeth be consigned to a life of unhappiness, but he was not about to let another man raise a child of his.

The problem was, he still didn't know how to make a marriage between himself and Mary Elizabeth happen. His sister hadn't replied to his letter, so he had no certainty that she would help him, given her husband's shipping business and his need to remain neutral when it came to the British. Then there was the difficulty of getting them both to New York, for he was certain the authorities would be searching for them from the moment they both disappeared.

Why, he thought, irritated, did he go to New York to wed Mary Elizabeth? He must have had a good reason, but for the life of him, he couldn't fathom it. New York was days of travel away, difficult to access, even if the authorities were not watching for an eloping couple. There were other towns closer where he could hope to find a minister to marry them. And yet he had gone to New York and he and Mary Elizabeth had been wed there.

Why New York? True, his sister and her husband lived there. True too, it was far enough away from the influence of George Strand that a minister could be convinced to marry them without her father's consent. Still, if he hadn't known that he was supposed to marry in New York he wouldn't be focused on spiriting Mary Elizabeth there.

He frowned. If New York wasn't his idea, then was his present being influenced by the future? Faith's mother, Chloe, had been clear that he would wed Mary Elizabeth in New York, but what if Chloe had been mistaken or had made it up to divert him? What if they were supposed to marry here in Lexington, in his parish church? He hadn't even considered asking Reverend Turner to marry them. Why? Because Chloe had told him that he would marry elsewhere.

But if she had made up the information about New York, she might also have misinformed him about the success of his plan to wed Mary Elizabeth. True, the name Elizabeth seemed to have become entrenched in the family between his time and Faith's. Elizabeth was a common name, however. It could simply be an accident that Faith's sister was also an Elizabeth.

He stared up at the dark velvet of the sky beyond the shadowy branches of the pines and maples under which they lay. He would not believe that Chloe had lied about his marriage to Mary Elizabeth. If he accepted that she'd been truthful on that subject, then he must also accept her statement that they were wed in New York. That meant he had to make arrangements to get himself and Mary Elizabeth there as soon as possible. He hoped his sister would help him, but if not, he would find a way on his own.

A breeze ruffled the treetops. Mary Elizabeth murmured in her sleep and moved against him. He tightened his hold on her shoulders reassuringly. He would have to wake her soon, but having her nestled against him was a stolen pleasure he wasn't yet ready to give up. He went back to plotting their elopement, her even breathing soothing his concerns while it stimulated his thoughts.

By land or sea? He still hadn't made up his mind. There were dangers in both methods. To his mind taking a ship from Boston harbor was by far the quickest way to get them both to New York. It was also the most dangerous, from the point of capture. Both Boston and New York harbors were funnel points with limited access and exits. It would be easy for Strand to keep watch and to stop passengers from boarding a ship in Boston and for him to have all ships from Boston searched upon arrival in New York.

Travel by land had other dangers, speed being the foremost. Once his elopement with Mary Elizabeth was known, George Strand would set Colonel Bradley and his dragoons to hunt them down. And he'd be able to do it too, since coach travel was so much slower than travel by horseback.

All in all, despite the problems, Andrew thought that he was best served planning a sea voyage.

So be it. He would ride into Boston tomorrow and make the arrangements. His first action would be to check with the courier he'd used to send his letter to his sister. Perhaps there was a reply that hadn't yet found its way to him. He hoped there was. He'd like some firm indication that he was doing the right thing.

The breeze stirred the tree branches again and Mary Elizabeth shivered in his hold. He knew it was time for them to part, but he didn't want to. He had a sense that this night was special and he wished it to continue forever. His practical mind told him he was testing fate, that each moment he and Mary Elizabeth lingered in their bower risked their discovery. He kissed her cheek, then nibbled her ear, nuzzling her awake.

She stretched luxuriously, like a satisfied cat, and smiled at him. "Andrew?"

"I need to get you inside, love," he said, kissing her cheek again.

She turned her face so their lips met and his gentle, affectionate kiss heated into something more. Their tongues touched, their bodies demanded. He pulled away, breathing hard. "Mary Elizabeth..."

She put her finger over his mouth. "Shh. I'll go in. Soon. But first I want you to kiss me again and touch me here." She took his hand and placed it on her breast.

Beneath his palm her nipple puckered. He swallowed, feeling his resolution evaporating. He moved his hand, letting his palm rub her sensitive place. She arched into him. "We risk all, love."

"If Mama had missed me, she would have called the alarm already," she whispered. "The danger comes with my return to the house. If I am caught then, what does it matter if we make love or do not, before I go in?"

Put that way, Andrew couldn't argue. Nor did he want to. He let his reservations float away and put his mind to pleasuring the woman he loved.

CHAPTER 13

The breezes of yesterday had brought gray clouds and the promise of rain, but it held off as Andrew rode hard for Boston town. His first stop was the courier he used to send messages to his sister in New York. He was in luck. A reply to his letter was waiting for him. He thanked the clerk and retreated to a corner of the room where he slit open the seal and quickly scanned the contents.

What he read reassured him. *The minister at my church is no friend of England and is sympathetic to your cause,* she wrote. *He will help you procure a special license and is willing to marry you as soon as possible. Make haste. You are both welcome to stay with me. Affectionately, your sister, Jane.*

He refolded the letter and slipped it into his coat pocket. So, Chloe was right. His wedding would take place in New York. Now, how to get himself and Mary Elizabeth there? He returned to the counter where the clerk presided and asked if he knew any ships leaving Boston bound for New York over the next few days. He was rewarded with the names of three ships and their captains.

He was about to leave when the clerk said, "There is also a captain who sails a schooner out of Lynn you might find helpful. We sometimes use him when we need a fast ship to get our messages to their destination quickly."

His hesitation and disapproving sniff had Andrew raising his brows. Lynn was a small harbor north of Boston, but it sounded as if this captain used the town's location and size to run a clandestine operation. "Why are you reluctant to recommend this ship?"

"The captain is...not as scrupulous as some others," the man said.

"A pity," Andrew said, not surprised. "Thank you, sir, for your assistance. I bid you good day." The clerk nodded and Andrew headed for Boston's docks.

"Two passengers? You and your wife?" The merchant ship's captain raised his bushy gray eyebrows. He was seated at his desk in his cabin on board the ship. The desk was walnut, polished to a high sheen. The top was clear, logbook and papers safely stowed in compartments or drawers. Like the desk, the rest of the cabin was beautifully maintained and scrupulously clean.

Standing in front of him, Andrew gave a firm nod. "That would be correct, sir. We have need to be in New York City with all speed and I am reliably informed that it will be your next port of call and that you have berths available."

"Aye..." the fellow said. "I do at that. But—" He stopped, stared at Andrew for a long minute, his expression frowning. Then he drew a deep breath and reached for a sheaf of papers in one of the drawers. He shuffled the papers, studying them. Andrew waited, watching him, wondering why this man whose reputation was excellent, would dither so over the booking of a cabin. He was afraid he knew the answer, and he didn't like it.

After a thorough check, the captain straightened the papers and replaced them in the drawer. He cleared his throat. "I'm sorry, Mr. Byrne. I thought I had a cabin available, but I find I do not."

"You have nothing available? Or are you unwilling to sell a berth to me?"

The captain pursed his lips and looked away. Then he shrugged and shook his head, clearly unwilling to say more. The interview was over. Andrew nodded and left. He would have to seek out the next name on his list.

He had the same results with the other two captains. Frustrated, he decided to ride for Lynn and see if the captain of the schooner would help him.

The schooner's captain agreed heartily, but as Andrew negotiated the arrangements, he found himself thinking of the clerk's warning that the captain was devious. He also couldn't help but notice the fellow's greasy, straggly hair, missing teeth, and dirty coat. This was not a man he would entrust with his person under normal circumstances, but time was of the essence, so he shook the man's hand on the deal, promised to return the next day, and headed back to Boston.

On the return ride he started to think about the gleam in the captain's eyes when he mentioned that he was sailing with his wife. His reservations grew. He decided to make one last effort to find a more reputable ship in Boston before he returned to Lexington. He headed to a well-known tavern in the harbor area. He'd ask the barkeep for suggestions. He might be more knowledgeable than the clerk had been.

The tavern was remarkably busy, even though it was past midday. Andrew made his way around the long rectangular tables, populated with shipping agents and sailors alike, to stand at the wide polished bar that stretched the length of the room. He leaned against the gleaming oak surface, idly watching the customers, while he waited for the barkeep to notice him.

"What's your pleasure, sir?" The man had thinning hair, which he tied in a queue rather than wear a wig. His face was round, his expression neutral. He wiped the surface of the bar with an absentminded care that boded well for the quality of his food and drink.

"Ale," Andrew said. The man nodded and went off to pour it out. When he returned Andrew had payment ready and as he was handing it over he said, "I am seeking a berth to New York for myself and my wife, but I have had remarkably little luck. You wouldn't happen to know of any ships heading in that direction, would you?"

The man shot Andrew a penetrating look from under frowning

eyebrows. Andrew dropped the coins in his hand. He had included a sizeable tip in the amount. The barkeep looked down and his fingers closed slowly around the money. Andrew sipped his ale and waited.

Finally, the barkeep seemed to come to a decision. He dropped the coins in his till, then returned to wiping his countertop. His tone was conversational as he spoke, the expression in his eyes shrewd. "Not surprising, sir. All of the captains have been warned not to provide transport for a young couple, else they will find themselves afoul of the law. I expect the captains you spoke to were just being cautious."

Andrew set the tankard onto the bar carefully so as to hide his dismay at the barkeep's words. "A warning you say? Who issued it?"

"An Englishman, backed up by a troop of soldiers." The man wiped his bar harder. It was clear he had no love of the British.

"Indeed," Andrew said. "Was it a Colonel Bradley, by chance?"

"Aye, that's the fellow. Hand in glove with that...with George Strand—he's the one offering the reward."

Seriously alarmed, Andrew said, "What reward?"

"Did I not mention that, sir? Seafaring men, they tend to be independent, see? Warnings and threats, they only go so far. But a fine reward for nothing but information? Why, that's a temptation few can resist."

Horrified, Andrew stared at him.

The barkeep nodded toward his tankard. "Finish your ale, sir, then you'd best be off."

The man's suggestion shook Andrew out of his immobility. He picked up the tankard, drained it, then reached into his pocket for his purse. Pulling out a gold coin, he flicked it toward the man. "My thanks, barkeep," he said, before he strode out of the tavern.

He rode hard for Lexington. If what the barkeeper had just told him was correct, there was every likelihood that George Strand had already been informed that he was searching for a ship to take him and Mary Elizabeth to New York. If Strand knew his destination, they would never be able to reach the city.

Worse, Strand now knew that he was actively searching for a way to elope with Mary Elizabeth and that he intended to do it soon. Strand would not be satisfied with keeping him from finding a ship. He'd do something more to stop him, but what?

As he rode for home, Andrew discovered the answer. Strand had set up roadblocks on all the main roads out of Lexington. A coach lumbering along his route caused him to slow his mount and pull the horse to one side as the big vehicle passed. The driver looked down at him from his lofty perch and shouted, "Lobster backs ahead, friend! Looking for lone, dark-haired riders. I'd be wary!"

Andrew acknowledged the warning with a nod and a salute. He waited until the coach was away, then he took to the fields and a round-about route home.

It was past five when he reached Lexington. He didn't bother going to his farm, but left his horse with a grim-faced Ron Aiken. "The green's full of British dragoons and they're searching for you, Andrew. What have you done?"

"Planned an elopement," Andrew said.

Understanding leapt into Aiken's eyes. "Strand got wind of it."

"Apparently. I need your help, Ron. I have to speak to Mary Eliza-beth, privately, before Strand has his lapdog, Bradley carry her off to Boston. Can you find her for me? Get a message to her?"

To his surprise, Aiken shot him a reckless grin. "Easy enough to do. She and her mother are at the rectory, as is my sister and some other ladies. What do you want me to tell her?"

Andrew thought for a minute. "Tell her to find a reason to go into the church. I'll meet her there."

Aiken nodded. He and Andrew slipped out of his house by the back way. Avoiding the watching troops, they approached the church from behind. As they neared, Aiken nodded and veered off for the rectory, while Andrew headed for the church. Inside, he took a few minutes to say a respectful prayer, then he settled down to wait.

He'd taken up a position near the door with the idea that he could grab Mary Elizabeth as soon as she entered and pull her into the shadows to ensure they had privacy while they talked. He knew it would take Aiken a few minutes to deliver his message, so as time passed he wasn't initially worried. Then he heard the voices and realized that just outside the door an argument was taking place.

"Mama, I simply wish to say a prayer or two. That is all. Why would you feel that was not appropriate?"

"It is perfectly fine, Mary Elizabeth, as long as Colonel Bradley accompanies you."

Andrew almost groaned.

"Mama," Mary Elizabeth said, "Colonel Bradley would be quite bored!"

"I would not," said the colonel's deeper voice. "Your father has entrusted me with your safety, Miss Strand. I intend to fulfill my duty as ordered."

Andrew's heart sank. Bradley would never allow Mary Elizabeth to speak to him and in fact, he'd probably order his men to arrest him. There was no point now in subterfuge. He flung open the great double door and stepped outside.

Into the light.

CHAPTER 14

*A*ndrew looked cautiously around him. He knew he was still on the church porch, but he also knew he was in the twenty-first century, not his own. The porch looked much as it had in his time, but beyond it was very different. Where there had been a broad church-yard opening up from the front doors, now there was a paved sidewalk that was separated from a main street only by a narrow strip of grass. The huge old maple tree that had once shaded the church was long gone, sacrificed to the building of the roadway.

In all the years that he had followed Faith's Beacon into the future, he had always found her at that one place on his property where there was a grove of trees in his time and a house in hers. Finding himself in her time at this moment, in this place, was unexpected—and a problem.

Time was short. At this very moment Colonel Bradley might be whisking Mary Elizabeth away to some location from which Andrew would be unable to rescue her. He almost turned and walked back into the church, but he hesitated. Perhaps this was the opportunity he needed. What better place to hide Mary Elizabeth for a few hours than in the future where none of her pursuers could follow? He took stock of the current situation and made his plans.

Cars were parked on the side of the road in front of the church. He didn't recognize the vehicles, but he did know the people standing near them. At the base of the stairs leading down from the church doors Daniel Hamilton and a stranger were standing near Chloe Hamilton. Though the stranger was casually dressed, Daniel was wearing a dark blue suit, white shirt, and blue tie, what Faith called business attire. He had his hands on his hips and he looked annoyed. But then, as far as Andrew knew, the man was always annoyed. Despite his concern about what was happening on his side of the Beacon, he grinned to himself. His arrival was sure to take Daniel's irritation and raise it to incendiary levels. Good.

Opposite Daniel, Chloe was frowning, lips pursed as she listened to something Daniel was saying. She was wearing what Faith called a pantsuit, made from some kind of light material. The trousers were a warm cream color, the blouse, a lovely sea green. The jacket matched the trousers and was buttoned at her waist. It draped over her hips and created a professional look. Her frown deepened and she shook her head. Whatever Chloe and Daniel were arguing about, she wasn't giving an inch. Probably part of the reason for Daniel's frustration.

On the other side of the sidewalk, Cody was leaning against one of the vehicles watching the argument. His arm was around Faith's waist and she was leaning against him, her head on his shoulder as she watched her parents bicker. Liz was standing on the sidewalk, halfway between the two camps. Her expression was worried. All three of the younger generation were dressed in a semi-casual style, Cody in slacks and a front buttoned shirt, Faith and Liz in summer dresses.

It was Cody who noticed him first. He straightened and said something to Faith, who looked up, beyond the battlers, to the church doors. Her eyes lit with pleasure, then she glanced at Daniel and bit her lip. She said something to Cody and he grinned.

Andrew decided it behooved him to take charge of the situation. Fortune had dropped an opportunity into his lap, but he didn't have a lot of time, or he might lose Mary Elizabeth forever. "Well met, family!" he said, pitching his voice so that it carried over Daniel's quarrel-some tones. He ran lightly down the stairs onto the sidewalk.

"What the devil are you doing here?" Daniel said. He glared at Andrew, then his eyes widened as he looked at the stranger beside him. "My apologies, Reverend. I wasn't speaking to you, but to this disreputable...relative of my wife's."

"Honestly, Daniel," Chloe said wrinkling her nose. "Stop being so critical. And I'm not your wife anymore."

Clearly Daniel had irritated Chloe even more than he usually did. Andrew turned to face the minister. He was a young man with a thick head of dark hair. His thin face was adorned by dark rimmed glasses that added a studious look to his expression, but there was a kindness in his eyes that gave Andrew a good feeling. Perhaps he would be of some use in this crisis.

The minister was more casually dressed than the others, wearing a front button shirt, open at the collar, and a pair of blue jeans. If Daniel hadn't identified him as a man of the cloth, Andrew would never have realized he was one. People in Faith's time dressed considerably less formally than in his own. He bowed politely and said, "Good afternoon, Reverend. I am Andrew Byrne, a relative of Miss Faith's. It is my pleasure to meet you."

The minister blinked and studied Andrew, who realized the man must be wondering about his clothes—riding coat, brocade waistcoat, linen shirt with ruffles at the wrists and an ornately tied neck cloth, breeches and riding boots—all so very different from the minister's own apparel. But he smiled and held out his hand. "Taylor Aiken. Nice to meet you, Byrne. That's an old family name around here. There was an Andrew Byrne who fought in the Revolution with my ancestor, Ronald Aiken."

"Bloody hell," Daniel muttered. "The fat's in the fire now."

"Daniel!" Chloe said, a warning in her voice.

"Fought in the Revolution, you say?" Andrew allowed himself to be distracted from his primary purpose. The word revolution implied an attempt to overthrow a government, a *successful* attempt to overthrow a government. Could it be that the demands of his fellow colonists had escalated from seeking changes in their current system to breaking away from Great Britain completely?

A thrill raced through him. Taylor Aiken used the word as a proper noun, the name of an event; one which everyone but Andrew was so familiar with, it didn't need explaining. Revolution. Separation from Britain. When would it happen?

Unaware of the questions his comment had roused, Taylor nodded and said, "He did. They were together at—"

"What's that awful smell?" Daniel said loudly.

Andrew shot him an annoyed look. Daniel was once again doing his best to make sure Andrew received no clues to his future.

The Reverend Aiken broke off politely at Daniel's interjection. Cody nudged Faith and they left the car to join Andrew and the others. Liz came with them. When they were all assembled, Daniel pointed at Andrew and said, "It's him."

"It's his horse, Dad. Andrew must have come from riding." Faith leaned over and kissed him on the cheek. "Welcome, Andrew. In case you haven't guessed, we're here tonight to discuss the wedding with Taylor."

Such informality. So strange to hear a man of the cloth referred to by his first name, with no indication of his rank or title. Andrew liked it. "I will not intrude then. However," he hesitated. "I find myself in something of a bother."

"A bother?" Taylor said. He looked like he'd never heard the term.

"When are you not," said Daniel, with a lift of his brow.

Andrew ignored him, focusing on Faith instead. "I need to visit."

"Now?" Faith asked, frowning.

Andrew nodded. "And I need to bring a guest."

"Mary Elizabeth!" Liz breathed. Her eyes were wide. She glanced at her mother. "But is that possible?"

Chloe frowned too. "It is, but it's difficult. Andrew, is it Mary Elizabeth you want to bring to the fu—with you?"

He nodded. "If I do not she will be lost to me forever."

"Is this an elopement?" Taylor asked. "Or an escape?" He was frowning now too.

"Why do you ask?" Daniel said, fixing a penetrating gaze on the reverend.

Taylor shrugged. "It's odd. My ancestor, Ronald Aiken, left diaries. I've been studying them with the thought of writing a history of his involvement in the Revolution. He talked about his friend Andrew Byrne who was in love with a Mary Elizabeth Strand. She was the daughter of an English official and her father thought Byrne was a rebel and forbade his daughter from seeing him. She disappeared from this very church, then later turned up married to Andrew Byrne."

"And did they live happily ever after?" Andrew asked. He was grinning. He couldn't help it.

"As to that, I can't say," Taylor replied with a smile. "Ronald doesn't mention the status of their relationship, though he does mention that they adopt—"

"Yes," Faith said. "Where do you need me?"

She'd deliberately broken in before the innocent Taylor Aiken could say too much more, Andrew thought regretfully. But she was right, time was passing and he needed to stay focused on the matter at hand—getting Mary Elizabeth safely into the future. "Inside the church." He looked at Taylor. "Is there still the doorway near the altar that opens into a passage that leads to a side door?"

The minister's brows rose above the rims of his glasses. "It sounds as if you know the building well. The doorway is still there. In fact, according to my ancestor's diaries, it's where Mary Elizabeth disappeared."

Daniel groaned. "This has to stop!"

Cody took Faith's hand and said, "Come on. We'll go inside and wait by the doorway."

Andrew clapped Cody on the shoulder and said, "Thank you, my friend!" Then he turned and took the steps two at a time. At the large oak door, he paused. Saluting Faith and the others he pulled it open and walked back into his own time.

CHAPTER 15

$\mathcal{M}$ary Elizabeth paused at the steps to the church. She stared up at the wide double doors, fear clutching at her, knotting her stomach, clogging her brain so she couldn't think.

"Has having Colonel Bradley with you tempered your desire for quiet meditation, daughter?" Lady Elizabeth asked.

Mary Elizabeth glanced at her mother and saw that her brows were raised and her eyes flashed her a warning. She felt herself coloring. In truth, it wasn't praying she was interested in, but Andrew Byrne, and she was here at the church because his good friend Mr. Ronald Aiken seemed to think she would find him inside.

Mr. Aiken's message had been whispered in her ear as the gathering at the rectory broke up. Saying that she wanted to pray had been a spur of the moment excuse, one that she thought her mother would accept. Except it hadn't quite worked out that way. Now her mother was deliberately testing the truth of it, and she feared that Colonel Bradley would find Andrew inside, waiting for her, and he'd do something dreadful to Andrew.

She looked at the big oaken doors again and knew that if she admitted she wasn't interested in saying a prayer, Colonel Bradley would go into the church anyway. If Andrew was there, he was doomed to be captured. Or worse. Perhaps if she went into the church with Colonel Bradley, the man would not be so quick to harm Andrew in front of her.

She swallowed, then said as calmly as she could, "Of course not, Mama." She lifted her skirts as she climbed the shallow set of stairs to the double doors. She would find some way to warn Andrew.

Colonel Bradley ran lightly up the steps, brushing past her to ensure he would reach the entrance ahead of her. He bowed to her as he pulled the door open. "Allow me to enter first, Miss Strand, that I might be certain no danger lurks within."

She almost stumbled, saving herself at the last moment. "Surely a church is the safest of places to be, Colonel. I doubt you need to be on guard in this building."

"I disagree," he said.

"Colonel Bradley must do as he sees fit to protect you, Mary Elizabeth," her mother said from behind. She had followed Mary Elizabeth up the steps. "We will wait here until you have deemed it safe, Colonel." A worried expression clouded her eyes and her mouth was set.

The sinking feeling in Mary Elizabeth's stomach grew worse. Her mother thought there would be violence if Colonel Bradley found Andrew in the church, but she believed there was no way to stop it. She must do something.

"But Mama!" she cried, desperate to warn Andrew as Bradley opened the door and marched inside. "This is ridiculous. There is no one inside the church at this hour!"

Colonel Bradley didn't close the door behind him. Doubtless he wished to have the people gathered outside watch as he vanquished his supposed adversary for Mary Elizabeth's hand. She watched as he strode into the gloom, then paused, probably to let his eyes adjust to the diminished light. He eased his sword from its scabbard and she gasped, raising her hand to her throat in fear.

"What is it, Mary Elizabeth?" her mother asked. "Is there someone in there with the Colonel?"

She shook her head. "No, Mama. The colonel...He has raised his sword in a house of God." She looked over at her mother.

Lady Elizabeth's eyes widened. "Ridiculous man." She shook her head. "Quite improper. What is he thinking?"

He was thinking of dispatching Andrew Byrne. Of course, her mother knew that, too. While she might not want Mary Elizabeth to meet with Andrew, she did disapprove of the colonel's willingness to resort to violence. That heartened Mary Elizabeth. She returned her gaze to the inside of the church. The shadows had swallowed up the colonel and there was no sign of Andrew. "I'm going inside."

"Dearest, Colonel Bradley asked you to remain here," her mother said. But her protest lacked conviction. Lady Elizabeth was clearly doubting the need for Colonel Bradley's supposed search of the church.

"Colonel Bradley has wandered into the vestry or one of the other rooms. The church itself is empty. I will be safe enough." Mary Elizabeth smiled at her mother and hugged her. "Mama. You know I am not happy with this marriage Papa has arranged. I do not love Colonel Bradley, indeed I hardly know the man. I must find a way to make my peace with a life that will be very different from the one I would have chosen." She hesitated, then said softly, "That is not my only concern. I care deeply for you, dear Mama, and once Colonel Bradley and I are married I will be separated from you for many years while you are here and I am in England."

Lady Elizabeth sighed. "The separation is not something I would wish, but your father has aspirations—for you, and for himself," she admitted. "Your Andrew is an honorable man from all I've seen of him, or heard. If he is in there waiting for you, say your good-byes and find the serenity you need to go forward."

"Thank you, Mama." She hugged her again, then stepped back. Turning, she entered the church.

Like Bradley, she paused a few feet inside to allow her vision to adjust. She also looked around. Disappointment washed over her. She had hoped that Andrew had somehow avoided Colonel Bradley's inspection and that he would appear to her once she'd entered, but there was no movement in the large chamber. She walked toward the altar, slowly as if she were a bride joining her bridegroom on her wedding day. But there was no groom waiting for her there, not today. And when she did marry, the groom would not be the man she wanted.

She slipped into the pew before the altar and sat, bowing her head and closing her eyes. She didn't pray. She couldn't. She just let misery wash over her as she wondered how she was going to cope with the rest of her life.

After a few moments she heard the impatient clatter of booted footsteps. Colonel Bradley, somewhere in the dim reaches of the church no doubt. She sat up, listening carefully. She thought that he was in a side chapel and wondered if he had cornered Andrew there. Panic had her rising to her feet and rushing forward.

She had passed the altar and was almost at the side door, which opened to a passage that led outside, when the air stirred near her. She looked around, but there was nothing, no reason for the sudden draft.

Then Andrew's dear voice said, "Mary Elizabeth!"

Her gaze followed the sound and hope surged through her. "Andrew?"

He was standing behind her and to one side, closer to the altar than to the passage door. He nodded as she said his name, and smiled.

"Where were you hiding?" she whispered, still very much aware that he was still in danger. "I thought Colonel Bradley had chased you from the building. I saw him pull out his sword—"

"The good colonel *thinks* he is pursuing me. He'll find out soon enough he's wrong. We have little time. Listen to me carefully, Mary Elizabeth. Do you remember when I told you that I can travel to the future?"

He'd talked about a special portal, what he called a Beacon, drawing him through time, but truly? She hadn't believed him. She'd thought he was teasing her. At the time, she'd shrugged it off as just one of Andrew's unique quirks. Andrew was her Andrew. He didn't need to have some special ability to make her love him.

Now his expression was so intent, she had to wonder if perhaps he really did believe that travel to another era was possible. The thought frightened her and must have shown on her face, for he smiled in a reassuring way.

"Take my hand and no matter what happens—what you see, what you hear—don't let go!" he said. He touched her cheek gently. "Do you understand? You must stay with me and always keep your hand in mine until I say it is safe to let go."

She nodded her understanding, because that was what she thought he wanted. "But, Andrew—"

A clatter of feet sounded near the entry to the church. Mary Elizabeth glanced toward the doorway and saw her mother standing in the opening. Behind her loomed the larger figure of Colonel Bradley. He must have left the church from the little side door, thinking he was following Andrew, then circled the building from the outside and come out again at the church steps.

"She was to remain outside with you!" the colonel announced, outrage in every word.

Lady Elizabeth gave him a haughty tilt of her head. "Really, Colonel. There is no need to shout. I am standing right in front of you."

"*God's blood,* I didn't find the rogue. He could be in there with her now!"

"And if he is, Colonel, I am sure you will find him." Lady Elizabeth lifted the fan attached to a cord at her wrist and calmly plied it.

"Then let me pass, my lady, so I can ensure your daughter's safety and search the building properly." There was barely controlled impatience in the colonel's deep voice.

"Of course, Colonel," Lady Elizabeth said, but she didn't immediately move.

Mary Elizabeth realized that she and Andrew must be visible to her mother, just as her mother was visible to her. Her mother was stalling, giving her time for her good-byes with Andrew. A wave of gratitude

CLAIM TIME FOR LOVE | 285

and love for her mother flowed through her. If Andrew could move through a portal in time, in a few minutes she would simply disappear and her mother would not understand how it had happened. The not knowing would be a terrible burden for Lady Elizabeth and she ached with the thought of it.

"Andrew," she said. "My mother and Colonel Bradley...If we suddenly disappear..."

"Trust me," he said. He reached for the nearby door that lead to the corridor and opened it. He held out his hand. "Come with me, Mary Elizabeth, so that we might marry and go forward into our future."

There was tenderness in his voice and love in his eyes. She wasn't at all sure she believed he could travel into the future, but he'd asked her to trust him, so she would. As she put her hand in his she heard the thump of booted feet from behind. She peeked over her shoulder and saw Colonel Bradley was inside the church.

"Halt!" he shouted as he raced down the side aisle toward them.

"Andrew!" she cried, terrified that Bradley wouldn't be content with merely separating her from Andrew, but that the man was intent on killing him.

Andrew looked at her and grinned. Then he said, "Remember, don't let go!"

"I won't!" She scuttled after him as he took a path that led them near the side door. To those in the church they must appear to be going through it, but when she looked she saw that they weren't in the passage, but directly in front of the altar. Oddly, the altar cloth was a different color and far less ornately worked than it had been a few minutes ago. She frowned. The candelabra that had stood behind the altar, at either end, had also disappeared. What was going on? She looked past the altar and noticed that the walls were different too. Moments before they had been whitewashed a bright, almost harsh, white. Now they were a rather pretty ivory.

Andrew tugged on her hand, reclaiming her attention. "I have introductions to make," he said.

She looked at Andrew, then past him to a group of people clustered nearby. People who were dressed in the strangest clothes she had ever seen. Shockingly, the two younger women appeared to be wearing nothing but gaily colored shifts, while an older woman was dressed in men's clothing, in the form of an odd-looking pair of breeches, topped with a frock coat of some kind.

She blinked. Was it true? Had she actually travelled through time with Andrew?

The dark-haired man who stood beside one of the strangely dressed young women smiled at her in a friendly way. His clothing was casual too, with no coat or vest or neckcloth over his long-sleeved collared shirt, but his smile reassured her.

"Mary Elizabeth Strand, may I present you to my family," Andrew said.

There was a mischievous gleam in his eyes that she didn't quite trust, particularly since she knew that his only family in the area was an aunt and cousins who lived in Concord.

"My future family." He pointed them out and named them as he went. "Faith Hamilton and her betrothed, Cody Simpson"—that was the dark-haired man with the reassuring smile— "her mother and father, Chloe and Daniel Hamilton, and her sister, Liz Hamilton."

She glanced at him in a wondering way. "Future? So, it is true?"

He nodded.

She drew a deep breath. Andrew had told her that he had the ability to travel to the future by walking into a light he called a Beacon, but she had seen no blaze of light. She had no proof this Beacon of his existed. Yet, here she was, standing in a church that was the same, but not, talking to people she didn't know and who were clearly not from her own time. She wasn't sure she was prepared for this strange world, but there was a definite bright side to it. "If we are in the future, can Colonel Bradley follow us here?"

"Not unless he holds my hand, as you are, and I bring him with me," Andrew said, raising their clasped hands for emphasis. His voice softened. "You are safe, Mary Elizabeth, and will continue to be as long as you remain attached to me."

"What will happen if I let you go?"

"You will return to our time."

"You both should go back now," the man called Daniel Hamilton said. His eyes were narrowed. Mary Elizabeth sensed his annoyance and thought that he didn't like Andrew very much.

"Nonsense," said Chloe, the older woman in the man's clothes. She smiled. "I'm delighted to meet you at last, Mary Elizabeth. Andrew has talked of nothing but you ever since your family moved into the area."

Mary Elizabeth frowned at that and looked up at Andrew. "Do you come to the future often?"

"Once a week, for dinner and to clean himself up, twenty-first century style," said the blonde woman called Faith. "Andrew, what is your plan?"

"We'll wait with you until after dark," Andrew said. "Then we'll return to my time. My sister has arranged for the minister at her church to marry us. I still haven't figured how I am to get Mary Elizabeth and myself to New York, but I'm sure it can be done."

Mary Elizabeth loved his optimism, but she was a more practical person. "Colonel Bradley will not give up searching for me. He brought a troop of dragoons with him from Boston. I am sure he will be guarding the church and your farm, Andrew. How can we escape his net here, in Lexington?"

The dark-haired man named Cody stirred and she saw Andrew's gaze sharpen. "What have you to say to that, Master Scientist?"

Cody looked at Faith, who frowned, shot a look their way, then returned her gaze to her betrothed. Mary Elizabeth thought she saw her move her head a fraction, as if in silent agreement for what he planned to say. Cody looked back at Andrew. "By going to New York," he said.

Andrew's eyes lit up. "You would drive us there in Faith's horseless chariot?"

"You can't," roared Daniel. "It's not allowed!"

"They are supposed to be married in two days time," Chloe said. "They'll never reach New York City by then in their own time, even without pursuit by a bunch of dragoons."

"Oh," said Liz, clasping her hands together. "This is so romantic!"

"We've been talking," Faith said, indicating Cody and herself. "I don't think we are harming the timeline by taking them to New York. I think we're just fulfilling our obligation."

"I agree," Chloe said.

The man called Daniel stepped forward until he was standing right beside his wife. His cheeks were red and his eyes were angry. "This is absurd. What if you are wrong? What if by doing this, you do change the timeline?"

Chloe grabbed his arm. "Daniel, the children must be married in New York to ensure that Andrew's sister comes to know and like Mary Elizabeth. So that when the time comes she gives her babies into her care..." She broke off, looking guiltily at Mary Elizabeth who was listening to this statement with shock.

Andrew, however, said in a delighted voice, "That settles it. We must make use of Faith's vehicle." He set off down the center aisle, his enthusiasm growing with each passing moment. "You will be amazed by this modern carriage, Mary Elizabeth. The windows rise up and down through a mechanical motor fueled by the engine that powers the vehicle instead of horses. There is a wondrous machine inside the vehicle that provides music, and the interior is always cool and comfortable!" He patted her hand. "The coach will move very quickly, far faster than you have ever travelled before, but you must not be frightened. I will be there beside you."

Mary Elizabeth thought Andrew must be exaggerating once again, but things were moving so quickly that there was no time to do much else but nod her acceptance. Besides, maybe it was true. She was, after all, in the future with Andrew. Anything was possible.

Andrew paused, to look back at the others who were trailing behind. "I suppose Mary Elizabeth and I will be sitting in the rear seat? That Master Cody will be riding 'shotgun'?"

"Shotgun?" Mary Elizabeth said, alarmed. "Are there footpads on the road to New York?"

"Don't worry," Cody said coming up behind her. "It's safe. Shotgun is just the term we use for the seat beside the driver. No firearms are involved."

She looked at Andrew, wide-eyed. "The driver sits *inside* the carriage?"

He nodded. "Amazing, is it not? Once you have visited this time more often, you will not find it so strange. But..." He stopped. After a moment's hesitation, the others flowed around them and out the front door, leaving them alone in the cool quiet of the church. "Mary Elizabeth." He touched her cheek with the fingertips of his free hand. "By going to New York, by marrying there without your father's permission, you will be disowned. Are you absolutely certain?"

This was her last opportunity to change her mind, the biggest decision of her life. If she wanted, she could free her hand from Andrew's and return to her own time.

If she wanted.

But she didn't. She gazed into his eyes and saw the love glowing there. "Andrew, I love you. I shudder to even think what my life would be like if I hadn't made this decision." She smiled at him, at the concern she saw in his eyes, the caring in his gentle touch. "I made my choice before I walked into this church. I love you. I want to live my life with you. My mother will come round. My father may not. But whatever happens, you are my family now. Yes, Andrew Byrne, I am absolutely certain."

He bent and kissed her, long and with all the pent-up emotion of the last few weeks. When he raised his head, his eyes were gleaming with the devilry she loved so much.

"Then, Madam," he said. "We are bound for New York." He raised her hand and kissed her knuckles in salute. "Come. Your horseless carriage awaits!"

THE CAT CAME BACK

THE 9 LIVES COZY MYSTERY SERIES, BOOK 1

The cat bounded onto his chest. It was a brute of an animal, big as a small dog and heavy boned. He called it his house tiger because of the restless way it prowled through the rooms, almost as if it was exercising to gain strength in its healing muscles. He scratched behind the cat's ears absently and the beast settled on his chest, purring in a satisfying, soothing way.

God, that smells good.

Roy contemplated the glowing tip of the joint. "It does, doesn't it?"

I wish I could join you, but I can't.

The voice was clear and seemed to reverberate inside his head. Roy glanced around the room, but the cat was the only other occupant. He looked at the joint and said, "Oh, man," and started to butt it out. The cat tapped the back of his hand with its paw, claws in.

Don't do that on my account.

Roy looked at the joint again. "Are you going to stop talking to me if I put it out?"

No.

"Far out." Roy smoked in silence for a minute, while the cat breathed in his fumes. "So why are we having this conversation? You've been living here for over two weeks and we haven't spoken before. Why start now?"

I've been trying to get through to you for days. I have to go. I wanted to say good-bye and thank you.

Roy considered that. "Why do you have to go? Don't you like living here?"

The cat likes it just fine. He wants to stay. I can't.

That was interesting. "So there are two of you living in the cat's body?"

You might say we're roomies for now. Until I've completed my mission.

"And you talk to each other?"

We share thoughts, just as I am sharing my thoughts with you. Restless, the cat leapt onto the floor, then prowled to the top of the stairs that led from the living room down to the front door. His movements were lithe, controlled, decisive. Big and powerful, he was clearly a male in his prime, a male with a mission.

Roy believed in possibilities. He'd built his life visioning what couldn't be and making it happen. He liked to keep an open mind, but this was really pushing his limits. A cat on a mission, who was communicating with him telepathically. Yeah, sure. He contemplated the smoke rising lazily from the glowing tip of the joint. Maybe it was time to quit.

The gray and black tabby shot him a look that could only be described as disapproving. *I thought you would understand.*

A happy idea brightened Roy's mood. Maybe this conversation was his writer's imagination going out of control. His characters tended to take over the creative process once he knew them well. Maybe one had decided to give him a poke and let him know how he could sort out the problems in his current project. They were such a dull bunch, though. He would never have pegged one of them for being a talking cat. For that matter, even thinking up the idea of a talking cat. If he added a talking cat, how would he work it into the plot? Maybe...

The vision of a narrow alley, closed at one end, plugged at the other by a beat-up car that had once been someone's luxury ride, rose in his mind. He was there in the alley, huddled in the shadow of a dumpster that stank of rotting food. Someone was with him, someone he trusted. While his nose twitched with distaste, his eyes focused on the small, sealed plastic bag the other person was holding. The bag was filled with pills that were a rainbow of colors. Need, intense, powerful, demanding, slammed into him. He wanted that bag. Now.

His hand shook as he reached into his pocket for the ready cash he always kept on him. He should quit—and he would, when he was ready. For now he'd enjoy the rush that would take away the guilt over the mess he'd made of his life.

He had the bills in his hand when he sensed movement nearby. He lifted his head to look, but before he could see who was behind him something hit him, connecting with his skull with a vicious crunch. Agonizing pain shot through his head. He staggered forward, disoriented.

He heard a voice say, "I've got him. You grab his other arm."

Hands took hold of him, keeping him upright, forcing him to stagger forward. Each step was agony. The inside of his head felt as if a maniac wielding an ice pick was slamming it repeatedly. He concentrated on keeping his head still to minimize the jarring, but it was an impossible task. His vision wavered, dancing in a sickening way that distorted everything. He glanced at one of the people helping him. All he could see was hair the same blond color as his own above a pale, narrow face that was nothing more than a blur.

As he stumbled forward, he was pretty sure they were leading him out of the alley. Relief coursed through him. They were taking him out onto the main drag where they could signal for help. That was great. Still, it would have been better if they'd let him slump onto the ground where he could lie until rescued. Maybe he should suggest that.

"Here we are. Okay, ready now. Do it!"

The hands released him. As he swayed unsteadily, relieved he didn't have to plow forward anymore, his blurred vision showed him a car trunk gaping open before him. Confused, he looked around. He

294 | THE CAT CAME BACK

only had a moment to realize that rescue was not in his future, before he was hit from behind with another blow that sent him sprawling.

Darkness closed around him.

Gradually, the vision merged with reality. Shaken, Roy squished the joint into the ashtray. The cat came over and rubbed against his leg, purring loudly. Roy sighed as he reached down to scratch the cat behind its ears. "That was what happened to you? How did it end? Did you die?"

Yes. I'll spare you the details. They aren't pretty.

"How did you come to be living in the cat?" he asked.

I went home, to tell my family where I was, but I couldn't reach them. Only the cat seemed to accept me. He invited me in.

Available in Paperback and eBook from Your Favorite Bookstore or Online Retailer

ALSO BY LOUISE CLARK

The Nine Lives Cozy Mystery Series

The Cat Came Back

The Cat's Paw

Cat Got Your Tongue

Let Sleeping Cats Lie

Cat Among The Fishes

Forward in Time Series

Make Time For Love

Discover Time for Love

ABOUT THE AUTHOR

The author of the 9 Lives Cozy Mystery Series, Louise Clark has been the adopted mom of a number of cats with big personalities. The feline who inspired Stormy, the cat in the 9 Lives books, dominated her household for twenty loving years. During that time he created a family pecking order that left Louise on top and her youngest child on the bottom (just below the guinea pig), regularly tried to eat all his sister's food (he was a very large cat), and learned the joys of travel through a cross continent road trip.

The 9 Lives Cozy Mystery Series—*The Cat Came Back, The Cat's Paw,* and *Cat Got Your Tongue*—as well as the single title mystery, *A Recipe For Trouble,* are all set in her home town of Vancouver, British Columbia. For more information please sign up for her newsletter HERE.

WWW.LOUISECLARKAUTHOR.COM

facebook.com/louiseclarkauthor